BLOODLESS

BLOODLESS

ANDY MURPHY

Glenbridge Publishing Ltd.

Library of Congress Catalog Card Number: LC 94-72730

International Standard Book Number: 0-944435-33-5

Printed in the U.S.A.

To my husband, Jim, for his steady belief, my family for their love and encouragement, and Della, my professor

"PARADOX"

A statement or event that seems contradictory,
unbelievable or absurd, but that may actually
be true in fact.

December, 1952, 12:01 a.m. His hand trembled as he guided the expensive pen with its seamless stream of black ink across the last line of the innocent looking piece of paper. With this done, the three men who sat across the table from him looked at each other in silence. Nervously, Walter Fitzgerald Hampton pushed his chair away from the table rising to his full six feet, two inches in height. His rounded shoulders seemed to be carrying a weight that pulled them forward. The formality of handshakes took place, and without any additional words, Walter Hampton left the room as quietly as he had entered. Quickly, almost running, he made his way down the hotel corridor toward his rented suite. The luxury of the room greeted him as he entered. Leaning back against the door he felt beads of sweat trickling down the back of his neck saturating his shirt collar.

"It's for Annie," he whispered silently. His neatly packed suitcase, containing one day's worth of clothing, seemed singularly naked on top of the king-sized bed that had held his restless body the night before. It was over now. He had done what he had to do. Money. Always for money. Life was created to worship it. Without it, you lived in bleakness—at the mercy of those who possessed it. Walter Fitzgerald Hampton

1

would never be at the mercy of anyone else ever again. Annie would have all that she wanted. She was beautiful and young. He was twenty years older; a deeply shy man who never dreamed life could be so sweet and enticingly passionate. He would possess her now. The money, twenty million dollars, guaranteed it.

For the first time in days, a slight smile appeared across the thin man's face as he allowed himself to remember the details of the past twenty minutes.

"They are bastards of the worse kind," he spit out. "What I do, I do for love. What they do, they do for greed."

His body tensed as his mind struggled to believe his spoken words. In the harbor of his soul, he knew his words were only feeble attempts to justify what could not be justified.

"We're all bastards—the future will prove us all to be bastards."

The truth stung as he said it out loud for the first and last time. Moving to the bed, Hampton unlatched his suitcase and placed a single white envelope in the inside expandable flap. Now all that was left to do was to wait.

At nine a.m. the next day Walter Hampton would arrive at the National Bank of America and complete two transactions—the renting of a safe deposit box in which a single, sealed envelope would be placed— and the transferring of newly deposited funds to a transcontinental service exchange in Zurich. At ten a.m., he and a strikingly beautiful, younger woman would be passengers on TWA flight 612, a nonstop flight from New York to Switzerland. Their tickets were one-way.

◆ ◆ ◆ ◆ ◆

November 9, 1982, 8:00 a.m. She felt a warm tingling as the reddish-brown liquid entered her body by way of a silver needle plunged deeply into a pale, blue, thin vein in her left arm. Her narrow shoulders shivered slightly as her huge brown eyes followed the doctor-ordered "gift of life" fluid draining from its plastic bag down the clear tubing into her waiting body.

Taylor Addison did not want a blood transfusion. She was afraid of blood, especially blood donated from strangers. She had begged her doctor just hours before to allow her family to donate their blood for her. Her words fell on supercilious ears as the doctor, with apparent God-given control, dismissed her request citing *the safety of the screened blood supply.* *"You're being silly about this blood thing,"* the doctor dryly replied.

Three pints of blood gathered from three different male blood donors took less than an hour to enter Taylor's blood stream. No one knows for sure when the cover-up began. And Taylor Addison would die before the truth was ever to be known. . . .

◆ ◆ ◆ ◆ ◆

May, 1986, 7:30 p.m. It was never meant to happen. The twice convicted petty thief was only sent to scare her. . .

"Why did I ever threaten them? Why didn't I just leave the papers and walk away?" the weary, slightly built woman thought as she sat slumped over her kitchen table. She had just started a letter to her sister. She needed to tell someone close to her what was happening to her life. She had to know there was one person who would believe her. She couldn't tell her daughter; she didn't want her to worry.

Her gleaming formica kitchen table was filled with bills and past-due notices. The balance in her savings account fell way short of being able to cover her monthly household obligations.

It was all gone—her savings, her job, and worse than that, she feared, her reputation. If she couldn't get a job in the next week, she wasn't sure what she was going to do. She was more than just a little afraid. It had gone way past harassment.

Everything she worked so hard for these last five years was slowly being wiped away. *They* took it away from her. She knew it—she just knew it. Everything was adding up now, and the trail was leading right back to *them.* How did it all get so far out of hand?

She had been so excited when she learned she had beaten out all the other applicants for the job. For the first time in her career, she was going to get to work for a real cause. It all seemed so unreal to her now.

The letter to her sister was started with a simple statement—a statement that needed explanation.

"I'm not sure what I am going to do. I feel there is no way out for me. . ." The thought would not be completed as a noise in her garage startled her. With everything that had happened to her recently, one would have thought the woman would have picked up the phone and called the police. But she didn't. It was the last mistake Anna Cable would ever make.

The crime was never meant to happen—but then, no one would ever know a crime had ever been committed in the first place.

1

September, 1986. The surface of the faded flat gray concrete highway was deeply pockmarked. It was an ugly stretch of expressway even when it was freshly poured some thirty-five years ago. Cheap grades of cement and layer after layer of pencil-thin patching asphalt had earned westbound Interstate 31 the deserving title of Acne Road from the long-haul truckers who daily assaulted its poured pavement.

The peeling white dividing lines slapped the balding tires of the mud-splashed Hamilton Regional bloodmobile station wagon as it sped across the highway's darkened belly. The speedometer registered eighty-five miles per hour, the last possible speed the transportation vehicle was built to reach.

The driver was little concerned with the marked police car he had just passed so quickly. The cops would not stop a blood center vehicle—after all, its cargo of fresh blood screamed a guarantee that someone's life was about to be saved.

It was almost dusk when the station wagon pulled off the road at the last truck stop before reaching the Hamilton exit. In easy, experienced motions the driver steered the vehicle to the far side of the parking lot. The lot, as expected, was nearly empty. The Red Hen truck stop served bad food and overpriced gasoline. Its reputation kept most of the long-haul truck driver traffic away. Crawling quickly over the front seat of the car, Terry Milo, the heavyset, balding driver, began placing the pints of freshly donated blood deep inside the darkness of a green trash bag. Sweat quickly gathered at his temples. In a matter of minutes, 150 pints of fresh blood were pulled from their coolers. Turning his bulk around, Terry climbed back into the driver's seat. Easing the station wagon's gear out of Park, he headed the car and its cargo to the main parking section.

The blood center driver would buy himself a cup of coffee, and on the way out, stop at the huge trash dumpster located at the rear of the truck stop. Quickly, almost gracefully, the heavy trash bag filled with lifesaving blood would be tossed into the bowels of the dumpster. No one would be following these actions. The green blood-filled bag would settle deep into the belly of its new surroundings. By the end of the week, the dumpster would be emptied and its contents hauled to a huge landfill in Rockton, Illinois, about 300 miles from Hamilton, where it would be plowed into the ground with a million other green trash bags. It was a perfect place to house a secret.

2

The day had been a disaster for Michael Bryan. Kiley Matson, the blood center's distribution manager, had grossly underpriced an entire shipment of out-of-state apheresis blood platelets destined for Florida, and the pricing error hit the desk of Dr. Silvers before anyone was able to pull the evening's shipping report and retag it. Someone would pay dearly for this costly "liquid gold" error if the good doctor was to be satisfied. This mistake cut into the executive level of quarterly bonus earnings, and nothing was ever to cut into those unrecorded earnings of pure profits. It was so easy to make money with this type of an operation. Indeed, the blood banking industry, as Michael Bryan had come to know it in a short two-year period, had deceived its way into the hearts of a believing public who didn't know enough to ask questions, and had bluffed a media that never suspected there was a need to question this secret, protected industry.

His eyes suddenly caught sight of the latest campaign poster taped to the back of his closed office door. In large red letters the words, "Please donate blood now, a life depends on you!" stirred his ulcer. Working in an industry that motivates with statements frequently and seasonally placed to instigate a guilty frenzied response through fear tactics made him uncomfortable.

At this moment, though, Bryan didn't have time to grapple with right and wrong. He had spent the better part of his day negotiating with the foul-mouthed, hot-tempered collection mobile chief, Herk Golden, who had threatened to organize a union and a walkout of on-site staff. And, to top it off, Grace Tende, the director of personnel, was pressuring him big time to hire a director of public relations. The position had been vacant for over three months. There was one last person waiting outside his office door to be interviewed. The hiring process for this important position had gone on way too long. Michael Bryan was tired. As assistant executive director for Hamilton Regional, it was part of his job to "weed and seed." Finding just the right person to fill the position of director of public relations had turned into a nightmare. One hundred and fifty-two résumés had flooded the personnel office the day after the ad ran in the Sunday edition of the *Daily Voice*.

Rubbing his pounding temples, Bryan walked slowly to his office door, stopping for just a moment to take a deep breath before he met this one last person whom Grace Tende had insisted he see at 5:30 in the afternoon.

"If it's one more supercharged idiot with a pocketful of press releases, I'm going to personally strangle Grace," he thought as he roughly turned the bronze handle to his office door.

Sitting quietly in the chair outside his office was a very attractive woman in her late thirties. He was not expecting a woman. The name on the personnel sheet clearly read J. Carter Egan. Discarding the J, he took the name Carter to be masculine in gender.

"Carter Egan?" Bryan asked in a questioning tone.

"I'm Carter," the voice returned, obviously used to the gender mix-up.

There was something very warm in her wide-set brown eyes. He felt his body relax as he clasped her outstretched hand. Her smile was full and very natural. He motioned her ahead of him as they entered his office. She walked quickly and gracefully to the chair that sat directly in front of his wide, uncluttered desk. Michael Bryan liked everything neat and orderly. His papers were never strewn about in an untidy fashion. They were always neatly sorted in order of importance to the right side of his desk. Stacked trays marked "incoming" and "completed" sat on the left-hand corner of his work station. Order was important to him. The only thing that Michael Bryan could control in his job was the order on the top of his desk.

"May I offer you a cup of coffee?" he asked.

"No thanks, it's a little late in the day for me," Carter replied.

All the other candidates had jumped at the offer of coffee. Her answer, for some strange reason, threw Michael Bryan off his stride. He opened the manila folder that held her two-page résumé and began checking off her qualifications line-by-line. The office was quiet while Carter Egan waited for questions.

Looking around at the surroundings, Carter noticed the pictures of sailboats that hung ever so straight on the office walls.

"You must be a lover of sailing?"

Michael's blue-black eyes quickly looked up from the sea of ink on her résumé as he sought just the right opening question.

"What?" he replied.

"You must like sailing," Carter repeated as she motioned to the pictures on his office walls.

Taken back by her casualness, the question had taken a moment to register.

Caught off guard again, he fumbled for words. Looking at the pictures on his walls as if for the first time, his eyes betrayed an expression of one who had not noticed something he loved for a long time.

"Yes, I guess I do love sailing. I don't get to do much of it anymore. There is just so much. . ." his words trailed off.

"Work?" she finished.

A smile, exposing even white teeth, spread across his face.

"Yes, work," he repeated.

Comfortable again, Michael began the interview.

"Can you tell me what you know about blood banks, Ms. Egan?"

"It's Mrs. Egan," she quickly inserted. "To be really honest, I know very little about blood banks. On the other hand, I'm a quick study, and I really do want to work in the medical field, especially for such a good cause," she candidly answered.

Her warm smile easily repeated itself. He liked her answer. "At least she's honest about not knowing crap about what we do," he thought. The other p.r. candidates had all launched into long-drawn-out explanations about their visions of blood banks. Their answers sounded like memorized versions of the statements written in the brochures they had read just minutes before walking through his door.

"Do you have many causes?" he questioned.

"No, not really. But I want one. I think people are at their best when they find something to believe in. Especially when it comes to handling public relations. I very much want to work for a company that inspires me to believe in it," she answered.

Her answers were direct and spoken with conviction. He believed her. That's what he was looking for—someone who could make a person believe. More important than that, someone who could make the media believe.

The hair on the back of his neck felt alive. It was always a good sign for him in people situations. As he continued his questioning, he mentally moved closer to this p.r. prospect.

He liked what he saw. She was very attractive and her body language was good. She sat relaxed in her chair. Her soft green eyes met his in a direct fashion when she spoke. When she laughed, it seemed genuine.

Her royal blue silk dress was tailored, but very feminine. A single strand of white pearls hung around her neck. Her shining blonde hair was cut to a medium length and combed in a casual style that softly, and very becomingly, framed her round face.

He liked her look. He knew Ben Silvers, the center's medical director, would more than like her look. But it wouldn't be Silvers who would have the final say; it would be Silvers's co-director, Gerald Thomas Preston. Preston had served on Hamilton's Board of Directors from its inception. Less than five years ago, he had moved into the controller's position after his sudden retirement from GENCO, a medical supply company with close personal ties to the blood center. A power struggle developed almost immediately between these two men. Dr. Silvers had total control over the blood center's daily operations. He didn't want to answer to a controller regarding his research projects and their operational costs. Silvers took his war to the board, but he forgot one crucial fact: Preston had recruited most of the board's current members. When Preston placed his calls asking for support, he was braced by personal information that key board members did not want to deal with publicly. The board responded to Preston's pressure; co-director's job descriptions were enforced. Silvers, as medical director, and Preston, as executive director, were to share jointly in the governing process of the blood center. However, the real power fell to the executive director because he was given the financial reins and therefore controlled the medical director's ambitions. Not an easy task, but one that Jerry Preston enjoyed much more than he dared to show.

Dr. Silvers was furious at the board's decision. He knew Preston had taken him to the cleaners, but he was smart enough to realize there would be another time. He would wait. There were many ways to operate a blood center. He would keep his own secrets, and one day he would hand Preston his head on a platter. It was just a matter of time.

The interview sped by quickly. Not once in over an hour had Michael glanced at his watch. Conversation was interesting with this woman, and he found himself sharing thoughts that had nothing to do with what he had scripted out as form questions for the candidates. Normally, Michael did not like start-up tête-à-têtes, but J. Carter Egan had drawn more words out of him than anyone else had in quite some time.

When he did glance at his watch, he was astounded to see that it was almost 7 p.m.

"Good heavens, I didn't realize it was so late," he apologized with a bit of red creeping up from the starched white, buttoned-down shirt that framed his expensive custom-cut blue pinstriped suit jacket.

"That's quite all right. I've really enjoyed the conversation and your insight into blood banking. I definitely feel I have a better understanding of the situations you address in this operation." She stood up, aware that the interview had reached its limit.

Bryan extended his hand and genuinely thanked her for coming in, adding that he would be calling her soon with a decision on final candidate selection.

"We hope to have someone in place within the next three weeks," he stated.

"I hope to hear from you," Mrs. Egan responded with that bright, easy smile.

He escorted her to the now-locked front entrance of the building, he felt sure that this was the last person he needed to interview for the p.r. position.

Grace Tende could stick any and all other résumés up her choice-cut ass as far as he was concerned. This was the applicant that would pass the test. He'd bet his sailboat on it. And above all, he valued his sailboat. He'd only bet it on a sure thing. J. Carter Egan was a sure thing.

Walking up the back stairs to his office, the stench hit him. "My God, I'm glad they didn't start cooking flesh when she was in here," he mumbled to himself as he climbed the stairs two at a time trying to escape the nauseating smell coming from the new Tissue Bank. "We've got to get a better venting system in here," he thought.

The Tissue Bank was opened at the direction of Gerald Preston, not Dr. Ben Silvers. Preston attended a conference in Seattle, and it was there that he saw a Tissue Bank operation in place. The dollar signs excited his imagination when he learned about the huge need for skin and bones. To be the Midwest supplier would add a fortune to the center's bank account. Plastic surgeons would pay large sums to have human skin and bones readily available, which Preston soon learned were in critically short supply nationwide. To be a chief supplier of tissue and bones was an opportunity Preston could not pass up.

On the spot, with executive right granted to him by the board for such situations of expansion, Preston bought the needed processing equipment and called for an immediate enlargement of laboratory space to house the new Tissue Harvesting and Processing Center.

Dr. Silvers was surprised by his co-director's savvy. He was also angry that he had passed up the trip to Seattle and had not been the one to discover such a medical opportunity. Silvers immediately demanded control of the operation. Preston had no problem with this. "Just get it up and running" was his only demand of Silvers.

Dr. Alice Crane, assistant medical director, was put in charge of the Tissue Bank's lab operations. She knew nothing about tissue banking, but lack of knowledge had never stopped her before. What she didn't know, she would fake until she did. Her medical sheepskin inhibited ordinary people from asking too many questions—a tactic widely used in the medical field.

Dr. Crane was a quick learner, and she was determined to get this project off the ground for Dr. Silvers. He had hired her with only one stipulation—cover my back and do as I say. She desperately needed the salary and all the perks that went with the position. As a former navy doctor, she was accustomed to taking orders. Now, at the age of 62, and looking much older, she needed just a few more years of decent income before she could retire and get out from underneath all the pressures of life that were now affecting her health.

Dr. Alice Crane was not your typical physician in appearance. To see her once was not to forget her easily. The laboratory staff, which reported directly to her, frequently found more than one occasion to poke fun at her behind her back. Gray, thinning dull hair rimmed a plump, round, no-neck face. Short and dumpy, she waddled as she walked. The sound of her thighs slapping together alerted staff well in advance of her actual physical presence. Her faded green eyes, open to just slits, gave the crew the leeway to nickname her "ET." She was aware of the reference and the jokes made at her expense. She packed her anger away and stored it for any occasion that could allow her to get even, an art she had mastered. She vented her anger through the telling of a dirty joke, especially when the content of the story pertained to anal sex. Four letter words became her "specialty." If she could shock you, she could bring you down to size. This was how she coped with the shortcomings in her life.

Reaching for his office door, Michael found himself out of breath. "I've got to cut back on smoking," he thought as he walked toward his desk. The ringing of the phone interrupted his speculation about his out-of-shape physical condition.

"Bryan," he answered.

"Michael, where is Bennie? He was supposed to be home an hour ago," the high-pitched, whiny voice screamed in his ear.

"I'm not sure, Barbara. I think he may have stopped at St. Margaret's on his way home," he calmly lied.

"This has got to stop, Michael. You have got to help him cut back on his hours. He is going to kill himself working like this," she went on.

"I should have such a schedule," he thought, knowing full well that Barbara's husband, the good doctor Ben Silvers, was probably downstairs right now getting his nightly blow job from his own personally hand-picked director of nurses. Quite appropriate, he silently thought.

"I'm sure Ben will be home within the hour, Barbara," Michael added, trying to be heard over her ongoing raging on the other end of the phone.

As usual, Barbara Silvers hung up on him. Michael began gathering his nightly paperwork. Reports on inventory discrepancies were popping up right and left. Substation nurse managers were screaming that posted month-end unit numbers did not match station tally boards that they each personally kept. Yet, the paperwork inventory was consistent with the counted blood inventory received and processed in the center's main laboratory.

"How could we be losing eight hundred units of blood a week?" pondered the weary assistant executive director. Something was wrong here. On top of all this, Bryan knew that Preston was less than pleased with the time it was taking him to find a p.r. replacement. It was the role of this position to stir the media to on-the-air emergency pleas for blood. The center had gone nearly two months without an emergency blood appeal, and the end result was beginning to affect their secret *Glass* account.

"Glass" was a code word used to refer to a type O blood inventory. The *Glass* inventory, which was exclusively narrowed to only type O blood, was kept well-stocked by regular, phony, emergency blood appeals. This blood was sold at a higher-than-market price to out-of-state hospitals desperate for the precious O type blood. The secret value of this O type blood inventory was worth well over a million dollars per year to the center. Only four other people beside Bryan knew of the Glass account: Dr. Silvers, Preston, Dr. Crane, and Kiley Matson.

Michael forced his briefcase shut. It would not hold any more papers. As he walked to the door, his eyes once again caught sight of his beloved sailboat. Eight more months would have to pass before he could once again feel the joy of sailing. This season was going to be different. He was going to sail at least three evenings a week and every Saturday. If Betsy didn't like it, Betsy could take a hike. Besides, how far would his wife get without his American Express card?

When the lights went off in Michael Bryan's office, the only other light on in the building, besides the twenty-four hour laboratory section, was in the office of the director of nurses, Elizabeth Monroe. Elizabeth had wanted to turn the light off thirty minutes earlier, but Dr. Silvers preferred to have it on. His wife of ten years always insisted that they leave the lights off when having sex. He could not control his wife but he could control his director of nurses.

Elizabeth introduced Silvers to pleasures that he had never felt before, especially in the daylight hours. The quiet director loved nothing more than to find an excuse to pop into her medical director's office during business hours on the pretense of business. The excitement of having sex in his office with people just on the other side of his unlocked door caused the good doctor's heart to beat at what he was sure was an unsafe rate. "Dying in this manner would surely be worth it," he often thought as the intense pleasure flooded his loins.

Elizabeth assured him that once he learned to relax, she could do things to his body that he had never imagined possible. She would give him what he wanted and more. All he had to do was supply her with what she needed most in all the world.

For all his bluster and self-projected macho image, Ben Silvers was inexperienced in matters of sex. The same could not be said for Elizabeth Zandra Monroe. At forty years of age, she had just signed the papers on her fourth divorce decree. She was neither friend nor foe with her just divorced ex, Frank Monroe. She was, at this point in her life, just indifferent. Another bad choice. She could find the best used car on any lot, but when it came to men, she consistently picked the obvious lemon. She had a taste for the fast side of life. Big and raunchy men were a challenge, and she loved a good challenge. They also had a way of making her feel superior. It was a feeling she needed.

The wild ones had definitely taken their toll. Her once natural rich auburn hair was now a brittle-looking red. Her thin face was becoming deeply lined from a combination of dry skin and hard living. Her deep-set blue eyes were surrounded by dark circles. She hadn't looked at herself carefully in a mirror for over a month. It wasn't that she didn't care, but more directed at the image she could not bring herself to see staring back at her in the mirror. Once a very fine nurse, her own mirrored reflection presented her with a truth she couldn't face as a person, let alone as a nurse. Regardless of what had happened to her in the past, she always found a way to be in control. These last six months had changed all that. She was not in control. Little by little, she had given in.

In one smooth motion, Ben Silvers rolled off the office couch moving Elizabeth gently to an upright position. Standing stiffly above her, he quickly pulled up his suit pants, straightened his tie, and ran his fingers through his dark curly hair. Walking slowly, he stepped around the books and over the papers piled in the middle of the extremely cluttered office floor. Reaching Elizabeth's metal desk in the left-hand corner of the room facing a blank undecorated wall, Silvers quickly opened his locked burgundy-leather briefcase, which was resting on its side. The extremely expensive attaché had been a birthday present from his wife. In a few moments the doctor turned to face Elizabeth and for the first time in eight hours, the light came back into her eyes. It was now her turn to be satisfied. She had never known such a master.

3

Gerald Thomas Preston slowly edged his company-provided blue Cadillac down the narrow driveway leading to his spacious two-story home nestled in Sydney Cove. Less than fifty homeowners held title to the half-million, one-acre tracks of land developed for exclusive estate living. Gerald and Nancy Preston were included in the lucky fifty.

Sydney Cove was a quick twenty-minute drive from downtown Hamilton. The city with just under a million inhabitants, was a quiet midwest metropolis known for cheap housing and affordable taxes. It was a good place to settle and raise a family. The phrase "middle class" could have started in Hamilton as the majority of its residents fell into that category. Gerald Preston was not middle class by any means.

Five straight shots of expensive scotch washed down into an empty stomach were having an effect on Preston's ability to navigate. Five years ago, it would have been different; the alcohol would not have hit him so quickly. But five years ago, his stomach would not have been empty. Today, he was dieting, a diet consisting only of endless cups of black coffee. High cholesterol was in part responsible for the diet, but closer to the truth was his need to appear youthful, trim, and appealing. The appeal process was directed toward someone younger—someone he could not get out of his mind.

"Why in the hell can't she leave a light on?" Preston uttered as he struggled to find his gold house key in the darkened entryway. Exasperated at having to search for a key in the first place, he felt a mounting anger as he unlocked the double doors and staggered onto the rum-colored, Italian marble flooring so carefully chosen by his wife some fifteen years earlier.

The house was cold and dark. Nancy Preston was, as usual, not present to greet him. He noticed a slim line of light escaping from beneath her white, gold-trimmed bedroom door as he made his way to his den. There would be no gentle knock on her door or soft call to say he was home. Communication of this sort had stopped over ten years ago. Conversations now were few depending on how sober Nancy wanted to be. It had been over six weeks since the Prestons had even appeared in the same room together, let alone engaged in conversation.

Preston's large round fingers quickly found the brass light switch in his den. With one upward movement, his area of the house was flooded with soft, muted lighting. Its rich decor was perfectly and completely masculine. The walls were paneled with expensive mahogany. A white stone fireplace with large French doors on either side dominated the outside wall. Hunter green carpet complimented the comfortable oversized multicolored plaid davenport and loveseat arranged in a conversation-style setting. There was no television set in Preston's den. He wanted no part of an intrusive outside world. Current events were not welcome. He did install a twenty-thousand dollar surround-sound stereo system, though. Music was very important to Gerald Preston; music held his past. And right now, the past was what kept him going.

Preston slowly moved to his own rhythm of performing his now nightly ritual. He removed his suit coat, loosened his tie, and kicked off his shoes. Walking directly to his wet bar, he located his favorite brand of imported Scotch, Chivas Regal, and poured himself a double. Tonight, though, he filled the crystal glass nearly to the top for a triple. One ice cube was added.

Picking up the stereo's remote control, he hit the play button. The instant sound of a woman's soft rich voice filled his ears.

"What's new? How is the world treating you?" The words were too much for him this evening. He quickly shut the music off. The power of a remote. "If only people could be handled this way," he thought. "Turn them on when you want them, shut them up with the press of a button." It was an appealing thought.

Heavily and clumsily, Preston lowered his two-hundred-and-forty pound body to an outstretched position on the couch, deeply indenting the overstuffed cushions. Raising his gray, balding head up to greet the crystal glass with thin pursed lips, he gulped down his last drink of the evening. The glass fell from his hand, landing silently on the thick carpet.

His subconscious memory drifted. Silvers's words once again flooded his thoughts as if running in sound bites. *"Damn it, Preston, we'll lie through our teeth if we have to—We've got to keep a lid on this—It could destroy us—Cover it up, cover it up."*

Sobering words kept him from falling asleep in his usual manner.

"How in the hell did I get in the middle of all this?" Preston's mind raced as he struggled to clear his head. Slowly, painfully he allowed his subconscious to drift back to the day the *"monster"* had been created. It was begotten nearly twenty years ago. The events leading up to it were still crystal clear in Preston's far-from-sober memory.

Unexpectedly, the American Red Cross had closed all its blood drawing facilities and left the central part of Hamilton County and its thirty hospitals high and dry. At the time, ARC viewed their blood operations in this area as profit-losing divisions. "Disaster Relief," with appealing and sensational fund-raising opportunities, was to become the wave of ARC's future endeavors.

The executive directors for the then-deserted area hospitals and key civic leaders, including Gerald Thomas Preston, banded together and quickly mounted a plan to form a central blood drawing operation. The role of this regional blood center would be to supply area hospitals with blood and blood components and to increase its service to the territory as time and blood inventory allowed. The cooperating administrators agreed that each of the area's hospital pathologists would hold the right to serve as board representatives, with six nonmedical board members selected by the executive committee. Preston was to be one of the chosen six. It had taken six hours of acrimonious debate to reach this decision. Hospital administrators are not known for friendship as each hospital CEO ran a highly competitive operation, competing for doctors with lucrative patient practices and programs to draw public attention. Blood and blood components were their only mutual interest. And each of these hospitals wanted more than its fair share of this liquid gold.

The second decision made that day included the hiring of a pathologist from Lincoln, Illinois, Dr. Filimore Quanto, to serve as the blood center's first medical director. Preston, who quickly recognized an opportunity to assert himself and be viewed as a fair-minded and contributing board member, suggested that a neutral physician with no local ties to any of the participating area hospitals, was the way to approach this new blood supply system. The smaller county hospital administrators did not trust their big city counterparts, especially Seton Memorial's Bud Mybeck.

Seton Memorial Hospital was the largest hospital in the state. Mybeck ran his hospital like a bulldog and was never shy about throwing his weight around to get what he wanted. He was loved by his hospital doctors because he would stop at nothing to get them what they wanted. Ethics were never a part of his business habits.

Dr. Quanto's selection was supposed to balance the scales and prevent the larger blood-demanding full service hospitals in Hamilton—especially Seton Memorial—from dictating a priority blood control system. For this new alliance to work, the size of a hospital and its blood demands could not control the flow of blood. Ideally, all hospitals were to work through a "community responsibility" philosophy. Under this concept, it would become the responsibility of each community served by the blood center to donate a percentage of blood, based on population, throughout the year. The blood center would utilize these freely donated community blood donations to provide the transfusion needs of any person living in the center's defined territory.

It was also mutually agreed that the new blood center would quickly drop the American Red Cross credit system. This was Gerald Thomas Preston's financial gift to the overall operating plan. The ARC credit system guaranteed an individual or family free blood if they donated at least five pints of blood during the course of a single year. Under this system, a financial gain was not possible. The new blood banking operation would indeed be different; Preston would see to that. The just-established regional blood center, christened Hamilton Regional, would now charge a processing fee, which was publicly stated as needed to cover the cost of recruiting, drawing, testing, and preparing the blood for distribution to the area hospitals.

On paper it presented an excellent mission statement. The blood would be donated for free by faithful blood donors. The not-for-profit blood center would charge a small fee for processing the blood, and the hospitals would, in turn, bill the cost to the recipient's insurance company. How could anyone argue with such a fair community process? The board agreed with Preston and unanimously harmonized that they had just created the best system yet to handle the urgency of the gathering of the "gift of life."

Dr. Quanto, the hand-picked neutral player, soon recognized that the picture presented could be manipulated to his new center's financial advantage. In just a few short days after Hamilton Regional was operational, Bud Mybeck, accompanied by Preston, paid Quanto a private visit. Mybeck's hospital had an insatiable thirst for a padded blood inventory. His multiple daily operating surgeons were concerned that their blood supply would be subject to restrictions with this new system. The "Gods of the Scalpels" did not want to schedule their operating hours around a blood inventory. An *"understanding"* would be necessary between Seton Memorial and the blood center. Mybeck and Preston were not at all concerned that such an arrangement could not be worked out. Filimore Quanto would have his price. Every underpaid pathologist did. In less than one hour, Quanto would agree to secretly pad Seton's inventory orders. A slight price reduction was also agreed upon because of the volume of the guaranteed orders. If three hundred pints of blood were ordered, six hundred pints would be shipped. Mybeck would get what he wanted: a guarantee of more than enough fresh daily blood for his operating rooms. Preston's medical supply company, GENCO, would be granted an exclusive contract to supply the center with its blood bags, and the blood center would profit from a noncompetitive, guaranteed shipment order from the state's largest user of fresh blood.

Quanto smelled an early retirement. Preston warned Quanto that it would take aggressive donation actions to draw the amount of blood needed to supply the preset orders, but Hamilton County was known for its generous and ever-faithful blood donors. Quanto was confident he could get the job done. Preston, of course, would make himself available at all times to help Quanto *"manipulate"* the board in areas of critical support.

All of this would be done secretly. Separate billing rates would be established per hospital and inventory levels at each hospital would be kept confidential.

In the end, the smaller county hospitals, who needed less blood and therefore ordered less, would pay a much higher rate for blood. So much for community sharing.

Filimore Quanto, with Preston's full knowledge, would also create another legacy to leave to all the other administrators following in his footsteps. Given no special title, a percentage bonus account for blood sold out-of-state, at double the going rate, would be paid directly into the top director's personal expense account. It was called a "service fund" in the annual report. Needless to say, this "resource sharing" fund, as it would later be dubbed, would add thousands of dollars to the top administrator's yearly salary. As greed increased, a special account known as the *Glass* account, which housed only O type blood for out-of-state sales was created as a sort of insurance package. It was an account not listed in the Annual Report. The blood center's pathologist would never again be underpaid.

"A well paid administrator was a willing partner in all matters of needed cooperation," reasoned Gerald Thomas Preston, who, at the time, was simply looking out for his own company's exclusive blood bag supplier agreement. Little did Preston know at the time that one day, five administrators and nearly twenty years later, he too would be on the receiving end of "resource sharing."

When Hamilton Regional Blood Center opened its doors for business on March 16, 1966, the media embraced it with open arms. Gil Havens, a top public relations executive in Hamilton, at the urging of Mybeck and Preston, was recruited to fill one of the six public board seats. Flattered at the invitation, Haven's public relations agency, at an inflated fee rate of $175 per hour, laid the groundwork for the Holy Grail image. The old-time public relations specialist carefully spoon-fed an unsuspecting media a preconceived foundation for future media blood appeals: "Blood cannot be manufactured. Humans are the only known source. If the public doesn't respond to the blood center's immediate call for donations, a tragedy will surely occur."

An uninformed public bought the media's well-intentioned educational story. For the next twenty years, Hamilton Regional would operate at will, amassing a steady flow of blood donations and a bank account that would cause even a Fortune 500 company to blush. The media continued to support this illusion.

Tonight, though, Preston was not in the mood to gloat over his past handiwork. It had been another bitter day filled with arguments and power struggles. Preston's drinking had begun to have an effect on him. His conscious mind had always been able to blot out unpleasant thoughts but was now in a mode of constant recall. Preston restlessly shifted his weight on a couch, which normally brought him much comfort. The turbulence of the day weighed heavily as his thoughts drifted back to a conversation that still haunted him some four years later.

"The NAABC has facts and figures to back it all up," shouted Silvers as he paced back and forth in Preston's office shortly after arriving home from the secret emergency conference called by the National Association of Accredited Blood Centers in Atlanta.

Hepatitis had long been a silent killer running loose in the public's blood supply, but the public never seemed to pay much attention to its yearly death count. This time hepatitis looked liked small potatoes when compared to this virus-type carrier that was now known to be present in all body fluids. The documented information reviewed by the nation's top blood banking medical directors was so scary that all handouts were destroyed at the end of the meeting.

"We're not going to do anything for the time being. It's a matter of sitting on our asses and pretending this killer disease doesn't exist," a highly animated Dr. Silvers ranted while a stunned Gerald Preston sat rigidly in his executive chair, not really believing what he was hearing.

"My God, Ben, there are thousands of blood transfusions performed on a daily basis."

"Don't you think I know this, Jerry? A red-faced Dr. Silvers cut Preston off in mid-sentence. "My God, the ramifications of this virus are staggering. We're talking about millions of lives here. Jesus Christ, if we just looked at the hemophiliac population alone, you'd be talking about the future eradication of a nation of helpless people depending on blood products for their survival. That's a joke—survival."

Preston's face was taut; his arched neck near paralysis. An energy of fear was wrapped around the emotional body of the medical director.

Two double windows suddenly invaded Silvers's ambivalent conscious. The warm, sun-drenched external world would slowly ameliorate his turmoil. After a few tacit moments, the medical director regained his controlled composure and continued.

"The NAABC will stall long enough for us to get our public statements ironed out. We'll, of course, downplay exposure methods and take advantage of the stats that show this to be a homo-plague. God knows the Bible-carrying public will not be alarmed at a bunch of queers dying," Silvers added, in a much less emotional tone of voice. "From now on, we will never publicly state that blood is safe. We'll play off the statement that blood is 'safer than ever' or 'as safe as humanly possible.' I'll get a memo out tomorrow to our p.r. department. From now on all public statements are going to have to be absolutely rigid in this statement. I don't intend to be the object of a fucking lawsuit."

Preston nodded his head silently in agreement.

"If we are never quoted as saying blood is safe, we'll protect ourselves as an industry from any preconceived public notion of false advertising. And from now on, neither one of us will make any public statements."

Preston turned in his chair to face Ben Silvers.

"What else do you know about this virus? How is it contracted? How long till we have a screening test?" Preston's questions came in rapid order like a scared child.

Silvers did not immediately respond to his co-director's questions allowing a black silence to fill the room.

"Damn it, Ben—" Preston finally spit out, demanding an answer.

"I know enough right now to tell you that I'm scared to death of it—even its name, AIDS—frightens the shit out of me."

"AIDS," repeated Preston softly, as if putting a face on the monster just discovered.

"Acquired Immune Deficiency Syndrome," Silvers clarified.

"The documents that we reviewed went back to 1972. Apparently, the National Association of Disease Control has been following it for quite some time. It's all been very hush-hush. They've identified multiple cultures of the virus. It's an intelligent sonofabitch virus, Jerry. It can mutate at will under a microscope. It's been isolated in body fluids, but that doesn't mean it can't be airborne in certain circumstances—like TB," the doctor's voice trailed off as if not wanting to say the rest of his thoughts out loud.

Ben Silvers turned from his spot by the window. In a slow, reluctant motion, he headed toward one of Preston's expensive executive chairs that had been custom ordered for his office suite. The sound of the doctor's body collapsing heavily into the stationary gold-colored velvet chair pierced the stillness that had captured Preston's office. It was rare for these two declared adversaries to occupy time and space together. All told, records would show that Dr. Silvers had probably spent less than ten minutes in his co-director's office in the last year.

Silvers, at the age of forty, was considered to be a handsome man. Nearly six feet tall in his stocking feet, the vain doctor prided himself on his trim waistline and broad shoulders. He exercised regularly and carefully watched his diet. His tanned face, set off by a square jaw, showed the strain of his newly acquired secrets. Deep-set, chocolate eyes stared at Preston's navy blue carpet. Slumping deeper into the chair, the community's most powerful medical director ran his hands through his close-cropped curly, dark-brown hair.

Medicine was not Ben Silvers's first choice of occupation. He had wanted to be a pilot. Less than perfect vision put an end to his dream of aviation. In the Silvers family, all males were expected to follow in their father's footsteps, and Dr. John Ambrose Silvers made this clear when Ben was a young child. As a boy, Benjamin Quinn Silvers lived for the moments when he could sneak off and read his books on airplanes. He would save his allowance and splurge only when he could afford the custom model airplane kits found only in Ollie Terrel's cross-town hobby store.

The young boy's hands would piece together the small plastic parts until the seamless body of an airplane was created. Only on rare occasions did the eager boy work from the kit's instructional diagram; instead, he preferred his own system of touch and feel. At ten years of age he was fitted with his first pair of glasses. At fifteen he realized his love—his only love—would forever be just out of his reach. Eyesight, good eyesight, was a top requirement in learning to fly an airplane. At sixteen Ben put away his models and with deep bitterness buried himself in schoolwork. His once warm, easygoing disposition gradually turned volatile, thriving on feelings of power. He found pleasure in verbal combat, and his hostility only masked his deep personal inadequacy.

His father, who suspected his son would inherit his nearsightedness, was secretly pleased with the turn of events. There would never be an open discussion of Ben's career choices. He would continue the family tradition and become a doctor, but not a general practitioner like his father. Benjamin Quinn didn't want the daily intimate contact with human beings; he preferred working with the components that make up living, breathing things. He would be a pathologist, but not just one of many. He set a quest for himself shortly after graduation from med-school to rise through the ranks in blood banking to reach the ultimate goal of commanding the top, most powerful position of all. Benjamin Quinn Silvers would one day be the Director of the National Accredited Association of Blood Centers. His ambition became a disease within for which there would be no cure.

Preston broke the momentarily self-imposed silence.

"If this is to be a homo thing, should we change our health questionnaire and block them from donating blood?"

"No. We are not going to change anything," snapped Silvers. "We are not going to do anything that would cause greater attention to this virus—at least not right away. We have some time to work through our position. The public and the media are still locked out on this information. Besides, it's not just a homo thing," Silvers added.

"My God, you mean it's in the straight population as well?" a visibly shocked Preston shot back. Silvers's answer was not what Gerald Thomas Preston wanted to hear.

"Yes, it's definitely been diagnosed in the hemophiliac population, and at this moment our research doesn't have enough positive data to forecast what the picture looks like in our own heterosexual population.

"I can tell you this—America's blood and plasma supply is definitely infected with AIDS, Jerry, and for every day we're in business, no man, woman, or child on the receiving end of a blood transfusion can knowingly be exempt from possible exposure to this deadly disease."

"Should we shut down then, Ben?" Preston righteously asked.

"That's absurd, of course not," Silvers responded. "It's for sure we don't have anything to stop this disease right now, and if the data reports are on target, we're out of the ballpark for the next ten to fifteen years in finding a cure for this disease—hell, maybe we'll never find it," Silvers added, pausing for just a few seconds to catch his breath.

"Our responsibility to supply blood on a daily basis isn't going to change, Jerry. Blood banking is a precarious operation. Blood has never been safe—and it never will be. There are so many diseases to be considered when you're dealing with any liquid drained from a human body. Hell, everyone associated with medicine has had to deal with the death rate of hepatitis—it's a mega killer. We don't have anything to really stop it either, and that knowledge hasn't shut us down. Why should AIDS be any different?"

"There's good news for blood banks," Silvers went on, shifting the conversation to the financial aspect of AIDS.

"The cost of adding another screening procedure is going to set the industry back a pretty penny. But there are no laws yet forcing a deadline to implement such a procedure. Blood banks can buy months of time."

Preston's hands moved nervously over the arms of his chair while he waited for Silvers to continue.

"When we get a screening procedure, we can simply double our processing fees to the hospitals. No one is going to complain about a price increase, at least not publicly. Let the hospitals raise their fees to the patients and the insurance companies can take it from there.

"It's very important to remember that when this does break, blood centers will stand together as a united body. We'll tie the plasma centers and the homos together." The doctor's distaste for the plasma drawing operations showed. "The mere fact that those centers pay people to donate blood and plasma will work to our advantage."

"Ben," Preston interrupted, "You know as well as I do that we also have a ton of homos donating blood. In fact, five out of the top ten blood donors we honored at that damn donors recognition dinner last month were queers." The color in Preston's face had all but disappeared.

"The public doesn't know that," Silvers countered. "Don't faint on me, Jerry, I'm not done filling you in yet," Silvers added with his normal sarcasm again present in his voice. Sitting up straight in his chair, Silvers continued to talk. He didn't really want to share all this with Preston, but he knew they would have to come to some kind of a truce if their profitable livelihood was going to survive these next few years. There was no way Silvers was going to let Preston claim five years from now that he didn't know the blood supply was tainted with a deadly disease. Legal advisors present at the secret meeting were up-front with advance advice for protection against public lawsuits. Lawyers would soon be a large part of day-to-day blood banking activities. Right from the beginning, he and his co-director partner would be joined at the hip with all the raw, dirty data concerning AIDS. Silvers would make sure of this. There would be no such thing as innocence.

Slowly, speaking in a near whisper, Silvers seemed to take an almost evil enjoyment in the task of updating his associate. The broad base of high-risk populations rolled off Silvers's tongue in an almost supercilious manner.

"Homosexuals, bisexuals, IV drug users, prostitutes, hemophiliacs, and past recipients of blood transfusions. . ."

Silvers's dark, brooding eyes waited for the magnitude of his statement to register on Preston's face, and as soon as he saw just the right amount of fear in place, he casually added a closing statement that was meant to put his pompous partner over the edge.

"There is no such thing as an unexposed population, Jerry. No one is immune from this disease—it's worldwide. Only the world doesn't know about it yet. It's our secret. Anybody, from any walk of life, can be a walking, spreading carrier of certain death. Sex and blood—that's what we're up against, and we all know there's no substitute for either one."

Preston had heard enough, at least all that he thought he should hear. His bulky frame bolted from the tailored chair. His arm motions sent a direct signal to Dr. Silvers to say no more.

The good doctor ignored the signal.

"We don't want a panic on our hands. We'll wait until the media gets wind of all this and then, and only then, will we start a national public information campaign. We are going to push the homo issue up-front and connect the hemophiliac's component supply to the plasma centers. The media will take a big bite out of this. This will give blood banks time to fall back and lobby publicly for an AIDS screening procedure. All this will help us protect ourselves from future negligence lawsuits. The public won't understand the difference. They'll relate a screening procedure to a test. It will be a soft defense but will help to settle any panic about the blood supply once we have the screen in place. We're probably talking a good eighteen months out while all this crap is being tossed around by our idiot media friends." Silvers had no time for the media. The media asked questions—direct questions. Only the media would dare question the medical brotherhood.

Preston's lips were drawn tightly. Anger, disbelief, and pure shock shone in his eyes.

"And how reliable will this screening procedure be in identifying the virus once we get it?" Preston asked, his voice rising barely above a whisper.

"Who knows? From what we're seeing right now, there can be a tremendous lag time from the moment of exposure until the identifying antibodies start to form. And we also have to factor in the testing time and possible slip-ups in tech testing and screening. We're going public with a six-month-after-exposure statement, but that's just for p.r. purposes. Hell, Dr. Caitte, the guru with the Office of Disease Control, had data that registered a possible ten-to-fifteen-year development time from the exposure date to the antibody formation, and to top it all off, there is a certain percentage of the population who will be carriers of this virus, but will never form antibodies within their genetic system. It's a crapshoot as far as I'm concerned."

"My God! All this sounds just short of being criminal!" Preston flared as he paced back and forth in front of Silvers.

"This is a deliberate camouflage—no, it's worse than that. It's a direct plot to deceive the public by withholding the barefaced truth about this disease!" Preston was now agitated. "How in the hell do you think we're going to get away with all this?"

"Fuck the righteousness, Jerry. This is exactly what we as a blood banking community are going to do. It's the real world—the medical world. We're not doing anything that is against any law. Look at it as our duty to protect the public from information they can't handle," Silvers shot back.

"Hell, we don't even have all the data on AIDS yet. Do you know what would happen if we dumped all this at once on John Q. Public? Hysteria! That's what would happen. Hospitals would empty, blood banks would be deserted, people would be running wild in the streets accusing their neighbors, strangers, even their families of exposing them to AIDS. We would have absolutely no way to control the public's reaction. By handling it this way, we are in control of the situation. Physicians have been in the business of dealing information out as needed since the beginning of time. It's our right to judge what is right for the public to know and what isn't. This is our call and make no mistake about it—we will make it."

"*We? We?* Who in the hell are you including in this *we* stuff? And what about the truth? Ben, what about the truth?" shouted Preston.

"Goddamnit—keep your voice down, Jerry. The truth is what we say it is. And you are now part of the *we,* like it or not. If you can't handle all this, you goddamn better resign and get the hell out of blood banking." Silvers had grown accustomed to using his best authoritative medical voice on his co-partner.

"Is there anything else you need to tell me, Doctor?" Preston asked with obvious contempt as he walked toward his desk chair.

"There is one more piece of the pie that you need to be aware of," added Silvers. "Research to date confirms a two percent rate of unknown transmission origin with this disease. That figure could climb once we have more data. This is a piece of the puzzle we're going to have to keep a tight muzzle on even if it means we out-and-out lie about it."

The look in Dr. Silvers's eyes punctuated his determination. Preston recalled a message he was given many years ago by Morley Habing when he had questioned the ethical judgment of a physician.

"Lies were not lies when spoken by a physician, as somewhere in time *they* were given a divine right commonly referred to as the "adjusted prevarication privilege." Ordinary citizens would never think to question information generated from a medical source. The public were believers—innocent from such possibilities as deception from a profession they held in esteem above all others.

Preston had only one final question for his medical counterpart.

"How many people will this AIDS disease kill, Ben?"

"How do I know? Do I look like a fortuneteller?" replied Silvers as he rose from his chair and headed toward Preston's closed office door.

Turning the solid brass handle, Silvers paused just long enough to send one more parting message to his associate.

"Do you have any stock in Sidwell Laboratories, Jerry?"

Startled at the question, Preston quickly replied with a simple no answer.

"Well, you should start buying it as soon as you can get to the bank. Sidwell will get the bid on developing the screening procedure kit for the virus. Its stock will skyrocket as soon as it becomes public knowledge. We blood bankers have to take advantage of opportunity. Don't say I never gave you anything, Jerry."

Silvers's smile was deliberate and exaggerated. His words hit Preston deep in the pit of his stomach. The door closed leaving the executive director alone in his office. For the first time in his long career, Gerald Thomas Preston felt impotent with this new knowledge.

He felt nothing but rage for Silvers and the situation he now found himself in. The packaged truth, soon to be spoon-fed to an unsuspecting and always believing public, would be wrapped in a bright red ribbon with the seal of blood banking integrity stamped across it—a guaranteed, genuine, truthful, apocalypse.

Preston had never been one to let the bending of the truth bother him, especially if the end resulted in the padding of his own pocketbook. He had spent most of his career looking the other way while men he considered to be pompous and arrogant, wearing the almighty physician's cloak, used their pedestal of power to rule over those not blessed with the calling. How dare the mere mortals question an unquestionable statement of truth. It came from the gods, therefore it must be.

Before the executive director left his office that evening, he carefully scribbled a reminder on his desk calendar. It read very simply. "Call broker tomorrow—a.m.—Sidwell—$50,000."

Tonight, nearly four years later, Preston tossed and turned on his sofa unable to stop thinking about those long-ago revealed truths. Included in those restless memories was a whole new subject—*"Lawsuit, negligence, Taylor Addison."* The words exploded like deep black ink on stark white paper.

It was almost dawn before the liquor, mixed with emotional exhaustion, finally allowed Preston to fall into a deep sleep—a sleep that came with dreams too frightening to remember.

4

A new director of public relations was hired for Hamilton Regional. Carter Egan got the job. She had sailed through her one and only interview with Dr. Silvers and Executive Director Preston with a flawless presence. They were impressed, just as Michael Bryan had been, and for all the same reasons. Dr. Silvers was especially drawn to her. He liked her look, her quick sense of humor, and above all, her lack of knowledge concerning the blood bank industry. Her obvious desire to find a noble cause to believe in was just what the doctor ordered. He would be her teacher. She would be taught only what he wanted her to know about blood banking and its ongoing crusade for faithful donors. He would mold her to fit his public and private agenda. She would do quite well with *adjusted prevarication.*

"A perfect person for the job of public relations," Dr. Silvers espoused while making a mental note to take full credit in front of the board for her future public relation successes.

Preston liked her maturity and the way she made him feel at ease. His gut feelings told him that she would be a good fit for the local media hounds to warm up to. God knows her predecessor, Anna Cable, who was perceived as being cold and unconvincing in her public appeals for blood, was disliked by the local press. Hiring Anna was a mistake and one that would not be made again, especially not now when the ability to make one believe was crucial to their future blood banking operations.

J. Carter Egan desperately wanted this position. Her gut feelings told her she had made a good impression on the two co-directors who would have the last word in selecting Hamilton Regional's new public relations director. She left her hour-long interview feeling that this was a career move that would really challenge all her professional skills, especially in the area of media relations. She wasn't sure what her selection chances were, but she knew that she had given it her best effort. The next day, she received a call from Michael Bryan with an offer of employment. She crossed her fingers and rejected the first salary offer of twenty-five thousand dollars. She countered at thirty. The blood center accepted her counter.

Driving to the center on her first day of employment, she was filled with starting day jitters. The blood banking world was indeed foreign to her. Was she making the right career move? And just who and what was Hamilton Central Regional Blood Center? She had asked her husband, Patrick, and several close friends and business acquaintances about this center. Their answers had nearly all been the same. They didn't know anything about blood banks or this company other than the fact that Hamilton's bloodmobiles showed up several times a year for blood drives, and they always seemed to need blood.

This time, Carter Egan was dedicating her energies to a new cause with a company she really knew nothing about. She wasn't sure how her husband really felt about her giving up a very good job at this time in their lives.

"It's your choice and it's your time. It certainly seems like a worthwhile cause," Patrick offered during their dinner conversation after her first interview. He knew she had grown tired of working in her current marketing position. She had been with Aaron Engineering for over seven years. Patrick knew the challenge in her position was gone, and above all else, J. Carter Egan lived or died by challenge.

Today, though, she was not going to have a lot of time for these doubts. A few minutes after her announced arrival, a distinguished looking woman with silver hair cut extremely short and wearing a white lab coat greeted her in the lobby.

"Are you J. Carter Egan?"

"Yes," replied Carter, extending her hand for the customary greeting.

"I'm Bertha White, Director of Laboratory Services for the Center." Her smile seemed warm but just a bit forced. "Michael is running just a bit behind this morning. Why don't you follow me, and I'll guide you up the maze to his office."

Carter nodded and quickly fell in line behind the already moving lab director. They swiftly made their way in silence to the executive wing of the center. Michael Bryan was just walking back toward his office when he spied Carter and Bertha White exiting from the front stairwell.

Michael apologized for not meeting her downstairs. "Today started off like hell and I've got a million things piled on my desk. Hope you don't mind if Bertha gives you the orientation," a preoccupied assistant director offered.

"Of course not," Carter replied, feeling a bit awkward but obviously wanting to put her new boss at ease.

"When you're all done, why don't you stop by my office and we'll touch base?" His smile clearly conveyed a thank-you for her understanding. Looking at Bertha, he directed her to proceed with a schedule that had obviously been discussed earlier.

For the next three hours Carter Egan was kept busy. Her guide set a fast pace through the center. They seemed to meet one person after another who bore the title "director."

"How many directors are there?" Carter asked halfway into her tour.

"About fifty too many" was Bertha's reply as she absorbed the new hire's reaction to her comment. Bertha paid close attention to Carter's observations, picking up on her remarks and questions as they passed from department to department. She judged Carter to be smart but naive—a perfect match for what was required of a Hamilton public relations director. Time would change all this, she thought, remembering her own innocence when she first started at the blood center some twenty odd years ago. Bertha had mixed emotions about public relations people. "They are nothing more than damn slaves. . .always subject to someone else's whims, she thought." As a functioning department, Bertha felt they were the last to know and the first to go. Security of employment was only as strong as yesterday's press releases, or in the blood banking business, yesterday's response to an emergency blood appeal. Bertha was still angry at the way Anna Cable, Carter's predecessor, had been dismissed from her position. No warning, just a quick call to a meeting. She didn't even return to her office. The next day, maintenance packed up all her personal belongings. Since she had failed to return any of Bertha's calls, one could only guess what had happened.

Bertha had saved the tour of the blood laboratory for the last part of Carter Egan's orientation. Slowly descending the back stairwell, which took them deep into the bowels of the second basement of the building, Bertha began her vivid explanation of the blood processing operation.

Never having seen such an operation before, Carter could not quite imagine the picture Bertha was trying so hard to set up for her. It wasn't until they opened the large double doors to the processing laboratory that her words had impact.

Blood was everywhere. It was like a battlefield. Only missing were the bodies of the dead and wounded. Strewn over the white counter tops of square sorting tables were hundreds of plastic bags filled with various shades of blood. What looked liked ordinary, white Sears washing machines lined the long outer wall to the left of the double doors. These processing machines would cause the different components in blood, such as plasma and platelets, to separate when set at various spin rotation speeds. The separated platelets looked to Carter like floating red strings in a pale, almost yellowish liquid. Some bags seemed to have more *strings* in them than others. Motorized wire rack containers kept the extremely valuable platelets in a state of constant motion.

"Once we get these platelet babies separated from whole blood, they have be kept in motion to prevent them from doing what they do naturally—clotting," the lab director emphasized as her hand gently tapped the metal container as they passed by.

"Since we can't freeze platelets, they have a short shelf life of three to five days. . ."

"Do we have any problems with platelets not getting into motion after separation?" Carter interrupted.

Bertha's dark eyes flashed. "God help any tech who leaves a batch of platelets unattended. As director of this operation, I'd fire them on the spot for not attending to their job."

The uniform grind of the several dozen spinning rotators filled with the precious supply of blood clotting platelets seemed to hum in a harmonized, almost sorrowful rhythm.

But the rhythm was interrupted in the form of the ghastly casualness of spilled blood. There were eight different stainless steel sinks in the laboratory. Most were filled with discarded blood bags whose dripping contents had splashed various shades of red up the silver contrasting side walls of the sinks. Blood stains from mishandled or leaking blood bags dotted the countertops and the pale white linoleum floor. A wave of nausea enveloped Carter. A huge blood stain on the laboratory floor had been set off with a chalk outline of a human body drawn around it.

"Laboratory humor," Bertha stated, as she noted the pale look on Carter's face.

"Does the public ever come down here, Bertha?"

"Sometimes," she answered with an obvious look of displeasure. "They usually faint or throw up about halfway through. If I had my way, the blood processing would be off limits to the public. They don't understand half of what you p.r. guys are rattling on about, and it's just a waste of our time when we have to stop and try to answer their questions. We work against the clock down here, and anything that interrupts puts us behind the eight ball."

Carter made a mental note to ask Bryan if they should continue to conduct public tours of this end of the center's operation. Bertha was clearly not in favor of it, and perhaps she had good reasons to justify her feelings.

Bertha caught the look of questioning in Carter's eyes.

"Perhaps things might be different with this one," she thought as she moved toward the nearest exit. They had entered the processing laboratory at the ten a.m. break time. Seeing this area void of any living human beings, only heightened the austere atmosphere of this part of the laboratory operation for Carter.

There was a definite smell in the processing area. Carter wasn't sure if it was the smell of blood or chemicals, but it was a smell that would offend a sensitive nose. Carter's stomach still felt a bit queasy. Two of her five senses, sight and smell, were working overtime right now. She would definitely have to overcome her distaste for this area.

Leaving the processing area, Bertha guided Carter down a narrow hallway leading to the testing area of the blood center. The sign on the door was marked "Testing—Authorized Personnel Only." Upon entering the room, the half-dozen or so techs sitting on tall stools pushed up to chest-high counter tops turned to stare at their uninvited guests. It was not a friendly atmosphere. Heads turned back almost in unison with neither a nod nor any other kind of a greeting signaled.

Bertha gave her canned lecture on the testing process of blood in almost whisper tones. "Blood must be processed completely within a twenty-four-hour time period. The shelf life for blood, Carter, is about thirty five days," Bertha stated as they passed slowly behind the techs. "Blood is a funny thing, Carter. The fresher it is, the more impact you get. Blood at the end of its shelf time is less vital—of course, you don't want to state that publicly. . ."

"Why not?" Carter innocently asked. It was a good question.

"In our business, Carter, we need to be careful about what we pass on. Blood is easily misunderstood. For your knowledge on this subject, blood is at its best when it is fresh out of a vein. Toward the end of its shelf life, some of its magic has worn off. And then you get into the problem of having to give more blood to the patient, which means more exposure to possible disease. Fresh blood requires less blood. Is any of this making sense to you?" Bertha asked in a still near-whisper tone.

Carter nodded her head in an affirmative manner even though she didn't quite understand. Bertha continued on with her lecture, and Carter wasn't sure at this point if the hushed voice was used out of respect or out of fear. Carter did pick up on the simplicity of the blood testing processing and how much the process relied on human interpretation. It seemed to Carter that the margin for error in identifying disease in blood definitely relied on the concentrated skills of the technician performing the test. With that thought, Carter now understood the hushed tone in Bertha's voice. With so much at stake, you certainly wouldn't want to interrupt their concentration level. Carter was relieved when Bertha concluded her remarks on this area. Turning to leave, Bertha was almost struck by the swinging lab door as it was suddenly in motion.

A muscular young man with jet black hair and an almost ghostly complexion that nearly matched the shade of his freshly pressed white lab coat was unexpectedly standing in front of them blocking their exit.

"I've been looking for you, Bertha. Quality Control says we've got a slip-up. We've passed on twenty units of infected blood. They weren't caught in time, and five will get you ten they've already been transfused."

The words stunned Carter. She scanned Bertha's face looking for a reaction. There was none.

"Why don't you come see me later, Reymond. We can discuss this then." Her manner was calm and very businesslike. From all outward appearances, this tech could have just told her it was raining outside. Infected blood—not caught—passed on for transfusion—the words still stung Carter's ears.

Reymond caught the glare in Bertha's eyes.

"Sure, Bertha. I'll look you up later," he stated as he looked Carter over.

"Reymond Alexander, this is Carter Egan. She's been hired to replace Anna Cable." The introduction was short and to the point. Bertha was on the go again.

Carter smiled a professional smile at Reymond Alexander and followed Bertha out of the area. The unwanted displeasure Bertha had with Reymond's remarks had not gone unnoticed. She could hear laughter coming from the room they had just left. A strange feeling of uneasiness touched Carter's sense of being as she hurried to catch up with her tour guide.

"Don't let Reymond's remarks throw you off, Carter. He knows better than to spout off like that. Hell, you could have been a reporter."

"Bertha, did we really send out contaminated blood?" Carter asked as she hurried to catch up with the fast walking lab director.

Bertha suddenly stopped, causing Carter to nearly run into the stoutly built woman.

"Listen, Carter. There are some questions you should ask and some you shouldn't. I only wished I'd had the opportunity to say this to Anna—just pretend you didn't hear that conversation. If you're meant to know about the inner workings of the laboratory, word will come down to you from the top. Keep out of what goes on underneath that level, otherwise. . ." Bertha did not finish her statement as she caught herself just in time.

"Mustn't taint the new hires," she thought as she left the sentence unfinished. Carter sensed she should let well enough alone and not pursue the issue—at least not now. The two directors began their climb up the back stairs toward the executive wing.

Suddenly, an odor, so foul it was indescribable, filled the stairwell. Instinctively, Carter put her hand up to her face covering her mouth and nose. "What is that odor?" she asked, half gagging.

"It's the Tissue Bank. They're cooking skin," Bertha answered, following Carter's hand motions. The last twenty steps were taken two-at-a-time. Carter had been especially impressed with the new Tissue Bank when Michael Bryan had given her a lengthy explanation on the need for human skin and bones and how Hamilton Regional was to be the only one in the Midwest with such an operation. The unbelievable smell of cooking skin was never mentioned in his explanation. At this moment, Carter was not sure if she would have taken the position with this company if her nose had been exposed to the smell of human skin processing.

Without saying a word, Bertha White directed J. Carter Egan to the nearest women's restroom. The sound of Carter regurgitating did not cause Bertha to smile. Instead, as much as she didn't want to, she felt a bit ashamed of herself for treating Carter the way she had all morning. She had not gone out of her way to make Carter feel at home or even welcome. Bertha judged Carter to indeed be a nice person, attractive, bright, and obviously searching for a cause. The center desperately needed a good public relations director. Anna Cable was gone, and it was time to bury old alliances to people who weren't coming back. Bertha sighed deeply. "Poor Anna, if only there had been a way to help her." Bertha White pushed the thought aside. It was safer this way.

Waiting for Carter to emerge from the bathroom, she made herself a promise to help Carter learn as much as was safe for her to learn about the technical aspects of blood banking. It was the least she could do for the newcomer. When Carter emerged from the rest room, Bertha smiled and told her not to feel discouraged.

"Blood banks are full of sights and smells, Carter. It took me awhile to get my sea legs. You'll do it. Just give yourself time. Don't rush it," she said.

Carter felt for the first time that morning a genuine feeling of warmth from Bertha. She was glad, as she certainly didn't want to start off on this director's bad side. It would be important for her to learn the technical aspects of the laboratory.

"If I have to wear a clothespin on my nose, I'm going to learn to adjust to the smells of this building," Carter thought as she followed Bertha back to Michael Bryan's office.

Bertha handed Carter off to Bryan's secretary, Michelle Burch, who quickly moved Carter on to the personnel department. Grace Tende was truly glad to see Carter. This position had been vacant way too long. The rest of Carter's day was spent filling out forms and viewing orientation films. At 3:30 p.m. Michael Bryan rescued her from the personnel department. He apologized profusely for his lack of attention on this her first day of work. The warmth of his smile and his obvious embarrassment at such a happening was easily accepted by Carter.

"Would you like to get settled in your office?" Bryan asked as he took her by the arm and gently led her down the hall toward her permanent quarters.

"I would, Mr. Bryan," she said.

"Michael," he corrected.

They were soon greeted by Shelly Nisen, Carter's new secretary. Introductions were made, and Carter was left to her new surroundings. The large supply room separated the p.r. department from the bank of offices where the "bigwigs" were, so stated Shelly. Carter spent the rest of what was left of the afternoon talking to Shelly. She felt an immediate bonding with her appointed secretary and made a quick judgment they would work well together. Shelly seemed to know her way around, and her experience would help Carter with her initial adjustment period. Shelly also appeared to have an easy manner about her with a dry sense of humor to match. In her late thirties with strands of gray flickering through her brunette hair, Shelly's hazel eyes sparkled as she spoke in rapid fire delivery. As the 4:30 quitting time rolled around, the new public relations director had to acknowledge a bit of fatigue as she gathered her things to leave for the day. The pair walked down the back stairwell together, which took them to the rear employee exit.

"First days are always energy drainers," Shelly stated. Go home and have a couple of beers and put your feet up," she called out to her new boss as they left the center for the day. Carter laughed and waved good-night. As the very new p. r. director's car pulled out of the center's employee parking lot, her secretary's thoughts were filled with less than pleasant reminders of a similar day spent with Anna Cable. Anna was also eager to learn—too eager. Somewhere along the way it all went wrong. Just what happened, Shelly didn't know. And to be honest, she didn't want to know. She needed her job. She had learned a long time ago to keep her nose out of matters that didn't concern her. Anna Cable had stumbled into something that she shouldn't have and. . .

Shelly quickly shifted her thoughts. None of this was her business. Anna Cable was gone and that was yesterday. The blood center had secrets. This Shelly knew to be true.

"I wonder how long this one will last?" Shelly questioned under her breath. "How long till she stumbles into. . ." She again aborted the thought. To survive at this center, a person had to learn to disconnect thoughts. The blood center Shelly had come to know from the outside fringes of operation did hold certain secrets—powerful secrets most people would never believe even if exposed to them.

"Out with the old, in with the new. Long live the evil empire," To Shelly Nisen it was just another day at Hamilton Regional. To J. Carter Egan it was just the beginning.

5

Patrick Egan was especially quiet during dinner. Carter had so much to share with her husband that he couldn't have gotten a word in edgewise if he had wanted to. She compared her first day on the job with that of her first ride on a roller coaster. As she spoke, Patrick couldn't help but admire his wife's soft and glowing features. It was always like that whenever she involved herself with something that really challenged her. The Egans had been married for almost ten years. There were no children. Carter was simply unable to conceive. When the doctor had informed her that she would never be a mother, a deep depression set in lasting over two years. There were thoughts of adoption, but they never got past the talking stage. There was something about bringing forth a child from the womb, her own womb, that unnecessarily drove Carter in regard to motherhood. Anything less felt wrong. Maybe it was her relationship with Patrick that made the bridge to adoption impossible for her cross. She sensed Patrick deep down did not want to adopt a child that wasn't from his own seed. Whatever, her longings to be a mother were dealt with and quietly put away. It was a painful time in the life of J. Carter Egan. A time of suffering.

To Patrick, children were never really that important. His research in chemistry and his wife, in just that order, were Patrick's priorities. Level-headed and very logical, Patrick approached life with very defined attitudes. He liked a sense of order in his surroundings, and Carter was so good at providing it that deep inside his soul he viewed a child as a threat to the environment they had created for themselves. He had never really shared this secret with Carter. It was the only secret Patrick would ever keep from his wife.

Carter's first day was clearly filled with many unexpected turns. As she related Reymond Alexander's comments to her husband, Patrick caught a flicker of anxiety surfacing in Carter's very pretty face.

"Hey babe, you're going to have to get used to walking on the edge in this job. Remember, you're working at a medical facility now, and accidents do happen in laboratories from time to time. This won't be like your job at Aaron Engineering," Patrick cautioned, "sludge is a lot different than blood."

"I know, but still—the thought of contaminated blood being transfused into innocent. . ."

"Don't get yourself worked up in a lather now, Carter. You don't really know if that happened."

Patrick was always so logical. He was right. She really didn't know if the blood had gotten out. Now was not the time to worry about things she couldn't control. Learning this business was not going to be easy. No sense making it any harder. Carter smiled at Patrick and returned his wink. Being slow to rattle was one of the things Carter admired most about her husband. She wished she could learn to be a little more like him.

Patrick could sense that his wife would become deeply involved with her job responsibilities, and this time, for selfish reasons, he was glad. Quince Industries, Patrick's employer, had just landed a huge research contract in Ankara, Turkey. The opportunity to be the project's lead chemical supervisor was his for the asking. The only drawback for Patrick was the estimated length of the project; one year, perhaps two, of solo duty was required. Families would not be allowed to accompany the team to this remote foreign location, and there would be long stretches of time between communications. Patrick already knew that Carter would be supportive of his decision to accept this assignment. There had been many separations of this kind in their marriage, but the duties only lasted for two to four months. This would be their longest separation. Patrick did not like to be away from his wife. He liked starting the day by seeing his wife's face opposite his at the breakfast table. He liked falling asleep with the scent of her body filling his senses. She was part of him. It would not be an easy assignment, but he would accept it. A research project of this importance did not materialize often.

Patrick waited until Carter had related all the details of her day before sharing the events of his day with her. Carter reacted to Patrick's opportunity exactly as he knew she would—she was supportive. The look in her eyes as they discussed the year's separation revealed only a portion of the inner turmoil she was feeling. The couple talked into the wee hours of the morning. Their conversation was not about how much they would miss each other, but rather on the order of all the necessary things that would have to be done before Patrick left the country. In less than thirty days, Carter would see her husband off at the airport.

Letting go of him as he held her just moments before final boarding was more than painful. It took her breath away and left her feeling torn—almost split inside. There was also a look in Patrick's eyes that Carter had never seen before—it was the painful look of regret. He had already started to miss his wife. If Patrick Egan could only have known what was in store for his wife these next ten months, he would never have left her. Not in a million years.

Sitting at her desk on the morning of Patrick's departure, Carter placed a small check-mark next to the day's calendar date. It was to become a daily ritual for her. She had survived separations before—she would survive this one. By now, Carter had been onboard at the blood center just under four weeks. She had crammed as much in during this time period as she could possibly absorb. It made Patrick's leaving a bit easier to handle. Whenever thoughts of his impending absence pressed her, she would simply pick up another book or technical paper and push the moment away. Patrick had been able to see his wife's efforts to be cheerful and supportive, but it only made it harder for him to think about leaving. He was glad she had this new job. It would bridge the time, however long the separation was to be.

Shelly Nisen interrupted the personal moment.

"Madison Boggs is on line two for you, Carter. Do you want to take it or should I tell her you'll call her back?" the good secretary quizzed her boss.

The name Madison Boggs brought Carter quickly back to reality.

"No, I'll take it," answered Carter with a slight smile on her face for Shelly's thoughtfulness.

Madison Boggs worked for channel WIXL. She was the evening news anchor for the local CBS affiliate television station in Hamilton. Madison was regarded by those in and out of her profession as a different kind of television reporter. She researched her own stories and went out on location to broadcast them. Her stories always gave the impression of news reporting at its best. Her office closet was filled with awards won for high quality television journalism. None of these awards would ever see a nail in place in Madison's office for public display. She didn't feel the need to be surrounded by awards touting her achievements, unlike some of the other reporting staff at her station who filled their walls with paper-framed awards and ribbons of first place. Getting the story and getting it right mattered to Madison Boggs. She had a strong distaste for the "modern information age" of television. Her negative opinion of *"journalism,"* which drives the news media to seek celebrity-oriented entertainment pieces, dedicated foremost to delivering advertising images to targeted groups of consumers for a profit, was voiced frequently in editorial meetings. Madison's male counterparts were more than cautious when vying with her over story selection. The good-old-boy system went out the window when she nailed the evening anchor position. There would be no co-male anchor. She didn't need one. She could carry the ratings. A professional in every sense of the word, Madison possessed an engaging and, for the most part, pleasant personality. She could also display a fierce temper and a tenacious streak. Her reporting instinct was based on old-fashioned "gut" reactions. She could sense a story and separate fact from fiction with an uncanny skill. Off-camera, in those few moments of personal life away from the station, Madison Adams Boggs was very much a private person. A good book, a lively conversation with her small circle of nonmedia friends, a cheap bottle of wine, and an early morning run before all the madness of the city landed on her reporting shoulders, for the most part, satisfied her. As for the public side, Madison indeed presented a pretty picture—tall and slender with dark shining chestnut hair framing a complexion-perfect oval face. Her large green eyes were naturally outlined by thick black eyelashes. When engaged in deep conversation, her green eyes could lock onto a person and hold them prisoner. Dimples in both cheeks enhanced her flawless smile. On camera, viewers were drawn to her easy-to-watch delivery, but it was the "perfect" in her appearance that bothered Madison. She was never comfortable when described in print as beautiful. It only reminded her of the uneven playing field women in her profession had to fight daily. Men weren't judged so harshly on their appearance in the media, but women were.

As for her name, no one was quite sure how she got it. Speculation among friends who knew her father varied. He had wanted a son after four daughters. "Madison Adams" was his choice.

In the beginning, Madison was aware that she was hired not just for her reporting talent, but for the way her face filled that small viewing area captured by the lens of a never-too-gentle television camera. She was also ambitious enough in the beginning to use this birth blessing to open doors for her in the world of talking heads. Ten years later, she had managed to rise to the top anchor position at WIXL. In her time slot, Madison Boggs consistently garnered the highest Arbitron ratings in the six and eleven o'clock evening newscasts. She was wise enough to know that this level of achievement made her a moving target. Anchors were always on the bubble; always looking over their shoulders or across the anchor desk at the latest find by news directors always pushing for higher ratings. Fresh faces were constantly arriving on the scene. Madison knew this better than most since she had moved into the much coveted anchor chair vacated by Bill St. Angela.

St. Angela was a twenty year institution at Channel 11. Evening news wasn't evening news if it wasn't delivered by the very male anchor. A veteran reporter, he recognized talent and good reporting skills the first time he allowed Madison to share his airspace. It was his idea to mentor her as his replacement. His parting words to Madison were implanted deep inside her journalism soul.

"Look for the story that's not being told, because to survive in this ugly world you have to be a bulldog. Don't get close to people, and once you've set your jaws in action you better damn well know what you're about to bite off as you might end up having to swallow it."

Perfect prose it wasn't, but good advice it was. Replacing a landmark like St. Angela would not be an easy task for anyone, especially in this tough, competitive midwest media market. Madison was intensely aware of this. A schedule was outlined well in advance of her mentor leaving giving the newcomer plenty of exposure time to the evening news viewers. Madison Boggs started off with *Medical Updates*, a soft news spot that guarantees public interest. Matters of health are key components of a balanced newscast. Health spots are also easy to sell to potential station advertisers. And those advertising dollars are what make the world of television so competitive. *Medical Updates* and Madison clicked. The public couldn't get enough of her. Every local organization in town wanted Madison Boggs to speak to them. She quickly became what most of her counterpart news hounds wanted to be—a local celebrity.

Part of her was happy—the attention was a powerful sensation. Part of her was not so happy—she had lost her privacy. Everywhere she went she was on display. The public takes ownership of those they create and support. If they interrupt your lunch date with a request for an autograph, the interruption is not looked at as intrusive. Familiarity, wanted or not, goes with the territory of fame. Next to movie stars, news personalities rate a certain amount of adulation from a public that allows them to invade their privacy each night while they are eating dinner or lying in their beds. Madison held her fans in high regard. She never singled out a story simply for ratings. She didn't set out to make news but chose the more difficult path of reporting news. She recognized the significant difference between the two. The ratings didn't dip when she replaced Bill St. Angela. In fact, the ratings went up one whole percentage point.

Time, and stories, had gone by rather fast. Her marriage this past year at age thirty-six to a local businessman had received almost as much coverage in the local newspapers as the presidential election. Madison was happier than she had ever been. The only thing that could possibly make Madison happier would be to turn the dipstick in the packaged home-pregnancy test kit blue positive.

But at this moment, Madison was concentrating on a press release that had just come to her attention. The not-for-profit company letterhead triggered memories of a telephone conversation she had some months earlier with a man who would not identify himself. At the moment, she had no clue as to the connection—just a gut thing. The conversation was strange from the beginning and did not make any sense. The caller's voice was deliberately muffled and his sentences were run together like riddles.

"Boggs here," Madison answered as always.

"I like to watch you on TV. I like the way your mouth moves when you say certain letters," the slightly feminine male voice quietly stated.

The thought of another jerk getting his jollies off while talking to her on the phone quickly ran through Madison's mind. She was almost tempted to hang up and get on with her day, when her gut told her to continue.

"Do you have something to say, sir?"

"This is the Red Man."

"The Red Man?"

"Yes, the Red Man.

"Well what does the Red Man want?"

"There's madness in the world—madness that's right under your beautiful nose, only you can't see it."

"What kind of madness are you referring to, red man?"

"If I told you, it wouldn't be a secret anymore would it, Miss Boggs? You know I have to keep the secret, don't you?"

"Is there a particular reason why you called me, or are you just wasting my time?" Boggs answered politely.

There was silence on the other end of the phone line. His soft breathing hung in the air as Madison waited to see where the conversation was leading.

"Someday, I might have to share my secret with you, Miss Boggs."

"What kind of secret are you talking about, sir?"

"Life and death secrets, Miss Boggs, bloody life and death secrets." With that said, the phone line went dead. In her line of work, strange conversations such as these were not so unusual. Anonymous calls were also, for the most part, not taken seriously.

Hamilton Regional Blood Center was a company that Madison had little firsthand experience in covering. She knew about blood and its many uses, but she had little knowledge of the daily workings of the community blood center. Usually a street reporter was given such releases, but this time, her news director sent it her way. Saving lives, blood donations, and emergency appeals were all she could conjure up about the blood center at the moment.

Madison placed a call to the contact person, J. Carter Egan, whose office had distributed the press release to WIXL in care of her attention.

"This is Carter Egan. May I help you?"

"Yes Carter, this is Madison Boggs with Channel Eleven. I understand you folks are having a blood shortage?"

"Well, yes we are having difficulty right now. Thank you for responding to our appeal."

"How bad is it really and how come you guys can't keep up with the supply? Is it still the AIDS thing?" an always direct Madison Boggs questioned.

"We dropped below our necessary three-day unit reserve level yesterday," Carter answered with a certain amount of concern present in her voice. "If an emergency should occur, we wouldn't be able to supply our sixty-five area hospitals, let alone handle a run on blood. I'm afraid it's quite serious at this point," Carter answered with belief in her statement adding, "It is difficult to convince the public of the very real need to donate blood on a regular basis. We need to collect at least five hundred units of blood a day just to handle the needs of our area hospitals. Unfortunately, there are too many days when we are unable to draw that many units of blood from the communities that we serve. We do our best to keep up with it, but blood cannot be manufactured. Our cries for help are very real," Carter added. She did not address the AIDS issue.

Madison couldn't find one thing in that explanation to challenge. As a rule, Madison took statements from public relations people with a grain of salt. They were always touting their needs in some manner. Madison's intuitive response signaled that this one truly seemed sincere in what she was saying. There was even an edge of urgency in her voice. The thought of someone dying on an operating table because there was no blood available was a frightening thought. Besides, hundreds of leukemic and cancer patients, especially children, depended on blood components for their daily treatment programs. Madison Boggs had seen firsthand the many uses for blood, thanks to her days on *Medical Update.*

"We'd like to send a crew down at noon for a live broadcast. Would your medical director be available for an interview?" Boggs asked.

"Dr. Silvers is extremely busy today, and he has asked me to handle all requests for media interviews, since I have been selected as spokesperson for our center," Carter answered.

"Sure, I guess it doesn't matter. If you're the spokesperson we'll go with you," Madison replied, not really sure why a medical facility would choose to be represented publicly by a nonmedical representative, especially in this era of AIDS and its association with the blood supply. It was just a passing thought to this news reporter.

Carter's first contact with the veteran newswoman went well. Hanging up the phone, she immediately began making arrangements for all media interviews to take place that day in the Distribution Center where the television cameras would have the most to work with. This section of the Center contained the huge glass refrigerators that housed the blood supply waiting for shipping orders. This morning, those massive ice chests were all but empty. Just a month into assuming the position of Director of Public Relations, Carter found herself coming face to face with a direct order from her medical director to issue an emergency blood appeal. She was being thrown immediately into the role of public spokesperson and media liaison. She was savvy enough to realize that good interviews needed more than just two talking heads. Background sights that could help generate an emotional appeal for any story was also part of a good public relations presentation. It separated the pros from the amateurs in the eyes of those ratings-conscious street reporters who needed visual background action to highlight the content of their story. Visuals were important in the world of the electric media. The blood center had plenty of visuals to offer in support of capturing a good story.

All the local television and radio stations had responded to Carter's urgent press release. Her television interviews were scheduled about fifteen minutes apart, giving time to rotate the various media crews with their cameras and lights in and out of the Distribution Center. Carter had placed an earlier call to Kiley Matson, manager of the distribution area, asking that he make himself available to answer any on-air questions concerning the blood center's distribution operation. Kiley was more than happy to be in the media spotlight. Tall, good-looking, and a smooth communicator, Kiley was every reporter's dream interview. He knew the operations side of blood banking, and he had a charming way of simplifying tough technical jargon. He also loved to flirt with all the good-looking female reporters.

Radio interviews were scheduled later that day in the main room of the center's blood donor drawing area. Radio would not benefit from the visuals of an empty glass refrigerator. Instead, for a good radio interview, a living breathing human being was needed to voice action over the airwaves to the imagination of the drive-time listeners. Most of the donors present in the donor chairs did not mind giving an interview under such circumstances. People like to be made to feel important. People also like to appear in the media. Later, when Carter had a deeper grasp of what was needed to orchestrate a full media appeal, she would always place a call to the Center's top, five-gallon donors, eligible to donate within that time period. Gallon donors were always more than willing to talk with the media about the need to donate blood. They were also relaxed and would not be prone to fainting during the interview. Their obvious faithfulness in giving blood on a regular basis would serve to pressure the average Joe Public, who was irregular in donation pattern, into making a special trip to the nearest blood donation center during this public appeal time. First-time blood donors, who might either faint or throw up, were screened heavily before being chosen to do a media interview during a critical appeal. Last but not least, was to place the reporter in the donor chair for a live, on-air interview for a first person, blow-by-blow scenario of what it's like to give blood.

Rarely did Carter ever have to suggest this reporter-donor angle. Reporters were eager to be seen in the role of "volunteer for a good cause." It served its purpose for a well-rounded human interest story with personal reporter appeal. People, for the most part, are decent human beings who faithfully respond to an urgent public appeal based on the very real needs of others.

Carter got through her first of many-to-come emergency blood appeals. She was given high marks by Silvers and Preston. Over three thousand units of blood were donated in a two-day time period. Michael Bryan was torn between public elation and private frustration. He was happy Carter had handled the situation so professionally and that his instincts in hiring her in the first place were correct. He was very relieved to see how swiftly she had bonded with the local media, especially Madison Boggs, who had never personally responded before to any of their past blood appeals. If Carter could generate this type of continued media support through other emergency appeals sure to be called, her future would be bright.

On the dark side—away from the lights and cameras—a laboratory was in shambles. Preston and Silvers would not okay additional staff or overtime for the processing end of a blood emergency.

As he had many times in the past, Michael Bryan went to his superiors and asked for additional staffing in the testing and processing laboratories. His concerns fell on deaf ears.

Michael was sternly reminded of the cost to keep the substations open past noon on Saturday. All facilities would be closed on Sunday, unless the field reps, who marketed the blood programs, could get the Army to volunteer their already identified O blood typed soldiers stationed at nearby Ft. Schneider. If this could be arranged, the main facility would be open from ten a.m. to two p.m. to accommodate the donation process. As far as extra staffing, "costs were high enough and any overtime would eat up a delicate payroll that needed to be contained if they were to make their quarterly budget."

"We'll stick to our normal routine of identifying O's and processing the other, less-in-demand types of blood, as time allows. See if you can't get the day shift to volunteer some extra p.m. time. Surely they won't want to see us have to dispose of blood because they can't get their job done," the pair stated almost in unison knowing full well that each blood emergency resulted in the secret disposal of hundreds of pints of unprocessed, donated blood, which couldn't be cleared through the system in the twenty-four hour time period needed to process and test each pint of blood. Time was the real enemy and since the emergency wasn't real to begin with, the end result could be looked at by Silvers and Preston as simply a matter of overtime logistics. The blame would not lie with them. There was no guilt on their shoulders for they were able to place the fault within the system.

In the system, the day shift was normally staffed with five processing technicians that included Bertha White. The evening staff was bare-boned to a staff of three. There was no way a volunteer effort was going to accomplish the timed processing of some two to three thousand extra units of blood that an emergency blood appeal could generate. This situation was not new to Michael Bryan or Bertha White. It occurred with each emergency blood appeal. Bertha, who was close to retirement, had given up fighting for extra staff with this administration. She knew she had come very close to being fired after her last go-around with Dr. Silvers, and with her husband battling cancer of the esophagus and dependent on her insurance benefits for his cancer treatments, she could ill-afford to lose her job at this stage of the game. Bertha made up her mind that whatever happened was no longer skin off her nose. She and her day crew would put in the back-to-back fifteen hour days during an emergency appeal with no additional pay for the effort. The laboratory staff could not be faulted for their desire to process the blood so freely given in such emergency times.

"Let the bastards account for blood being dumped because there weren't enough hands to process it, let alone run the necessary tests," White bitterly thought as she filled the belly of the laboratory's autoclave with the unprocessed, untested blood. Within seconds, hundreds of pints of blood would feel the intense heat of the autoclave's burning oven. The plastic bags once filled with the gift-of-life liquid quickly turned to ashes.

As Laboratory Director, White's power to do the right thing only went as high as her supervisor. She was simply following orders now— their orders. One more year and she was out of there. Time couldn't pass fast enough for Bertha White.

Unfortunately, Michael Bryan did not have the luxury of a fast-moving retirement clock. As Bertha's direct supervisor, he gave the order to destroy the blood. For whatever reason, be it out of respect for those who donated or guilt for not standing up to the evil pair and forcing a staff increase, Bryan would assist Bertha in the late evening disposal of blood. Afterwards, he would stop by Del's Pub, which was located just two blocks from his north side home, and try to wash away the awful taste of disillusion with multiple bottles of strong imported German beer followed by generous shots of Irish whiskey. Most generally, the ritual included Del driving him home in the wee hours of the new dawning day. Betsy, his wife, never understood this behavior in her husband of eleven years. Never deeply in love with Michael, she found ways to avoid any situation that could result in direct confrontation of feelings. Feelings, especially those of Michael, were of no interest to her. She had worked to get her life just the way she wanted it. She was perfectly satisfied.

Michael Havens Bryan was an easy touch. He came from a well-to-do family with strong social ties and connections in all the right places. As his wife, she had all the right charge cards accompanied by the sleek white Porsche and the family house on Devington Boulevard. Tennis on Tuesdays, bridge on Thursdays, shopping on Friday, and dinner parties on Saturday suited her ambitions. She would have discarded Michael long ago if it were not that she needed his family attachment for the good life she was now leading. To dissolve this marriage would cost her dearly in the social routine she had settled into so well. It did not matter to her that she was living above Michael's own income. These little incidents of drunkenness were just slight matters of inconvenience. They would disappear with the morning sun. She would set a pillow and a blanket out on the living room couch for her drunken husband. She did not want to be disturbed by noise in the middle of the night by a fumbling man who might want to force himself on her. She had gone through that on one other occasion. It would never happen again. Whatever caused Michael Bryan to resort to such crudeness was of no interest to her. As for Michael, his feelings were buried deep within his soul. He knew the shallowness of his wife's love. He had walked straight into her trap from day one with his eyes wide open. He thought he could change her. Like all men, the challenge was the best part of the courting game. He knew she was a "money hound." His friends had all warned him. He simply didn't listen. Whatever it was that attracted him to Betsy Colebert in the first place had long since escaped his memory. He blamed it on the moon. He had always been a sucker for a full moon and a pretty face. He had met Betsy under a full moon and an open sail. The moonlight beamed off her full smile as the wind softly caressed and carelessly tossed her long golden hair about her shoulders. Her laugh was soft and gentle. She spoke openly of all that she wanted from life. She was not poor, but came from a caring middle class family. To Betsy, middle class meant having limits. Limits on shopping sprees, limits on social standing. She didn't want to stand on the edge always looking in. She wanted a place in the middle of all that glowed from the deep color of money and all that it could give. She didn't want limits. Michael remembered that he wanted to give it all to her. Eleven years later, they were still together in name only. His job with generous salary, arranged by his father's friendship with Gerald Preston, kept his debts about even. He hadn't looked at a full moon in the same way for over ten years. And his idea of a pretty woman was completely different now. Time and logistics can kill so many things. This Michael Havens Bryan knew for a fact. A bloody, moonless fact.

6

It didn't take Carter long to realize the seriousness of the discord between her executive director and her medical director. Unfortunately, she, like Michael Bryan, fell right smack in the middle of the madness created by such a dividing atmosphere. It was the kind of madness that could not be easily described to an outsider. It was subtle, yet driving. It permeated every action, every decision that took place within the center. It was an atmosphere destined one day to explode. Everyone waited with apprehension for that day to arrive.

Carter also found certain areas of the blood center's operation to be less than genuine when it came to dealing with the public. One of those areas was the telephone recruitment department. It was all but closed to her now—as she had been told pointblank by the director of that department, Mary Jane Wilson, to leave this part of the center's operation out of her public relations efforts. The incident happened shortly after Carter had spent a morning listening to the phone operators recruit apheresis donations for the center. Carter was furnished with a script and told the telemarketers always followed it when contacting this special donor base. What Carter accidentally heard did not in any way follow that script. One operator pressed a story of a small child desperately needing platelets.

"If you can't come in this afternoon, this child may just not be able to receive his leukemia treatments. The center is so low on platelets, we're on an emergency standby—." Carter had heard nothing of an emergency standby. At that time, the platelet inventory was more than adequate to handle their hospital orders.

When she questioned the supervisor, she was told she "must have misunderstood" what the operator was saying. It was at this point in the conversation that Carter's observation time in this department was cut short.

Carter went directly to Kiley Matson. If anyone knew of an emergency standby situation it would be Kiley. Kiley listened as Carter explained what she had just heard. His face masked his feelings as he began to explain the system to Carter.

"Carter—listen to me. We are in a hard driving business here. There may be times when some of the tactics we use seem less than genuine to you, but believe me, if we don't apply the pressure, our well can dry up faster than a Vegas desert."

Kiley went on to explain how important apheresis donors were to his supply and demand operation.

"Look at it this way, Carter. We have a select base of typed donors who agree to the cause of donating their blood for platelet extraction on an as-needed basis. The process to do this is fairly simple. We set 'em in a chair, put needles in both their arms, and over the course of three to four hours, we drain out only the needed platelets or white cell components for a so-called specific type cancer or leukemia patient from one arm, while returning the rest of the bloody liquid we don't need through the other arm. What does it matter if the platelets go to someone here or someone in Florida?" Carter couldn't answer that question at that moment. Her mind was filled with questions about the procedure—right or wrong would come later when she had time to think about what Kiley had just said.

"Is this procedure safe—I mean, it sounds kind of dangerous?"

"It's so safe, Miss p.r. director, we could haul these donors in here every thirty-six hours if we needed too," Kiley concluded with charm dripping from every syllable.

"Are there ever any problems—I mean do these donors ever have reactions of any kind?" The question was innocent.

"None that you'll ever talk about, baby," Kiley answered not realizing he had sent up another red flag for Carter to think about later.

"If we have this kind of an emergency going on right now, Kiley, how come I am not aware of it—I mean there was nothing on our flash report to—"

"Carter, darlin'—don't get all hot and bothered. It's just a tactic we use once in a while when I get a chance to swing a good deal for large volume platelet shipments."

Carter's face displayed the quizzical look of someone who hadn't the foggiest idea of what he was so casually spitting out about their shipping operation. He had clearly stepped over the line here with his little educational talk with the public relations director. He thought Carter had been taken into the circle a little more than this. "Anna had certainly been given a different orientation than this one," Kiley thought as he began to backtrack.

"Carter, just take it at face value. Believe me, the blood is going to good use, and we're breaking no laws in our telemarketing department."

Carter backed off pressing the issue further. Kiley's face told her the teaching lesson was over. Maybe she was overreacting to a situation she really didn't understand just yet. The cause was there—and Carter felt truly dedicated to the cause of saving lives. Maybe when she understood the system a little better, she could discuss this again. She and Kiley would not talk again for several days. But they would talk again. The occasion came unexpectedly three weeks later.

"Hey kid, got a moment?" the deep rich voice of Kiley Matson rang out as he quickly shut Carter's office door behind him.

"Kid" was a common term of greeting used by Kiley Matson.

"I guess I do," Carter quickly answered, glancing at her watch. They had just ten minutes before the start of their morning flash meeting.

"What can I do for you, Kiley?" Carter softly declared with a smile.

"Oh boy, what could you do for me—hmmm," Kiley teased back. Kiley's quick and often sexual play on words did not fluster Carter. For some reason, she felt at ease with him. This was not the case for most of the other female directors who were constantly at odds with him.

Carter laughed out loud, shaking her head in amusement at the always-trying-to-be-provocative distribution director.

"Did you come in here to waste my time, Mr. Matson, or is there really something on your mind above your belt?" Carter fired back. Kiley's deep laugh again filled the room.

"I like you, J. Carter Egan. You're not at all like the rest of your predecessors," Kiley answered, glad that he had found someone who did not take him any more seriously than he took himself.

"Predecessors—that word reminds me of dinosaurs and other prehistoric animals," Carter shot back.

"Trust me darlin', they were dinosaurs—big and ugly dinosaurs who roamed the halls yelling for more blood, only to fall helplessly into the trap set for them," Kiley answered.

"And what trap is that?" Carter asked.

The room was silent for a moment. Kiley's dark eyes narrowed and the smile almost always present dissolved.

"That's for me to know and you to find out," Kiley finally answered with his smile reappearing.

"So, Mr. Matson, what brings you to my office?" Carter asked once again.

"I really just wanted to tell you that I think you handled the emergency really well. You've got a touch with the media, kid, and trust me when I tell you how much we need that touch right now," Kiley seriously answered.

"The word from the poop deck tells me that you are doing your homework," Kiley continued.

"I think I should take that as a compliment," Carter teased.

"Oh no—compliments are given far and few around here. God forbid that word should get out that I was ever engaged in compliments, especially to the very sexy p.r. director," Kiley's natural smile was again present. "It would ruin my reputation," he quickly added.

"Any other words of wisdom for me before we head out to our morning flash meeting?" Carter asked, rising from her chair ever conscious of the time and the meeting that demanded their attendance.

"I just wanted to apologize if I seemed flip with you when you came to see me about that misunderstanding in telemarketing the other day. I'm so used to joking my ass off around here just to get through the day, I failed to take in the fact you are relatively new to our operation and may not see things the way us seasoned veterans do."

Kiley rose from his chair and headed toward Carter's closed office door. Grabbing the handle, he turned back to face Carter.

"J. Carter Egan, I like you. I think you really do believe in all this hocus-pocus stuff. Keep it up—who knows, you may even make a believer out of me," Kiley answered, his face reflecting a somewhat out-of-character sincere expression.

With those words spoken, Kiley opened the door and quickly exited.

As Carter headed down the hall toward the small conference room where the 8:30 a.m. meeting was to take place, she couldn't help but feel there was more to Kiley Matson coming to her office than had transpired this morning. What did he want? Was he trying to tell her something? Whatever it was, the message was not clear. J. Carter Egan did not do well with fuzzy messages.

Carter quickly took her assigned seat at the conference table. All the directors were placed at the table according to their political status. The closer you sat to the executives, the more power you were perceived to have. Carter was assigned a seat next to Gerald Preston. At the head of the table sat Kiley Matson. It was his meeting to lead.

"Good morning, ladies and gentlemen. Shall we get started?" he asked, not waiting for an answer.

"We're in pretty good shape right now thanks to the response of Carter's emergency appeal," Kiley began.

"Inventory levels across the board look great. We've gotten good response from business with several first-time donation drives scheduled for later this week, which means our resource sharing can continue. Let's hear it for emergencies!" he added, with typical Kiley sarcasm.

Grace Tende, personnel director, made her usual frowning gesture. Tende never approved of Kiley's light approach in directing meetings. It was nothing personal, just a difference in style.

Elizabeth Monroe, who was late for the morning meeting as usual, smiled ever so slightly as she quickly sat down next to Michael Bryan.

Dr. Silvers sat unusually still—fingering the daily report that Kiley had prepared for the meeting. His eyes never left the white sheet of figures.

Gerald Preston was also distant this morning. Usually, the two men used this meeting for their morning ritual of arguing over mindless issues.

Seeing that there were no open issues left to discuss, Kiley began the motions of ending the meeting.

"Okay, ladies and gentlemen, you all have my permission to return to your monotonous daily drudgery called work. I, on the other hand, will move on to my daily buying and selling of precious corpuscles. Life on Wall Street, how sweet it is."

Dr. Silvers turned to his co-partner and in a quiet, almost whisper voice, spoke intimately into Preston's ear. Preston nodded his head in obvious agreement and quickly turned toward Carter Egan.

"Carter, dear, would you mind staying after for just a few minutes? Michael, you too, please."

"Of course," Carter replied, lowering her body back down into the conference chair. Her body language did not reflect the nervousness she felt at the sudden request to remain. Michael's face showed no emotion. His body seemed relaxed, almost as if he were prepared in advance.

It took a few moments for the gathered directors to exit the room. The look on Dr. Silvers's face showed a quick trace of anger as he waited impatiently for the group to leave.

Finally they were alone. The room was painfully quiet. Carter felt a cold sensation pass over her shoulders. This sensation had occurred to her only one other time in her life. It was followed by awful news—the death of her father. The memory caused her to sit up rigidly in her chair.

Dr. Silvers began. "Carter, we have received some very disturbing news this morning," he paused, as if choking back on the words that had to follow.

"We are being sued. A young woman from Grandville claims we were negligent in our blood screening process, and she is now claiming we are responsible for her contracting the AIDS virus." His words were cold and edged with bitterness. Carter had never seen such a look in a person's eyes before. It was obvious the doctor was trying very hard to retain his temper and speak in a very controlled manner.

"Of course, she has absolutely no grounds for such accusations, and she will never collect a cent from us. We are in the absolute right here. I *will not* allow her to drag us through the mud with her—"

"Ben, this is not the time for ranting. Carter has got to be prepared for what lies ahead of her," Preston cut in.

Preston's "what lies ahead of her," hit Carter immediately.

Sensing it was not time to react with questions, she waited for the pair to continue.

Silvers drew his hand up to cover his mouth, a nervous habit performed when he was trying very hard to control a stream of foul language. Preston continued.

"We have a very clear path to take in this public lawsuit that I am afraid is destined to draw a lot of press," he slowly stated, watching Carter's face for any signs of trouble.

"Our lawyers will be here this afternoon to brief you thoroughly on this case, because as the center's spokesperson, you will, from now on, be the only person allowed to speak to the press."

"Time is on our side," he continued, "and I am sure we will, in a matter of time, put this issue to rest. She simply has no case against us. We did everything by the book—*by the book*," Preston repeated.

"How were we negligent?" Carter asked, speaking for the first time.

"Damn it, we were not negligent in any way. The donors were all healthy and they met our criteria—they met our criteria," Silvers spit out, repeating himself as well.

"Carter, this is a most unpleasant situation," Preston said, taking back control of the conversation. "I can't begin to tell you how distressing it is to be at the mercy of those individuals who seek large sums of money from institutions such as ours. But it is a sign of the times with all the media hype and so on. I am only afraid we are at the beginning of a new era of recklessly filed lawsuits by individuals who seek fame and fortune."

Carter glanced across the table at Michael. His eyes were steeled in the direction of Preston and Silvers. She thought she saw a tightening in her supervisor's jaw, but it lasted only an instant. It was as if he felt her gaze and killed whatever emotions were building inside.

The sound of the conference room door opening stopped the conversation. Dr. Alice Crane made her entrance quickly, settling in a chair at the end of the long square table.

"Sorry I'm late," she huffed as she struggled to regain her breath. "I have all the files, Dr. Silvers," she stated, as she roughly slid the manila folders down the length of the polished meeting room table to her bosses.

"Everything is now in order," she announced, smiling ever so slightly.

"Thank you, Dr. Crane," Preston answered.

"You did as I asked, Alice?" Silvers questioned.

"Yes," she answered.

Michael Bryan moved sharply in his seat. It was a motion that seemed to be mixed with anger and fear.

"Carter, you need to know the history of this woman who is suing us," Silvers stated, as he continued to look at the papers just given to him by Dr. Crane.

Apparently satisfied with what he had received, Silvers closed the file and slid it into his briefcase. He carefully zipped the black leather case shut. It was fairly obvious whatever documents he now possessed were extremely important.

"Her name is Taylor Addison. She lives upstate in Grandville. She's worked in real estate as a clerk in a rather small office. She was married—I'm not sure if she still is. We know she received three units of blood that came from our distribution center. She was being treated for ulcerative colitis by Dr. Fairbanks at Union Rivers Hospital, and apparently her condition warranted the need for a blood transfusion, which I might add, she freely accepted."

Carter was riveted to Dr. Silvers's every word. The room felt colder to her as his carefully chosen words settled into her mind. Preston felt the need to add to the last sentence spoken.

"Obviously, Carter, you are familiar enough with our donor criteria to know the process we follow and the care with which we screen our donors," he added.

Carter moved her head up and down in an approving nod. She knew the donor criteria very well. She had helped in rewriting the questionnaire with Dr. Silvers over the objections of Dr. Crane, who felt a layperson had no business handling such matters. It led to a very bitter discussion which ended in hurt feelings on Dr. Crane's part.

"How many donors did you say were involved?" Carter asked.

"Three," Silvers answered, in unison with Dr. Crane.

For the next thirty minutes, Carter listened to the co-administrators as they set forth their strategy to deal with this new situation. Blood centers were simply never sued. The public never crossed those Holy-Grail lines of true belief. The brass ring had never been pulled. This was, for all apparent reasons, a staggering, unthinkable act. The arrogance displayed by the administrators clearly showed a confidence in obtaining a quick dismissal of negligence by any chosen medical panel.

"This will never come to court," Preston finally stated, leaning back deep in his chair. Indeed, the due process of law was definitely in the blood center's court. According to Dr. Silvers, an unbiased medical panel would be selected to hear the deposition statements of both parties. This was to happen before the matter could be moved to the court system. Of course, the center hoped to end the matter at this level. The blood center was to be represented by the powerful law firm of Javis, Smith, Crohn and Lavens. Dr. Silvers and Dr. Crane would each have a separate attorney from the firm for representation. The law office would also supply an attorney for Gerald Preston, in addition to the blood center's own attorney, Martin Ball. In all, four different attorneys would join forces for the side of the defendants named in the lawsuit. It was a mighty show of force. A force with deep financial pockets.

John Stansbarry, an aging practicing attorney, from the small town of Port Smith, would represent Taylor Addison.

For the next thirty minutes, Carter would listen to the trio. Michael Bryan made no statements. The briefing finally reached the point of conclusion.

"We'll stop for now, Carter. The attorneys will be here at two p.m. to fill you in on all the details you'll need to know to handle this matter in regard to the press," Preston relayed in his most formal dismissing manner.

Carter pushed her chair back and was rising to her feet when Michael Bryan's voice filled the air.

"I believe you forgot to share one piece of information with Carter that she really needs to know before she comes face to face with the media."

The trio of executives stared at the assistant executive director as if he had just spoken in a foreign language.

"Forgot what, Michael?" Preston quizzed.

"You forgot to tell Carter that Taylor Addison is also five months pregnant." Bryan's words hit Carter deep in the pit of her stomach.

"Oh my God—no," gasped Carter, visually showing an emotion of shock and concern.

A look of displeasure instantly appeared on Preston's face. This was one small part of the pie that they did not want to address at this moment. His assistant had obviously crossed a line that was not meant to be crossed at this stage in the game.

Dr. Silvers exploded. "We didn't forget to tell Carter anything—it simply isn't relevant. It makes no difference to us if she's pregnant or just using this ploy to gain more public sympathy."

"And we have no assurance that she didn't get AIDS from having sex with many different men. As a matter of fact, she should be asked to name all her past sex partners. We should have the right to make her disclose this information. It's important to our position of innocence," Dr. Crane added, tagging on to Dr. Silvers's statement.

The knot in Carter's stomach tightened. This was far more complicated than was first set out for her. Her first thoughts turned to the media. She knew the media would jump on this story like sharks in a feeding frenzy—not just the local media, but the national press corps as well. The thought of Taylor's pregnancy hit Carter in a way she never imagined. She felt terrified as if a huge black cloud had wrapped its dark energy completely around the room where they all sat. She didn't want to think about the child or the mother who was carrying it so naked in her womb. A womb that could be filled with a disease so deadly. . . .Carter shifted her thoughts back to the media—these thoughts she could handle.

For the next several moments all three of the executives addressed Carter at once. Each had his own motivation for speaking with a separate point to make. Carter was still reeling from Bryan's bombshell.

Finally, Gerald Preston put an end to the siege of aggressive voices.

"Enough, I say, enough!" his voice pierced the air, bringing quiet to the room.

Raising his arms, he motioned for Carter to sit back down. A look said the same to the others.

Michael Bryan was the last to sit down. His whole being shook as he lowered himself into the conference room chair. He was obviously, for reasons of his own, very disturbed by this entire situation. Carter did not miss the body language.

"I'm sorry, Carter. This unfortunate situation has all of us up in a lather. It's just so difficult to be placed in such a position. Obviously, Dr. Silvers and Dr. Crane are upset, as am I, at having to defend ourselves against such mean-spirited charges as this woman—and I might add, my sympathy does go out to her—but nevertheless, she's bringing about a very trying situation that should not be happening. We did no wrong here. We are not guilty of any such negligence as she is asserting in her petition to win a large financial settlement from us. Her motive has to be greed. I simply cannot explain it to you in any other way," Preston's voice trailed off.

Silvers and Crane made no further attempts to speak. They also did not make any eye contact with either Carter or Michael Bryan. Their silence testified to their anger.

"Can you make your schedule available for the two o'clock meeting?" Preston asked, looking directly at Carter in a most fatherly manner.

Carter nodded her head and asked one key question.

"Dr. Silvers, will I have access to the donors' criteria information that will obviously be questioned?"

Dr. Crane answered the question.

"Carter, by law, we must keep the donors questionnaires confidential. Rest assured, Dr. Silvers and I have reviewed the donors' health questionnaires and found them all to be eligible and qualified donors. It's nothing against you, but we cannot breach the donors' confidentiality. We will be forced to forward a copy of the health questionnaires, with the names of the donors marked out of course, to all attorneys involved."

"If the attorneys can see this information, with the names marked out, I don't see why I should not be able—"

"Carter, it is just a matter of rules and regulations here. You're going to have to trust us on this one," Silvers said in a very kind fashion. "Maybe somewhere down the road, when we all get more comfortable with what we can and cannot do, I'm sure we could let you review the health statements. But until I'm absolutely sure that the center is following the rules to the tee, I don't want to take any chances with this woman's attorney being able to show Hamilton Regional stepping over the line with NAABC regulations. I hope you can bear with us—I mean, this is the first time a blood center has ever been sued. We're all a little nervous here." Silvers ended.

The explanation seemed to satisfy Carter. It was a mistake and one that would return to haunt her.

Nodding in acceptance, Carter rose from the chair to leave. As she approached the door, Silvers's voice captured her attention once more.

"Carter, can you handle this with the media and all? Can you put aside your obviously caring feelings for a pregnant woman and defend our names?"

Carter turned, looking directly at Dr. Silvers.

"Yes, I can. We did nothing wrong as a blood center. It's just an unfortunate and tragic situation. With all my heart, I wish I could do something about it, but the truth of the matter is—we committed no negligence, and I can defend that. I can defend that," she replied. She closed the door quietly as she left their company.

Dr. Crane was the first to react to Carter's parting words.

"And there, gentlemen, goes our best defense. She believes—and if she believes, so goes the press."

Preston ignored Dr. Crane's comments turning his immediate attention to his assistant who was lighting his first cigarette of the day.

"Michael, I wish you had let the attorneys brief Carter on the girl's pregnancy," he stated, with no trace of emotion in his voice.

"It's better this way," interjected Silvers, who quickly gathered up his briefcase and walked out, not waiting to hear Michael Bryan's answer.

Dr. Crane shot a parting dirty look at Bryan and made her exit felt with a slam of the door.

"I'm sorry, Jerry, I just felt she should know now—beforehand," Bryan said softly to his superior and father figure.

"You are going to have to distance yourself from this situation, Michael. Of course, we all feel bad about the girl, but we should not be made to pay for something we had no harm in bringing about," Preston added, raising his voice for conviction.

"Carter is going to need your support and your guidance, Michael. This is not going to be an easy assignment. The moment the media gets wind of this lawsuit, all our lives will change—for some time, I suspect. For some time."

Gerald Thomas Preston drew his weight up heavily from the chair and headed his large frame toward the door.

"Jerry, are we guilty of anything here?" Bryan questioned out loud for the first time since hearing about the lawsuit.

Preston stopped, but did not turn around.

"Of course not, Michael. We are guilty of nothing that can be proven."

Preston's large hand cupped the door handle. He paused as if there was more he wanted to say. Michael Bryan waited, his eyes fixed on the back of the man who had hired him. There were to be no more words. In one motion, Preston turned the handle and made his exit into the hall leaving Bryan alone in the room with his answer, his cigarette smoke, and his conscience. All three of these elements would one day prove to be deadly.

Gerald Preston stood at his office door leafing through his morning telephone messages. The meeting with Carter and the others over the lawsuit had unsettled him. When he came to the name Morley Habing, a chill went down his spine. That name had been absent from his life for over thirty-five years.

Closing the door and locking it from the inside, Preston went straight to his desk. Once he was seated in his custom-made chair, he dialed the number his secretary had written down on the pink return message sticker. The phone rang two times before it was answered.

"Hello."

"Morley? This is Gerald. What can I do for you?"

"Hampton is dead. I just received a cable this morning," Habing, a former board president of the National Association of Accredited Blood Centers, answered with a level of nervousness not usually displayed in his generally calm, deep baritone voice.

"You sound upset, Morley."

"I am, Jerry."

"What for? It's been over thirty-five years. If there was going to be a problem, it would have surfaced before now." Preston replied.

"I hope you're right, Jerry. I hope you're right."

The phone line went dead in Preston's ear. "Thirty-five years," mused Preston, as he hung up the phone allowing his mind to drift back in time.

"My God, what a difference it would have made today," he thought. "What a difference."

7

The coffin was plain. Silver in color—void of brass or any other elaborate decoration that spoke of wealth. The church was quiet as mourners came to pay their last respects to a man who had been generous but distant to all of them during the course of the last thirty-five years.

His only son sat alone in the front pew. His head was bowed but there were no tears. Remorse did not lay on his shoulders. Only regret. Regret of the worst kind. He was never close to this man he had been taught to call Father. His mother had died two days after his birth, a fact that was destined to drive a wall between them for the rest of their lives. The father was only to love one person in his lifetime—his wife. His beautiful, passionate Annie. It was she who wanted children. He gave in only because she begged him so often. He could never really resist her wishes or her desires. She was staggeringly beautiful. Dark hair, ivory skin with a smile that burned into your memory. She was full of motion and rarely seemed to be still. She inspired within Walter a desire to learn about all life's simple treasures, not just books and numbers and formulas. Annie was life and goodness and magic.

He, on the other hand, could be described as average in looks. He was not handsome. Tall and thin, with a receding hairline that began in his early twenties, Walter Hampton was certainly not the picture-perfect escort you would put with the beautiful princess. They met by chance on a busy street corner. It was Annie who began the conversation, and it was Annie who asked him to join her for lunch. No one really knows how the love affair began or why it would last. What bound the two together was constantly questioned by everyone who would come to know them. They had settled in the small town of St. Gallen, just north of Zurich. They paid for their mansion with American currency. In six months, Walter Hampton had outlined a very detailed plan to add to his fortune. As for his wife, Annie would live the life of every woman's dreams—fine clothes, jewelry, trips to faraway places. Walter lived to make her happy.

63

When she finally was with child, her whole world seemed to light up. She was infinitely satisfied. She would tell her staff each morning that she was the most happy person in the whole world, and it was all possible because of Walter. He gave her everything, including a limitless love of the heart.

Annie's death was devastating to Walter. He wanted to love the son that his wife bore him, but it was as if his heart shrank and feelings were beyond him. It would take the father several weeks before he even gave a name to his son, Thomas Erin Hampton. Annie had chosen it. There would be no christening, no formal birthday parties, no happy holiday celebrations for the little boy—not ever. His father just didn't have the heart to think about it. The servants and special nanny would do their best to bring joy to the holidays, but the small, and oftentimes frail boy would never know the magic of his mother who surely would have brought all such occasions to life. The truth of the matter would also reveal that he would never know anything about his parents: who they were, where they came from, or his family ties. It was as if they entered the world alone, together. No relatives or family heritage was ever to be mentioned. Today, thirty-five years later, he sat in front of the casket that held the body of his father. A father he never knew or dared to love.

In the same afternoon, according to his father's wishes, the will would be read. As expected, everything went to Thomas. The only shock was the amount of the estate. Five hundred million dollars. Twenty million was held in cash in a special revolving account to be released to his heir at the time of his death. The rest was tied to vast stock and real estate holdings. The only surprise was an envelope that was to remain sealed for thirty days after his death. The carefully worded instructions stated that his son was to be given the envelope and the rest would be up to him. It was a strange reading. Thomas had no idea what was in the white envelope that had turned yellow with age. Whatever it contained had been sealed away a long time ago.

"Shall we set a date for you to receive the property, sir?" asked the attorney, who had taken care of the Hampton's personal affairs for the last thirty years.

"I don't know, I guess I will be back sometime around the twenty-ninth. Do you have any idea what this is all about, Quinn?" Thomas asked, as he held the envelope in his hand.

"No, sir, I do not. All I know is that your father would oftentimes remove it from the safe deposit box and hold it in his hand. It always seemed to make him sad. I believe it must have something to do with your mother, Thomas. But to be honest, it was a subject that was never discussed," Quinn Careton answered, taking the envelope back from Thomas and placing it once again in the wall safe.

The two men left the house together leaving the huge mansion to the care of the servants. Thomas Erin Hampton chose to drive the forty-five miles to Zurich for the night. The house held too many painful memories for him to even think of staying.

The bitterness of the scotch whiskey burned his throat as he sank heavily into the king-sized bed in his luxurious suite. He had never known any other kind of surroundings. His father had always been generous to him, making sure he never wanted for anything of a material nature.

Tonight, though, he would have given the last of his millions to have known any feelings of love from the man he so resembled.

"An envelope. A single, dingy envelope. What the hell did Walter leave for me?" pondered the son, as he lay staring at the fireplace. "Does it contain the names of relatives who exist in America? Was there some deep dark secret that had been kept hidden all these years? Family, it must be about our family," Thomas concluded, as his mind raced with secrets to be revealed.

The flames danced with color, and the warmth of their glow soon touched his body relaxing him. It had been a long day. A day that ended with a certain amount of mystery. It all would keep, at least for now. He had gone this long without knowing his father; another thirty days would not matter. The son fell asleep with the glass still in his hand. A single white envelope, and his father's face, would haunt his dreams.

8

Reymond Alexander was the only tech still left in the testing laboratory. It was well after hours. The bench light, which hung directly over his area, was the only light still on. The laboratory, normally well-lit during the day, took on a dark appearance this evening. The room was cold and ever so still.

Small sample vials of collected blood from the center's daily blood drives sat in plastic containers holding twenty samples each. They were positioned to the right of Reymond Alexander's work station. The long day of testing caused Reymond's shoulders to ache. He could have left when the other techs did, but something deep inside him wouldn't let him go. There had been too many mistakes lately. Mistakes that should never happen in a blood center laboratory.

A perfectionist by nature, Reymond Alexander was considered a pain in the butt by most of the other bench techs—anal-retentive to an obsessive level. At one time, Reymond's word ruled the testing laboratory, but that was before Dr. Ben Silvers appeared on Reymond's turf.

The test sleeves of donors' blood were now ready for final processing. Paperwork to coding, blood samples to refrigeration for freezing and storage. Donated donor blood samples were retained for a period to retest as a back-up if testing results were questioned. Lately, there had been many donor sleeves that needed backup testing. Returning to his bench, Reymond gathered up the remaining sets of blood vials that had been carefully rechecked and set them in the cooler. In a matter of hours, Quality Control would scan the tests and match the coded blood bags for delivery to the hospitals.

Methodically, he cleaned the stainless steel sink, removing all traces of the red liquid deposited there throughout the day. The now empty vials were placed in an orange hazardous waste trash bag marked for disposal. Quietly, Reymond set them outside the testing laboratory door. At midnight, the gathered orange bags in the hallway would be picked up by maintenance and sent to Seton Memorial for waste processing. There would never again be a trace of their existence.

Today had been another especially hectic day. The computer again went down for no apparent reason. The new system recently purchased at a tremendous cost was proving to be a nightmare for the laboratory. The blood center promoted the system to the public as flawless at the time it was purchased, touting it even in their annual report as a computer-controlled labeling process ensuring the quality control of the inventory of blood. The system, even when it worked, was still controlled by the skill of the people who used it. The computer program that had been created for the center was full of operating bugs, and there was no one at the center with enough computer knowledge to head off the program disasters that were occurring almost every day.

There were many causes for such breakdowns. The blood center did not have a perfect system. No blood center did. Computers could also be manipulated, a fact that is so often overlooked.

For Reymond Alexander, computer glitches, such as today's, scared him much more than he would ever let on. The testing lab felt the pressure of trying to process huge quantities of blood, schemed from phony emergency blood appeals. This facade of being short of blood did indeed endanger the whole order of processing in his laboratory. Several times in the last few months bad blood had made it through the system and had been forwarded to the area hospitals. An anxious Bertha White worked feverishly trying to fix the errors. All the techs knew the odds of contaminated blood being allowed through with a false negative or safe result doubled with this kind of intense pressure present in the testing process. Silvers was pushing too hard for profits. That's what all this amounted to in Reymond's eyes—profits. Before Silvers there was the occasional call for blood to beef up the inventory—lots of blood banks in the industry played the game; but lately the appeals were coming one on top of the other. It wasn't right. They were heading for a major disaster one day. The thought sent a chill down Reymond's spine.

"I don't know why I bother," Reymond fussed as he cleared his area and prepared to leave for the evening. "Nobody else works half as hard as I do—it's as if they could care less. If I were still in charge—" The thought brought a bitter taste to the gaunt looking tech's mouth. Silvers and Reymond had clashed from the very first day of the medical director's reign.

At their first meeting, Reymond corrected Dr. Silvers on a process in front of the rest of the laboratory techs. The confrontation was heated with Reymond finally backing down even though he knew Silvers was wrong. The incident left Silvers feeling intimidated. Although Silvers would never admit it to anyone, Reymond's obvious knowledge in the testing area made him more than a little uneasy. Certain things would have to be done from time to time in this area, and Silvers did not want to tangle with someone who might question his orders. The medical director had made up his mind on the spot to fire Reymond the next day. Grace Tende had to use all her skills as personnel director to counter such a happening. There were no real legal grounds to do so at this point, and the threat of a lawsuit, painted so vividly clear by the personnel director, quickly backed Dr. Silvers into a retreat. If he couldn't fire Reymond, he would take away his power base by demoting him from manager to bench tech. Grace could not prevent this, even though she tried to per-suade the new medical director not to start off his first days at the center with such actions. Reymond had worked hard to achieve this position. He was considered to be the best testing manager the center had ever had. He had devoted his life, such as it was, to the center. Eighteen hour days were normal for Reymond to work in his laboratory. He checked and rechecked his bench techs' work. It was no secret that Reymond was thought to be next in line for Bertha White's job when she retired.

The personnel director's arguments only seemed to anger the medical director more.

"I don't give a damn if he can look at a pint of blood and tell it's infected. I don't want him as a manager under me. He doesn't know his place. I want him set back down. We don't need a manager in testing anyway. Bertha White can oversee both operations. We're top-heavy in this area as it is," Silvers stated as he waved Grace Tende out of his office. This was Grace's first lesson in dealing with Benjamin Silvers. It was a bitter one. The demotion was the final result of this first meeting. Silvers really thought Reymond Alexander would leave when he was demoted. He didn't. Because of Grace Tende's defense of Reymond, she too, found herself on Dr. Silvers's list of perceived enemies within the center. A fact that did not bother her one bit.

Those were many bitter days ago, and tonight, Reymond was still devoting more than his share of time on behalf of the center.

"Silvers won't be here forever," he thought as he removed his starched white laboratory coat, turned off the lights, and began moving quickly down the hall toward the distribution area where he would leave through a back door. He paused just long enough to look at the long row of glass storage refrigerators, which held the inventory of freshly processed blood waiting to be forwarded to the hospitals. His beauties were all there, sitting so innocently with their proud label of "Gift of Life" adornment.

"Goodnight my lovelies," Reymond whispered as he walked out the back door. A smile would cross his face as he pulled up the collar of his thin Windbreaker. "Silvers was ambitious—and that ambition would take him away from Hamilton Regional." The thought warmed his body to the cold air.

Reymond Alexander was going home now—just in time to catch the late evening news. Another obsession tormented Reymond's life—Madison Boggs. The newswoman was very much a part of the strange world he had created for himself. One day their paths would cross. It would be a day Madison Boggs would never forget.

As he made his way toward the employee parking lot, his slow-moving shadow pitched itself up the outside wall of the blood center. His mind once again involuntarily called up the image of Dr. Benjamin Silvers. Almost as if he had been kicked in the stomach, the anger returned. He leaned against the side of his car.

It was never fair, never fair. Silvers would one day regret the day he had destroyed Reymond Alexander's world. It might take time, but it would happen. As Reymond's car pulled out of the employee parking lot, the night clerk began his duties of filling the Styrofoam containers with the stored blood bags from the refrigerators. In just a few hours, the drivers would back their station wagons into the service area and begin loading their cargo of hundreds of units of tested blood destined for needy hospitals. The Styrofoam containers were marked with the center's trademark stickers.

In just a matter of hours, Reymond's worst fear was about to become a reality.

9

Carter was glad it was Friday. It had been a very long intense week. The briefings with the attorneys had stretched into four days, tying up her schedule for hours at a time. There was so much they did not want her to say. She was being coached on presenting a clear defense of innocence. Each session would begin with a gentle reminder by the attorneys that they were not "coaching" her, but simply preparing her for her deposition with John Stansbarry, the attorney retained by Taylor Addison to represent her.

Carter looked tired. She had not been able to sleep at night and she deeply missed her husband. It had been several weeks since she had last spoken with him. This whole situation with the lawsuit and the multiple attorneys questioning and requestioning her was most unpleasant. Making friends at the blood center was also hard. Everyone seemed to be so territorial. Grace Tende was the exception. Carter was developing a friendship with the personnel director, and she found herself relying on Grace's advice almost every day. They had set a lunch date for today, and Carter was looking forward to the break. Grace had been with the blood center for fifteen years. She knew the operation, and she knew the personalities of each of the players. She was respected by everyone because, above all else, she was considered to be very knowledgeable in her field and very honest in her professional work habits. Even Jake Silby, the manager of the mobile fleet, who had gone nose-to-nose with Grace on several occasions, felt a warm spot for her. Dr. Silvers was the one exception. But Dr. Silvers was also afraid of Grace Tende. She had cleaned up his personnel messes all too often. His more than one dalliances with his nurses usually ended up in Grace's office. Because she was so good at what she did, the matters were soon disposed of and the threats of sexual harassment never materialized.

Grace was also a bit of a mystery to everyone. Blonde, softly attractive, somewhere in her forties, she carried herself with an air of sophistication and mystery. No one ever remembered seeing Grace Tende rattled, no matter what the situation. Her personal life was just that—personal. Still single, no one knew for sure if Grace Tende had ever been married or was even dating someone on a regular basis. At the blood center, where gossip was always a favorite pastime, Grace Tende was more than just a curiosity. There had only been one real involvement in Grace's life. She had fallen in love with one Dr. Thompson Moran. The affair had lasted nearly six weeks or until Grace discovered a truth Moran had not been able to share with her. He was married—unhappily, but nevertheless, married. Grace broke it off with deep pain in her heart. She buried herself in her job and tried not to second-guess her decision.

Gerald Preston especially liked Grace Tende. He had fallen in love with her the first moment they met when he was still head of GENCO. Grace soon became aware of his feelings after she had accepted a luncheon engagement, one she thought was to be a business meeting. As it turned out, the other staff members from GENCO did not appear, and she was alone with Preston in the restaurant. Ever the gentlemen, he made his feelings for her known in a most elegant manner. Tastefully, softly, and with proper care, he expressed his longings for her. She was not offended, but rather flattered. With kindness and consideration for him, Grace made it very clear this kind of a relationship would never be. It was not an easy situation but required great care. She did not want to hurt him, but she was unwilling to engage in a relationship with a married man.

When the lunch was over, Preston still had his dignity. His love for her did not burn out over the years. Today, as her direct supervisor, it was painful for him to see her every day and know that she would never be his. But it would be even more painful for him not to see her every day.

Grace Tende liked Carter Egan the moment she met her. So much so, that she almost stood in the way of her hiring. She didn't want to see Carter get hurt. People got hurt at this blood center, especially if they were innocent.

The intercom suddenly came alive in Carter's office.

"Carter, this is Grace. Can you pick up, please?"

"Yes, Grace," Carter quickly responded, picking up the telephone and cradling it between her chin and shoulder while she continued signing supply requisition orders.

"Can you get away now for lunch?" Grace asked.

"I don't see why not," Carter replied. She quickly cleared her desk and grabbed her coat. Carter met Grace at the back door, and they decided to grab a bite to eat at the cafeteria on the second floor of Gibby's department store, a few blocks away. It was a favorite spot for Grace who would often combine a quick clothes shopping expedition with the daily necessity of eating lunch.

"I'm starved," Grace said as she dug into her salad.

"Me too," Carter replied as she eagerly attacked her sandwich. The lunch was a good relief for Carter, who was feeling the pressure of her job. As the two women conversed easily, the food quickly disappeared from their plates.

"Grace, I have a question to ask," Carter said as she pushed her plate to the side. "Is it my imagination or does Dr. Silvers hate Reymond Alexander? I mean he literally spits his name out every time we talk about the testing lab."

"No, you're pretty much dead on. Silvers has had it in for him from day one. It's a shame. Reymond is really one of the center's most dedicated employees. I wish there was a way to help the situation, but I'm afraid both men pretty much feel the same way about each other," Grace replied.

"There seems to be a lot of unrest among the staff. Do you think we will ever see a union organized?"

"I don't think so. It's been tried, but somehow the vote never comes through. I'm not so sure a union would solve all our problems, I mean—"

"As long as there's so much unrest at the top, I can't see how anything will change," Carter said not realizing how negative she sounded.

"I see it hasn't taken you all that long to catch on to the real problems at the center," Grace laughed as she finished her coffee.

Ever aware of the time, Grace looked at her watch.

"Carter, I need to replace my lipstick. I can pick it up downstairs at the cosmetic counter if you have the time."

"I'm not on any tight deadline. I need to buy some new eye shadow myself."

With the check split, Carter and Grace made their way down to the main floor. The cosmetic counters at Gibby's were always tastefully displayed. Carter followed Grace to the Clinique counter. The sales associate working the counter was busy with an inventory count. Her back was turned to the approaching customers.

"Excuse me, but could you help me?" Grace asked, trying to get the clerk's attention.

As the young woman wearing the white smock turned to face her customers, Grace instantly recognized her.

"Jody—well my goodness. It's nice to see you," Grace said with obvious surprise in her voice.

The young woman's smile disappeared. Her attractive face was now set in a hard look. For a moment, Carter thought she was going to walk away.

"I didn't know you were working here, Jody," Grace continued trying to cover up her own flustered appearance.

"How is your mother, Jody?"

"She's still in a coma, thanks to you and yours, Miss Tende."

"What are you talking about, Jody? Your mother is in a—"

"A coma, Miss Tende," Jody Cable repeated with obvious bitterness in her voice.

"Jody, I had no idea Anna had even been sick."

"She wasn't sick; she tried to kill herself."

"Oh my God!" Grace was clearly shocked. The young clerk's eyes were filled with tears. Quickly she regained her composure. In a cold voice she asked Grace Tende what she needed from her cosmetic counter.

"I—I need a refill for my lipstick."

"What color?"

"Amber Rose."

In a matter of moments, the replacement lipstick was placed on the counter in front of Grace.

"Will that be all?" The voice was cold and edged with bitterness.

"Yes, Jody. I think that covers it for today." Grace handed over her charge card, and the sales clerk walked around the corner to ring the sale.

Carter had picked up on the name Anna immediately. Could this be the same Anna that she had replaced at the center?

"Grace, this may be none of my business, but you seem upset.

Is this young girl related to Anna Cable?" Carter asked.

"Yes, Carter. Jody is Anna's daughter."

"Please sign here," Jody Cable asked as she returned with Grace's receipt.

Grace quickly added her signature to the top copy.

"Jody. I'm really very sorry about Anna. I didn't know, believe me. Is there anything I can do—I mean, can I visit her?"

"Stay away from my mother! Just leave her alone. If it wasn't for you and that center, my mother would be okay." The young woman was very upset now, and another sales clerk quickly came to her side.

"I'm sorry to have upset you, Jody. Really, I'm very sorry."

Grace turned and quickly left the counter. Carter picked up her purchase and hurried after her friend. The look of hate on Jody Cable's face would stay in Carter's memory. Something was very wrong here. What had happened? Would Grace be able to tell her? Or was this going to be another deep dark secret of the center? There were so many things just not quite right at Hamilton Regional.

Grace was visibly shakened as they made their way through the crowd.

"What was that all about, Grace?" Carter gently asked.

"I'm not sure, Carter. To be honest, I'm really not sure. Anna Cable was such a nice person—very bright, very convinced of our cause. Something happened to her, though. I had no idea she had tried to commit. . ." Grace did not finished the sentence.

"Listen Carter," Grace stopped in the aisle near the exit, "if anything starts to go wrong for you at the center, I hope you will come to me."

The remark seemed strange at this point.

"What could happen to me, Grace? I mean—I work at a respected blood center for heavens sake." Carter's words were so innocent. Grace could not say any more at this point to her new friend. Things just might be different this time. The words of Jody Cable were still ringing in her ears. Grace made a mental note to pull out Anna's personnel records as soon as she got back to her office. The brisk walk back to the center was made in silence. Carter quickly picked up her work where she left off. In a little less than an hour, Shelly appeared at her door. She had a very disturbed look on her face.

"Boss lady, you had better come down to the lobby as soon as possible," the secretary stated, with an urgency in her voice.

"What's the matter, Shelly?" Carter asked.

"The media is pulling up outside in droves. Look outside your window and you'll see what I'm talking about," Shelly responded.

Carter made her way quickly to the window. The ground below her looked like a media mine field. Clearly marked television vans were everywhere. The reporters were positioning themselves in front of the building trying to get a clear shot with the Hamilton Regional Blood Center sign prominently displayed as they did their standups. They most definitely wanted their viewers to know where they were broadcasting from tonight.

Carter's heart began to pound. The lawsuit must have hit the court records. They were public records and monitored on a daily basis by all media sources. The moment Carter knew was coming was clearly here.

Suddenly, all three lines on her phone lit up. She could hear Shelly just outside her office picking up the calls and placing them on hold. Walking to the doorway of her office, Shelly signaled to Carter that the calls were all from the media. They wanted to talk with someone about a lawsuit. Shelly looked bewildered. Carter did not.

Carter closed the door to her office.

"Now is not the time to panic, Mrs. Egan," Carter said out loud. "Now is the time to powder your nose and get your ass down to that lobby. You know what to say—you know what to do. Now let's just get on with it."

Carter left her office and took the front stairwell down to the lobby. In a matter of moments she was surrounded by reporters all wanting a statement regarding the lawsuit, which had just been made a matter of public record. The nursing staff looked stunned by the ferociousness of the reporters. They were all talking at once, almost shouting at Carter.

Elizabeth Monroe heard the commotion from her nearby office.

"What's going on out here?" she asked a nearby phlebotomist in the process of drawing blood from an equally interested volunteer donor.

"I don't know. Maybe we have another blood shortage," the phlebotomist replied. "I've never seen those guys in such a fury," she added, with the blood donor nodding his head in agreement.

Elizabeth Monroe knew better than to approach Carter. There was no way she wanted to be put in a position of answering any reporter's questions. Quietly, she retreated back into her office. Her eyes quickly caught sight of her black file cabinet which stood in the corner of her office. Her mind flashed back to the blue folder that Silvers had given her taped shut. Elizabeth had no idea of the importance this file folder held. Ben had given it to her earlier and told her to put it in a safe place as it had something to do with a lawsuit. She closed her eyes and took a deep breath.

"I wonder if that folder has anything to do with the situation that brought those reporters here? Don't ask questions!" she told herself. "Everything happens for a reason and some things are better off left in the dark."

With those thoughts silently spoken, she went back to work on the daily schedules blocking out the sounds on the other side of her door.

The reporters voices were rising in unison. Carter realized that the situation was way out of control. The reporters, who were normally friendly and polite, were throwing question after question at her. They were hostile questions.

"What does the center have to say about the lawsuit?"

"Are you going to settle out of court?"

"Will the baby have AIDS?"

"Will Taylor Addison die? If so, how long does she have?"

"Who are the donors? Are you going to make their names public?"

"Are the donors homosexuals?"

"Is it true the blood supply is completely tainted with AIDS?" There was no way Carter could answer these questions in this format and not come out looking guilty as hell no matter how she answered.

"Please, if you give me a moment, I will try to respond to each of your questions. Will you please help me?" Carter said, holding her hands out to the press in an innocent gesture.

Whether it was the look on her face or the fact that they were inside the walls of a revered shrine, the pack of reporters backed off.

"I will grant each of you time and answer your questions to the best of my ability with the information I have. Can we all please move to the conference room?" Carter asked.

The questions subsided and the reporters motioned their cameramen toward the conference room door.

"We'll have more room in here," Carter said as she opened the door into the large street level conference room which was used only for board meetings.

The cameramen went to work arranging their large cameras on tripods. A bank of lights was centered in the middle of all the action. When the last of the lights was plugged into the nearby wall sockets, the conference room took on a ghostly, almost surreal atmosphere. The lights were blinding and the heat being generated quickly made the room feel like a sauna. Microphones were arranged by the handfuls directly in front of the podium where Carter now stood. Carter felt on fire and freezing at the same time. Her face felt as if it were shaking— jumping with nervous twitches. To the naked eye, it was not apparent. To the press, Carter seemed composed. Finally, they were ready. A voice from the back of the room that Carter recognized as Madison Boggs started the questioning.

"Why isn't the medical director down here with you? Will he answer our questions directly?"

"Dr. Silvers, because of the lawsuit, is not able to answer any questions at this time. I have been appointed spokesperson and will speak on behalf of the blood center. I'm afraid I will have to do for the time being," Carter responded.

"Can you tell us what you know about Taylor Addison's condition and what kind of a chance does the baby have?" Kelly Dillon from Channel 31 asked, raising her voice to be heard.

"I'm afraid I cannot answer questions in regard to Mrs. Addison's state of health," Carter answered.

"What can you tell us, Carter?" Chet Lampert, a print reporter for *The Daily Voice* shouted out from the far corner of the room, obviously upset the questions were being very carefully answered with no real juicy quotes to take down for his daily readers. Lampert was an aggressive street reporter who wanted to land a columnist's position. This story, he felt, had the potential for national headlines.

"In regard to the lawsuit, the blood center wishes to state that there was never an action of negligence on our part. Our center did in fact process three units of blood from three healthy donors who met all the criteria for blood donation at the time of their presentation. We would also like to state at the time of their donation, AIDS was an unknown virus, and there was absolutely no screening test available. In accordance with our process, all known screening tests for diseases which can be identified with blood were used. The blood center feels deeply for the situation Mrs. Addison now finds herself in, but in no way do we consider ourselves guilty of negligence. We do not have any evidence at this time to confirm how Mrs. Addison contracted the virus." Carter read from a prepared statement from the attorneys and signed by Dr. Silvers and Gerald Preston. The room went wild with the last statement.

"Are you trying to say that Taylor Addison did not get AIDS from a blood donation as she is now claiming?" Madison Boggs asked.

"What I am saying is we have not had a chance to review the lawsuit and all its charges," Carter responded as Philip Jarvis, Silvers's attorney had instructed her.

"Is there a question about Addison's sex life?" Chet Lampert immediately shouted out.

Carter's eyes immediately locked onto Chet Lampert. For just a moment, a bit of anger flashed across her face. Carter paused and looked down at her feet. When her eyes returned to the crowd of reporters, she carefully began her answer.

"At this time the blood center has not had an opportunity to review the lawsuit or to investigate all the surrounding bodies of evidence as needed to assess the charges. In reviewing our records, in regard to this donation process that resulted in a transfusion, we have not uncovered any, and I repeat any, areas of negligence. This is a tragic and unfortunate situation, and our heart goes out to all those who are dealing with the complications of AIDS." Carter made her statement with restraint but with obvious belief.

Several more questions were put to Carter. They were basically the same questions only phrased differently each time they were asked. Carter handled the questions sincerely and gracefully. The reporters sensed that Carter was being held hostage by absent, accused executives, and was doing the best she could under very difficult circumstances to answer on their behalf. Whatever it was about Carter, the media liked her. And more importantly, they believed her—after all, there was no test for AIDS at the time Taylor Addison received her transfusion. That was a stinging statement of truth.

As quickly as the mob of reporters gathered, they dispersed. One by one they went racing out the door to get back to their studios. Bits and pieces of the accused and the victim would be edited together just in time for the evening news. The public would see the victim telling her story and the accused reinforcing their innocence. Whoever came across best in their twenty-second sound bites would win the viewers' sympathy. The public would decide who was guilty or telling lies. Faithful blood donors who knew the process would respond to Carter's aired quote that there was not a screening procedure in place at the time this woman received her transfusion. Others would remember Carter's quote that all the donors were properly screened and passed the health questionnaire in regard to donation eligibility. Sympathy would be felt for Taylor Addison, but the blood center would come out looking like the wrongfully accused. Carter did her job today. She did her job very well.

"Point, set, and match," Dr. Silvers rejoiced after he watched the evening news later that night. While Barbara served him an extra slice of his favorite banana cream pie, he promised himself that he would tell Carter tomorrow how great she looked on television. He went to bed early and went straight to sleep. He felt a feeling of security. Carter gave him that security. Taylor Addison and her unborn baby never entered his mind.

That same evening, Grace Tende paid a visit to Michael Bryan's office. She closed the door as she entered. This conversation was to be private. Very private.

"Carter did a great job handling the media today. Don't you agree?" Michael pleasantly asked his personnel director.

"Yes, Carter is great with the media." There would be no more small talk.

"Michael, I can't find Anna Cable's personnel records in my files. Would you happen to have them?"

The mention of Anna's name stiffened Michael's back.

"Yes, I believe I do, Grace. What's the problem?"

"I don't recall turning them over to you, Michael. How did you get them?" Grace asked with a quick tartness.

"Don't you remember, Grace. I asked you for her file the afternoon she was fired."

"No, Michael. I don't recall such a conversation. Until this moment, I hadn't realized Anna had been fired. I thought she left on her own because of—"

"She was let go, Grace. She—" Michael stumbled here. "She just couldn't do the job the way Silvers wanted it done."

"I never got that impression of Anna, Michael. She seemed very capable."

"She never melded right with the media, Grace. Come on now—don't tell me you don't remember her clashes with Silvers. She couldn't get the press in here."

"Maybe there wasn't a real reason to bring the media in, Michael."

"Grace, let's not get started here. We've been through this before."

"Did you know Anna Cable is in a coma?"

"What? What are you saying?" Michael asked with a stunned look.

"Anna Cable tried to commit suicide, Michael. I ran into her daughter, Jody. She's working in cosmetics at Gibby's. She seems to blame me, Michael, and the center for whatever happened to her mother."

"Did she tell you why, Grace?"

"No. The conversation didn't get that far. I mean—the girl was obviously very upset."

Michael leaned forward in his chair, his features strained. It was clear this news had taken him by surprise. Grace's intuition told her that whatever happened to Anna Cable was connected to the center. What could possibly have happened to push Anna Cable into trying to take her own life? The thought would not leave her.

"Grace, I hate to cut this short, but I have another meeting to make this evening." Michael stood up and began to push papers into his briefcase. This conversation was clearly going nowhere tonight.

Grace felt a growing anger as she headed toward Michael's door. As she reached it, she stopped and turned toward her supervisor.

"Michael, will you be returning Anna's file to my office?"

"No, Grace. I think it needs to stay with me. We can talk about this at another time."

"This seems very unusual to me, Michael. I mean—I'm the personnel officer for the center, and it's my role to hold employee files in my office."

"Grace, I understand your role at the center. But for reasons that don't concern you, I will hold onto Anna Cable's personnel file."

"Michael, what did Anna do to cause all this?"

"She put her nose in places where it didn't belong, Grace. Just like you're doing right now." Michael's voice carried the early traces of anger. His face was flushed and his jaw tight.

Grace closed the door without saying another word.

"Damn it!" Michael spit out as he threw his briefcase down hard on the top of his desk. "Why in the hell couldn't Anna just go along? Why did she have to take what didn't belong to her and threaten the program? It shouldn't have come to this—Herk and his goons shouldn't have pressed her as hard as they did. But who would have thought she'd try to. . ." The word suicide stuck in his throat. "My God—what have we done?"

At Hamilton, some questions are better left unanswered. Anna Cable was one of those questions.

10

Madison Boggs did not lead off with the lawsuit on her evening news. Her reporter instincts were working overtime in regard to this story. "It's not ready for headlines," was her editorial quote to her news director. Instead, she led off with the announcement pertaining to the city just landing a major sports tournament that would bring national attention to Hamilton. She was the sole supporter for this story lead. But, as usual, Madison won. She had clout in the newsroom. She was also rarely wrong in such matters.

"Thanks for joining us this evening. See you tomorrow night at six and eleven," said a smiling and beautiful Madison as the news director gave the signal to roll the credits. Unhooking her microphone and gathering up her cheat notes, Madison pushed her chair away from the stage desk. The lights were still glaring in her eyes as she stepped down from the platform and made her way back to her small office. It was a few minutes past eleven o'clock. Madison was tired tonight. Her usual energy was just not there. "Maybe I'm coming down with the flu or something," she thought as she opened her desk drawer to look for some aspirin.

The loud shrill of the telephone pierced the quiet of the office. Automatically, Madison reached for her phone.

"Boggs here—can I help you?" It was her standard telephone answer.

"Humpty-Dumpty sat on a wall. Humpty-Dumpty had a great fall. All the king's horses and all the king's men, couldn't put Humpty together again." The voice was one she recognized.

"Is this the Red Man?" Madison asked.

"You have an excellent memory, Miss Boggs," it was the slightly effeminate male voice on the other end.

"That's what I get paid for. What can I do for you tonight?"

"You didn't use the story tonight. Everyone else used the story. It really is a very good story."

"What do you know about the story, Red Man?"

"More than you do, Miss Boggs."

"What is there about the story that interests you?" Madison asked, sensing the call was leading somewhere.

"You'll never know unless I help you, pretty lady."

"What won't I know?"

"The truth."

"And what is the truth?" Madison pressed.

"Humpty-Dumpty sat on a wall, Humpty-Dumpty had a great fall. All the king's horses and all the king's men couldn't put Humpty together again."

"Who is Humpty-Dumpty, Red Man?"

"The most evil person in all the world, Miss Boggs."

"What are you trying to tell me? Do you know something about Taylor Addison?"

"We will talk one day, Miss Boggs. We will talk. One day you will need my help." There was sadness in his voice.

Madison wasn't quite sure where to take the conversation next. If she pushed too hard, she might lose the call and the connection. Anonymous callers were always difficult to manipulate. They controlled the situation. Something all reporters hated—for someone else to control the situation.

"You looked nice tonight, Madison."

"Well, thanks Red Man. When do I get to see you?" Madison hoped for a break. She sensed her mysterious caller had important information, and she wanted to do more than play word games over a phone.

"You saw me today, Miss Boggs."

A strange, uncomfortable sensation nestled in the back of Madison's neck. Nausea was now in her throat. The room was suddenly very warm; she felt faint.

"What is this?" she thought, as she tried to refocus on the call. Sensing something was wrong on the other end, the caller brought the conversation to an end.

"I'll be seeing you, Miss Boggs with the beautiful mouth."

"Wait—I have a question to ask you," Madison hurriedly interjected, trying to regain the connection they had before she almost passed out. Her question was not to be answered tonight. The caller hung up.

Ed Morton, her news director, stuck his head in Madison's office.

"You still here?" he asked.

"Yeah, I'm just leaving." She returned the phone to its cradle.

"Are you okay? You look kind of green around the gills," Ed asked, concerned at the paleness in her face.

"I feel like hell, Ed. Maybe it's the flu."

"Maybe you are working too hard, Madison. Why don't you take a few days off—God knows you've got enough vacation time stacked up."

Madison did not take regular vacation time off. Long weekends maybe, but never more than that.

"Maybe you're right, Ed. Some time off may be good for me," Madison answered, shaking her head as if she really was thinking about it.

"Ed, I have been getting phone calls from a nut who calls himself Red Man.

"Red Man?" Ed mocked.

"Something tells me this guy is sitting on something big—I don't know why, Ed, but I have this feeling he's tied to the blood center." She ignored Ed's mocking.

"The blood center?" Ed repeated. "What makes you think that?"

"I don't know for sure. Just a few comments in our previous conversation and his questions tonight about me not covering the story," Madison answered.

"You mean the lawsuit?" Ed questioned.

"Yeah—the lawsuit. I don't know, Ed. Maybe I'm all wet here, but my instinct tell me something is not right in Denmark down there."

Ed's dark eyes captured Madison's visceral concern for her story that was only partly formed. But the other stations had broken the story.

"How come you didn't go for the story? Madison. I mean, it's not every day a pregnant woman files a lawsuit against a blood center, especially one located right here in Hamilton."

"I want to wait until I can talk to the girl, Ed. I mean—sit down with her, minus the lawyers and the prepared statements, and find out all the details. Later on this week I've got a one-on-one with her. The story will be better done without all the splash of the lawsuit."

Ed did not answer. His mind was working on putting sense to her feelings.

Madison gathered up her purse and switched off the lights in her office.

"Hell, Ed. When I start questioning the blood center, it's time for me to take a vacation." A forced, artificial smile appeared, but it could not mask her feeling that something sinister was unfolding, but she could not penetrate the fog.

"Go home and get some sleep, kid. You'll feel better tomorrow," Ed teased as he ruffled her hair. They had been friends for a long time. He believed in Madison and her instincts. As they walked silently out to the parking lot, Ed planned to pull any files he had on the blood center and to file a Freedom of Information request for their financial holdings. So much for instincts. Maybe she was on to something here. Maybe the story was not ready for headlines, at least not yet.

11

The sun peeking through the mini-blinds bothered Elizabeth Monroe. It was early morning after another bad night. Her body felt hammered and beaten. Her head was pounding and her stomach churning. The sound of the ringing phone caused her to sit up straight in her queen-size bed. Reaching for the intruding noisemaker, Elizabeth's eyes focused on the face of a smiling baby picture in an antique silver frame. The sight always took her breath away. Her shaking hand reached forward and placed the framed face down on the night stand. The phone continued to ring.

"Hello," she answered with a voice sounding still half asleep.

"So, how's Liz this morning?" the familiar voice asked.

"Elizabeth is tired and trying to sleep." Her voice turned from sounding sleepy to sounding irritated. She hated the nickname of "Liz." "This is my day off," she added for reference.

"Well, get up, sunshine. We're going to spend the day at the lake." He did not ask if she wanted to or if she had other plans. When he called, she was to be ready. He was the master.

"Ben, I really don't feel like going to the lake today. I have some personal things I need to do and. . ."

"I'm the only personal thing you need to attend to, my dear. How could you have forgotten that so soon?" A deep laugh followed.

Elizabeth did not answer.

"I'll be over to get you in two hours. Dress warm, it may be chilly." The steady hum of disconnection rang in her ear.

Returning the phone to its cradle, Elizabeth eased herself down between the covers once again. The sun was full up in her immaculately kept bedroom. Elizabeth's home was small, beautifully furnished and always kept letter-perfect, unlike her tornado-blown office. The smell of fresh coffee brewing seeped slowly into her bedroom. Rising quickly, Elizabeth reached for her robe lying neatly at the end of her bed.

"Mom, is that you?" Elizabeth called out while walking down the hall toward the kitchen.

"Yes, dear," her mother answered.

"I didn't hear the door open," Elizabeth replied, neither mad nor surprised at her unexpected visitor. The aroma of the coffee, and her need for it, quickly filled her senses.

Myrtle Thomas smiled warmly at her daughter. Her stocky frame moved around the kitchen with familiar ease. She had already set the breakfast table for two and was in the process of mixing eggs and milk for her daughter's favorite, French toast. Elizabeth had always been a picky eater, but French toast was always a winner in the eating battle. Kitten had also loved her grandmother's French toast. Kitten was Elizabeth's only child. She died at the age of one year and six days. A flu-like virus and a tragic mix up in the emergency room at Seton Memorial took the child's life away in a mere ten days. Elizabeth, her mother felt, would never recover from her daughter's death. Myrtle Thomas was absolutely correct.

"You look absolutely awful, dear. You're not sleeping again, are you?"

Elizabeth did not answer but nodded her head in a confirming manner. A cup of coffee was poured for Elizabeth and the proper amount of sugar added. The ceramic mug felt warm to Elizabeth's hands as the aroma of the rich grounds slowly swirling up from the steaming coffee touched her sense of smell.

"Mom, why is your coffee so much better than mine?" Elizabeth asked in the process of tasting her first cup.

"Because I make mine with freshly ground beans, Elizabeth. It only takes a few extra moments. . ." her mother continued to tell her the exact steps to take just as she always did. Elizabeth smiled and listened just as always.

The breakfast was half-eaten as her mother knew it would be. But at least her daughter had some good food in her stomach and not just coffee and cigarettes.

The kitchen was cleaned and returned to its normal neat order. Myrtle had gone into Elizabeth's bedroom and made the bed and returned her granddaughter's picture frame to its upright position.

"I'm on my way, dear. Do you need any groceries? I have to go to the store later," her mother asked.

"No, I'm okay for now, Mom. Maybe next week we can go shopping together."

A quick kiss on the forehead and Myrtle was gone leaving Elizabeth alone once again. She did feel better—at least for the moment. The kitchen clock spoke to the hour of needing a shower and finding warm clothes for the trip to the lake. Ben did not like to be kept waiting.

"Perhaps today will be a good day," Elizabeth thought as she stepped into the waiting hot shower. Lingering for nearly fifteen minutes beneath the steady stream of water brought a healthy glow to the body of Elizabeth Monroe. She did have a great body. A body that Ben Silvers enjoyed.

She was applying the last of her makeup when she heard the familiar sound of the Jeep Cherokee pull into her driveway, which ran along the side of her house next to the bedroom window. Quickly finishing, she grabbed her navy pea coat from the closet and made her way down the hall and out the kitchen door. The driver threw open the passenger door of the Jeep.

"You look great, Liz."

"Thanks, Ben," Elizabeth replied as she settled into her seat. The car was put in reverse and slowly backed out of the driveway. In a few minutes they had made their way through traffic and were on the ramp leading to the Interstate heading north to Ben's lakeside cabin, a cabin his wife did not know he owned. Ben's hand was now resting on Elizabeth's thigh and moving slowing up and down in caressing motions. This action had aroused him and made him press down harder on the accelerator of the car. Ben Silvers had liked the feel of Elizabeth. He had been instantly attracted to the director of nurses. Elizabeth, on the other hand, did not share the same instant attraction. Ben Silvers was cocky and flip with her in their first conversations. She avoided his presence, and when she was called to his office for a one-on-one, she kept a stony professional tone in her voice at all times. A conference in New York City changed all that. She didn't really want to go and used every excuse not to make the trip. Silvers stated quite firmly that this conference was a top priority and that, as director of nurses, she had to attend to document the changes soon to be set forth by the NAABC. It was critical to their center to keep abreast of current regulations, especially in this the age of AIDS. If nothing else, they needed to document the participation of their center on both their résumés. Elizabeth felt trapped but nevertheless, she could see the merit of her attending the conference, even if it meant she had to share time with Silvers. The conference was not heavily attended, and the sessions were long with little of the hyped evidence of learning they had all been promised. She was apprehensive on the last evening of the conference when she found herself sharing an elevator with Silvers. He invited her to a quick dinner and simply would not take no for an answer. The dinner was not as horrible to endure as she imagined it would be. She was surprised at how different he was away from Hamilton Regional. He possessed a quick sense of humor that had never surfaced in their normal working environment. In a matter of a few hours, Elizabeth Monroe found herself changing her opinion of Dr. Benjamin Silvers. He was also the perfect gentlemen. This she did not expect. When they returned from New York, Elizabeth felt herself more relaxed in his presence. Silvers knew, if he was going to score with Elizabeth, it would have to be on her terms—at least at first. The moment arrived late one evening when they were working on updating donor criteria codes. Elizabeth did indeed make the first move. Silvers's inexperience in sex surprised her and in a way gave her a feeling of false superiority. This feeling would disappear as the months went by, and her eager partner introduced her to an experience she had never had before—liquid morphine. If it was a deliberate act of introduction or a simple response to help her with the nightmares of her past, she would never know. Ben Silvers was a man with many surprises. Today was just another day of surprise.

The usual hour drive to the cabin was handled in just under forty-five minutes. The couple hardly made their way into the cabin before the intense desires of the male figure were satisfied. They would spend the day having sex. Sex complete in its many moments of pleasures. For Ben, the hours spent were unlike any others he had ever known. For Elizabeth, the time was used as an escape to touch and be touched. To separate her mind from memories buried too deep to surface but too horrific to forget.

As the sun began to set, Ben rose from the day bed and began to dress.

"Let's stop at the inn and have dinner," he said. The words struck Elizabeth immediately. Ben had never offered to take her out in public before.

"What's the occasion, Ben?" She asked as she began to assemble her clothes from the various spots where they had been discarded upon arrival.

"Does there have to be an occasion, Elizabeth?" Ben returned, not looking at her but paying attention to the combing of his hair in the mirror. Elizabeth did not answer.

Soon they were sitting at a quaint table in the inn overlooking the basin end of the lake. She was truly hungry and for once was glad to be spending time together with this man in a normal setting. Elizabeth was not in love with Ben, but she had come to know a side of him that no one else knew. She was still attracted to his good looks and his brilliant mind. His passion with her was tender and strong. She was also his teacher. She taught him to enjoy sex. She taught him about his body and his releases of emotion. This was her power over Ben Silvers.

Ben interrupted their quiet.

"Guess who called me this morning?"

"Who?" Elizabeth asked.

"Fritzsimmons Garret."

"The President of NAABC?" Elizabeth was impressed.

"He's getting ready to retire and guess who just may be a candidate for his job?" Silvers's smile left little doubt as to the answer.

"Are you serious?" Elizabeth sat back suddenly in her chair and smiled. Ben Silvers had talked of nothing so deeply as one day working his way up to this prestigious position. It was his ultimate dream.

"Yeah, well, it seems he wants to juggle the chairs up a bit at the corporate level. He wants to participate in picking his successor, and the NAABC is looking for someone who can continue to bring fresh money to their sizable piggy bank. You and I both know I'm just the guy who can do that." Silvers grinned after he sipped deeply from his glass of wine.

"What ever happened to his long-time assistant, Sterling—something?"

"Sterling Howard," Silvers stated drily. Sterling was not someone Silvers liked. Sterling Howard was too stuffy—too dedicated to run things by the book. He was nothing like Fritzsimmons Garret.

"Howard doesn't have the guts to run the association. Fritz knows that. My track record beats his any day. As soon as we settle this mess with the lawsuit, Fritz wants me to fly to New York and do a little mingling. I'm probably going to be spending a little more time traveling, you know, getting to know the coast guys. They all know who supplies their damn blood banks." The comment was stated with pride as Silvers had earned a solid reputation for putting together an efficient shipping operation.

"Did you see the news last night?" he asked changing the subject.

"Hmm, no. I didn't turn on the television."

"Too bad—you missed Carter handling the lawsuit with the media." His voice was full of good humor.

"Obviously, you are pleased with Carter's performance," Elizabeth's voice had just a tinge of cattiness. Ben picked up on Elizabeth's response.

"Carter's great with the media, Elizabeth, and she is our saving grace against this bitch causing us trouble." Ben's voice had taken on a hard edge that disturbed her and was unwelcome.

"The girl is not a bitch, Ben. She has AIDS and she is going to die." Elizabeth hoped that Ben would soften with the tragic circumstances facing the pregnant girl. But the girl's fate did not faze Ben. His jaw tightened as his hand squeezed his wine glass.

"I can't seem to make you understand how serious these charges are, Elizabeth. I'm in a situation that could damage my entire career—a career that I've worked very hard to build. I'm not going to see it all washed away because your idiot nurses failed to do what they should have done in the first place." His words were bitter now and laced with sarcasm. "It was your idiot nurses who screwed up, Elizabeth. Your goddamned idiot nurses." Ben spit out, his voice rising.

"What are you talking about, Ben?"

"Edwin Shell, that's what I'm taking about."

Elizabeth's mind raced to put a face with the name just thrown at her. As Elizabeth stared across the table at Ben, her mind drew a blank trying to place a face with a name that obviously was at the root of Ben's anger. Sensing that he had said too much already in disclosing the name of Edwin Shell, Ben began a retreat from the conversation that had led to an immediate change in the evenings disposition.

"Forget it, Liz. Let's just finish our dinner," a fake smile slowly spread across his face. The lines in the corner of his eyes were still hard and his face still flushed. Elizabeth knew when to press forward and when to hold her tongue. She would not pursue the conversation at this moment. Later, as they were driving home, Elizabeth dared to continue.

"Ben, that statement you made over dinner about my nurses being the cause for your trouble with the girl—what do my nurses have to do with it?"

"There's no need to go into this now, Elizabeth," Ben answered very calmly.

"Ben, if you are in trouble and my nurses are the cause of it, I need to know right now. How can I help you if I don't know what's going on." Elizabeth was angry. Angry for many different reasons.

Her words did not fall on deaf ears. Ben was listening. Elizabeth would need to know what was going on if the plan was to work. He would have to trust her as well as Alice Crane. He could rely on Alice Crane. Could he really rely on Elizabeth Monroe? A feeling of smugness suddenly draped itself over his shoulders.

"Liz, let's not waste our time talking about this. Do you still have the blue folder I gave you for safekeeping?"

"Yes, it's in my office file cabinet."

"When you get a chance, just open it up. I think you will get a pretty clear picture about what we need to do." The "we" in his statement didn't quite make sense to her at that moment.

The Jeep was now turning quietly into her driveway. Ben killed the engine and began to unzip his light-weight corduroy pants. His body ached with a strong erection. Elizabeth playfully placed her hands around his manhood increasing his desire. She lowered her head to his lap and softly kissed his exposed member in slow easy motions. Six months ago, this action would have caused Ben Silvers to explode. Tonight, with Elizabeth's teachings, he had learned how to control his release to prolong his pleasure.

The windows of the Jeep were completely steamed with moisture by the time Elizabeth exited. Her hands fumbled with the keys to her back door. The warmth of the kitchen touched the coolness of Elizabeth's cheeks as she finally entered her home. She discarded the navy pea coat on the living room couch. Turning the lights on in her bathroom, she opened the drawer beneath the sink. Taking out a syringe and a blue rubber strap, she reached up into the medicine cabinet and extracted a packaged needle. In a few moments she would feel her peace and her demons would come to rest. Before she gave into the dreams of the night, her mind flashed to the sight of the blue folder she had put in the back of a black file cabinet in her office at Ben's urging. Names and faces all began to weave in and out of her consciousness until they ran together as one.

She barely made it to her bed when the full effect of the "master" took over. Her body felt on fire as her mind embraced the feelings of pure pleasure—a pleasure only Ben could give her. As she controlled him, he most certainly controlled her.

Without question, Elizabeth Monroe would be part of Ben's plan. There was no longer a choice for her.

12

Kiley Matson had spent the better part of his day with the telephone glued to his ear. He was in his "wheeling and dealing" mode—a process that cemented his job security. Matson's role had been defined early when his *gift for talking people into things and out of things* surfaced. He was the driving force behind the center's out-of-state resource sharing operation.

Matson had developed a strong following with other huge blood centers located in both coastal zones: New York and California. These two areas alone accounted for more than half of the amount of transfused blood used in the country. The blood centers that were responsible for supplying these prolific, blood-using hospitals had significant problems in securing enough blood and blood components to handle the demand. Kiley Matson was their "ace in the hole," especially since the liberal supply of donated blood coming into the United States from Europe, which amounted at one time to an importing of nearly 65 percent of all blood used, had been completely closed down since the AIDS epidemic.

Kiley Matson was not smiling when he finally hung up the phone. His posted inventory of O+, O– blood was down from his usual comfort zone of 4,000 units to 1500. The *Glass* account was rapidly depleting and he was having to stall future resource sharing orders. This would most definitely show up as a loss in projected sales for the month, a fact that would send the good twosome up the wall. There was never to be a decline in posted sales profits.

Kiley was also bothered by another trend that made his job even more difficult. Blood drives were not posting their usual high numbers, especially among factory workers. Normally, the manufacturing plants were the center's bread and butter. Workers who volunteered to donate blood during the course of their scheduled shift received a value incentive of time off the job. In some cases, there could also be a dollar bonus incentive. It all depended on the terms of agreement established between company management and the blood center. Many unions paid their members "cash on the barrel head" immediately after their donation process. None of this was known publicly but it existed and ran smoothly most of the time. Lately, blood centers were moving even further into the open, sweetening the incentives for getting people to donate blood by offering free tickets to concerts, ball games, and other public events. Chances of winning trips, such as cruises or Hawaii vacations, were beginning to surface, and always with full media support. One blood center on the east coast had even publicized a donation promotion where the *hook to donate* was a raffle chance on a $250,000 house. This center received a generous gift of the house by a builder who was a devoted fifty-gallon blood donor. People were lining up at the outreach locations by the dozens to have a chance to win; all they had to do was donate their blood. For years such practices were frowned upon by the national association of blood centers. The reason was clear—the safety of the blood supply. People could be motivated to conceal or deny a health issue that might prevent them from the opportunity to win something. Most people do not thoroughly understand the importance of their health history when it comes to donating blood. Add to this misunderstanding, the naive belief that the blood centers have tests for everything, and if something would be wrong with their blood, it would be caught in the testing process. Plasma centers who pay for blood face the same problems with the safety of the blood supply.

Jake Silby poked his round face into Kiley's office.

"How's the ball game going today?" Jake asked, ever the kidder.

Jake Silby was just the person Kiley wanted to see. Not answering directly, Kiley motioned Jake into his office. Jake came in and closed the door behind him.

"What's cookin'?" Silby lowered his frame into the metal chair that served as Kiley's guest seat.

"Jake, my numbers don't add up. What's going down with the drivers?" Kiley asked with obvious knowledge of past situations that led to the same findings in his control sheets.

"What are you hinting at, Kiley?" Jake replied with an edge now in his voice.

"Are your drivers dropping units again? Is that clear enough for you, Jake?"

"Bullshit, Kiley. You're pulling stuff right out of the air. My drivers don't drop."

"Screw the pat answers, Jake. This is Kiley Matson you're talking to. I know the shit you're pulling. What's the beef this time?" Kiley fired back.

Jake Silby moved his body to the edge of his hard metal chair. He had been friends with Kiley Matson for over ten years but not good enough friends to confide information that could come back to bite him in the ass. Matson was controlled by the higher-ups, a fact that did not escape the manager of the mobile fleets. Herk Golden, Silby's boss, would have his head if he even thought he was talking to Kiley Matson about more than the weather. Matson and Golden had a bitter relationship, and lines were clearly drawn between the two men.

"I'll tell you what's going on, Kiley. Our mobile buses are falling apart, our drivers are paid less than scale, and there hasn't been a decent cost-of-living increase in over three years." Silby's frustrations started to show as he got up from his chair. "What we need is a union to come in here and clean out the bullshit."

"Look, Jake. I understand all that, but don't think you can get the union in here by dumping. Tweedledee and Tweedledum will air your asses out to dry—they've done it before and they will certainly do it again."

"Well, when you can't fill your precious orders and the rope tightens around your neck as well, we'll see who controls the powers that be. You could be a force for our guys, Kiley. You could be." Jake quickly exited Kiley's office. The conversation had nowhere to go and they both knew it.

"Shit," Kiley yelled as he threw his pencil down hard on his paper-strewn desk. Once again the ugly image of the union was raised. Twice before the drivers had tried to muscle the union in, convinced that their power would bump up their salaries and give them clout in management matters. Both times, when the final votes were tallied, the union movement lost. Power and money in all the right places bought the votes and would certainly buy them again. Herk Golden loved for the union issue to come up. He profited handsomely with selective incentives provided by the purses of the executive level. Herk controlled the drivers, most of whom needed their jobs to survive. He was given total control of hiring his crew, including being allowed to bypass Grace Tende's background checks. More than one of Herk's drivers had backgrounds that came complete with police rap sheets. Herk Golden was their passport to staying alive on the streets, and so, whatever Herk wanted, Herk got from his men. One day, maybe, he would let the union have a fair shot at organizing, but not right now.

Nevertheless, for Kiley Matson, the drivers dumping blood put him in a terrible bind—a bind of the worst kind. Kiley now had only two recourses left—call another emergency or buy cheap blood from the *"black zones"* to fill their own local hospital orders. The black zones, as they were referred to by those who were in the business of buying and selling blood, were those areas in the country where blood was available for shipment because of lesser hospital demands. The service centers in the black zones were also known to work out trades with paying plasma centers that were not too particular about their donor base or in following the NAABC screening regulations. Blood from the black zones could be looked at as risky. But they were popular to some buyers because they sold their excess blood products several dollars less per unit than a premium zone such as Hamilton Regional. A premium zone was considered an area where the number of reported AIDS cases ran lower than the national average and the donor base was 100 percent volunteer. Kiley lived or died by his ability to fill his local hospital orders, and at the same time, satisfy his out-of-state orders where he could jack up the price of each unit of blood at a considerable profit for his center. This is where the center made its real profits—resource sharing. If you could supply, you could pump those liquid gold dollars straight into the bank.

The coastal hospitals had no loyalty when it came to buying blood. Obviously, they preferred receiving blood from the premium zones, but if push came to shove, and their local contacts could not supply their orders for blood, the phones were going to ring in a black zone that day. But first, they were going to ring Kiley Matson to see if his magic touch of supply could fill their needs directly.

Kiley prided himself in responding to each and every phone call. He developed a "push and shove" method, as he liked to call it; buy blood cheap from a black zone, retag it with Hamilton volunteer shipment markers, and resell it directly to the coastal hospitals at a higher market price. They got their blood; he got their dollars. So what if a small NAABC procedure was tampered with? Only blood centers knew where the blood was drawn and the donors' names. The centers controlled the paperwork. The NAABC required area distribution blood centers to tag the origination site on each unit of blood. In turn, the hospitals were required to control and record the names of the recipients. The records were kept separate in this manner to handle the perceived "confidentiality. The procedure protected the donor from liability. Donors names were never to be released by blood centers to anyone. To change this "protection system" of the volunteer blood supply was a question never open for discussion. Donors would stop donating their blood if they ran the risk of being identified and later sued by a recipient claiming their blood was responsible for contracting a disease.

In Kiley's mind, blood was by no means safe, no matter where it came from. So why sweat the small stuff? So far, his method had worked smoothly. As long as the coastal blood centers did not know they were being directly cut out, Kiley was "in like Flynn."

Timing was everything in a "push and shove" situation. The hospitals needed blood, and if they had a way to get it without hassle, tested and ready to transfuse, they would pay the price and keep their mouths shut to their local blood center distributors.

Michael Bryan was Kiley's next visitor.

"What's up with the inventory, Kiley? Our control sheets are out of whack. I've been going over them for the last week and. . ."

"The drivers are dumping again," Kiley answered before Bryan could finish his question.

A look of anger immediately appeared on Bryan's face.

"Those sonsofbitches. I'll fire the lot of them."

"Why don't you just spend a little money and fix up the mobiles and give them a ten-cent raise per hour, Michael? You know the fleet is operating on a shoestring purse. Hell, it doesn't take a rocket scientist to figure out how to pacify these dumb asses," Kiley cut in.

"There's no money. . ." Bryan started to say.

"Bullshit. Cut the canned crap, Mike. You and I both know better than that. There's plenty of money—plenty. God knows I bring a fortune into this place on a daily basis. You and I are not reaping the good life, though, are we, little brother?" Kiley's remarks were laced with inside knowledge and cattiness. Kiley knew that Michael Bryan was making several thousand dollars more a year than he was, thanks to his relationship with Preston. This bothered Kiley Matson a lot.

Michael Bryan knew when to argue with Kiley Matson and when to back off. When it came to personal issues such as money in whose pockets, Bryan knew better than to try and push for a fair conversation. Kiley Matson distributed the direct dollar payments to the executive level, a level which he was part of. Michael Bryan was on Kiley's turf when it came to the financial end of this operation.

"Look, Kiley, I am doing the best that I can. I'm in the process of trying to negotiate for better pay for everyone, but it takes time, and units dropping all over the place don't help anyone."

Kiley Matson looked at Michael Bryan and nodded his head. This conversation was not new. Kiley knew that Bryan could not stop the latest tactic by a disgruntled crew of drivers.

Time and a twist of gentle persuasion by Gerald Preston was the standard mode of correction for this pesky, recurring problem. The phone rang in Kiley's office. "Kiley Matson here."

Michael Bryan made his way to the door, closing it behind him as he headed for Bertha White's office. At least he had verified the dumping problem. He also knew that tomorrow morning Kiley Matson would be asking for an emergency call from the public relations department. It was how the system worked. It was all perfectly legal and tidy in all matters of operation—but it turned in his stomach like food poisoning.

"Blood—only humans can supply it—manipulate it, and profit from it." Michael thought as he pressed on to settle another matter that was among his headings of responsibilities within the hallowed walls of the blood center.

The sudden urge to be sitting topside on his sailboat with a stiff breeze at his back hit Michael Bryan where he still had feeling left. There had been an ad in *The Wall Street Journal* that morning that had gotten his attention big time. A marina was for sale in Seattle. The asking price was a little over three hundred thousand. He could not get the ad out of his mind. Bryan made a mental note to call his father later in the day. Perhaps there would be a way to get himself out of this mess. Betsy, of course, would not want any part of this new life; the thought caused Michael Bryan to smile for the first time in many days.

Bertha White swung her legs under her metal desk. Reymond Alexander scooted a peeling gray metal chair across the room to sit at Bertha's right hand. They were looking at computer inventory control sheets. The numbers were not matching up. Several hundred appeared to have been processed out of order, supposedly impossible with their new automated computer process.

"I've checked these bar codes a hundred times, Reymond, and I still can't pinpoint the break," Bertha said matter-of-factly to her trusted tech.

Reymond did not comment but continued to scan the sheets.

"I'm afraid we've had a major breakdown here. God help us if any of these jumbled units were contaminated. It would take us forever to reboot and pull the testing samples for comparison," she stated with just a hint of concern surfacing in her voice.

"Don't panic, Bertha. It could just be the idiot computer acting up again." Reymond's voice was calm as he continued to look at the print-out sheets.

"Just the two people I hoped to find," Michael Bryan cheerfully stated as he entered Bertha's office.

Bertha motioned for Michael to grab a chair as Reymond acknowledged his presence with a smile. Reymond liked Michael Bryan. Bryan had always treated him fairly and with respect—something he felt he did not get from too many people.

"What's going on?" Bryan asked.

"It could be nothing, Michael, and it could be a disaster." Bertha's voice showed little emotion.

The hair on the back of Michael's neck stiffened.

"What's the problem, Bertha?"

"Quality Control is reporting the testing sleeves of several units are in fact now testing positive. Somehow, several pints of bad blood got turned in the system and made it through to the hospitals without testing. We can't find their test results in order to identify them at this point.

"The computer could have eaten them, Michael. We've been through this before," Reymond quickly added.

"How many units are we looking at, Bertha?" Michael asked.

"Close to a hundred, maybe."

"Jesus Christ, Bertha—that's unbelievable," Michael replied quickly following up with another question.

"How soon till you're able to verify?"

"Not today, that's for sure. Not today." Bertha's answer was not what Michael wanted to hear.

"Before we press any hot buttons, let me work on the back-up. If we did go down, I might be able to trace the failure through the default system," Reymond interjected. His words seemed to offer a reprieve for Bertha and Michael. They agreed to turn the matter over to Reymond for the time being.

"I'll pull someone off of the line and replace you for the afternoon testing run, Reymond. Stay put in here as long as it takes to give us some answers," Bertha directed.

Leaving Reymond alone in Bertha's office, the two supervisors headed out the side door.

The cool air brought an immediate rush to Michael's lungs. Reaching for his cigarettes he extended his pack to Bertha as she supplied the lighter. Inhaling deeply, the pair did not speak for a few minutes. Finally the silence had to be broken.

"How serious is this, Bertha?"

"It could be a disaster, Michael."

"Is there enough time to recall the units if we have to?" he asked.

"It depends on when and where they were delivered. If they were sent to one of our large hospitals, chances are they have already been transfused."

"Jesus Christ—what a mess."

"Yeah, well you and I both know we have a snowball's chance in hell at getting a recall," Bertha continued.

Her words rang with painful vibrations in Michael's ears. They had been through this several times in the last two years. Bertha had identified a recall situation concerning less than a half-a-dozen units only to be told to process the request directly through paper channels to Dr. Crane's office. They were both fairly sure that the notification process stopped at her desk. There were no laws on record in Hamilton that forced its blood center to notify area hospitals of contaminated blood. A courtesy call to the hospital pathologist relating the incident was standard procedure and it would occur at the center's discretion. It would then be up to the pathologist to follow through to the physician treating the patient who received the blood transfusion. Depending on the doctor's judgment, so went the notification. The public was not aware of this and if it should ever come up, all parties would say that notification did take place. Most of the time, physicians justified the delaying of notification with statements relating to the age and condition of the patient they were treating. Since a large portion of blood transfusions were given to the elderly and the very seriously ill, the physician deferred to the more important issues at risk. A contaminated unit of blood was not of uppermost importance. Most of these patients would not live long enough to suffer the effects of an HIV contamination. Hepatitis was a different story. How many people have received infected blood and died in the process of their recovery because of undetected hepatitis complications is simply not known. Rare are autopsies done on such patients. Causes of death are usually listed under the original diagnosis of admitting factors, not from the complications of treatment, which would include blood transfusions.

A gust of cold wind caught the tips of the cigarettes the smoking pair held in their hands sending a spray of ashes through the air. "I guess it's time to quit, Michael," Bertha said as she brushed the ashes from her sweater's sleeve.

"Even God is trying to blow out the smoke." She laughed as she pulled open the heavy metal side door.

"I'll see you later, Bertha. Give me a call if Reymond finds the break." Bryan walked swiftly up the back steps toward his executive level office.

"What the hell could be next," he thought. "What the hell could be next."

The marina in Seattle was once again in the front of Michael's mind. Somehow, some way, Michael Havens Bryan had to find the money to buy back his life. By the time he reached the top of the stairs, he had made up his mind. It could be done. If he had learned anything from Gerald Preston, it was that all things were possible. All things.

13

Reymond Alexander spent the better part of the afternoon scanning through the computer's main back-up system. His motions were precise. Reymond's worst fear had indeed surfaced and was staring him coldly in the face. "How could we let this happen?" he repeated silently over and over again, as he searched the control sheets. "Why didn't Quality Control catch this sooner?"

Reymond knew the answer even if he didn't want to say it out loud. The rush to get it done. The goddamn rush.

The constant computer breakdowns had them relying far too heavily on manual coding. QC just couldn't keep up with it. A manual processing of blood always had to be rechecked, but they were so far behind—God knows how many units slipped through. It would take even more time to identify and track the substandard units as understaffed as they were in that department.

"God help us if any of these are HIV or Hepatitis positive."

One thought did cross Reymond's mind, though. If this was as bad as it looked, Silvers could be in a real sticky situation with his county hospitals. It doesn't take much to turn a bunch of hospital administraters into a screaming pack of hyena all demanding replacement for an inept medical director. Reymond allowed himself a smile.

By 5:30 p.m. Reymond had pulled all the default back-up sheets he needed to present his case. When Bertha White walked into her office, Reymond motioned for her to peek over his shoulder.

"Did you find something?" She asked.

"Sure did," he stated with dark concern present in his voice.

"We have a break, Bertha—a big one."

"How big?" his supervisor asked not knowing if she was really ready to hear the answer.

"Sixty so far," came his answer.

"Oh my God! Please tell me it was all whole blood units?"

"Nope! It looks like the sixty were divided into components, Bertha."

"Oh no," Bertha said in a low, almost painful tone of voice as the realization of the situation hit home. For some reason, Bertha's mind flashed to the blood center's campaign literature statement—*"A single unit of blood can be separated into as many as five different blood components. Thus, your one donation can help as many as five different individuals who need the gift of life."*

"How can we tell the public that sixty units of blood broken into platelets, plasma, and other components has now infected some three hundred unsuspecting blood recipients?"

"What did you just say, Bertha?" Reymond asked as his attention was still occupied with the report.

Bertha did not answer Reymond Alexander. Sensing that she was stunned and a little rattled at this moment, he cautiously continued to relate his findings.

"The damn computer has gone down four times in this span of time, Bertha, and the manual processing was never backed up by a QC check. The bad blood got wrapped up with the good and shipped untested," Reymond relayed as he continued to pull up data from the computer. "We're in such a goddamned hurry to process those blood babies that we've got our delivery carriage in front of the safety net." His words hit home with Bertha. The last emergency had put a large strain on processing, and Quality Control was thrown for a bloody loop when the computer shut down in the middle of the media alert, forcing a manual system of registering and coding. They simply overlooked their own system of checks and balances.

"They must have sent units through without waiting for the lab tests to be registered and tagged to the paperwork," Bertha finally stated out loud, while trying to mentally walk herself through the processing system. This kind of error could occur. It wasn't supposed to, but it could. It was commonly referred to as "human error" caused by a frantic rush to deliver.

"Are we looking at any HIV's mixed in with these?" Bertha asked as she stood helplessly waiting for an answer.

"Some of them are, but I don't know how many yet. I think I can track most of them—given a few days, but I can't get all of them—at least not tonight," Reymond answered as he continued to feed commands into the computer.

"We have one more problem to face, Bertha. The unit numbers that were added late with positive reactions for disease will have to be matched against stored sample numbers. If they are out of order bar code wise, we may have to retest the last two or three thousand units across the board," Reymond added with just enough sincerity in his voice to produce genuine concern.

The staggering facts of Reymond's words hit Bertha square between the eyes.

"That's almost impossible. We'd be better off to just recall the donor population for the last month." Bertha added.

"Silvers will drop dead when he hears about this, Bertha." Reymond answered trying to contain any traces of joy from his voice.

"We are not going to tell him, Reymond. This information has to go through protocol channels—that means we direct our findings to Dr. Crane." Bertha answered very matter-of-factly, not showing the deep emotions she was now feeling.

A look of surprise passed over Reymond's face. He did not realize the protocol procedure included Dr. Crane. This was a new rule and one that Silvers had engineered only recently.

"She'll scream a bloody bitch," Reymond answered. And you know she won't initiate a recall for weeks—hell, maybe not at all if she thinks she can get away with it."

"So be it, Reymond. So be it."

For just a few seconds, Reymond felt nauseated. The techs would be blamed for this. Everybody knew they were trying to beat a system that was never meant to be hurried along like cattle. Blood testing took time and precise measurements. One man was inflicting this pressure on his department—Silvers. Before Silvers arrived—accidents like this never happened.

The look on Bertha's face clearly showed the pain of responsibility she was feeling. After all, she was the laboratory's director. She was ultimately responsible for everything that went on in the bowels of the basement.

"Would Dr. Silvers hold her responsible and dump the whole mess in her lap?" Reymond pondered silently. This thought had not occurred to him before. Reymond quickly put it out of his mind.

"I'll just have to take steps to keep her clear, if and when the time comes to point the finger at someone," he reasoned as he continued to pull information up on the computer screen.

"I'd better go find Dr. Crane, Reymond. Please see how much more tracking you can do." Bertha softly closed her office door behind her as she headed out to find the assistant medical director. In all her years of service to the blood center, this was truly the darkest day Bertha White had ever spent.

"How could we have let this happen?" she said to herself as she brushed past two of her lab techs so lost in thought that she failed to return their greetings.

"How could we have let this happen?" she repeated as she reached the bottom of the stairwell that would take her up two flights of stairs to the executive level. Grabbing on to the stair railing, the weight of the last few minutes seemed to hold her feet to the ground. Tears suddenly welled up in the proud woman's eyes. Never before had she cried at the blood center—today would be the exception. Bertha pitched forward and rested her head on the wooden railing.

"Bertha, what is wrong?" the voice of Grace Tende quickly caused Bertha to try to regain her composure.

"It's nothing, Grace." Bertha used her sweater sleeve to wipe away the tears from her now pale face.

"Don't give me that, Bertha. In all these years I've never seen you cry—is it Dr. Silvers?" Grace questioned with just a trace of anger showing.

"Believe it or not, Grace," Bertha quickly replied while she put her body in motion again, "this time Dr. Silvers had nothing to do with it. Nothing whatsoever."

Bertha White had no way of knowing how wrong she was. How very wrong.

14

The afternoon reports were beginning to blur in front of her eyes. Carter had spent the better part of the day catching up on paperwork and proofing the latest brochure she had written to help educate the public on the need to donate blood.

The pamphlet design had turned out better than she had hoped. She made a mental note to bump up the firm of Dietrist and Richards to the top of the list of preferred art vendors.

There really were certain aspects of her job that she loved. Creating descriptive and colorful brochures was one of them. Carter seemed to have a knack for taking very technical subjects and translating them into clear and easy-to-read text. Not all public relations directors could do this. Carter was surprised by the knock on her door. It was after six-thirty, and she thought she was alone on the third floor.

"Come in," Carter replied.

Grace Tende's face was a welcome surprise.

"What are you still doing here?" Grace asked.

"I guess I'm doing the same thing you are, Grace. I'm trying to catch up and get ahead of the game," Carter answered with a warm smile.

Grace settled her tall frame into the padded upholstered chair that sat in front of Carter's desk.

"How about knocking off and going across the street for dinner?" Grace asked her new friend.

"That's the best offer I have had in some time, Grace. Just give me a minute to clear my desk. I'll meet you at the back door in ten minutes," Carter cheerfully replied, glad for the company over the dinner hour. Lately, she had come to realize that dinner time was when she missed her husband the most.

Grace smiled, agreed to the time, and then left to clear her own desk. Ten minutes was all it took for Carter to bring her office to a close. Slipping on her thin raincoat without its lining, she wished now she had chosen a warmer coat. The weather had turned cold quickly as it could do in this part of the midwest. As she walked past the assistant medical director's office, she saw Bertha White sitting at the edge of Dr. Crane's desk. They were speaking in very low tones and were so absorbed in their conversation that they did not respond to Carter's good night farewell.

"Bertha looks so pale," Carter thought as she continued on down the hall toward the back stairwell that would take her to the rear exit of the center.

Carter and Grace arrived at the back door at the same time.

"Perfect timing," Grace cheerfully called out glad to be heading out the door for the day.

Grace slid into the passenger seat beside Carter. Carter drove smoothly up College Avenue and over to Tremont where they could see the large marquee of the Fillmore Inn against a softly setting sun. Carter's blue Pontiac pulled into the small parking area next to the restaurant and, luckily, into a recently vacated parking space close to the entrance. The approaching winter wind blew their hair and chilled their faces as they quickly made their way inside the trendy restaurant.

The warmth of the cozy place soon settled in, and the new friends were taking turns discussing the different events of their day over a glass of wine. As hectic as each of their lives was, they still found the energy to laugh and to try to take each hurdle less seriously. Carter and Grace were both dedicated to their careers, a common bond for their friendship.

"Grace, can I ask you a question?" Carter asked almost timidly.
"Sure, Carter."

"Since you've been at the center longer than most, has it ever been operated in a. . ."

"In a more civilized manner?" the personnel director answered. Reflecting for just a moment, Grace continued.

"When I first came to the blood center—good grief—it's been over fifteen years now," Grace paused thinking out loud how quickly time had gone by.

"Anyway, to answer your question—yes, there was a time when Dr. Morris was our medical director. Dr. Morris was a jewel. He was liked by everyone and pretty much ran the center on a sort of part-time basis.

"Part-time?" I don't see how you could run the center on a part-time basis?"

"Well, believe it or not—it was feasible. But, of course, that was before we really got so involved in resource sharing and the. . . ." Grace did not continue her sentence. Instead she shrugged her shoulders and let the answer die.

"Is there that much money in resource sharing?" Carter continued.

"If you're good at it—yes there is, Carter." Grace's answer held just a trace of sarcasm. Carter did not miss this rare display of insight into the internal operations of the center.

"What makes us so good at it, Grace? I mean, we seem to constantly need blood, and donations are so hard to keep up on a regular basis," Carter questioned.

"Kiley Matson," Grace quickly answered.

"Kiley?" Carter replied with a quizzical look on her face.

"Kiley. He's a real wheeler-dealer on the blood circuit, Carter. Sometimes I worry about the deals he makes."

"What do you mean?" Carter was eager to hear more about Kiley.

"To be honest, Carter. I can't really put my finger on it. I can only tell you my gut tells me we sometimes bend the rules a bit."

"Like how?"

"I'm not sure—I can't really explain it. Have you ever heard them talk about the Glass account?"

"Yes—just a couple of times during our flash meeting," Carter quickly volunteered.

"Well, I'm not sure what significance this account has on the center's revenue, but I believe it does have something to do with income to the center."

"What kind of income?" Carter questioned.

"Extra income, Carter. Income that generates some pretty hefty quarterly bonuses for the big four—Preston, Silvers, Crane, and Bryan," Grace answered washing her answer down with a deep sip of red wine.

Carter did not ask another question. Her mind was trying to sort through all that she had just heard.

"Carter, I want to share something else with you."

Carter's eyes told Grace she would keep whatever it was to herself.

"The other day, when we ran into Jody Cable at Gibby's, I came back and went to my file to pull out her mother's personnel records—they were gone. I mean, every trace of information I had on Anna Cable was nowhere in my personnel records."

"Are you sure you just didn't misfile them, Grace?"

"I'm positive. I went to Michael and asked him if he knew anything about Cable's records, and he stumbled all over the place. I finally got out of him that he had taken her personnel file. That's as far as I got. He had another meeting to go to, and I left.

"Why would Michael take personnel files out of your office, Grace? I mean, is this a blood center policy?"

"No! Records have never been removed before—at least not since I've been there." Grace reached up to rub her eyes. This subject had obviously been preying on her mind. The mysteries were beginning to mount about certain blood center operations. Carter was glad to have someone like Grace confide in her—it made her own questions much easier to ask.

"I just can't get Anna Cable out of my mind, Carter. I asked Michael if he knew about Anna attempting suicide and from the look on his face, I'm sure he didn't know that something like this had happened to her. Carter, I think the Center. . ."

Before Grace could finish her sentence, a tall, distinguished looking gentlemen interrupted the conversation.

"Grace—how are you?" he asked extending his hand toward Carter's dinner partner.

"Thompson—my goodness, is it really you?" Grace replied with an obvious look of pleasure surfacing in her pretty face.

"It's been nearly three years and four months, Grace. You haven't changed a bit—you're still as beautiful as ever," Thompson Moran replied.

"Carter, this is Dr. Thompson Moran, Medical Director for the State Board of Health," Grace said with her eyes still on the handsome man's face. "Carter Egan is our new public relations director, Thompson," Grace added for reference.

"Hello," Carter replied as she extended her hand to the stranger.

"It's a pleasure to meet you, Carter. I think I remember seeing you just recently on the evening news," Thompson politely replied as he gently shook Carter's hand. His hand was strong like a surgeon's hand, yet he didn't grip Carter's hand so tightly as to crush it as some men do when they shake hands with a woman. He knew how to touch a woman, Carter registered as her feminine instincts surfaced.

"Carter's been on TV a lot these days," Grace added, reinforcing the correctness of Thompson's statement.

"It's very nice to meet a friend of Grace's," Thompson replied as he pulled up a chair joining the two women. He had not been asked to join them, but something told Carter that this man did not wait to take the lead on anything that mattered to him, and Grace Tende obviously mattered to Thompson Moran.

"So you're the new kid on the block?" Thompson teased Carter. "Your predecessor applied for a p.r. position at the Board of Health, not long after she left the blood center, I think. For some reason, she didn't get the job. I'm not sure why—she was certainly qualified—I mean if she was good enough for Grace to hire, she had to know her business."

Grace smiled ever so slightly. The subject of Anna Cable was difficult now for her to talk about. Thompson sensed he had stepped into an area of conversation that was not welcome at this table. He quickly changed the subject.

"So how are things at the blood center these days?" questioned Thompson almost too politely.

"About the same, Thompson," Grace answered with a smile.

"Is our friend Silvers still howling at every full moon?" Thompson asked with a full smile.

Grace did not answer the question but smiled and shook her head.

Thompson's deep warm laugh filled the air. He had touched on a subject he knew would draw a touch of red to Grace's face. Carter had heard about Thompson Moran one afternoon when she and Gerald Preston were discussing the politics of blood banking. She couldn't remember at the moment all that Preston had said, but she vaguely recalled the conversation to be positive. Preston seemed to respect Moran, even to the point of being just a little bit afraid of his power in the position he was in. Carter wished now she had paid more attention to Preston's exact words.

For the next hour the trio seemed to converse on many different subjects, each one more interesting than the last. Thompson Moran seemed so alive and so knowledgeable. When the subject turned to art, a sudden feeling of fatigue crept into Carter's body. It wasn't the subject but the time of day. Looking at her watch Carter was surprised to see it was nearly 10:30 p.m. The day had started very early, and it was time for Carter to go if she were going to rise and shine tomorrow at six a.m.

"Grace, I hate to be a party-pooper, but I'm afraid it's getting to be past my weekday bedtime." Carter was a little embarrassed at being the first one to mention leaving.

"Oh my goodness, it's almost eleven," a startled Grace said as she looked at her watch for the first time that evening. Grace had lost track of time and "who wouldn't," thought Carter when you're talking to a man this interesting. In this short time Carter had come to approve of Thompson Moran. She couldn't help but sense there was a chemistry between her friend and this interesting and attractive physician.

Thompson asked if he could take them to their cars, but Grace explained the situation and thanked him for his offer.

"May I call you again, sometime, Grace?" Thompson inquired as he helped Grace put on her coat. Grace paused and looked at Thompson with a look that Carter could not quite read.

"I'm afraid. . ." Grace's full answer was cut off in mid-sentence by the handsome medical director.

"I've been divorced for over ten months, Grace," Thompson answered as if he knew that Grace was about to say no to him.

A soft smile embraced Grace's face and her blue eyes deepened in color.

"In that case—yes, Thompson, please do call."

The winter wind again made Carter sorry she had not selected a warmer coat. It was a mistake she would not make tomorrow no matter what the weatherman said on the morning news.

"Thanks for having dinner with me tonight, Carter. It was delightful to eat with someone so interesting," Grace said as Carter pulled up next to her car in the center's employee parking lot. The center's lights were still on in the laboratory section, and their bright reflection helped to light the area.

"I liked Thompson, Grace. He seems to be a very nice person." Carter spoke directly sensing that Grace wanted her opinion.

"He is nice, Carter. We've known each other for some time, but he was married and I just don't get involved with married men—it makes no sense."

"He reminds me a little of Patrick," Carter added. "The way he has so much to say on so many subjects." Carter laughed at her remark as she knew Patrick would if he were there.

"It's hard to be separated from someone you love, Carter," Grace matter-of-factly stated as if she were speaking from experience.

"Yes, it is. But you just make the best of it," Carter replied, her voice showing emotion.

Grace reached over and gently squeezed Carter's hand.

"You'll get through this separation, Carter. Just keep remembering all the good times and the clock will race ahead."

Grace's face took on a serious look. Something was bothering her. "Grace, what's wrong?" Carter asked.

"I keep remembering the remark Thompson made about Anna Cable applying at the Board of Health and not getting the job. Anna had a master's in communication. It just struck me funny. If I remember that job opening, Anna should have been a good match for the job qualifications—and to my knowledge, no one from the Board called me to check on Anna's references."

Carter digested Grace's comments. She didn't really know anything about Anna Cable, but Grace surely did.

Grace smiled and made a remark about thinking too much at such a late hour. The two friends ended the evening vowing to repeat the experience very soon. Carter waited until Grace's car engine kicked over before she pulled away. The two women exited the parking lot, leaving Dr. Alice Crane and Bertha's cars behind.

Carter couldn't help but wonder why Dr. Crane and Bertha were still at the center at this late hour.

"Maybe the two of them were having dinner?" Carter mischievously thought, laughing out loud at this painted picture in her mind's eye. "Oh Lord, I feel sorry for Bertha."

As Carter and Grace drove away, the lights in the laboratory section darkened. It was only a matter of moments before the lights in the executive wing switched on. The lights would stay on until just before dawn—long after Bertha White had left.

15

The morning flash meeting was exactly as Michael Bryan had pictured. Kiley Matson threw out all the red flags as he usually did when crusading for an emergency call. Gerald Preston was the first to ask questions.

"Is the inventory in *Glass* at a critical level?" Preston asked casually. The word "Glass" registered with Carter.

"It's draining, Jerry," Kiley replied informally in addressing the executive director. Not many people at the Center, including Michael Bryan, dared to address Gerald Preston as "Jerry" in public.

"How many orders are backed up?" Silvers questioned with no apparent edge in his voice at this point.

"We could end up losing forty or so by noon. There's at least thirty orders that need to be blocked," Kiley answered.

"There's no way we are going to lose those orders, Kiley." Hold those orders and stall in delivery time if you have to." Silvers again responded calmly. He turned toward Carter.

"Carter, we are going to need for you to call out the media again."

"Of course, Dr. Silvers." Carter was distressed that the center had again found itself unable to supply its own hospitals with the precious supply of blood in less than three weeks from the last emergency.

Carter had wanted to return to the subject of what they referred to earlier as the "Glass" account, but the opportunity did not arise. Instead, Kiley dismissed the meeting without any floor discussion and quickly left the room.

"Carter, I need to speak with you for a moment. Can you come directly to my office?" Dr. Silvers asked as he headed down the hall toward his office.

"Of course, Doctor," Carter replied falling in line behind him.

Closing the door behind them, Dr. Silvers settled quickly into his chair. He smiled broadly at his p.r. director.

"Carter, I'm excited this morning. Something wonderful has happened in the last few days that will put us on the map."

"Good—I mean, what is it?" Carter smiled excited at the prospect of some good news happening for her center. The AIDS lawsuit had put everyone in a bad mood these last few weeks.

"We have an opportunity to land a large grant straight from the offices of the National Association of Accredited Blood Centers. Our HLA laboratory will be working on very important data that is absolutely top-secret. I wish I could fill you in at this point, Carter, but I can't. It is absolutely necessary that we keep a lid on any information that pertains to this project. I know how goddamned nosy people are here, but this time, I've ordered a complete blackout on the activities of our HLA projects. If anyone, and I mean anyone, inquires about the work Siam Qua is doing, you need to come straight to me."

"Can I speak to Siam about what he is doing so I will have a firm understanding of the project?" Carter broke in.

"No, not yet. Siam is not to be bothered by anyone. In time, I'll let you know when you can speak to him. Just keep this under your hat for the moment, Carter."

"Who else knows about this?" Carter asked.

"Preston, Crane, Michael, you now, and of course, Siam."

"Carter, I can't begin to tell you how profitable this could turn out to be for our blood center. To be selected as one of three outside sources to work on such an important bone marrow. . ." the doctor's words stopped.

"This project is very important to me, Carter. You should know in confidence, I have a very good chance of being selected to replace Fritzsimmon Garret when he retires this spring as acting president for the NAABC. This project, if it succeeds, won't hurt my chances one bit." The look in his eyes made it very clear to Carter that her medical director had aspirations that were not meant to be tampered with by mere mortals.

"Carter, all I ask of you for now is to get the media support and do your best at helping us keep our blood supply at a secure level. Our center is looked at as a premium center in our ability to supply our area hospitals with blood. It's critical at this point that we be able to live up to that image." His words were electrified with urgency. Carter's thoughts raced ahead to the phone calls she would need to make to the media if she was going to put forth an effective emergency campaign.

"Don't worry about the media, Dr. Silvers. They won't let you down." Carter smiled at Silvers as she rose to leave. There was a question she wanted to ask, and the climate seemed right to ask it.

"Dr. Silvers, just what is the Glass account? I've heard Kiley mention it a couple of times." Carter's question caught the medical director off guard.

"It's nothing for you to worry your pretty head about, Carter. It's just an inventory term we use. Forget you ever heard it, okay?"

The answer unsettled Carter. The look in the medical director's face told Carter to let the subject alone. Carter smiled and left Silvers's office. She would ask this question again at another time. A deep frown was present as he picked up his phone and dialed the distribution office number.

Kiley Matson answered. "Matson."

"Listen, Kiley. Carter was just in my office asking about the Glass account. I'm not ready to let her in on this part of our operation yet. Maybe somewhere down the road—we'll have to see how she adapts. In the meantime, ditch any references to Glass at Flash—do you get the picture?"

"Loud and clear, chief. Do you want me to spin a story?"

"No, not just yet. I told her it had to do with inventory. Back me up on this if she approaches you with it. Okay?"

"I hear you loud and clear." Kiley smiled as he hung up the phone. "She's catching on quicker than Anna did," Kiley thought as he gathered up the day's orders.

As Carter walked the short distance back to her office, she couldn't help but feel she'd seen another side of Dr. Benjamin Silvers—an emotional side. It felt good to witness a side that cared very much for other human beings. "Dr. Silvers needs to be seen by more people like this," she thought. "Perhaps I've been too hard in my judgment of this man."

For the rest of the day, Carter went about her business driven by that early morning conversation. The media were indeed roused by her emotional appeal. Twenty reporters and cameramen showed up at the center to air the public appeal for blood.

"AIDS, and an unfortunate lawsuit have nearly crippled the blood center's blood supply."

"Donations have dried up."

"The public seems to be afraid to donate."

These were a few of the lead-in sound bites that led off the evening news. All the stations but one carried the headline news story. Madison Boggs aired the story, but not with headlines. At the close of the evening broadcast, her station flashed an emergency appeal request. Madison Boggs was now working on something more than a gut feeling. She had found a source on the inside. Or rather, the source on the inside had found her.

The caller had identified himself as a former employee of Hamilton Regional. He was a young med student who worked part-time in the distribution department. The male voice had made it clear that the blood center was involved in the shipment of blood out of state at a cost to the local blood supply. Big bucks were the driving factor here for the blood center, the student implied.

The problem for Madison Boggs was to prove that this was indeed a procedure the blood center used for their own financial gain. If the blood center was laying the blame on poor area blood donations, and using the excuses of AIDS and public lawsuits to "cry wolf," then Madison did have a story to tell. To Madison's surprise, though, there were no laws being violated—only a situation of questionable public ethics. If she could somehow prove that the blood center was in fact shipping blood out the back door and calling false emergency appeals to make up the difference, she just might have a story for the evening news. The caller could not offer Madison any solid proof of such actions ever taking place, only his word that he had personally observed such shipping procedures. And that he had been ordered by a supervisor to remove blood from the open inventory refrigerators right before emergency appeals went up. He had also heard other rumors that he was not yet ready to share with Madison. He promised the reporter he would stay in touch. One day he just might come in with several other employees and talk to her. He made it clear because he was a student, he did not want to appear full face on camera. Madison guaranteed him she could block his face and alter his voice. No one would be able to guess his identity. But the caller had doubts and would have to think about it. He was not sure he wanted to cross the line as a whistle blower. He had his future to think about.

"This would not be an easy assignment," Madison thought as she hung up the phone. She would need help from someone on the inside who was willing to supply her with reports and documentation. Since the caller was not ready to come forward at this time, all Madison had was the filtered down words of a faceless accuser. Without evidence in hand, this person would surely be labeled a "disgruntled employee" by the powerful blood center and suffer an immediate loss of credibility in the public's mind.

"I wonder how much of this Carter Egan is aware of? Maybe she is part of the whole charade? Madison's instincts rebelled at this last thought.

The story was not ready for airtime. It would take time and patience. Madison had both.

16

John Stansbarry tapped his pencil heavily on the wooden desk. Things were not going smoothly in his process of preparing questions for the blood center's depositions that were to take place in less than two days.

It was like looking for a needle in a haystack. His instincts told him something was there, but just what and how to find it was not coming together as he had hoped. In filing the papers for the lawsuit, Barry, as he was called by his family and close friends, knew he would be going down a road not frequently traveled by many small town lawyers.

Three things about this case bothered Barry. One: Taylor Addison had requested that her family be allowed to give blood for her. She was denied this right, a right that was clearly within reason to expect. Two: a brother and two sisters matched Taylor's blood type and would have been compatible blood donors for the transfusion, which was not deemed to be a dire, lifesaving emergency to begin with, but more of a procedure to "pink-the-patient-up." *Pink-the-patient* is a term used to describe a method to infuse a person's system with oxygen-bearing blood cells, which usually results in an increased feeling of energy and well-being for the patient. Last was the poorly copied paperwork that sat staring him in the face. How could he get any insight into the health history of these donors if he couldn't clearly see how they answered their health questionnaire at the time they gave blood? He had expected the donors' names to be marked out, but he had not counted on the entire questionnaire being illegible. His requests for clear copies had been repeatedly stonewalled.

"Do you want me to pick up some sandwiches for dinner?" Tovey Stansbarry asked his uncle.

"Hmmm—whatever," Barry replied not looking up from the sea of paperwork strewn across his desk.

Tovey neatly placed his reading glasses on top of his worn law books and stood up swinging his suit coat over his broad shoulders. The evening light caught the reflection of Tovey's bright red hair creating an even deeper shade of red. Tovey was Barry's nephew—his favorite nephew if the truth were to be told. He had joined Barry's law practice just six months before—two days after his law graduation from The University of Virginia. He had thought about pursuing other firms, but his heart told him the only place he wanted to be a part of was at the side of his uncle, John Tovey Standsbarry.

"I'll get us a couple of burgers and maybe a salad," Tovey said as he left the office to pick up their evening meal, which, these last few weeks, had consisted mainly of hamburgers and French fries from The Cozy restaurant, located two doors down from the office of Stansbarry & Stansbarry on the main street of Port Smith.

Barry did not acknowledge his nephew's words. His attention was on Taylor Addison's case. John Stansbarry was in his early sixties. A head full of white hair and the most piercing blue eyes gave him an appearance easily remembered. His face was tanned and his body sturdy from his youthful days of working the land on his father's farm. He was bright and possessed a dry sense of humor. The study of law was a natural for Barry. He loved everything about it including the musty smell of libraries where he buried himself in learning. He had gained a reputation as a tough courtroom lawyer who came well-prepared. He fished and hunted with most of the sitting judges in the surrounding counties and never asked for favors. If you were his friend, you were his friend. He didn't need favors from sitting judges. He was a good attorney, but he was a small town attorney.

Taylor Addison was to be a very different client. The first day she walked into his office he was struck by her frailness. Everything about her seemed so soft, so tender. Her eyes were a deep shade of brown, which were sometimes mistaken for an inkwell black. Her skin was pale white—a pale that spoke of suffering. Obviously pregnant, she carried herself a bit stiffly, as if trying to keep her balance. But first appearances are often deceptive. This was the case with Taylor Addison as she was not a weak woman. Quite the contrary. When you got past her physical appearance, you met the strength of a woman determined to win a battle—a battle she felt she should never have faced.

"Are you John Stansbarry?" Taylor asked with a voice soft enough to command his immediate attention.

"I am," he replied.

"I need an attorney and I'm told you are a good one."

"Well, that's only some people's opinion, Miss." Barry's face displayed one of his broad smiles.

"Do you think you are a good lawyer?" Taylor countered with no sign of emotion on her face.

Barry hesitated a few moments before he answered Taylor's very direct question. He could see from her face that she was indeed serious about the whole matter of needing an attorney.

"I know the law and I respect it. I don't play games with it and I don't take a case unless I believe in it. To be honest with you, I'm not really sure what makes a person a good lawyer. I can only tell you I do my best. Sometimes I win and sometimes I lose. And there are those days when I feel I should have stuck to farming." Barry's answer was straight and truthful; there was no trace of a smile.

The room was quiet for several seconds. Taylor's eyes never left Barry's face.

"Do you mind if I sit down?" she asked.

"Of course not. I'm sorry my manners are so poor," Barry quickly said with a touch of red coming to his cheeks. Once seated, she continued. "I would like for you to be my attorney, Mr. Stansbarry. I don't have much money but. . ."

"Before we get to dollars and cents, perhaps we should get to the meat and potatoes," Barry injected. "Just what kind of a problem do you have that you need the services of an attorney?" he asked.

"I have AIDS, Mr. Stansbarry. I know that I am dying and I also know that I may not live long enough to see this matter through, but I know that I should not have gotten this disease in the way that I got it. I'm also going to have a baby and I don't know what will happen to my child," she paused as she struggled with her composure. "I'm not a woman who cries easily, Mr. Stansbarry, so don't be afraid you are going to have to handle a lot of tears all the time—it's just that these days I find myself so all alone in my belief. . ."

"What is your belief, Miss?. . ."

"I'm sorry, my name is Taylor—Taylor Addison. My belief is that I was made to take a blood transfusion that was infected with this AIDS virus. I didn't want this blood to come from strangers. It could have come from my family. I wouldn't be dying today if my family had been the ones to give me blood," Taylor stated in a quiet, controlled voice—a voice soft and vulnerable.

Barry had been studying Taylor's face as she spoke. That she had just told him she had a deadly virus did not frighten him. AIDS was until this moment only a word to John Stansbarry. Taylor Addison was the first person he had met face to face that had this disease. She did not fit the stereotype he pictured as an AIDS victim.

"This AIDS virus is a tough illness, Miss Addison, but you really don't know for sure if you will die from it. I hear people are living for very long periods of time. . ." Taylor interrupted him.

"If you've got money and can bypass the long waiting line for treatment programs—you can buy yourself a few extra days of life. But if you've got AIDS, Mr. Stansbarry, and you're poor, you are going to die faster. I don't kid myself; I am going to die and maybe my baby is going to die, too. I only want to live long enough to see my baby and to know that it will be taken care of after I'm gone."

"Who do you want to sue, Miss Addison?"

"The place where I got the blood." Her answer was to the point.

"What about your doctor?"

"Dr. Fairbanks is a good man and I know he didn't know that I was going to get AIDS when he ordered that transfusion," Taylor replied hesitantly, not sure of this part of her problem.

"He's part of the problem, Miss Addison. If you're really determined to go so far as to file a lawsuit, the whole situation and all parties involved need to be considered here, including the hospital where you received your transfusion."

"I don't know all about this, Mr. Stansbarry. I only know I shouldn't have gotten that blood."

"When did this transfusion take place, Miss Addison, how long ago?"

"It's been almost four years—November 9, 1982."

"I see. Well, if my memory serves me correctly, the blood centers did not have a screening test for this disease at that time."

"But they knew about the disease then, Mr. Stansbarry, and they did nothing to stop people from donating that shouldn't have been blood donors in the first place," Taylor quickly countered with anger rising in her cheeks causing her face to flush a deep red.

"I asked for my family to be my blood donors. They would not have given me a disease that is now going to kill me and my baby." Taylor's words stung with the bitterness she was now living with every day.

"I've lost everything, Mr. Stansbarry. My job—and most of my friends have backed away from me—my insurance was canceled and I can't even find a doctor who wants to treat me. All I have left is my family and my dignity. I will not roll over and play dead. I deserve to stand up to them, face to face one day in a courtroom and ask them why? Why didn't they do something about this disease before it was too late for people like me? I had a choice here, Mr. Stansbarry, and it was denied.

Because of this, I'm going to die." Her voice was once again softly controlled.

"May I ask you a few questions, Miss Addison?"

"Yes."

"Are you married?"

"I was. My husband was killed about three months ago," Taylor answered with tears welling up in her eyes for just an instant.

Her answer came as a surprise. He had guessed that she could be divorced or, for that matter, not even married. John Stansbarry was shocked to learn that his new and vulnerable client was a widow.

"I'm sorry, Taylor. May I call you, Taylor?"

"Yes, please do."

"How did your husband die?" Barry gently asked.

"It was a car accident. He—he died instantly."

"I need to ask you several direct questions, Taylor. Are you sure you are up to this right now?"

"Yes, I'm sure. Ask your questions."

Barry paused for just a few seconds, waiting until her eyes were cleared of tears and her jaw set once again in stubborn determination.

"Are you sure you contracted this disease from a blood transfusion?"

"I'm positive."

"Forgive me for these next few questions, but I must ask them."

"Okay," came the reply.

"Have you ever used drugs or shared a needle with anyone else using drugs?"

"No!"

"Have you or your husband had multiple sex partners?"

"I've only been with one man and that was my husband, William. I—I don't believe he had sex with anyone before me. I mean, we grew up together, and it was always just the two of us. William was so shy— I—I just don't think he could have been with anyone else." The tears were present again; her answers were spoken honestly and with no offense. Barry found both truth and pain in her words.

"I believe you, Taylor, and I am sorry if I appear to be insensitive in this line of questioning, but you must know you face a rocky road if you file a lawsuit against a very powerful and tightly joined medical community such as the people you will name in this suit. These questions are mild compared to what they might throw at you—and trust me when I tell you, they will attack you on every front you can imagine, and can't imagine at this time."

Barry's words did not seem to ruffle Taylor Addison.

"I know what they will say about me, and I know that they are powerful and smart. But I'm right, and that is what the law is all about, isn't it? If a person is right, then shouldn't the law stand up for them? Isn't the law for people just like me?"

Taylor's words were so powerful that Barry couldn't answer her immediately. In his years of practice he had seen far too many *right* people end up destroyed in the hallowed halls of justice.

"That is what the law is for, Taylor. It's what I believe law is all about," Barry answered as he digested what had just transpired in his office.

"Will you take my case, Mr. Stansbarry?" The girl asked once again.

"I'm not sure I'm the one you ought to select, Taylor. Perhaps a law firm from a more mainstream practice. . ."

"I do not want a big city attorney. I want you," Taylor interrupted not realizing that John Stansbarry was trying to avoid agreeing to take her on as a client. It wasn't that he didn't want to help her. He did believe she was telling the truth and that she had grounds for some sort of a lawsuit. But he doubted his own strength to go up against the power of an industry that could well afford to hire the most powerful of law firms. He would be outmatched in research and in resources. It truly would be David against Goliath. Would Taylor be best served by Stansbarry and Stansbarry?

"If it's a matter of money, I have a small insurance policy that carries a $5,000 death benefit. . ."

"I'll take your case, Taylor, and there is no need to discuss any monetary issues at this point," John Stansbarry heard himself saying. There was something about the look in her eyes that gave him belief in himself.

That first meeting seemed so long ago. Tonight he was anything but ready to take on Goliath. He would only get this one shot at this bunch. Taylor's right to have a directed donation by her family was on their side. But as far as the law went, there were no laws in place to cover this kind of a situation. At least, none that his research could turn up. Still, there was something else missing. Something that was right under his nose and for the life of him, he just couldn't find it.

"Here's your hamburger—plain with onions and pickle on the side," said Tovey as he brought in the take-out order that would serve as dinner for the two men.

"Tovey, something is wrong here, but for the life of me, I just can't find it."

"Well, we have the documentation that the three male donors have questionable backgrounds with two admitting to being active homosexuals and the third one admitting to being a bisexual. There could be negligence on behalf of the blood center for not screening those risk categories out sooner than they did," Tovey replied between bites of his hamburger.

"Negligence is what we have to prove and right now they have all the points going for them. You and I know the blood banks should have started some sort of an elimination screening procedure long before they did, but there are no laws stating they had to," Barry answered. "I also checked on the directed donor policy the center had in place at the time of Taylor's transfusion. According to the records, the center allowed directed donations. But off the record and out of the public eye, they did their best to discourage this type of donation process. I was told by a pretty good source that blood banks were afraid directed donations would interrupt their free flow of blood and curb their blood supply. If people were to hold back donating for themselves or friends or family, the blood supply could quickly dry up."

"Have we any idea when those clear copies of the health questionnaires are coming in?" Tovey asked.

"I called again today—same answer—soon."

"Couldn't we get the State Board of Health to intercede in this matter for us? Don't they have some power over these centers?"

"Their power is as limited as ours, it appears. They told me they didn't have clear copies either," Barry answered. "Whoever heard of a photocopy machine having a terminal problem with outputting clear copies?" Barry spit out. "Let's go over what we have again in those codes, Tovey."

"Has the medical panel been selected?" Tovey asked.

"Yes, as of this morning we have three pathologists from three separate hospitals. Two of them live in Hamilton and the third one is from St. Joseph County."

"All of them are pathologists?" Tovey questioned.

"You got it. Nice and neat, isn't it?" Barry was angry and it showed in his voice. "That's pretty convenient, isn't it, Tovey?"

"This doesn't quite make sense to me, Uncle Barry. Why don't we have any other kinds of doctors? I mean it seems like a brotherhood here."

The two men finished their sandwiches and continued to pore over the papers and records that were so foreign to them. When the lights finally were shut off, it was well past midnight. In two days they would meet the officials of the blood center face to face. It would not go well. Most of John Stansbarry's questions were denied answers by the objections of the blood center's attorneys. The questioning of Carter Egan was especially difficult as most of the questions put to Carter were objected to by all three sets of blood center attorneys. As much as he didn't want to, Barry liked Carter Egan. She was obviously the only one who felt any remorse about Taylor Addison's condition. It showed in her eyes and in her voice. Unfortunately, though, Carter's testimony was very strong on behalf of the blood center. Her belief in their strict system of health screening was very convincing. On paper, it read even stronger: "the donors met the health criteria, and there was absolutely no screening tests available at the time these men donated their blood."

Dr. Silvers and Dr. Crane were cold in their testimony. Their answers were limited to a simple yes or no. No elaboration was allowed as their attorneys objected to every single question that was put to them. The deposition was brought to a close when John Stansbarry did something he had never done before in a hearing—he lost his temper and walked out. Something else happened that day—John Stansbarry had been manipulated. Philip Javis had played hard ball in his repeated objections to every question Barry attempted to have answered. Javis was hoping to provoke such a reaction from the less sophisticated attorney.

Tovey Stansbarry had never seen his uncle so upset. The ride home to Port Smith was spent mostly in silence.

"I fell for it, Tovey. Hook, line, and sinker. They put out the bait and I bit it off like a minnow in a sea of sharks."

"Philip Javis is a piece of work, Uncle Barry. I just wish we could have had some real time to put the questions to those doctors. I certainly never expected to have Javis raise so many objections to even the simplest of what should have been routine discovery questions," Tovey said trying to make sense out of what had just happened.

"Smoke screen. Javis just threw up the biggest smoke screen in deposition history, and I let my temper pull me into the fog he was deliberately creating. Those three *unbiased* medical panel physicians are going to have nothing to read that could make them think a negligence issue could indeed be possible," Barry continued as he steered the car down the exit ramp toward Port Smith.

"Taylor deserves better than this, Tovey. She's going to get lost in the system just like a lot of other innocent people who are at the mercy of a God-awful powerful industry that sits in judgment on their own kind."

"Uncle Barry, I can't help but feel we're sitting on something so wrong here. I mean, the whole thing just doesn't lay out right. I'm going to do some checking on the three doctors who have been selected by the medical board to be on this panel. I want to know if they have any connection to this blood center. Any connection whatsoever," Tovey's statement would serve as a determined promise.

"And if they do, Tovey, we could push for an early court date. It's going to be a long uphill battle before we get to trial, but by God, we are going to take this to the last possible. . ." Barry stopped in mid-sentence. Taylor Addison did not have the luxury of time on her side. At the outside, she had another six months at most, according to her doctors. The pregnancy had indeed weakened her. If she could carry the baby to term, she had little chance of ever seeing its first birthday. She'd be lucky to hold the little one in her arms for more than a few days. Time, and a disease too violent to predict, was their enemy. These next few weeks would all have to count.

"Tovey, we are going to need to arrange a deathbed statement from Taylor as soon as possible."

Tovey nodded his head without answering. He hated the thought of setting this up. The rest of the ride home was quiet. The small town lawyers had faced the giants and the giants had put it to them. If Taylor Addison died before they could bring her case to a public trial, and it certainly looked as if this was going to be the way it was, they would have to use a pre-taped statement from Taylor to speak to the jury. Taylor had a right to have her day in court, even if all the odds of winning were stacked against her. John Stansbarry, the small town attorney, made two promises tonight—Taylor Addison was going to win her case, and never again would he let the city boys get the best of him.

In a few weeks, the medical panel would meet. Their decision would have an immediate impact on Taylor's case. It was to be an impact that should never have been felt.

17

The lines were so long in the reception area that Elizabeth Monroe had to revert to a number system. Another critical appeal for blood was working, and the faithful blood donors were again pouring in the center's front door as well as its satellite branches. Carter was giving media interviews as fast as the television and radio crews could set up their equipment. Her captured sound bites, with desperate pleas for blood donations, were being aired every hour on the hour. Between interviews, she volunteered her time at the cookie station where individuals who had just gone through the donation process were taken to have freshly squeezed orange juice and store-bought cookies. Donors were always asked to stay a few minutes after donating blood so they could be given a light refreshment to help replenish their lost body fluids. First-time donors oftentimes would have reactions after losing just under a pint of blood. Nausea, lightheadedness, feeling faint were some of the physical problems the "cookie ladies," as they were called, looked for. Usually such reactions would pass in a few minutes, but it was the blood center's policy to try and keep each donor for at least fifteen to thirty minutes. The blood center certainly did not want someone who had just given blood to get behind the wheel of a car and pass out. Liability was an issue here.

Some blood donors would sail through the donation process with no signs of ill effects. Others would have no immediate reaction but would develop a cold, sore throat, or have flu-like symptoms within a few days after their donation. Most would never tie their recent blood donation to this kind of illness. And neither would Carter if she had not overheard Dr. Crane telling her own secretary not to donate blood ever again for this very reason.

"Some people's immune system simply can't take the loss of a pint of blood. It makes them vulnerable to colds and flus they probably would not have come down with had they not given blood." Dr. Crane didn't want to lose the services of her very capable secretary again. As for the

126

multiple gallon blood donors, Dr. Crane had also expressed concern with the long-term effects to their systems.

"We don't have enough dedicated research to tell us if those individuals who donate blood five or six times a year are more subject to bone loss or anemia as they grow older. It's a process with a double edge. We want their blood, but we don't know what problems we may cause these people later on," Dr. Crane would tell Carter one day when she was in the process of completing a paper for one of Dr. Silvers's future medical publications. He had hoped to receive private funding to plot out his suspected findings. Of course it would be kept confidential. The blood center did not want to stir up any controversy that would reduce this steadfast category of faithful blood donors.

This paradox seemed funny to Carter. If blood donors could face serious health issues by giving blood, she felt the center needed to be straightforward and tell them so. It is one thing to go blindly into a situation and another to do so with all the information at hand. After all, this was a volunteer process.

Carter had so many questions. It seemed every time she posed such questions, she was given an answer carved by the same hand. "Carter, the public wouldn't understand," or "we're waiting on findings from the NAABC to confirm this theory," the good doctors would always reply. At times, Carter felt she was being patronized any time she asked a question which questioned blood center policy. It was demeaning, and increasingly disturbing.

The weekly directors' meeting was just getting under way when Carter managed to break away from her cookie duty to attend.

Every Wednesday all the department heads met with the executive level. They were expected to give a detailed report for the week on their department activities. Some meetings were short and sweet and other meetings would go on for several hours. One such meeting occurred three weeks earlier. The problem began when the question of supplying free coffee to each department area surfaced. Gerald Preston had gone off on a tangent on this subject. Because he was against it, Dr. Silvers immediately decided to be for it. The debate set a record for trivia and would go down in history in the memory of those present who were forced to sit through it. Everyone, including Grace Tende, who could usually keep things on track, got caught up in the madness of this discussion. Not one person present, though, would be able to tell you how the meeting ended or what was resolved.

This Wednesday's meeting was about to affect Carter in another way. All the department heads were present except Kiley Matson who, the group was told, was busy in Distribution.

"Shall we go around the room, ladies and gentlemen," Preston began as usual. For the next few minutes each director gave a mini-report on his or her department's progress or lack of it. Carter was sitting next to Bertha White this morning. When it was Bertha's turn to report, Carter was surprised to hear Bertha pass.

"I really don't have any updates today," the laboratory director stated in a flat voice and very out-of-character.

Neither Dr. Crane or Dr. Silvers questioned her lack of reporting. Carter felt something was very strange here.

"Carter, how is it going with the media?" Gerald Preston asked accepting Bertha's pass. This, too, was out of character for the executive level.

"The media is once again supporting us," Carter answered. "We have standing room only downstairs, and our branches are reporting the same kind of response conditions. I think we can safely say our media appeal is working."

"Great! responded Gerald Preston, obviously relieved.

"How soon do you want me to call the emergency appeal off, Dr. Silvers?" Carter asked innocently.

"Not until I tell you so, Carter. We are nowhere near the level that I want us to be. We have a good response going and there is no sense not taking advantage of it," the doctor answered.

"But we've drawn over three thousand units in less than a day and a half. I thought our safe level was fifteen hundred?" the p.r. director questioned.

"The safe level is where I tell you, Carter. And I've not told you it's safe yet, have I?" Silvers answered with deep sarcasm in his voice.

Carter felt the blood rushing to her face. His answer and tone of voice had taken her by surprise.

"I'm sorry, Dr. Silvers, but I'm afraid I don't understand our policy here. I was under the impression we were only to keep an appeal going until we stabilized our inventory for a three-day blood supply. We are nearly a week in advance. . ."

"Since when have you become the expert in blood banking, Carter? I will tell you when to call off the media. Just keep doing what you are doing and let me worry about our inventory." Benjamin Silvers had indeed spoken. Carter's instincts told her not to press the issue—at least not here, in front of the other directors, who were by now all looking intensely at her waiting for her reply.

"I'm sorry, Dr. Silvers, I certainly didn't mean to question your judgment. I guess I misunderstood our safety level." Her apology was spoken as a true public relations person would speak—ever the diplomat, never embarrassing your direct superior.

"Carter, I'm sure Dr. Silvers did not mean to imply you were questioning our policy. We just need to have a deeper inventory in position to keep our resource sharing orders filled. As we all know, we serve many masters here. Our public is very broad with a very strong demand for blood. We must help those who cannot help themselves," interjected Gerald Preston, wanting to glaze over the harshness of Dr. Silvers's criticism of Carter.

"I'm not sure why we are sending so much blood out-of-state at a time when we obviously can't meet our own territorial needs?" questioned Grace Tende.

The question put to the executive level brought a deadly silence to the conference room. Grace was not known to discuss policy ever at a mere director's meeting. Her question was obviously very direct and meant to draw a response that would be heard by all present. Gerald Preston's face clearly displayed his surprise at hearing Grace Tende questioning the tactics of the executive level.

Gerald Preston was the first executive to recover from Grace's bombshell question.

"Of course we are supplying our hospitals first, Grace. But we must also be a good neighbor and respond to those areas that can't help themselves," he answered in his usual polite manner that also carried the tone of authority.

"I can understand being a good neighbor, Mr. Preston," Grace interjected, "but it seems to me we should be more concerned about not over-burdening our own donor population, not to mention our own internal staff, with repeated blood emergencies. I mean, do we have an emergency in our area or does New York, California, and Florida have the emergency?"

Dr. Silvers pitched forward in his chair. His eyes had narrowed and his face was etched with color rising up from his neck. His hand trembled as he repeatedly clicked his ball-point pen open and closed. Elizabeth Monroe, who was sitting across from the doctor, moved sharply in her seat. She had seen that look in Ben Silvers's eyes far too often these days. A look of intense anger that was about to explode. She wanted desperately to reach across the table and take hold of his arm. This was not a gesture the director of nurses could ever do openly. Instead, Elizabeth tightly gripped the arms of her chair, hoping that her eyes could draw his attention before it was too late. If he would just look at her, she could signal him to just let it pass.

Dr. Crane's voice was unexpected.

"Of course, the emergency is here in our own back yard, Grace. We have been under the gun ever since the AIDS crisis hit and now with all the publicity about this damn lawsuit, people are just falling behind in their regular donation patterns."

Dr. Crane's answer shifted the weight of this subject away from Dr. Silvers. She, too, had seen the anger flooding up in Dr. Silvers, and she, better than most, knew it was best for her to address this issue with the fair-haired personnel director than to allow an emotional outburst from Dr. Silvers that could contain some very damaging evidence—evidence that only a few select individuals now possessed. Silvers talked too much when he was led by his temper. Gerald Preston recognized Dr. Crane's attempt at keeping her superior out of the flow of this conversation.

"Grace, I hope Dr. Crane has put your mind at ease," Preston quickly said, taking control of the meeting once again.

"And Grace," he continued, "we are only shipping *off-blood* types to our out-of-state networks—you know, the excess A's and B's and such. Blood types that are not so much in demand by our own area hospitals."

Grace did not speak but simply nodded her head as if she now understood the situation clearer. The room was now very tense. Dr. Silvers began gathering the papers he had spread out in front of him during the meeting.

"I believe we are going to adjourn for today. Dr. Silvers and I have a business appointment shortly, and we need a few moments to prepare. Thank you all for coming," Preston said, serving notice for the faithful department heads to call it a day.

Grace Tende motioned for Carter to wait for her in the hallway.

"Oops!" Grace said with a half smile on her face. "I guess I dipped into waters that are not meant for mere mortals." The two began their journey back to their respective offices.

"I don't know, Grace, I still have a feeling. . ." Carter was interrupted by a voice from behind her.

"Carter, could I have a word with you now?" Michael Bryan said in a quiet tone of voice.

"Of course, Michael." Carter responded to her direct supervisor.

"I'll see you later, Grace." Carter turned into Bryan's doorway.

"Give me a call when you get some free time, if you get some free time," Grace responded, obviously knowing that Carter's schedule was terribly hectic during an appeal.

Carter quickly settled into a chair in Michael's office directly opposite his oak desk. She always felt comfortable with Michael, and yet, her female instincts had picked up vibrations that this man was in many ways a very unhappy person.

"I've got some fresh coffee here, Carter, would you care for a cup?" Michael asked as he poured the black liquid into a ceramic mug.

"No thanks, Michael, I've had way too many cups already," Carter answered with a smile.

It could be said that Michael Bryan and Carter Egan had become friends. There was an easiness between them, the kind that allowed for good conversations and honest opinions. Michael sipped his steaming coffee as he walked around his desk. A few seconds went by before Michael began.

"Carter, I want you to know that I think you are doing a wonderful job with all the responsibilities that go along with your job, especially these media appeals."

"Thanks, boss. I needed to hear that after today's meeting," Carter answered still feeling the sting of Silvers's outburst.

"Don't let that sonofabitch, excuse my French, get you down, Carter. You had every right to ask that question," Michael quickly returned.

Carter could see by the look on Michael's face that he genuinely did not like their medical director. Carter, on the other hand, did not have such strong feelings against Dr. Silvers; she simply found him to be a difficult personality to deal with.

"About the shipping out-of-state, Carter. We do a lot of this resource sharing—it's a large portion of our business."

"Do we take care of our hospitals first, Michael?" Carter interrupted wanting an honest answer.

"Yes, of course we do, Carter," Michael quickly replied not looking directly at her. "We are supplying nearly sixty-five hospitals here, and that is a tough job. I mean, we have to keep up the supply and, at the same time, maintain costs and staffing."

"Thanks, Michael. I needed to hear that. I mean, it would be so unethical if we were calling false alarms and claiming to be bloodless just using this as a screen to profit from out-of-state ventures," Carter said, obviously relieved. She truly trusted Michael.

As Carter stood up, Michael asked her a question that had nothing to do with the subject they had just been addressing.

"Carter, have you ever wanted to just be free?"

"It depends on what you mean by free, Michael?"

"I mean to just get up in the morning and do just one thing that you really loved doing."

"Michael, this is none of my business, but are you okay?"

Michael Bryan did not answer Carter directly. His eyes found the sailboat picture set so evenly on his wall. "Some days I look at that boat, and I can almost feel myself at the wheel with the wind hitting my face and the smell of salt water climbing up my nostrils." Michael's voice trailed off. The room was comfortably quiet. Carter knew that Michael Bryan was under intense pressure these last few weeks. She was, in a way, glad that he had shared this personal conversation with her.

"What keeps you here, Michael?" Carter wasn't sure if she should ask such a question but felt comfortable enough with the moment to inquire.

"The wench!" Michael stated laughing out loud at his answer.

"The wench?" Carter repeated laughing with Michael.

"I'm not sure, Carter. I guess I wanted to work for something—a cause—something that was bigger than anything else I've ever done." Michael responded not minding the personal question. "When I got out of school, I didn't know what I was going to do—I mean—an MBA these days won't even buy you a cup of coffee let alone land you a decent job." Michael paused for a moment. "My father really got me this job, Carter. He was a long-time friend of Preston's, and you know—he placed a call and I got an interview. The rest is history."

"If you weren't qualified, Michael, you wouldn't have gotten this job," Carter quickly said sensing that her boss was not taking credit for his own abilities.

Michael's blue-black eyes focused strongly on Carter. The emotion in his eyes told Carter he deeply wanted to believe what she had just said, but something was clearly preventing it.

"Carter, you are a very nice person. Patrick Egan is a lucky man." Michael stood up and began making motions to continue his day. The mood for personal conversation was over. His mind was once again riveted on the stack of work that needed to be addressed before the end of this workday.

Carter smiled at her boss and thanked him once again for taking the time to address an issue that was bothering her.

"I'll talk to you later," Carter replied as she started to head back to her own office.

"Carter, do me a favor. If you have questions about our operation, please bring them to me—not Silvers. Okay?" His eyes pushed for a yes response.

"Okay, Michael." His request was understood. He seemed to be trying to spare her from Silvers's unpredictable mood swings.

"Carter, things aren't exactly the way they seem in our business. You're too new to it to really understand."

This made Carter apprehensive. She realized more and more that there were secrets at the center—secrets that could send her down the path Anna Cable took.

"Michael, are you telling me we are doing things here we shouldn't?"

"No, that's not what I'm saying. It's just—I don't want you to get in a crossfire with Silvers. He can make your life pretty miserable."

"Did he make Anna Cable's life miserable?"

Michael did not answer for a moment. His handsome features frowned and his hands reached for a cigarette.

"What do you know about Anna Cable, Carter?"

"Really very little. All I know is she left here under some kind of dark cloud. We ran into her daughter the other day at Gibby's. . ."

"We?" Michael immediately questioned.

"Grace and I. We went to lunch there and we stopped to buy some cosmetics. Anna Cable's daughter was behind the counter. She told Grace her mother had tried to commit suicide. She seemed to blame Grace and the center for. . ."

"Stay away from Anna Cable's daughter, Carter. This situation could cause you nothing but trouble."

"Trouble—what kind of trouble?"

"Anna Cable stuck her nose in places where it didn't belong. She became a . . . let's just say Anna Cable was difficult to work with and leave it at that."

"What's going on here, Michael? What possible secret could Anna have uncovered that would cause such a fuss with all of you?"

"Who said anything about a secret, Carter? Anna just involved herself in matters she had no business in—that's all. You're not at all like her."

"Are you sure, Michael?" Carter's eyes held Michael's for just a moment. He didn't like what he saw. If Carter continued to ask questions, she could be in for a rough ride. Maybe even rougher than what Anna Cable got.

"Hey, don't look so serious. We're just a blood bank, Carter. This isn't the Mafia here. We just process blood for patients who need it to live. It's a great cause. One that you wanted to be part of, remember?"

Carter's face relaxed. His words hit home. She smiled and made her way out of his office. Michael felt a bit sick to his stomach. Carter's words had struck a nerve.

"Michelle, will you please hold my calls for the next hour. I need to catch up on some paperwork," Michael said as he held down the intercom switch that connected him with his personal secretary.

"Yes, Mr. Bryan," came the reply.

For the next hour, Michael Bryan was indeed busy on the phone. He placed three long distance phone calls to three out-of-state banks. The fourth call was placed person-to-person to a Swede Andersen in Seattle. When Michael hung up, his hands were sweating. It could all be done so easily. He had the access at his fingertips. Now all he had to do was to find the courage.

18

Siam Qua's hands trembled slightly as he carefully placed the glass vial containing the control marrow back in its locked storage unit. One last check of temperature and the heavy door would be swung shut and locked with a coded password only he and two other people possessed. Returning to his bench, Siam recorded all the test samples that had been used during the day. Thirty-one in all were listed. Carefully, Siam removed the latex gloves and lab apron, folding them in precise motions and placing them in orange plastic bags. A twist tie sealed the bag. The bag would then be placed in a two-inch thick steel drum.

Siam was tired. He had been working eighteen hour days for the last three weeks. The quiet and brilliant research scientist was nowhere near where he had hoped to be at this stage. Time was running out and Dr. Silvers was becoming increasingly frustrated with the results. "Perhaps it was never meant to be," Siam thought as he poured over his notes and lab results. The air in the laboratory was indeed stuffy. The air vents in this area had been sealed off, and the room smelled sour. Siam rubbed his temples and for just a moment leaned forward resting his head on his forearm as he fought off the fatigue of the long day.

"Have we any signs of progress, Siam?" Dr. Silvers asked, startling the tired research director who had not heard the lab door open.

"Oh, no sir, I'm afraid not," Siam responded regaining his composure at hearing his superior's voice.

"Damn it, Siam. How far out are we?"

"The results are less than we had hoped for. There is a gap between the time of core response and the time of initial rejection. I'm afraid the bone marrow has many separate loops for us to unravel before we can duplicate it. As it is, I feel we still have many weeks of carefully controlled testing patterns ahead of us before we even begin to pierce its identification system," Siam added with no emotion in his voice—typical of an experienced scientist.

"We don't have weeks, Siam." Silvers reminded the quiet Ph.D. who worked, not for money or power, but for the intense desire to understand all the mysteries of life.

Siam did not answer Dr. Silvers. His eyes recorded the criticism of his superior and his mind made a mental note to work even harder. Siam Qua did not like the feeling of failure. He had not failed at anything in a very long time.

Siam Qua was a brilliant young man who had fled from the Philippines to Canada shortly before he was awarded his doctorate in science in Manila. His credits were in place, but he did not have the credentials to prove his doctorate had been attained. He settled in Toronto where he spent nearly fifteen years working in small hospitals in the outer regions. Siam used this time strengthening his English and working on antigen-testing projects in which no one else was interested at the time. Siam's goal was to find work in a major scientific laboratory in the United States. Getting into America was another thing. What he lacked was a powerful sponsor—a sponsor with certain contacts. Siam Qua met Dr. Silvers at a medical conference in Quebec. The two men met by accident when Siam found himself sitting next to the doctor at a luncheon. Silvers was impressed with a paper Siam just happened to have in his briefcase concerning the field of Human Leukocyte Antigen testing (HLA). Silvers was fascinated with Qua's knowledge on this profitable subject. He hired Siam Qua on the spot to open such a laboratory in Hamilton. The required background checks and mind-bending red tape were worked through, and Siam Qua was awarded the proper medical credentials. Silvers would serve as Siam's sponsor. Silvers's network of powerful medical friends pulled more than a few strings to arrange all the needed documentation for Qua's entry into the United States. Siam Qua's dreams of working in medicine in America were finally realized. From that time his dedication to Benjamin Silvers never wavered. In less than five years, Siam had gained a national reputation for his work in HLA testing, a difficult field which makes it possible to match donor organs, tissue, and platelets with needy recipients. Qua's HLA lab was also used in paternity exclusion cases, an area that also brought in considerable dollars to Silvers's center. Silvers had signed multiple, exclusive national contracts directly aligning Hamilton's HLA laboratory with many hospitals across the United States, hospitals that could not afford the expensive equipment needed to house such an operation. This past year, Siam started to receive attractive offers to work elsewhere, offers that included Seton Memorial Hospital who wanted Qua to establish a freestanding operation in their department of special research. But Siam chose to stay put at Hamilton. His obligation and loyalty to Dr. Silvers was powerful, and at Hamilton he would be left alone to work on projects of his own choosing. Ordinarily, Silvers would not challenge Siam Qua on his research. The medical director's only requirement was to bring dollars to his center. Research dollars were very important to the blood center, and Siam Qua's name on a research grant proposal almost always prompted funding. Silvers recognized the importance of having someone employed who could drive those lucrative dollars into the center's bank accounts. Many of Silvers's "toys" were funded with research dollars secured by his HLA Director's name on the dotted line.

Tonight, though, Silvers was pushing for results. Results that Siam Qua did not know if he could produce in such a short time.

"Siam, we have got to be the first to create an all-compatible bone marrow blood product. If we can create the master cell and match its antibody response, linking a formula to diffuse the rejection response, we can state that we have the inside track on this research," Silvers said, making it all sound so simple. It wasn't. Siam knew the clock and his restrictions were working against him. Silvers wanted a top secret approach to this research. He lived in fear of outside spies penetrating Siam's lab and robbing it of any findings that could beat them to the punch of landing the million dollars in grant money that the NAABC was willing to pay to create a bone marrow product that would not need specific, person-to-person typing to match a waiting patient needing a bone marrow transplant.

Silvers had even ordered extreme precautions to limit the staff access into the lab area when the control serum was present by changing the code on the access door into the inner chamber of the laboratory, a step that Siam felt to be obsessive. Only Qua, Dr. Crane, and Dr. Silvers possessed the code to unlock the latch.

"Siam, I know I'm riding you pretty hard here. I guess we both know how important this project is," Silvers said as a form of apology for his testy response. Silvers knew he could not attack Siam if he was to get out of him what he needed. Siam was a genius and one of the few individuals Silvers considered to be superior to himself.

"Let's call it a night and start out fresh tomorrow," Silvers said gently touching Siam on the shoulder.

Siam nodded his head and in his quiet way began to secure the lab for the evening. Ben Silvers waited until Siam covered the last of the instruments sitting in precise order on his work table.

"Siam, I have something in mind that may be necessary for us to put together," Silvers began in a quiet voice. Qua did not look up but signaled with a nod of his head that he was indeed listening.

"We may need to bait our findings on paper. I have every confidence that given the right amount of funding, and time, you could be the one to break the path of donor rejection and find the key to break through the need to type the marrow specifically to each transplant." Silvers hardly stopped for breath. Qua's eyes were now locked on Silvers's face.

"The bone marrow program is so goddamned behind because we have to spend so much time and money matching the donor to the patient. When we break the barrier and can create a kind of all-compatible bone marrow—one that doesn't need to be matched—and can be produced here in our laboratory, we will have unlocked a gold mine. I mean, hell, more than that—you'll earn yourself a Nobel," Silvers ended with his biggest smile spread across his face. He searched Qua's face for any telling signs of his reaction to what had just been presented.

"You want me to lie about our progress?" Siam asked.

"Not lie, just stretch the truth. If we don't, Siam, someone else will. Just look at all the stretches of truth that AIDS brought out in our industry. Hell, every laboratory on earth created a paper trail that was just on the verge of uncovering the cure—all in the name of securing grant money for research. How many of those million dollar research projects have paid off? Hell, we all know that most of that seed money ended up in other pet projects that had little to do with AIDS research."

"Dr. Silvers, I have never embellished the results of any of my scientific research. I have always. . ."

Silvers interrupted the speech.

"Qua, we don't have time for righteousness this time. We're talking about a race here, a race worth big dollars for our center. Dollars I want. Stuff like this is done all the time. How in the hell do you think some of these other laboratories have gotten so big? They added on a little to their paper trail to get the goddamn dollars so they could go on and make their discoveries. It's how you do things in America, Qua. You've got to have the balls to go out on a limb." Silvers was now pacing in front of the lab table. His face was red and a look of irritability was clearly present. Siam Qua knew this look.

"I do not think I can do this for you, Dr. Silvers. It would not be ethical."

"Let's not talk about ethics, Qua. It wasn't ethical to lie about your medical degrees, now was it? It wasn't ethical to pay the committee a few extra bucks on the side to stamp your credential clean, now was it, Qua?"

Qua felt his stomach tightening. Silvers's words stung.

"Perhaps you have grown tired of the good life in America, Qua. Maybe you would like to go back to Canada or maybe you have a longing for your little village—Bagalot?"

"Baguio," Qua corrected. He had not said that word out loud for over twenty years. His life there was one of poverty and constant shame. His father and brother were crooks by his standards, trading in the black market and using the dollars to bully the people in his village. Drugs and violence repelled the quiet and extremely smart young Qua. His father had used blackmail money and drug profits to pay for Siam's schooling. He wanted to use Siam's degree for his own good. Siam Qua would indeed be a slave to his father's evil world. He had to escape. He could not go back.

"Look, Siam. Let's not go off here. You just need to pad your findings a bit to get our foot in the door. The NAABC is well aware of your work. All you have to do is write the paper. You can add the bells and whistles in such a way they will never question your documentation. Besides, they have nothing to compare it with at this point. If you say you have a crack open, but at this point, don't want to furnish complete data without funding rights, they're not going to question it. The money is just sitting there rotting away in some foundation fund. Why shouldn't we push it? You can do this, Siam."

Siam Qua did not look at Silvers but slowly nodded his head again. He knew Silvers well enough to know that he could not change the course of this conversation by confrontation. In time, perhaps, he could find the marker, perhaps even before the funding arrived. He would just have to devote more time, more energy. There was truth in what Silvers had just said—ethics was not always on the playing field when it came to securing large research dollars. Besides, Baguio was a place he did not want to think about. Perhaps there would be time to change Silvers's mind, but it was not going to be tonight. Silvers took Qua's nod to be an acceptance. He smiled at Qua and the tenseness in his body seemed to give way. The look was no longer present. The threat had passed. At least for tonight. As the two men left the laboratory a few minutes later, they did not see Reymond Alexander standing in the darkened hallway just a few feet away from the HLA doorway.

Reymond had heard that something very important was now housed in the HLA laboratory area. He had tried on two other occasions to enter the lab after hours when he spotted Siam locking up, but his code key was immediately denied. He had one more area to search for the master code that was now being used by only three people. Reymond didn't like secrets. Especially if the secrets belonged to Dr. Benjamin Silvers.

19

The raindrops were huge, splashing the windshield with large patterns of clear water. It was a cold rain—the kind that chills straight through to the bone.

The car's heater was not working properly, and Thomas Erin Hampton's custom-made, woolen sweater felt almost light in weight as the approaching winter temperatures penetrated its dark pattern of woven fibers.

"What a perfect day for this," Thomas Hampton uttered in character with the dreary day as he carefully guided the black BMW up the narrow driveway leading to the family estate. Pulling into the familiar circular entrance way, he killed his car's engine and coasted to a stop directly in front of the double doors, which had been imported from Italy so many years ago. Deep in thought, Thomas did not see the manservant approaching the driver's side of the car with a shiny black umbrella in hand.

"It's good to see you, Mr. Hampton," Claude Devoure, the tall Swiss keeper of the manor stated as he swiftly opened the car door holding the umbrella over Thomas's emerging body.

"It's good to see you, too, Claude," the younger man responded, genuinely glad to see the now elderly servant who had been, for the most part, his only playmate as a child.

"The rain's as cold as falling ice," Claude said, gently shivering as the two men made their way inside the dwelling.

The stately house greeted the pair with a rush of warm air. Thomas felt the same heaviness he always did when returning to this place, which held so many lonely memories.

"If only it could have been different," Thomas thought as his eyes took in the beautiful furnishings and paintings his mother purchased so many years ago.

"Thomas, it's good to see you," Quinn Careton said as he emerged from the library where he had been waiting.

Hampton smiled for the first time that day as he greeted the family attorney with a warm embrace. Quinn Careton was more than just a paid adviser to Thomas; he had truly served as a surrogate family member for as long as he could remember.

"Shall we get this over with?" Thomas asked bluntly with the anxiety of the long wait now showing in his eyes.

"As you wish, sir" replied the ever-proper Careton, who was in many ways just as anxious. The two men made their way into the library where Walter Hampton's wall safe was housed. In a matter of minutes, the yellowed envelope was extracted and placed in the hands of the son who was now the owner of its contained secrets.

"Shall I leave you alone?" Quinn inquired.

"If you don't mind, I would like for you to stay." The huge fireplace generated heat and produced a crackling sound as Thomas settled in a chair near its inviting warmth. Quinn Careton walked to the farthest window as if to give privacy to this moment.

"I'm not sure if I should even open this, Quinn. I mean—what if its contents. . ." The sentence was not finished as Thomas's eyes searched Quinn's face for advice.

"I wish I could help you. Believe me when I say I have no idea what is written there. I was only made aware of its existence a few months before your father died when he asked me to witness in person that he was adding to its contents. He never said a word to me concerning why he was reopening the envelope or what additional information he was adding to its original contents. But I do know your father was not a man to do things without great thought behind his deeds. I don't think he would have wanted to hurt you. He really did love you—in his own way," Quinn said, trying hard to be of help to the young man he had come to love as his own over the course of the last thirty years.

In one smooth motion, Hampton ran his index finger across the seam of the letter-sized envelope. To his surprise, it contained two thin sheets of cheap white linen paper carefully numbered, and a single silver key. The son immediately recognized the handwriting of his father. The message kept hidden for so long began rather simply.

> *To my son—my only son:*
> *There are things people may do in their lifetime they are not always proud of. Such things exist in my past. Your past, I pray, will never be burdened in such a manner. I am sorry to have caused you the pain of being raised with such a poor image of a*

father as I have been all these years. I now know it is time to share with the one person who bears my name the secrets of a past. I am not sure if you will find the strength to carry out my final wishes, but I want you to know, you should feel no guilt if you decide to throw away the key and let sleeping dogs lie. The key that I am referring to, should at this moment be resting in your hands. It will fit a safety deposit box located at the National Bank of America in New York City. The account number, which is also now in your name, is AC50361. I have only been to this bank twice in my lifetime—once, on the day that your mother and I left the United States for Zurich, and thirty-four years later to that very day. My last trip represents an anniversary of a date that I cannot forget.

I have left behind documents that may help you understand the actions of a man who was your father. A man who was very much in love with your mother. I have also left behind the answers to unlock the secrets of men you may find evil in deed. You, my son, like your mother, are innocent of my deeds. Your past will never be a burden to you as mine is now to me. I can only tell you that I have tried for years to justify my actions, but as I write this message to you, I must now face myself and tell you that evil can be defined in many different ways. Perhaps men such as myself, and those other individuals who are part of my past, are the most evil of all men—for we truly did know the difference. Money, my son, and all it brings, can rob a person of his soul.

I am not sure what action you may take once you are aware of all the secrets kept hidden for so long. I do not hold you responsible for any action, please know this. I can only hope you will one day forgive me, and perhaps, put my soul to rest.

With love, your father,
Walter Hampton.

For a few moments, Thomas Hampton sat staring at the pages of linen paper that now lay in his lap. The words written to him by his father left him even more troubled. At most, he thought the envelope would contain the deep dark secrets of his family's heritage. But the words written were linked with more than just heritage—they appeared to contain secrets of far greater importance. What evil was his father a part of? Who were these other men? What could be so important to his father that he would keep it locked away for thirty-five years in a remote safety deposit box? Why had he not shared this part of his life with Quinn Careton, a man whom he had trusted for so many years?

Was this just another ploy of his father? A ploy to hurt him once again. How much more would the son have to endure before the ghost of his father's distant love released him? Quinn Careton's voice broke the silence that filled the room.

"You look rather pale. Is there anything I can do?"

Thomas did not answer, but wordlessly handed Quinn the short letter.

The look of puzzlement on the older man's face when he finished reading the letter spoke a thousand words.

"Evil men and greed. None of this makes any sense to me at all, Thomas," Quinn answered, trying hard to find words that would speak to this situation.

"Most of my father's life was a mystery to me. As far as I'm concerned, this is just another slice of that mystery," the son answered.

"What are you going to do, Thomas? Will you go to New York?"

"I'm not sure. I need a few days to think about all this." The son moved to the large window overlooking the manicured gardens that Walter Hampton had carefully designed many years ago. For just an instant, Thomas could see the image of his father, the bent-over form tending to his roses. As a small boy, Thomas would sit behind the large hedge, which served as a dividing line for the gardens, and watch his father working the soil that bore his prize roses. Thomas would listen to his father's soft humming and envy those bushes for the attention they were receiving. Those memories seemed so very near at this moment.

"Thomas, if you need me to go with you, I will certainly arrange my schedule," Quinn carefully offered not wanting to pressure the young man into a decision.

"Thank you, sir. I appreciate your offer," Thomas replied with no hint in his voice as to what his decision might be.

The rest of the day passed in quiet fashion. The two men shared lunch and spoke on other business matters that were now the responsibility of the son. The letter was not mentioned again. The day that began in mystery would end in the same way. Thomas Erin Hampton stayed at the mansion that evening, his first overnight stay in more than two years.

Painfully shy and withdrawn, Thomas Hampton had done little with his life. Well-educated with a talent for understanding chemistry, mathematics, and physics, he had rejected the opportunity to teach after graduating from college, choosing instead a life of nomadic wandering as if looking for something or someone to hold him in one place.

"Purposely lonely" was how he was once described by one of his professors at Glenwich, an exclusive college, where he had earned a double degree in chemistry and physics in less than three years. Tonight, alone in his room, Thomas took out the letter and reread his father's handwritten message.

The words "With love, your father, Walter Hampton," struck the son deeply. Words so absent from his life were now written down on paper for him to repeat again and again. For nearly an hour Thomas wrestled with his emotions. Finally, he came to grips with what he had to do.

Carefully, Thomas folded the thin sheets of linen paper, placing them inside a small metal box that held other keepsakes accumulated over the years. The small silver key was placed in his wallet. The next morning, Thomas Erin Hampton called a travel agent and reserved a ticket to New York City. It was a one-way reservation.

20

The last several weeks had gone by rather quickly for Carter Egan. The winter winds of December were approaching and Carter had just returned from a NAABC conference in Colorado where one incident had proven to be deeply disturbing. She had been excited at the thought of traveling to Colorado and networking with other public relations directors who were experiencing some of the same day-to-day pressures. The meeting was to serve as an educational guide for Carter. Michael Bryan felt she might be able to learn new marketing ideas that would help in the recruiting of blood donors.

She was assigned to the newcomers committee and Ed Jordan was the chairman. Jordan also worked for a large regional blood center in the South as a director of marketing and public relations. Jordan was everything Carter despised. He was loud, opinionated, and it was his way or the highway. He had worked at the same regional blood bank for over ten years. Carter remembered Kiley Matson's references to sending Jordan's center so much blood on a regular basis that they had begun to refer to it as a "satellite branch."

At Carter's first committee meeting, Carter tried to overlook Jordan's, self-serving, egotistic attitude. It wasn't until he started bragging about his extended emergency calls that Carter's anger showed.

"Are you telling me your center deliberately stages false blood emergencies?" Carter questioned with the look of amazement on her face.

"Are you telling me you have never called a quickie?" Jordan shot back at her with a smile and a wink.

"Never—we've never done that," Carter returned.

Jordan did not answer but shrugged his shoulders. The room was quiet and several other p.r. directors diverted their eyes from Carter.

"Look, Carter—Carter Egan," he repeated as his eyes stared at Carter's name tag. "In our business, we have to motivate any way we can. I don't feel at all bad about asking for help from a public that sits on their butts and waits for us to yell emergency. If that's what it takes to keep my hospitals supplied, then so be it. Those of us who have been doing this longer than you have all "cried wolf" at one time or another. And besides, who is it hurting? Not those patients who need the juice to keep on going. I'd be surprised as hell if Kiley Matson hasn't dipped his ass in a little public manipulation. Everybody does it. It's the way it is."

Carter felt her face burning. She started to defend Kiley when Jordan asked the group another question.

"Just between us, how many of you have used the bloodless routine in your own back yards?"

To Carter's surprise, several hands went up. Sensing his deflation of Carter Egan, Jordan smiled and turned the group toward another seminar topic. Carter did not say another word during this session. Something was wrong here. Was she really this naive? Were her blood shortage calls always out of real need? What bothered Carter Egan most was the deep down feeling that Ed Jordan knew something about her center that she didn't know. What was worse was Carter's recent questioning of her daily reports. Blood inventories just didn't match up with Kiley's line-for-line reporting. There were little things on the morning flash sheets that were still mysteries to her, like the Glass account.

The word "bloodless" stuck in Carter's mind. It was a very good word. A word she would be aware of in the future.

The week went by fast for Carter. It was exciting to attend a medical convention, but it was also tiring. She slept most of the way back on the long flight to Hamilton. The conference gave her a lift from her normal routine, and she actually found herself looking forward to this week's Director's meeting. She wanted to share with the group those positive things she had picked up while she was at the conference. Silvers and Crane had entered the room laughing. This was a good sign for the other directors. Perhaps today's meeting would go fast and there would be no bloodshed. Carter had just settled into her seat when Gerald Preston asked for everyone's attention.

"Ladies and gentlemen, I have just received word that our lawsuit may soon be dropped as the medical panel has ruled in our favor. It was a unanimous decision."

Several directors broke into applause. Silvers was beaming. Dr. Crane looked as if she had just won a gold medal. Michael Bryan sat quietly in his chair next to Preston. His eyes did not make contact with anyone else. Carter thought he looked disturbed, almost as if he were not happy to be found innocent of such damaging charges. Elizabeth Monroe also seemed strangely quiet with the announcement.

"Ladies and gentlemen, it just goes to show you that justice does prevail. When you're right—you're right," Silvers said with laughter following his remarks. He looked across the table and winked at Elizabeth who pretended not to notice the familiarity.

The round robin of director's exchange went fairly fast. Carter gave an update on the conference, just touching on the highlights. Everyone seemed to be in good spirits. When it was Kiley's turn to report, the tone of the meeting took a somber turn.

"I hate to be the bearer of bad news, especially in light of the good news we have just heard here, but I'm afraid our inventories are falling at a rapid rate. Carter, it looks like you may have to call another alert tomorrow morning if today's drives don't score big. We could find ourselves bloodless again if we don't."

The word "bloodless" hit Carter in the stomach. It was no longer a new word to her. It was now a word that set off certain gut feelings. Feelings she didn't like.

"Kiley, are you sure we need to go out to the media again? I mean we seem to do this so often," Carter said, trying to conceal the distress she was feeling.

"Carter, if Kiley says we need the media—we need the media. Get your press releases in order this afternoon and we'll hit it fresh tomorrow morning," Dr. Silvers replied.

"Shouldn't we wait to see how today's. . ."

"Carter, we are going to need an alert out tomorrow morning. Just be ready for it, okay?" Silvers answered with obvious testiness in his tone of voice.

Carter dropped her eyes and did not reply. She was learning not to confront Silvers directly, especially with other directors present. When she looked up, she saw Bertha White staring at her. Something in Bertha's eyes bothered Carter. Was it a warning? Or was Bertha just embarrassed for her? The meeting was declared over in just under one hour. It was a short meeting by past standards. The mood of celebration quickly returned as the staff filed out of the conference room. Michael Bryan fell in behind Carter, and when he was close enough, he reached out and touched her on the shoulder.

"Carter, I need to speak with you," he said in a somber tone.

In a few steps the pair was safely behind Bryan's office door. "Carter, I feel I have to tell you something before you are hit with it by the media," he began. Carter nodded her head and waited for her boss to go on.

Michael Bryan took in a deep breath and stated softly, "Taylor Addison died this morning, shortly after she gave birth."

Carter's gasp was audible and a look of horror showed on her face.

"Oh my God, Michael. This is terrible." Carter's eyes filled with tears. She took in a deep breath as her body slumped forward in the chair. "How is the baby? Does it have the disea. . ." Carter didn't finish the sentence.

Michael Bryan did not speak, but his eyes told Carter he really didn't know how the baby was.

"Does Dr. Silvers and. . ."

"Yes, Carter. They know. The trio knows."

"You mean they knew about Taylor's death in there—at our meeting?"

"Yes—we knew it." Michael seemed to hold back his feelings. Carter found it hard to believe that they could act so nonchalant about Taylor Addison's death—to the point of not telling the center's directors, and only sharing the news of their so-called victory.

"Is Taylor's death the reason Preston said he thought the lawsuit would soon be dropped?" Carter asked, regaining her composure.

Bryan nodded his head in a confirmatory manner, but said nothing out loud. For a few moments, the two sat quietly without speaking. Finally, Carter rose to leave. Michael Bryan walked over to his large window and turned away. Carter said nothing more. The sound of Carter closing the door left him alone with his thoughts, thoughts that spoke to an innocent woman dying so far ahead of her time. He forced himself not to think of the child. He couldn't. He just couldn't.

Madison Boggs received word of Taylor Addison's death before the sheet was pulled up over her body. A news intern, working directly for Madison, had paid a hospital orderly fifty dollars to let her know any news concerning Taylor Addison's health. The orderly wasted no time in getting the news to Madison's contact. This time, Madison Boggs scooped the other networks with news of Taylor's demise. Almost mechanical in her delivery, Madison read her own written words with little emotion.

"Taylor Addison, of Grandville, died this morning at 8 o'clock in St. Joseph Hospital from complications attributed to AIDS. Ms. Addison had given birth to a son only hours before. The condition of the child and his

chances of developing AIDS are still unknown at this time. Ms. Addison had filed a lawsuit against the Hamilton Regional Blood Center citing negligence on their behalf. As irony would have it, the medical panel, who met just this morning to review the validity of charges against the blood center, found in favor of Hamilton Regional. In a prepared statement released just minutes ago, the panel of pathologists cited that the three donors in question had fulfilled the requirements for blood donors, met the health criteria standards, and were in good health at the time of their community donations. The medical panel concluded their deliberation with a closing statement documenting the absence of a screening test for the HIV virus at the time the donations did in fact take place. Taylor Addison would have been twenty-six on Wednesday."

Quick in-and-out reporting. This was news at its best; get the scoop and take it to the air first. At one minute past the last broadcast airing, the story would become history, and the frenzy over Taylor Addison's every move would be over. Fate was guilty in the death of Taylor Addison, so stated the medical panel. No one was at fault for her death. These things happen. Normally, Madison would retain no feelings toward events or people she spoke about over the airwaves. They were detached from her. But this time, she couldn't get the story or the person out of her mind. There had only been time for one face to face interview with Taylor Addison. She taped it one week after Taylor had become a public figure by filing a lawsuit against a major medical industry. Taylor was heavy with child when Madison met her. Outwardly, Taylor's appearance seemed strangely normal for a woman with AIDS. Only the dark circles under her large brown eyes gave a hint of her illness.

Taylor was understandably bitter and her remarks about the blood center were laced with caustic adjectives. There was something strangely haunting in Taylor's taped words that wouldn't let go of Madison's memory.

"I was told on a Monday that I was pregnant, and then on Wednesday the doctor called me and told me over the phone that I had a disease called AIDS. I shouldn't have gotten this disease. It was given to me—carelessly—by the blood center."

"Carelessly" was the word that kept surfacing all afternoon in Madison's mind. Ed Morton was sitting at his desk when Madison passed his office a little past six on her way out of the station for a quick supper before finishing with the eleven o'clock news.

"Hey, Madison, if you've got a minute, I've got something that might interest you," Ed called out to the rushing figure passing by.

"What do you have, Ed?" Madison questioned a little impatiently as her stomach was crying to be fed.

"Have a look," the news director said as he handed his anchor a copy of the blood center's financial statement.

Madison quietly read through the eleven page report of information secured through the Freedom of Information inquiry that Ed had requested several weeks earlier.

"Well, this is certainly interesting," she replied.

"You're damn right it's interesting, Madison. This information is staggering when you consider the source. Ten bank accounts—all spread across the U.S. and Canada with no less than $999,000 in each of them, and yet, these are the same people who are holding raffles to help purchase a new bloodmobile? Something smells here, Madison."

"There's nothing illegal about raffles, Ed," Madison replied still pouring over the center's financial report.

"Yeah, well, I guess there's also nothing illegal about the blood center holding back from the public their little tucked away greenbacks either," Ed shot back.

"I wonder what this figure is all about?"

"Which one?" Ed asked.

"The $400,000 noted as debt retirement."

"I don't know. Could be a reserve fund, a building fund, although there's nothing showing on this report that points to any accumulated debt. Maybe we should dig a little deeper on that one." Debt retirement was a clever way to list the executives' yearly incentive bonus. Gerald Preston had come up with this line item.

"This is absolutely amazing, Ed. These guys have a sweet thing going for them with this kind of profit floating out of there."

"Hold your tongue, Madison. Remember Hamilton is a not-for-profit corporation—it says so on every page—501C3 status. See, it's as plain as the nose on your face," Ed replied sarcastically.

"If you took away the not-for-profit seal, these guys would be listed in the Fortune 500 category," Madison added. "I had no idea there was so much money involved in blood banking."

Turning the page, she was suddenly taken with the documented information concerning salary levels.

"Good grief, Ed. Did you see how much the top four executives at the blood center make?"

"It's hard to miss, Madison."

"Their salaries come in at over a million dollars a year. $350,000 each for the two top dogs—let's see, that adds up to $700,000 for their level with $395,000 split between the two assistants. And according to this column, that doesn't include their perks—cars, American Express Cards, travel allocations for conferences. And look at this! Company cars are provided with *executive choice*." Madison was truly surprised at what she had just learned.

"They have to sell a hell of a lot of blood each week just to meet their executive level payroll," Ed added with little emotion.

"Middle management is not making that much money, though. It seems their entire group has only one person making over $40,000 and that's the director of nurses. The average salary is around $25,000 if my math serves me right. I had no idea these guys pulled down so much money, Ed."

"And neither does the public, Madison. But you can't torch a company just because they pull down top dollars in salaries and have bank accounts spread all across the country and were smart enough to shield it all under a 501C3."

"They're listed as a service industry."

"I guess serving up blood for hospitals is a service, Madison. I can't argue with that."

"But who regulates the dollars involved here. Who sets the limits for what these guys can and can't charge for blood?"

"I'm not sure if there are any regulatory guidelines for such charges, Madison."

"Well, their board must have some say in their salary levels. Surely, they review these things?"

"If you look at their board, it's filled with other doctors, and it's a volunteer board. They don't get paid for sitting on it. It does look good on their vitae, though, community service and all. I wonder how many of those board members actually show up regularly for the board meetings?" Ed observed as he read through the center's latest annual report, which listed all of its board members.

"Looking at this group of serving members, most of the docs sitting on this board earn far more dollars than those blood center directors. Hell, Madison, if the truth were known, these guys probably make one or two meetings a year at best, and when they do show up, five will get you ten, they eat the goodies served up by the p.r. department and vote unanimously on whatever the center's executives want them to. It's corporate America at its best, and who knows the difference? Not the public, that's for sure. And what's worse," Ed added, "even if we did unravel some things here, we probably wouldn't be allowed to take this industry on full speed."

"What do you mean, Ed?"

"The medical community is a powerful lot. They have tremendous influence in our advertising world. Shit, look at our total ad budget. Seven out of ten of our top advertisers are connected to the medical community. Every major hospital floats commercials nowadays. Those dollars are big time ad dollars. We couldn't afford to tweak them too hard or the higher-ups would have our asses in a sling," Ed stated with typical honesty.

As much as Madison wanted to disagree with Ed, she couldn't. No matter how much bullshit was floated, stating advertising had no direct control over editorial direction, the truth of the matter was simple: No advertisers—no news department. Ad dollars paid their salaries and kept them on a leash at the same time. Small affiliate stations didn't have the same deep pocket luxury as the major networks did when it came to dollars in hand.

"What are we doing here, Ed. We don't even know enough about this industry to nail a story together, let alone put them out of business."

"You're right. We don't know enough about these guys and neither does the public we're supposed to serve."

Ed's words struck a chord with Madison's gut.

"We feed these guys air time any time they call us, but when it comes to understanding their operation, we sit here with egg on our face and say—'Uh, I don't know.'"

"If we do put something together on the blood center, are you telling me it hasn't got a chance at airing?"

"I'm telling you it depends on what we uncover. As far as I'm concerned, if you turn up real news on this operation, Madison, and there's dirt in the bushes with bona fide witnesses to prove it, I'll go into editorial on your side."

Madison smiled for the first time that day. Ed suddenly noticed what the carefully applied makeup on Madison's face was no longer hiding her evident fatigue.

"You look tired, lady. How about me buying you a quick dinner? We need some time to digest this for a while. We can get a fresh perspective on this whole thing tomorrow. Hey, maybe we're overreacting to this because of Taylor Addison?" Ed offered as he reached for his coat.

"Maybe you're right, Ed. It's been a long day and I'm hungry as hell. If I don't eat soon, I'm afraid I'm going to pass out." Madison handed back the pages of the report, stood up, and headed for the door. A sudden feeling of nausea hit as she reached Ed's doorway, leaving her dizzy and obviously unsteady on her feet.

"Are you okay, Mad?" Ed replied as he quickly came to her side. "You look like you're going to faint. Sit down for a minute."

Madison leaned against the doorway, steadying herself as the wave of sickness passed over her. In a few minutes the nausea was gone. As the color poured back into her cheeks, Ed chided her about being on a perpetual diet.

"You could use some meat on those bones, kid." Are you up to a quick bite of dinner at the Eagle's Roost? Madison nodded. Ed held her arm for support while walking to his gray Buick parked in his reserved space at the north side of the station's parking lot. The Eagle's Roost was a hangout for media types who were on the run between airtime dead-lines. Madison was surprised to see Chet Lambert sitting at a table by himself in the far corner of the tiny restaurant.

"Hey Chet, are you saving those seats for anyone in particular?" Madison called out as they entered the eatery.

Chet motioned them over, obviously glad for the company. Chet was not liked by many in the media. Madison could care less what other people thought. She had always found Chet to be right on the money when it came to flushing out news. His tactics were not always the most ethical, but he got the story and usually, as much as she hated to admit it, got the story first.

"Congrats on the scoop, pretty lady," Chet said, obviously referring to today's Taylor Addison headline.

"Yeah, well, every now and then, TV does beat newsprint, Chet." Madison chided Chet knowing full well how uneven the playing fields were when it came to instant reporting.

Chet smiled and bit into his hamburger.

"Are you done with the lawsuit thing?" Chet asked.

"Are you?" Madison countered.

"Hell, I was done with the story fifteen minutes after I got it," the print reporter stated drily.

"I thought you were hot-to-trot on this story, Chet? Didn't I hear you comment about this being a national story?" Ed teased. Lambert shifted in his chair uncomfortably. "Yeah, well, my editor had other ideas."

"So what gives with your editor, Chet?" Madison quickly returned.

Chet's face took on a dark look. He didn't say anything for a few moments, as if trying to find a way to express something to Madison, and yet keeping it all off the record.

"You're a hotshot TV reporter, Miss Boggs. Do some digging on this one. Check out those old bloodlines." Chet Lambert quickly wiped his mouth with his paper napkin and stood up.

"Sorry to eat and run, but you know deadlines." Chet gave Madison one of his trademark smiles and left.

Chet's muscular frame quickly disappeared out the front door of the packed restaurant. True to his image, Chet had also left Madison and Ed with his bill.

"What the hell was that all about, Madison?"

"I'm not sure, Ed. But I think we were just given a clue."

"You know, now that I think about it, Chet came on hot and heavy when Addison first filed that lawsuit. He put the ink to the blood center with some pretty strong jabs," Ed added.

"Chet's a strange bird, Ed. I can't imagine him giving me a lead on a story—not with his ambition."

"Yeah, well maybe someone tied a knot in his tail."

"I'll see what I can dig up here, Ed. I'll pull up his inches at the library and see how much space he started out with and where it went." Madison dived into her salad with gusto.

"See, you're eating rabbit food again, Madison. How do you expect to feed that baby if you keep eating like that?"

Madison blushed a deep red. "How'd you know, Ed? I haven't told anyone."

"I have five boys, Madison. Which means my wife looked just liked you did earlier this evening—many, many times. Congratulations, lady. I couldn't be happier for you." Ed bit into his double cheeseburger.

Madison was indeed pregnant—three months. Her doctor had confirmed her suspicions just two days before. Perhaps it was the stirring of life in her belly that drew her thoughts to the fate of the young woman who had just been laid to rest that afternoon.

"Something tells me we could be on a real roller coaster if we dig any deeper into this story, Ed."

"You're a newswoman, Madison. You wouldn't have lasted all these years if you didn't have those characteristics that make you go for the kill."

"But we may have bitten off more than we can chew with this one. Especially if it turns up a lot of loose dirt on an industry that has been, up to now, lily white."

"Are you telling me that you want to back off this?"

"Not in a million years, Ed. You know me. I'm fearless." A small smile showed on Madison's lips. She was courageous and pursued her stories tenaciously, but she experienced fear often. She did not try to conceal her apprehension from Ed.

The news pair finished their dinners and returned to the station. Madison did her eleven o'clock standup exactly as before. She would call Chet Lambert first thing in the morning. She owed Taylor Addison that much. The word *carelessly* was a word not to be taken lightly in the English language. Especially when it was spoken with such conviction by a lady who died under the full belief of its meaning.

As Madison Boggs signed off the air, Elizabeth Monroe was returning to her office. When word reached her late that afternoon of Taylor Addison's death, it struck a strange feeling in the pit of her stomach. The blue folder in her locked cabinet was still a mystery to her. Something inside had kept her from opening the file drawer. True, Ben had blamed her nurses for this whole lawsuit mess; but what had they done? Did she really want to become a part of whatever was so important to Ben that he ordered her to bury it? She was in no shape mentally to take on more responsibility for anyone. Every day was becoming more and more of a huge lie.

Elizabeth did not turn on her overhead office lights. Instead, she switched on her desk lamp, which gave her office a dim but soft glow. Her hands trembled as she pulled the folder out from its safe haven. Using her scissors she cut the sealing tape from the binder. As her eyes focused on the printed copies of paper in the dimly-lit room, she steadied her shaking hands by laying the three sheets of paper across her desk. In one fierce moment of recognition, Elizabeth Monroe realized she possessed the original health criteria information sheets belonging to the three male donors who gave blood for Taylor Addison. Why had Ben given these to her? What was the need to lock them away? Hadn't he turned all of this information over to Taylor's attorneys and the State Board of Health? Elizabeth's mind raced for answers. She was about to breathe a sigh of relief as she saw nothing out of the ordinary with the first two donors' questionnaires, when suddenly her eyes focused on donor number three, which was marked clearly with a black marker pen at the top of the page—Edwin Shell. The name exploded in her mind. Ben had thrown his name at her on the way back from his lake house just a few weeks ago. Elizabeth held Shell's health questionnaire directly under the light. In an instant she saw what Ben Silvers was hiding.

"Oh my God! How could we have let this happen?" Elizabeth uttered in a low, almost moaning voice. As her eyes continued to read this donor's answers, she felt ill. As a nurse, she could not believe what she was seeing. Across from the second question where the donor was asked, "Do you consider yourself to be in good health?" Edwin Shell had checked the NO column. As her eyes continued to scan the columns of questions and answers, she found violation after violation. Edwin Shell had just had major tooth extractions two days before his donation. He was taking penicillin, aspirin, and antibiotics. He did not possess a doctor's release permitting him to donate blood this soon after such surgery. To top it off, the blood center's own in-house nursing staff, personnel she supervised, had failed to have either Dr. Crane or Dr. Silvers review this donor's NO answers as required by the blood center's own written criteria. Edwin Shell was most negligently allowed to donate blood. In all, Elizabeth found no less than ten direct violations of the center's policies on Edwin Shell's health questionnaire. He should never have been allowed to donate blood—AIDS or no AIDS. This donor was clearly not in the best of health and stated so in his own handwriting by checking that NO box. The penicillin, aspirin, and antibiotics were other clear evidence of the careless overlooking of safety guidelines that should have deferred Edwin Shell from giving blood. Negligence was clearly evident. Careless negligence. Negligence concealed.

Pinned to the back of Edwin Shell's questionnaire was a piece of paper that Elizabeth recognized as Dr. Crane's handwriting.

"Shell's blood went to three other individuals. I hope to hell they don't join the lawsuit."

Every fiber in Elizabeth's body felt on fire. "My God, it's a huge cover-up. We're involved in a cover-up in the death of that girl and probably three others."

Elizabeth wished she had never taken the folder from its dark hiding place. She didn't want to be a part of this. Grabbing tape from her desk drawer, Elizabeth quickly stuffed the sheets of paper back inside the blue folder. Her hands trembled as she started to retape the edges. Suddenly her conscience stopped her. For several minutes Elizabeth stared at the folder in her hands.

"We can't do this—we just can't do this," Elizabeth repeated. Maybe it was too late, but Elizabeth had a strong feeling that Taylor Addison's attorneys had never seen these health questionnaires. If they had, they would have given this clearly damning evidence to the medical panel, and there was no way in hell that those individuals could have found the center innocent. The center was anything but innocent.

It only took a moment to make clear copies. Sitting down at her desk, Elizabeth dialed information and asked the operator for the address and phone number of the offices of Stansbarry and Stansbarry in Port Smith. Elizabeth's neat handwriting carefully spread across the plain linen envelope she found in her top, right-hand desk drawer. In swift motions, the folder was resealed and placed back inside the cabinet drawer and locked up once again. She did not bother to turn off her desk light as she quickly left her office. Driving home, Elizabeth's mind raced. She had to think. She needed time to sort through all of this. Had Ben given her that file deliberately to make her a part of all this? Had Ben set her up to make it look like she was the one concealing this evidence from the attorneys? After all, it was one of her nurses who let this donor pass through their security system, a system that should have prevented Edwin Shell from donating. "My God! How had I let myself become involved in all this? she almost said out loud to herself.

The metallic sound of the mailbox lid banging shut frightened her. It was too late to stop it now or even to take time to come to grips with what she had just done. Her life was never going to be the same. She had to get home. She had to close her mind down. There was only one way. When Elizabeth entered her house, she headed straight for her bathroom medicine cabinet. As she reached for the package of fresh needles, she caught sight of her reflection in the mirror. She didn't like what she saw. This was not supposed to happen. How had she let herself become a worn-out, used up, drug addict? As the tears began to fall, the once proud nurse slowly slid down the wall with the weight of her body coming to rest on the snow-white bathroom carpeting. Curled up in a fetal position, Elizabeth spent most of the night fighting the forces that so controlled her body and mind. At one a.m., Elizabeth lost her battle with the demons. She gathered up the necessary paraphernalia to administer her addiction. Elizabeth expertly found her vein and, in a matter of moments, her relief. Ben Silvers had given her many secrets to keep. But this one was more than she could handle. How could Ben have spoken so bitterly toward Taylor Addison when he knew she was innocent. The blood center was negligent. Ben knew this. Alice Crane knew this. Who else knew the truth? Question after question roared in her head. Finally, the liquid poison took hold, and a certain calmness came over her. Tomorrow, after she had time to think all this through, she would confront Ben. Taylor Addison was dead, others could be dying. This was all wrong. The blood center could not be a part of something so evil. Mistakes were made. In all her years as a nurse she had seen things happen that medically should not have taken place. Her own daughter was taken from her because of a medical mistake. But it was not deliberate; it was an accident. A tired resident accidentally gave her baby girl suffering with the flu the wrong dosage of medicine. It killed her. It wasn't meant to happen. No one did anything deliberate. You could forgive accidents. How do you forgive a deliberate cover-up? She was a part of that lie now. A prisoner to the truth so powerfully wrapped around deliberate deeds of deception.

A veil of blackness mercifully set in, and Elizabeth Monroe was freed temporarily from the need to ask any more questions about this terrible evening of discovery. Elizabeth would not go to work the next day. She would call in sick. She needed time. Time to think, and time to dry out. But time was a luxury Elizabeth did not have.

The moon was full in the sky as Ben Silvers drove home from the celebration party spawned by the earlier announcement of the medical panel's ruling. What the outside world didn't know, was that the medical panel of three doctors had spent less than two hours reading the materials presented, and the deathbed video statement of Taylor Addison was turned off halfway through its showing. They ruled unanimously.

"It is our finding that the parties accused of negligence were in no way to blame for such accusations. Our findings in reviewing the presented evidence show the blood center processed the donors with the highest quality standards. Therefore, we feel the negligence issue is without cause and should be dismissed."

It took only fifty-one words to dismiss Taylor Addison and her charges of negligence. The brotherhood could find no reason to doubt its members. No reason at all. This was the way it was.

So tonight, Silvers, a member of the tight brotherhood of medicine, was feeling right with the world when he climbed into his bed as a vindicated medical director. He made love to his wife and a mental note to take Elizabeth back to his lakeside cabin as soon as he could arrange the time away. Everything was going to be okay now. It was over. Taylor Addison was dead and the panel had declared his blood center innocent of all charges. He could get on with his life. His cover-up had indeed held. Alice Crane would need to be thanked for her contributions. Perhaps a bonus could be paid to her from one of his research funds. He would arrange to have a check drawn up first thing in the morning. It was the least he could do. After all, what was the use of having these funds if you couldn't divert them to your own advantage. Ben Silvers used everything and everyone to his advantage. So far, he had gotten away with it. So far.

21

A light snow covered the ground as Carter Egan carefully backed her car out of the garage. The moon was still lighting the sky, casting its pure reflection upon glistening white snow flakes. Any other morning, Carter would have lingered to take in the beauty of this early morning postcard scene. Today, though, Carter was in a hurry. Her media alert was still in full swing, but the large volume hospital orders continued to drain their blood inventory. They simply could not keep ahead of the demand. Kiley Matson said that this was as close to being "bloodless" as the center had come in a long, long while.

Dr. Silvers had called Carter to his office just before she left work the previous night to share his concerns with her.

"We are being drained at an alarming rate, Carter. Our county hospital orders are up 120 percent from this time last year. Our reserve inventory simply cannot keep up with the demand." The doctor was no longer the angry, sarcastic person who jumped her bones two days ago during the managers' meeting.

"I am afraid we may be in for a run by our competition, United Components, to take over our territory. If our hospitals ever see us as being unable to fill their orders, their loyalty would be gone in an instant, and United Components would have their foot in the door so fast your head would spin," the good doctor said to his believing director of public relations. She did not know that before each emergency appeal, Silvers called the pathologists at his larger hospitals, telling them that the center was "simply helping the blood supply along" and that they should not be alarmed at the public appeal. "We have plenty of blood and can most definitely fill your orders," he quietly told them.

"This is the nature of our business, Carter," Silvers continued. "We can never rest on our past abilities to gather blood. We have to be constantly going after new donors if we are to keep the competition out of our territory. We're going to need to leave the media alert on for just a few more days. If we can just get to the 1500 level and stay there for at least a week, we can back off from our shortage call."

His words seemed genuine, and once again Carter saw a side of the medical director that she really liked. He was warm, caring, and appreciative of her efforts. He told her over and over how great a job she was doing with the media.

Silvers knew exactly how to push a person's hot buttons. He could be charming and speak with a certain eloquence to the cause of blood banking. He had a gift—a gift he used when he needed something. What he needed from Carter was her ability to haul the media out of their warm beds and into his lobby. Their support was worth their weight in gold to his blood center. He needed to have this heartfelt talk with Carter tonight. He had recognized how harshly he had treated her the other day. He could not afford to make an enemy out of Carter. He needed her. He knew enough about his public relations director to know she could be won over once again with just such a conversation, sprinkled with concern and appreciation. Carter was responding exactly as he knew she would.

The parking lot was almost empty when she arrived. The wind was blowing the white flakes about with enough energy to make her walk to the back door a chilly one.

The blood center could be spooky when it was empty. The hallways in the lower levels were dimly lit, and shadows pitched unfriendly figures up the walls as Carter climbed the stairs to reach her second floor office.

She had come in early this morning to finish up a new batch of press releases. With luck she could get them typed and ready to be faxed by the time Shelly got to work. The fax machine had made communication with the media just that much easier. The shrill ring of her telephone startled her.

"Carter Egan," she answered as always, not quite sure who could possibly be on the other end at this hour of the morning.

"You're a nice lady, but you are being used," the strange voice replied.

"I beg your pardon?"

"We're not short of blood. Just check out the back refrigerator."

"What are you talking about? What back refrigerator?"

"We'll leave a key out for you. Just go to the cabinet in the distribution storeroom and look under the plant that sits on top of it. The key will unlock the door in the back storage room. You will see what we're talking about. It's all there."

The voice on the other end was gone. Carter suddenly felt frightened. Who was it? How did they know she was in her office at such an early hour? Was someone in the building with her right now? If so, who?" Question after question stormed through Carter's mind. The voice had been heavily distorted. Carter couldn't tell if it were male or female. It had an almost electric tone. The voice sounded manipulated—the way you hear a voice on television being distorted when the station is deliberately masking it to protect the person's identity.

Anyone who has ever received an anonymous phone call could relate to the uneasy feeling Carter was now experiencing. Was this message on the up and up? Should she do as the caller instructed and seek out the key that would open a refrigerator she did not even know existed? For several minutes, Carter sat at her desk making no movement at all. Something inside seemed to take hold of her, pulling her body into motion.

"Let's just get this silly game over with," Carter reasoned as she decided to face the mystery given to her.

"I'll bet Kiley is behind this and is trying to pull another one of his jokes on me," Carter said out loud as she started down the stairs that would take her to the ground floor level and the distribution area. The Center seemed deathly still as Carter made her way down the hallway. She opened the door to the shipping area; no one was present. Walking past the long row of glass storage refrigerators, Carter was disturbed by what she saw. The glass coolers were nearly empty. Only a few bags of processed A-type blood were present on the shelves.

"My God, if this is all the blood we have left after our last run, we're in deep trouble," Carter thought as she continued walking toward the storage room. The door was unlocked. Entering, Carter's eyes searched the dimly lit room for the cabinet with the plant on top. Why anyone would put a plant in this room struck Carter as extremely odd, as there wasn't enough light or fresh air for anything living to survive in this room. But to the right of the door was an old gray metal cabinet with a plant in a clay pot sitting on top. The healthy green foliage was a dead giveaway. Someone had placed this potted plant in this area on purpose. It was far too healthy looking to live here permanently. As Carter lifted the obviously-placed decoy, she found a tarnished key resting beneath it. Finding the key scared Carter. Someone was playing mind games with her. But who, and why? Carter's eyes searched for the door that the key was meant to unlock, but there was no door. The room was square and filled with what looked like overflow file cabinets. A sudden noise from the other room caused Carter's heart to jump. Standing perfectly still,

Carter waited for someone to enter the small storage room. Nothing happened. The room was small enough for Carter to make it to the doorway in four quick steps. Pushing the metal door slightly ajar, she saw Terry Milo, one of the fleet drivers, shoving a cart filled with ice coolers across the room's uneven tile floor. Her movements caught Terry's attention.

"You scared me for a second, Mrs. Egan," Terry stated as he stopped midway to his destination. "I didn't know anyone else was here this early."

"I just wanted to get a jump on the day, Terry. I was looking for some old files," Carter replied. "I guess I'm not going to find them in here, though."

"Well there's not much kept in there anymore," he said as he motioned to the storage room Carter had just exited.

Terry went on with what he was doing. Carter walked to the doorway exiting into the hall. Where was this back storage room? Were there really hidden refrigerators? The day shift was now coming on duty, and the center did not seem quite so menacing. Looking down the hall, Carter's eyes searched for something she had never noticed before. There was nothing in that direction, she thought, walking back into the distribution area feeling somewhat stumped. Carter once again searched for a door. Convinced that she was now being used for someone's folly, the p.r. director turned to leave. Suddenly, her eyes focused on an area that a person would tend to overlook as separate from the distribution area. Because it was connected to the shipping area with a glass door, the immunohematology reference laboratory oftentimes was overlooked. It was a small area and its walls on one side were the glass walls of the Center's main storage refrigerators, which could be opened from either side. This reference lab provided assistance to member hospitals encountering patients with difficult-to-match blood types. It also housed an inventory of frozen "rare" blood for use in Hamilton County or elsewhere upon demand. This small lab had limited access. There was a door on the far left side of the reference laboratory that Carter had never noticed before. The doorway was not standard in appearance. Double panel doors were cut into the wall with no wood outlining their frame. A small lock hung down from the center of the silver hinges connected in the center of both doors. Carter pushed the glass door open and quickly walked around the high bench lab tables to the far left-hand corner of the room where she had spotted the overlooked door. The key felt warm in the palm of her hand as she slipped it into the waiting lock. Carter instinctively turned to see if anyone else was in the area. She was still alone. Slipping the lock free, Carter pushed open the right door panel just enough to allow some light in the darkened area she was about to enter. Reaching in with her left arm, Carter's hand found a light switch on the wall. Stepping inside and closing the door behind her, Carter quickly moved the single square button upwards flooding the area with light. The large narrow room was cold. Shiny stainless steel doors about two feet away stared back at Carter. There were six, floor-to-ceiling double doors in all. Carter moved to the double unit directly in front of her. The large handle was easily pressed downward. Opening the doors, Carter's eyes narrowed as the inventory of chilled blood was revealed. The units were clearly marked with shipping tags for out-of-state destinations. There were hundreds of bags of blood, all stacked very carefully in their chilled holding place. It was hard to estimate how many bags were in each refrigerator. Carter proceeded to open each of the double doors. The same sight greeted her each time. Before she could take an inventory count, Carter heard a noise to her left where she saw another exit for the first time. It was clear someone was coming in. Carter's instincts told her to hide. There wasn't enough time to make it back to the center door where she had entered. Instead, she squeezed her body between the wall and the last cooler unit on the right-hand side of the narrow square room.

"Somebody left the light on again."

Carter recognized Terry Milo's deep baritone voice.

"Yeah, well, we're not their baby sitters." Carter thought this voice belonged to Herk Golden, the chief of the mobile fleet.

"I'll be goddamned! Somebody left these doors unlocked," Herk exclaimed as he discovered the interior panel doors slightly ajar. Terry Milo said nothing but went about his business of loading his ice coolers with the daily shipment of blood. The opening of the refrigerator doors caused Carter to stop breathing each time a new door was unlatched and the two men edged closer to her. Together, Herk and Terry quickly and methodically removed the stored blood from their secret holding units. Soon, Terry and Herk's parked blood center station wagons were fully loaded for their first airport runs and outreach stations. Herk Golden was pissed as he waved Terry on. He was going to be delayed in his routine this morning.

"Matson is going to hear from me on this," he swore under his breath as he headed for Kiley's office after relocking the interior door of the storage area that he had found unlocked. Kiley's door was still closed. Checking the handle to see if Kiley was in yet, the locked door angered Herk even more.

"Goddamned executives. They all keep bankers' hours." Herk scribbled a note on a yellow sticky pad that he found on top of the nearest desk and pasted it to Kiley's door.

"Tell your lazy-ass staff to turn off the storage room lights after they leave and to lock the door. I found everything open this morning. Hell of a way to run an operation." Herk did not sign the note. Kiley would know who the handwriting belonged to.

Carter had not moved since the lights went off. The sound of the interior door being locked had almost paralyzed her. Was she trapped? The room was pitch dark and terribly cold. She would have to use her memory to find that wall switch. In just a few minutes, Carter's fingers again flipped up the plastic wall switch and light flooded the room. The thought of being trapped in a secret refrigerated storage area never crossed her mind when she came to work earlier this morning. The exit door had a roll bar across it. As her hands grasped the cold silver metal bar, she prayed it would open from the inside without a key. Her instincts were right as sunlight and cold fresh air greeted Carter as she quickly stepped outside. The events of the last thirty minutes had truly shaken Carter Egan. The caller was obviously right. She was being used. The blood center was not short of blood. There were thousands of units in those hidden refrigerators. They had plenty of blood. What was going on? Why were they doing this?

Carter walked around the back of the building. The morning wind had whipped small piles of deep snow across the sidewalks. Turning the corner, she quickly found herself near the employees' entrance on the ground floor level. This was the same door she had entered earlier that morning. Warm air greeted her as she stepped inside the steam-heated building. Her shoes were covered with snow.

"What brings you down here so early, Carter?"

Carter clearly was startled by Kiley Matson's voice.

"Oh, I wanted to get an early start on some press releases," Carter covered.

"Well, we certainly are down to rock bottom. Our late run has drained us," Kiley stated as his eyes studied Carter's appearance.

"Where's your coat, lady? It isn't summertime anymore," Kiley questioned.

"I just ran out to my car again for my briefcase. I thought I left it there, but I guess I left it at home," Carter returned, trying hard to cover herself and her morning activities.

"Got time for a cup of coffee?"

"Not really. I've got to get busy on those releases," Carter stalled. "I'll see you later at flash." With that, Carter headed up the stairs toward her office. The morning had left her shaken. Something was going on. Something she didn't want to be a part of. The key in her hand felt warm. She had been clutching it for the last thirty minutes, pressing it so hard to her palm that it had left a deep red impression.

Carter sat down at her desk in a state of shock. The worst thing that could happen to a person in public relations is to find out that what she believed in and pitched to the public and the media, was fraudulent. Calling false blood shortages was fraudulent in Carter's mind. The sudden ring of her phone interrupted her chain of thought.

"Carter Egan."

"Carter. Is that you? I can barely hear you." The voice of her husband flooded her senses.

"Patrick. Oh, Patrick. I'm so glad to hear from you," a stunned Carter replied to the warm voice of her husband.

"Carter, I'm. . ." The line crackled with static. She couldn't make out a single word her husband had said after he called her name.

"Patrick, I can't hear you," Carter spoke loudly into the phone.

The line was now completely severed, and the steady hum of the dial tone rang in her ear.

"Oh, please God—let him call me back."

For the next fifteen minutes Carter sat with her hand on the phone. The call was not to be forthcoming.

"Hey, boss. Can I get you a cup of coffee?" Shelly asked as she stuck her head in the doorway.

"Yes, please."

In a few minutes, Shelly was back with a steaming cup of black coffee.

"Shelly, can I ask you a question?"

"Sure, boss. What's up," the ever positive Shelly answered.

"I want this to remain just between you and me, Shelly. Okay?"

"Well, yes. I guess so," Shelly answered not sure what her boss was leading up to.

"Have you ever heard any rumors about false blood shortages being called since you've worked at the center?"

Shelly's eyes looked away for just a moment.

"Yes. Yes, I have." Carter waited for Shelly to go on.

"Mostly from the driver pool and a few techs in reference."

"What have the drivers said?"

"Just stuff. Stuff like they didn't believe we had any such thing as a real shortage because they were delivering too many units to the airport when we were supposed to be down and out."

"I see." There was a silence.

"Have you ever heard any talk from the people who work in Kiley's area?" Carter pressed.

"Nobody talks in Kiley's area, Carter. But then—anything can happen at this place. I need my job, so I see nothing and hear nothing. I probably shouldn't have answered your question, but I wouldn't want to see you go through what happened to. . ." Shelly stopped.

"What happened to Anna Cable?"

Shelly was now obviously very uncomfortable with the way this conversation was going, but she liked her boss and honestly did not want to see her end up the way Anna had.

"I don't know exactly what happened to Anna, Carter. Rumors fly so hot and heavy in this place you don't know what to believe half the time. All I know is that Anna found out something and she went to Mr. Bryan. Next thing we knew, she was gone. They called me and asked me to get her coat and purse. They wouldn't even let her come back to her office."

"But you have no idea what it might have been that she found out?"

"No, I don't. She took her morning report sheets with her. That's all I know. Mr. Bryan came up that afternoon and went through all her drawers and emptied everything out in a cardboard box. I just thought it was Anna's personal stuff. I haven't heard from Anna since the day she left. I've called her a couple of times, but she hasn't returned my calls. I heard she was having trouble finding work in Hamilton."

Carter's face displayed the stress she was now feeling.

"Carter, you've done a real good job for the blood center. There's so much you've brought to us we didn't have before—I mean the brochures and the way you treat the field reps—like they really matter. I would hate to lose you as a boss. Whatever is wrong with this center can't come close to the good we do for people. That's what keeps me here—the good we do for sick people who need blood." Shelly's words were sincere. She liked her boss and did not want to lose her. Shelly, with only a high school education, had worked her way up the ladder into a good secretarial position at the center, a position she did not want to lose by sticking her nose in places where it didn't belong. Lots of staff knew things at the blood center, but nobody ever talked about the secrets in a public way. The conversation had gone as far as it could go. Carter recognized it and immediately changed the subject directing Shelly to another task. Carter pulled the press releases from her printer and placed them in her holding file. As Shelly was leaving, she spotted the releases and asked her boss if she wanted them faxed out this morning.

"No, Shelly. I'll let you know when and if we have to go to the media again."

It was, by now, time for the morning flash meeting. Carter gathered her things and headed down the hall toward the conference room. As the other directors took their seats, Carter noticed that Elizabeth Monroe and Bertha White were again absent.

Kiley Matson was standing outside the doorway talking intensely to Dr. Silvers. The conversation seemed to be heated with Silvers shaking his finger in Kiley's face. Kiley didn't back away from the doctor. Instead, he lowered his voice and leaned in to just a few inches away from Silvers's left ear. Whatever Kiley said backed the angry doctor down and the tension of the moment cleared. Preston's appearance in the doorway helped steer them both inside. Kiley began his morning report as always with his usual glib remarks. His tone of voice became serious when he reached the daily inventory stats.

"I'm afraid we are still in a terrible bind this morning. We are down to all but a few units of blood. Our O's are completely depleted. We couldn't even fill our late-night runs, let alone think about filling this mornings orders. Carter, we are going to need to keep you on the airwaves."

Carter couldn't believe what she was hearing. What was Kiley doing here with this kind of a report? She had just witnessed thousands of units of blood being loaded into the center's vans, and there were still hundreds of units left in those back storage refrigerators.

Carter was savvy enough not to show any emotion at this point. A game was being played here, and Carter did not know all the rules. These next few minutes were very important for Carter. She had to present a calm profile right now. Too much was at stake.

Carter smiled and calmly nodded at Kiley. Nothing in her appearance gave way to the turmoil that was churning inside her. For the first time, Carter really looked at her morning report sheet with documentation of the blood center's daily inventory. Kiley had set up the sheet to give a total inventory of blood types, whole blood and packed cells shipped, platelets (random & pheresed), cryoprecipitates, and fresh-frozen plasma. He also included the daily scheduled blood drive totals with the actual blood donations secured for each day. Branches were also accounted for in this report. At the bottom of the sheet, Kiley documented the number of apheresis donors and units drawn from those procedures. This morning, Carter noticed a single typed R on the same line as the cryoprecipitate inventory. The number listed this morning was 1100. Total units available in distribution by all types totaled 250. Carter had a question.

"Kiley, can you tell me what the R is for on this line?" she asked pointing to the R on her report sheet.

Kiley looked a little off balance.

"Yeah, well that's our reserve."

"Is that our cryoprecipitate reserve?"

"Yes," Kiley replied.

"I didn't realize we could garner that big of an inventory in cryo's," Carter continued pressing for more information.

"It's a frozen product, Carter. We can store it." Gerald Preston added.

Michael Bryan took out a cigarette, a nervous habit during a nervous moment. Questions were not usually fielded off this report. The other directors present sat still as if waiting to be dismissed. Kiley did just that.

"Okay, boys and girls, we've got work to do and time's a-wasting. Carter, let me know if you are going to hold any interviews in the distribution area. I want us to look real pretty for those cameras." With those words spoken, Kiley made his usual speedy exit.

Carter had made up her mind. It was what she had to do.

"Dr. Silvers, Mr. Preston, and Michael, may I have a word with you?" Carter asked of the chief executives. Dr. Crane remained seated even though Carter had not asked her to stay.

In a few minutes, the other directors were gone from the room. Gerald Preston had not taken his eyes off Carter. Silvers sat in his chair going through his morning mail. He did not expect what was coming.

"I need to address an issue that has just come to my attention."

"Yes, Carter. What is on your mind," a very interested Gerald Preston asked.

"Dr. Silvers, do we in fact have a real blood shortage?" Carter's question was direct and to the point.

"Of course we have a blood shortage. I just addressed this issue with you yesterday, Carter. Why would you question me again?"

"Because this morning I received a call telling me the whereabouts of a certain refrigerator." Carter placed the old tarnished key on the table in front of her. Michael inhaled deeply from his cigarette. Silvers, Crane, and Preston stared intently at Carter. The room was deathly quiet.

"I used this key this morning and to my surprise, I found several refrigerators filled with blood—hundreds of units of blood, all tagged for out-of-state shipments."

"Carter, my dear. I'm afraid you are confused about what you saw," Preston stated in his best fatherly voice.

"How could I be confused about what I saw? I was just told by Kiley this morning that we are almost out of blood—I saw enough blood in those refrigerators to last us two weeks or better. What are we pulling here? And why are you lying to me?" Anger was present in the public relations director's voice.

"Of course we have a reserve supply, Carter. It's our business to operate in advance. It's how we've been able to keep our territory clean all these years. You don't see United Components in here, do you? We get our hospitals the blood they need and we do it without a hitch," Dr. Crane forcefully replied.

"We do it by calling false blood shortages, Dr. Crane." Carter shot back.

"Now wait a minute, Carter. Before we get to a level we can't control, let's talk about this," Preston quickly stated.

"Of course we keep a reserve supply. We need to resource share a certain portion of our blood draws. This makes good business sense. Those dollars allow us to keep making improvements at our center and to hire adequate staff to handle the operations side of this business. Blood banking is a business, Carter."

"I understand business, Mr. Preston. I can't understand how we can mislead our public in such a manner."

"We're not misleading our public, Carter," Silvers responded. "We are not the ones to blame here. If you want to blame someone, blame the donors who sit on their asses and forget to come forward on a regular basis. Do you think we'd be in the shape we're in if everyone that was eligible to donate blood did? Hell no. It's not our fault we have to prompt the public to come in here. It's their fault," Silvers concluded.

"If everyone who was eligible to donate blood did, the average person would only have to donate blood every five years. That's the real tragedy here, Carter." Dr. Crane added.

"I understand all the theories, doctors. But my question has yet to be answered. Are we, or are we not, calling false blood shortages?" Carter was pushing for a straight answer.

"Yes, Carter. I guess you could say we are calling false shortages." Michael Bryan's words were stunning.

Preston looked at his assistant with intense interest. Where was Michael going with his answer? Preston knew Michael well enough to know that he was not as dumb at this moment as the other two executives now thought he was.

"We've been given an enormous task of supplying hospitals out of our area. The NAABC called us several months ago and asked us to take part in a resource sharing cooperative. We live in an area that has tremendous support from its donor population in spite of what Dr. Silvers just said. Our donors do give more than their fair share. And for the next few months, this assignment is going to hit us hard. We have to produce an outlandish number of type O red blood cells if we are going to keep our coastal hospitals afloat. We have an obligation here. There is a shortage of blood. That's not a lie. Perhaps we are stretching it a bit with our own community, but there is a shortage and it's not false. I take full responsibility for not telling you about our situation earlier. I can fully understand how you must have felt this morning." Michael's words softened Carter's doubts. She desperately wanted to believe. Above anyone else in this room, Carter clung to the hope that Michael Bryan would not lie to her. For one brief moment, Carter was ready to accept this new information and go on, when something ever so subtle changed her mind. It was the sight of a slight smile flashing across Dr. Crane's face. Something inside told Carter she had just learned more than she ever wanted to know.

"I see," Carter finally replied. She would have to play their game if she was going to gain time to think this situation through.

"Well, of course that does explain. . ." Carter was interrupted at this point by Dr. Silvers.

"Carter, of course we should have told you about this earlier. I also blame myself for not sharing this information with you."

Preston rose to his feet. "Carter, I'm sorry this incident has so upset you, but I hope you can see we mean no harm here. We just have a job to do. We have an obligation to the public that we serve."

Preston's words soured Carter's stomach. Is this what happened to Anna Cable. Had she too stumbled onto this obvious fraud? How long has this type of operation been going on? Question after question raged through Carter's mind. She stood and headed for the doorway, turning just as she got to the entrance.

"I'm sorry if I came across in the wrong manner. I just didn't understand the situation," Carter said, feeling the acid build up in her mouth. She could not bring herself to look at Michael. Michael immediately caught this, but did not let on to the others.

After Carter had left the room, the three executives adjourned to Preston's large office.

"Do you think she believes us?" Silvers asked.

"Yes, I think Michael handled the situation beautifully. She has a trust with him and he handled it just fine," Preston stated as he patted his protégé on the back with a job-well-done gesture. Dr. Crane smiled and looked directly at Bryan.

"For a moment there, Michael, I thought you had gone off your rocker. You handled it well. I have to give it to you." It was the first time in a long while that Dr. Alice Crane had any kind words for Michael Bryan.

Silvers seemed content with the reassurance and confidence the others had in the situation.

"Who in the hell do you think supplied her with that key?" Silvers asked.

"I'm not sure. Maybe the same person that supplied Anna Cable with her insight," Dr. Crane added. Preston and Bryan did not respond. They had no idea who had tried to tip off the public relations director. It was a dangerous situation for them. Someone had far more information than they should. It was a situation that needed attention. Someone was working against them and obviously had an inside track at supplying information. Herk Golden would need another bonus from the executive kitty. If anyone could find the informant, Herk could.

When Silvers and Crane left Preston's office, Michael stayed behind.

"Jerry, I'm not so sure Carter really believed me. I thought I got to her, but yet, when she left the room she avoided eye contact with me and that's not like her. I think we might need to be careful here."

"Michael, why don't you take Carter to lunch. See if you can feel her out. I think you're wrong. I think she does believe you. Michael nodded and headed for Preston's office door.

"Michael, that was very nicely handled. My compliments to you. You really are learning quickly. Maybe I can retire quicker than I thought." Preston smiled at his young charge. Michael nodded and returned Preston's smile, closing the door behind him. Gerald Preston swiveled his desk chair around to face the large windows behind him. His eyes took in the snowy winter view. The loneliness of his life once again crept into his thoughts. Grace Tende and her beautiful face popped into his mind. Things could be so different for him if only Grace would give him a chance. Funny about life, he mused as he lit one of his expensive cigars. Money really can't buy you everything. Power and material things, yes. Money was good for those things. But money had its limits. This he knew for a fact.

After Silvers left Preston's office, he and Crane had shared another private conversation. Carter was not going to be allowed to turn into another Anna Cable catch-us-with-our-pants-down fiasco. If Carter were now suspicious of their operation, certain precautions would be required. Silvers wanted her watched. Herk Golden had just the man for the job.

Seated once again at her desk, Carter knew she only had a certain amount of time to make a decision. As a professional, Carter had three choices. She could stay at her job and look the other way. She could turn them in and perhaps never work in her field again, or she could quit and take her secrets with her. Obviously, her predecessor was fired for knowing too much. But Anna Cable had not come forward with any accusations to the public or the media. Carter wondered what if she were wrong? What if Michael were telling her the truth? Carter's temples were pounding with pressure. There were just so many "what if's" involved. Taking the situation apart and analyzing it brought little comfort. Carter found herself very short on facts. Were any real laws or regulations broken by the calling of false blood shortages? No. The whole situation was really ethical. The blood center was "crying wolf" in regard to needing blood. Nevertheless, the blood was going to people who needed it, regardless of whether they lived in Hamilton county or New York City. No laws were broken by such actions. Dr. Crane's statement about people only having to donate blood every five years if those eligible to donate would, kept running through Carter's mind. Was all this caused by the very public the center was in business to serve? Could it be avoided? Could the blood center get more people out to donate blood without painting pictures of fatal consequences? Questions that she had not addressed before now surfaced in Carter's mind. What about the holiday appeals? Were they for real?

Carter's memory recalled two conversations that had taken place shortly after she started work at the blood center. Dr. Silvers told Carter to mark her yearly calendar one week in advance of all approaching holidays.

"We will need to issue press releases with strong reminders for the public to donate blood. This is just standard procedure, Carter. People stop thinking about donating blood whenever a holiday rolls around. We have to jar their civic duty a little bit. Otherwise, we could find ourselves short of blood."

And yet, now that she thought about it, she distinctly remembered Kiley Matson complaining about his part-time job at Seton Memorial.

Kiley worked as a med tech in the operating room area. Part of his job responsibilities were to start iv's for surgery patients. The hospital had cut everyone's hours back with the approaching Fourth of July holiday, keeping only a skeleton crew available for emergencies. Kiley had made a big deal out of telling everyone present at the morning flash meeting how dead it was to work in a hospital over a holiday. His seniority usually put him at the top of the list to work at Seton during such times, if he wanted to. Although the holiday pay was good, Kiley said he had passed on working. "There's no action," he said to the group. "It's dead on holidays. The goddamned scalpel kings don't schedule surgery on public holidays!" he ranted, "They're off skiing in Vail or lying on their asses on some tropical beach with their families, leaving the poor scrubs to sit around all day hoping for some car accident to give them something to do."

Kiley's words made sense to Carter. Hospitals as a rule do not schedule major surgeries over a holiday period. The surgeons break their backs scheduling as many back-to-back surgeries as possible weeks before the holiday. Residents and on-call docs are left to handle the emergencies should there be any. Even cancer and leukemia treatments are bumped up to be scheduled either before or after a holiday. The whole goal of a hospital administration is to try and make each patient's life as close to normal as possible. Having surgery or receiving cancer treatments on a holiday does not fall under the heading of normal. Records would show that the use of blood in a hospital over a holiday period is usually down, way down.

"Holidays are also part of this facade," Carter reasoned as she thought through so many different images that she was creating for the public.

Who would ever question any of this? Hamilton Regional was not the only blood center putting out urgent appeals for blood. It happens on a regular basis all across the country. Holiday appeals had become a way of life for the blood center industry. The media never questioned the need, and the public, hearing the appeals, responded in a charitable way. It was a clever rub. It all went together like a wink and a smile.

Carter was drained. Looking at her wall clock she was amazed to see it was only 9:30. It seemed like it should be later—much later.

"Carter, have you forgotten we have an assembly this morning?" Shelly asked as she held open Carter's door.

"What assembly?" Carter replied trying to shake off her deep thoughts.

"We got a memo late yesterday afternoon. I think it has to do with the settlement of the lawsuit," Shelly replied noticing the depressed state of her boss.

"I guess I haven't had time to read my morning memos," Carter covered as she rose from her desk and joined Shelly in the walk to the large street level conference room where all such employee-type gatherings took place.

The room was packed to overflow. The four executives stood in the front of the room waving to the staff to crowd as many people in as possible. Finally, when the room could hold no more, Gerald Preston began.

"We want to thank you all for the wonderful job you have done during this especially trying time. As you may know, the medical panel selected to hear the evidence concerning Taylor Addison's lawsuit ruled in our favor. There was no negligence to be found on our part." Preston's words were interrupted by the clapping of the gathered staff. Smiling broadly, he continued.

"We especially want to extend our thanks to Carter Egan for the marvelous way she represented the center during this trying period with the media," another clapping interruption. Carter felt flushed as she found herself being congratulated by fellow staff members standing close to her.

"There was never a question we wouldn't be found innocent of all charges leveled against us," Dr. Silvers added taking the spotlight away from Preston.

"We are a proud blood center with a firm history of excellence. That has not changed. No one has the right to tarnish our record—not if we continue to do our job. I know this has been a difficult time for all of us, but it is over. In a few days no one will even remember the name of Taylor Addison. . ."

"But we will," interrupted Michael Bryan, "because Taylor Addison represents the public we serve—the public we must do our very best to ensure a safe blood supply for." The room was once again filled with applause. Silvers shot Michael a dark look. He did not like to be upstaged by anyone. Preston smiled broadly. He had just seen his assistant once again save the center from embarrassment. It also pleased Preston to see Silvers put in his place by someone other than himself. The meeting was formally adjourned by Dr. Crane who did not offer any words of wisdom. The crowd of gathered employees lingered, talking in hushed tones amongst themselves. The news of Taylor's death had touched them as a group. It wasn't just Dr. Silvers or Gerald Preston's lawsuit; it was theirs as well. They were a part of this controversy and had all been jarred by Taylor Addison's accusations of negligence. The "not guilty" verdict lifted a dark cloud from their heads as well.

Grace Tende caught Carter's attention. The two friends walked to Grace's ground floor office. "That was short and sweet," Grace replied as she settled in her desk chair. Carter walked to the window and did not reply.

"Hey, are you okay, Carter? You don't seem yourself."

Carter still did not answer causing Grace to repeat her question.

"Are you all right, Carter?"

"It's so pretty out there this morning, Grace. Snow always makes me think of Patrick—he really gets into it."

Grace assumed that Carter was really missing her husband this morning. But was this the only reason for her distant, almost odd behavior?

"I'm not a lover of snow. It's cold and wet and frankly, I prefer warm temperatures and dry roads," Grace kiddingly replied. "How's your schedule today? Do you have time for a quick bite of lunch around one o'clock?" Grace asked.

Carter again did not answer.

"Carter, what's wrong?"

"Grace, why do you work here?"

"What?"

"Why do you stay here?"

"I don't know. It's a decent job. We've got good benefits, and I guess you could say I'm comfortable. Why do most women stay put in a job, Carter?"

"Grace, there are some things going on here that are not right."

"Like what, Carter?"

"Like calling false blood shortages when we really have plenty of blood."

Grace did not respond. Her eyes searched Carter's face.

"How did you find this out, Carter?"

Grace's answer took Carter back. There was no surprise, no questioning in her response.

"Are you aware of what goes on here, Grace? Do you know we call these fake shortages and pump people up around holidays with scary media releases just to get extra blood into our center so we can send it out the back door?"

Grace was not one to mince words. "Carter, I've suspected such goings-on for some time. I have no real proof, but. . ."

"If you suspected it, Grace, why didn't you do something about it?"

"Carter, my suspicions are just that—suspicions. And they are only recent—ever since Anna Cable left. She had tried to tell me something on the morning she was dismissed, but we didn't get a chance to really talk. It all happened so fast. I was told by Preston later that morning that there was a problem with Anna, of a personal nature, and that they had come to a mutual parting of the ways. Apparently, according to him, Anna had fallen in love with Michael Bryan and was becoming a problem. He had no choice but to settle it as gracefully as could be done under the circumstances. Anna and I did not get to have an exit interview. It all happened so fast."

"What do you think Anna was trying to tell you?"

"I'm not sure. She had some reports in her hand, but all she had a chance to say was something about errors and evil men. None of it made any sense at the time. She was terribly stressed."

"Do you believe this is the real reason why Anna Cable left, Grace?"

"I don't know. Michael Bryan is a handsome man and plenty of the hired help here have huge crushes on him. But, as Anna's direct supervisor, Michael could have—well, it could have become a very nasty situation for all involved—especially if she was bothering him at home and doing some of the other things I was told she was into."

"Did Anna Cable ever give you any reason to believe she was doing such a thing, Grace?"

Grace thought about the question before answering.

"No, Carter. In fact, Anna Cable was just not the type in my opinion. She was too much of a professional. But I'm not a shrink, Carter. I don't know if Anna was making a nuisance of herself with Michael or not."

"Grace, I just found positive proof that this center is engaged in unethical conduct."

"What kind of unethical conduct?"

"We are lying to the media and the public when we tell them we are short of blood. I can physically show you thousands of units of blood right now—all tagged and waiting to be shipped. And yet, you heard Kiley tell me this morning we could not even fill our morning orders to the hospitals, and that I needed to get out another appeal to our media."

"Yes, I heard him. Can you definitely prove we have plenty of blood, Carter?"

"Can you come with me right now? I can show you proof to back up my words."

Grace nodded her head and the two women exited her office. Walking at a brisk pace, the two directors entered the reference laboratory.

"The refrigerators are back here, Carter quietly stated to Grace who was following close behind. Carter had slipped the key into her suit pocket earlier in the morning. Reaching inside her pocket, the small tarnished object was quickly recovered and inserted into the hanging lock. The two techs who were sitting at the high bench tables all but ignored the two lay persons intruding their territory.

Carter was not prepared for what was to happen. The key did not undo the lock.

"What's wrong?" Grace asked.

"This key doesn't work—It can't be," Carter replied, still struggling with the key in the lock.

"Can I help you ladies with something?" Kiley Matson asked, scaring the two women with his unexpected presence.

Seeing Kiley caused Carter to lose her composure for just a moment.

"I'm afraid you are both going to have to leave this area. You need to have on protected garb—you know the code rules, Grace. This area is restricted to all but select personnel unless you have some kind of business in this lab?"

The two women did not say a word and left the area with Kiley staring after them. The look on his face was one Carter had seen before but only when he was dealing with Dr. Silvers.

"Grace, I don't know how they did it, but they changed that lock since early this morning. I used this key then and it opened that lock."

Grace did not say a word but simply nodded her head. Carter followed Grace back to her office. Closing the door, Grace turned toward Carter.

"Don't bother to ask me if I believe you because it would be a waste of words. I do. You saw something this morning that obviously scared them enough to change the lock on that door. To be honest, Carter, I have not been down in that area since the remodeling three years ago. As I recall from the designs that I saw, extra refrigerator units were designed to fit in that location. I was told they abandoned that part of the construction due to the cost of the cooling installation. Nobody ever goes in that area."

The drivers go in that area, Grace. They load those vans every morning."

"Carter, you can bet your boots, Silvers and Preston know we were at that lock by now. If we're calling false shortages, Kiley must be in on it. He controls our inventory and acts as our agent of sale."

Carter suddenly remembered Kiley's and Silvers's heated exchange earlier this morning outside the conference room door. She also remembered Herk cussing when he discovered the interior door unlocked. Herk must have told Kiley about it, and the change of locks was done shortly after that. It all fell into place.

"Kiley is not going to let his empire be threatened, Carter. He wields too much power to let it go easily," the personnel director stated with years of observation to back up her instincts.

"I nailed them on calling false shortages this morning, Grace, after our flash meeting. I even showed them the key."

"Who did you talk to, Carter?"

"Silvers, Crane, Preston, and Michael," Carter answered.

"How did you leave that meeting?"

"Michael told me we were involved with a cooperative effort to help supply our coastal hospitals. It was all supposed to be hush-hush. I pretended to believe them. I guess that's how we left it—they thought I believed."

"Michael told you this story?" Grace seemed genuinely surprised by Michael's involvement in such a cover-up. She could believe Preston, Silvers, and Dr. Crane were involved, but for some reason, Michael Bryan was a surprise partner to this dark trio. Grace felt a sudden surge of disappointment. Carter and Grace spent the next thirty minutes devising a plan that would buy them time. Grace wielded some power with the executives. She knew a lot more than she should. If she could use her inside knowledge to keep them in check, she just might be able to figure a way out of all this for herself and Carter. At one o'clock, Carter left the center for lunch. At one-thirty, Grace Tende would follow. Both their departures were recorded. From now on, so would their every move. At this blood center, only a select few were allowed to have secrets.

22

It was a little after three when Madison Boggs called again for Carter Egan. She had phoned earlier but was told Carter had just left for lunch. Their conversation began casually. The two women had genuinely come to like one another. Earned respect was key in their professions. Both had worked hard to gain a reputation as a straight shooter who came to work prepared. Madison did not straddle fences—you knew exactly where you stood with her. Carter appreciated this courtesy, as not all media personalities were this way. Some will smile and act accommodating. But then when their story airs, your statements come out scrambled. The media can manipulate news in their handy-dandy editing booths. But this was not Madison's way. The news reporter had not called Carter to chat about the time of day. She had a purpose—a very direct purpose. It did not take her long to get to the point.

"Carter, I have to level with you. We received a call this morning intimating that you guys were not short of blood as your emergency appeal states. We were told you were shipping out very large orders. Is any of this true? Can you verify your inventory?"

This question, coming on top of everything else that had come to Carter's attention earlier, really shook her. Her hesitation confirmed the truth for Madison.

"Why are you asking for media support, Carter, if you have more than enough blood?"

"Madison, I want to speak to you off the record. Can we do that?" Carter asked.

Carter had never asked to go off the record before. Madison's instincts told her that Carter was on the edge of something. If she gave this p.r. director enough rope, she might just get more than she bargained for.

"Sure, Carter. What's on your mind?"

"Madison, I don't know who is calling you, but I do know that I can't tell you anything right now. If you run with a story like this, you will definitely hurt the blood center."

"Carter, if the blood center is not doing anything wrong, why won't you just answer my question?"

"It isn't that simple, Madison. There are so many things going on right now."

"What's going on right now, Carter?"

"I can't tell you anything, Madison. If I could, I would. But right now it's all such a mess."

"Carter, can you meet me for lunch this week?"

"I'm not sure."

"Why not?"

"I just can't right now—it wouldn't. . ." Carter did not finish her sentence. She was afraid she had said far more than she should have. Madison Boggs was a reporter. A very good reporter. Carter knew if Madison had a live body willing to come forward and face the camera with his or her accusations concerning false shortages, she would have said so in the beginning. Carter knew Madison was fishing.

"Are you afraid of something, Carter?"

"No."

"Are you hiding something?"

"Madison, I can't answer any of your questions right now."

"When can you answer my questions?"

"I need time to think some things through. It's not as easy as you. . ."

"What are you afraid of, Carter?" Madison was pushing.

"I'm not afraid."

"You sound it."

"You're mistaken, Madison. I'm fine."

"Listen, Carter, if you're in a jam down there, I can help you. All I need is a paper trail and your statement verifying what's going on. I can keep you off the camera. We can disguise your identity. If the center is pulling crap, the public has a right to know about it."

"Madison, I have to go. I have a meeting."

"How much time do you need, Carter?"

"I'm not sure, Madison. But if you just give me some time, I promise I will call you."

Call me, Carter."

"I will—I will."

Madison's dark eyes narrowed as she hung up the phone. She was on a fishing expedition with her shortage question. She had thought Carter would come up with some p.r. explanation, some quick "how dare you attack the center with such garbage accusations" and then launch into the usual "if people don't give blood, people are going to die statement." She didn't. Carter Egan was in trouble. But what kind of trouble Madison could only guess. The problem was—at this point, without Carter's help or someone else from the inside, she could only throw pot shots at the center. It wouldn't work. This center was surrounded by Teflon. Nothing would stick—even if it were the truth. Madison circled her calendar. She would give Carter a week. The story wasn't going anywhere without her.

Madison's call completely unnerved Carter Egan. Who was making these phone calls? Was it the same person who had called her earlier? Her lunch with Grace had at least given her someone else to turn to. Together, they might be able to gain time—and paper documentation to take to the board. The board was the key to forcing any changes in their current mode of operations, at least that's what Grace and Carter felt. As personnel director, Grace had access to most of the computer codes with the exception of Siam Qua's area. It would not be an easy assignment to print out hard copies of daily stats and shipping orders, especially with Kiley looking over her shoulder while she worked from the computer in his department area. But if she played her cards just right, she might be able to do it. Grace had also made it perfectly clear to Carter that from now on she thought the trio would be watching their every move. Kiley had surely alerted them that she and Carter were seen together in the reference lab. Perhaps curiosity had killed the cat.

"Carter, Dr. Silvers called for you while you were on the other line. He would like to see you in his office as soon as possible," Shelly informed her boss as she headed for the copy machine. The look on Shelly's face told her he had given the secretary no clue as to why he wanted to see her. This was a summons Carter had not planned on so soon.

Carter picked up several reports that were on her desk and headed out in the general direction of Silvers's office. She did not want to appear anxious. Several of the field reps were at their desks trying frantically to schedule additional blood drives on the month-end calendar. A blood shortage with full media backing gave the reps additional clout to prod businesses, previously dragging their feet, to schedule a blood drive. Guilt in full spotlight is a strong motivator.

Carter took a deep breath before knocking on Dr. Silvers's closed door. His voice beckoned her to enter.

"You wanted to see me, Dr. Silvers?"

"Yes, Carter, I did. Please come in."

Everything seemed pleasant enough at this point. For several minutes the conversation was casual. He approved Carter's latest brochure text on the Tissue Bank, and seemed genuinely pleased with Carter's outlined speech for his annual report address. As he handed her the corrected text of the annual report, Carter felt his reasons for wanting to see her were confined to simple business matters. As she was gathering her papers to leave, Silvers turned the conversation to more important matters.

"Carter, I hope you are feeling okay with all that went on this morning?"

Smiling, Carter nodded her head.

"Did you recognize the voice of the person who called you with that crap about hidden refrigerators?"

"No, Dr. Silvers, I didn't," Carter replied hoping this conversation would have a quick demise.

"I don't know where people get off trying to stir up something that is none of their business." Silvers was obviously still upset.

"I understand you and Grace were in the reference area this morning after our meeting," he continued.

"I wasn't there with Grace, Dr. Silvers. She came into the lab at the same time I did. She said she was looking for Bertha White."

"I see. Well, why were you there, Carter?"

"I wanted to check our inventory out, Dr. Silvers. Kiley said this morning he wanted me to go back to the media with another appeal, so I felt I needed to have a handle on our supply. I mean—our real supply, reserves included. After all, if someone called me this morning with a concern of hiding blood and accusing us of calling false shortages— who's to say they wouldn't call the media next and tell them the same story. I just wanted to be ready to handle. . ."

"Do you think someone from here would really call the media, Carter?"

"I think it's a possibility, Dr. Silvers."

"Carter, the public wouldn't understand our business. Our industry is constantly on the brink of turmoil. I mean—the whole operation is under intense pressure. We live or die by the whims of indifferent people."

Carter did not respond but her face reflected strong interest in what he was saying.

"Resource sharing could be easily misinterpreted by those on the outside, especially the media, Carter."

"Resource sharing is not that difficult to understand, Dr. Silvers," Carter blurted out, "it's just a means to help out other areas. It's a form of community service. I can understand that and I truly believe the public would understand. My only reservation about resource sharing is if we are led to call false appeals to keep up the shipments." Carter meant for her words to be conciliatory. The doctor's easy manner with her up to this point had given her a very false impression once again.

"You keep saying false shortages, Carter, so obviously you still think that is what we are doing," Silvers was suddenly angry. He felt threatened by Carter's words. "Well, let me tell you something, Miss p.r. lady. If that's what it takes to bring dollars and cents into this center, then so be it. How do you think we operate here, Carter? The United Way doesn't support us. Joe Blow doesn't support us—I do it. I keep blood running in and out of here any way I can get it. It's your job to back me up. What is it with you public relations people? You don't understand a damn thing about our operation, and yet you stick your nose in places where it doesn't belong and cause more trouble than you're worth."

The doctor's face had turned a deep shade of red. His shoulders were hunched forward and his hands were tightly clasped together, softly pounding on the top of his desk. This quick change of mood frightened Carter. Silvers was so explosive, so menacing when he got this way.

"Dr. Silvers, we don't have to engage in unethical practices to bring blood in here. We could go to the public and tell them the truth. We could tell them how hard it is to supply blood to the system. We could be up-front with them about the NAABC asking us to help out with the coastal supply. It's wrong to lead our community down the garden path by making them think they are not doing their duty with our blood supply when they are, in fact, doing far more than their share."

"The moment you tell the public the truth is the moment you bring a bunch of do-gooders through our front door asking a lot of questions. We've worked hard to separate the public from our private business, Carter. I have no intention of changing a system that works. Not now. Not ever."

"You may have to, Dr. Silvers. If the media ever finds out how we operate. . ."

"How are they going to find out? Are you going to tell them?"

The look on Carter's face expressed something to Silvers he was afraid of—this one might do just that. He could not let Carter think she could change his operation with veiled threats. He had to stop her from even considering such a thing. It was time to have his heart-to-heart discussion with this public relations director. It had worked with all the rest. It would work with her.

"Carter, let me wake you up here. If you ever think you can bring the media in here for anything less than to support us, I will pin you to the wall. I will swear on a stack of Bibles that you are a liar, a disgruntled employee trying to discredit our operation for your own gain. I'll show you to be a problem not only professionally, but personally. It's easy to do, Carter. All I have to do is set out a pattern for the media to go after. A few dropped sentences about you, and, shall we say, your handsome boss, and the press gets the picture pretty clearly. Especially with the fact that your husband is nowhere around, and you are, after all, a very healthy woman. No matter what happens after that, Carter, your lily-white reputation will be tainted, and you wouldn't be able to get a job as a garbage collector in this city. Remember, Carter, public relations people are only useful to a company as long as they can keep their mouths shut. The moment you gain a reputation as a whistle blower is the moment you kiss goodbye to your career. You should know that by now."

The doctor's words stunned Carter. His evil scheme painted a very true picture of what could happen to her. Telling the truth shouldn't work this way, but far too often it did. Silvers sensed he had scored a direct hit. He continued to attack.

"No matter what you think you might know about our operation, Carter, you are still just a lay person with no medical background. It would wind up being your word against mine. Against this blood center. Who do you think the public is going to believe? You, a flunky—or me, a trusted medical doctor running a trusted medical facility?" His words were powerful. "Resource sharing is our business, Carter. We've set it all up in a most respectable manner. Think about it. How many times have you discussed resource sharing with the media since you've been here? Do you think anyone would listen to you now if you try to change that explanation? Think about how many lives you would be jeopardizing if you tried to create a fuss about the way we operate. We've done nothing wrong here, Carter. So we ship units of blood out during an appeal. The public has been groomed very carefully for a number of years to accept our methods of operation without question. You can't prove any wrong-doing, Carter. No laws are being broken."

"What you're asking me to do is to purposely lie to the public, Dr. Silvers."

"I'm not asking you to lie, Carter. I'm just asking you to go along with a system that has saved a lot of lives and can't be replaced by anything else. People need blood—it's our business to see they get it, and if it takes a few nudges here and there, so be it." Silvers stood up and walked to his window keeping his back to Carter. For a few moments the room was quiet. Turning around, he walked directly over to the edge of his desk stopping in front of Carter. His closeness was unsettling.

"Carter, listen to me. You've done an excellent job for us. You have a way with the media. There are lots of opportunities for you here at the blood center. Once you learn what it is we really do here, there could be no limit to your success in helping our cause along. All I'm asking of you is to go along with me. Keep the pressure on the public. If we get the blood, who's being hurt?"

"I can't lie. . ."

"You've been lying, Carter. How many times have you been quoted in the press stating blood is safer than ever?"

"How many brochures have you written using those exact same words—safer than ever?"

"But, it is safer. . ."

"No it's not. It's even more dangerous than it was ten years ago. AIDS has brought us to a whole new level of transfusion problems, Carter. And it's no longer just blood—the danger now includes other businesses operating under our shingle like organ transplants. Yes, that's right—our bone marrow program, our Tissue Bank. All of it is subject to the same dangers as a simple blood transfusion. It's all the same, Carter." The doctor's face was now just a few inches away from Carter's as he continued.

"Blood isn't safe, Carter, but it still saves lives. It's all we've got. What are we supposed to do—tell the world blood isn't safe and then fold up our tents and go home? People are going to die without blood. Sure, some people are going to get bad blood from time to time, but there's a hell of a lot more that are going to live because you and I did our job and had the damn stuff ready and available for them when they needed it. Use your head, Carter. All this is part of a vicious cycle. But it's all we've got right now."

Silvers stood up and walked around his desk to his chair. Carter could not take her eyes off him. What else was he going to tell her?

"What about our statements. . ." Carter would be cut off in mid-sentence.

"Forget about all the statements. Blood is not and never will be safe. Think about this, Carter," the doctor continued obviously enjoying his teaching lesson, "right now there is another new disease being born at this very moment. And its lying there dormant in someone's blood stream as we speak. All it's going to take is for that person—that unknown person—somewhere on our planet, to have contact with another human being—and, bingo, we're on our way to another plague. We can't stop the creation of new diseases, Carter. And we sure as hell don't have the resources to screen them all out of our blood or organ supply."

Carter felt the color draining from her face. The doctor sensed he had done his job very well this time. He could see the fear in Carter's eyes.

"Carter, I'm sorry if this conversation got a little personal. It's just—well, I don't like to feel threatened—it causes me to play a little rough. I like you. I really do. You've got the class and intelligence this center needs to keep us above all the madness. How about forgetting our little misunderstanding and getting on with helping me do the kind of job here that we have to do? Perhaps you can look at things from my side now. I'm sure I don't have to remind you of the niche you've created for yourself in the public's eye. After all, you are the one they have come to depend on. It's your face they recognize in public—your name they ask for when calling our center for information. You've become a very recognizable person since you've started here, especially since the lawsuit put you out front as our spokesperson." The doctor's words drove home how closely Carter was now tied to the center.

Carter knew that she had to walk a very fine line at this moment. She was frightened by this man. He could do so many harmful things. Anna Cable's name flashed in Carter's mind for just a split second. Carter remembered what Grace had told her over lunch. "Whatever you do, play along with them." Grace and Carter weren't in a position to change anything yet.

"Dr. Silvers," Carter began in a soft voice, "you've given me a lot to think about. I don't want to cause the center any harm. I really do love my job. I guess I just didn't understand all the pressures we're dealing with."

Silvers smiled. Carter at this moment looked like a whipped puppy. He prided himself at being able to redirect a person's perspective. Carter just might be the best thing that ever happened to the center, the medical director calculated, as he held open his office door for Carter. He was finished with Carter for now. His pep talk obviously had an effect. As the public relations director passed by him, he couldn't help but catch the scent of her perfume. He liked whatever it was she had sprayed on her body. Perhaps in time, he and Carter could move to another level. Everything was possible in time. This he truly believed.

It took Carter only a few minutes to reach her office. Shelly had gone home by now, and the second floor was almost deserted. On her desk was a file folder. Grace Tende had put it there just a few minutes earlier. Carter put on her coat and tucked the folder under her arm. She was going home. It had been a long day for her, a day no one would believe. And that's what frightened her most of all. No one would believe. . . .

23

The mail was delivered early to John Stansbarry's office on this snowy winter morning. Usually when arriving at his law office, Barry gathered up the mail, newspapers and magazines left on his doorstep, and promptly deposited them on his nephew's desk. It became Tovey's duty to separate the incoming mail and pass on all those things meant for his uncle to see.

Today, for some reason, Barry changed his routine. A plain gray linen envelope with no return address caught his attention. It was postmarked in Hamilton County. Using his favorite letter opener, Barry slit the envelope open. It contained three white sheets of paper.

"My God, what do we have here?" the attorney said out loud as he quickly glanced at the papers in his hand. "Clear copies of the donors' health questionnaires. Those son-of-a. . ." With sheer disgust, John Stansbarry threw the copies down on his nephew's desk. "Now we get them." Barry did not finish his sentence as he headed for the small kitchen to put on his first pot of coffee for the day.

The sound of the office door opening brought a quick call to his nephew. "Is that you, Tovey?"

"Sorry I'm late. I stopped off at Aunt Anne's this morning to take her some of mom's jelly. Did you get the mail this morning, Uncle Barry?"

"Yeah, it's on your desk with all the other junk that I tripped over this morning. I don't know why we get so many magazines delivered to this office. We never read them. It's just a waste of money as far as I'm concerned," Barry stated as he wiped off the counter top where he had just spilled half a packet of sugar.

"What's this?" Tovey asked, as he scooped up the scattered sheets of paper from the top of his neat desk.

"Clear copies—courtesy of the blood center," Barry said as he made his way back to his desk with his freshly poured cup of coffee. "Timely, huh?"

Tovey was slowly taking in the information, reading each copy from top to bottom. When he came to the third sheet, his face paled. "What the. . ." Tovey did not complete his sentence.

Barry glanced at his muttering nephew, not quite understanding the look that was spreading across his nephew's face.

"Did you look at these, Uncle Barry? Did you look at these?" Tovey's voice was excited and pitched higher than Barry had ever heard it.

"What's the matter, Tovey? What are you looking at?"

Tovey didn't say anything but walked quickly over to his uncle's desk laying the sheet of paper directly in front of Barry, pressing the paper down to flatten it. With his index finger, the younger Stansbarry pointed to the second question listed on the sheet.

John Stansbarry was stunned as his eyes focused on the information now in front of him. The word "NO" clearly was checked. Barry read the question once again out loud.

"Do you consider yourself to be in good health? NO!" My God, Tovey, what do we have here?"

Quickly, Barry read each question, line by line out loud. He couldn't believe what he was seeing.

"Are these from the blood center, Uncle Barry?" Tovey asked as his uncle searched the other two donor's questionnaires for similar errors.

"It looks like the other two are okay—just this donor. . ."

"Who sent us these clear copies, Uncle Barry? The envelope they came in doesn't have a return address on it. There's no blood center logo on it either."

John Stansbarry didn't answer. His blood pressure was rising so fast that his face had turned a beet red contrasting noticeably with his shock of snow-white hair. An angry jaw tightened and the veins in his forehead bulged.

"I don't know who sent us these copies, Tovey. But I'd bet my life it wasn't the blood center."

For a few moments neither man said a word. What did not feel right—what never fit—was now in their hands, sending their minds soaring in disbelief.

"Check it out, Tovey. Get on the phone and call that secretary back at the blood center. Act casual. Just see if she did stick these in the mail to us."

Tovey quickly dialed the memorized blood center phone number. In a moment the quiet voice of Dr. Crane's secretary answered. Tovey covered his question very easily. In a few seconds he had all the answers he needed. Thanking the girl for her time, Tovey hung up the phone.

"Their machine is still out of order. She didn't send us anything." Tovey's face was flushed.

"Those sonsofbitches. They buried the truth, Tovey. They don't have a problem with any copy machine. Those copies were darkened deliberately. Shit! How could we have been so stupid.

We should have gone down there in person and demanded to see the originals. Where's my goddamn brains?"

"Who in the hell would ever have suspected these guys—these lily-white medical bastards to have tried to pull something like this? For Christ's sake, look at this," Tovey said as he held up the questionnaire. "There are at least five to six answers that clearly show this guy should not have been donating blood for Taylor or anyone else. Look here—he didn't even fill this line in where it asks if a donor is going to engage in strenuous exercise—it's blank. According to their own blood bank guidelines, all questions must be answered by a prospective donor."

John Stansbarry grabbed the questionnaire out of his nephew's hand. "My God, you're right," he said slowly as he reread the piece of paper, line by line.

"What are we going to do now?" Tovey asked.

"I'll tell you what we're going to do. We're going to get on the phone and get that medical panel back together. This time we've got the evidence that proves negligence. AIDS or no AIDS—this person clearly does not qualify to be a blood donor. They knew it, Tovey. They knew it all the time." John Stansbarry could not stop shaking his head in disbelief. They were now three phone calls away from justice. Just three phone calls away.

Tovey Stansbarry gathered up Taylor Addison's file and quickly assembled the telephone numbers of the three medical doctors who made up the panel. It was decided that Tovey would handle this task and his uncle would pay a visit to Taylor's parents. It would not be an easy visit.

As Taylor's young baby lay sleeping in his grandmother's arms, John Stansbarry went over what had happened that morning. The grandparents were stunned. They were gentle people—caring people who had worked hard all their lives. Taylor was their youngest child. She was special to them in so many ways. With her death just days behind them, their grieving hearts were almost too numb to comprehend all that the attorney was saying. Stansbarry's revelations were almost more than they could handle. They were innocent people. No match for such seemingly evil actions.

"Are you telling me, Mr. Stansbarry, that the blood center had this information all along?"

"Yes, sir. It surely looks that way."

"But, why? Why would they put my daughter through something like this if they knew they had made an honest mistake?" Taylor's father asked.

"Maybe they're not so honest, sir."

"But they're doctors aren't they?" They're doctors," the mother asked as she held tightly to her grandchild.

"Just because they're doctors, doesn't make them saints. All I can tell you is we're going to get that medical panel to reconvene. When they see this evidence, they'll rule on our side. And Taylor's day in court will have the power of this ruling on her side," Stansbarry answered so sure of his words.

"It isn't the money, Mr. Stansbarry," Taylor's father replied. It never was. Taylor shouldn't have died this way. They made her look so awful. She was the one who looked like the criminal. She questioned them, and they made her look like a. . ."

"Taylor was no criminal, Mr. Stansbarry," the mother interrupted. "Our daughter didn't deserve such a fate. They were careless—Taylor was right all along. They were careless—and she died because of it," the new grandmother sobbed with tears welling up in her soft hazel eyes.

The ride back to the office was a sobering one for John Stansbarry. Taylor Addison's dying words were as clear as if she were sitting next to him right now.

"You have to promise me you won't stop. You won't let them put me in the ground with no justice. I took a risk, John Stansbarry. Against all odds, I stood up for what was right. It wasn't just for me. Promise me you will see my case through to the end. Promise me you won't stop." Taylor's skeleton face was sweaty with intense pain as she looked at him. Her hand clung to the sleeve of his suitcoat. The look in her attorney's eyes told her what she wanted to hear. Taylor's last few days alive were spent in agony. She could bear the pain of the disease; it was leaving her child behind that broke her body in two with every breath. John Stansbarry had not slept well since Taylor died. It was as if she wouldn't let him.

When he walked into his office and saw Tovey's face, he knew something was wrong.

"So when do we get this show on the road?" Barry asked.

"You're not going to believe this, Uncle Barry."

"Not going to believe what?"

"They have no intention of reconvening. I called all of them—I told them we had new information that changes the whole outlook of the case. And they all refused to even let me tell them what we now had. They said it was too late to enter anything now. It was after the fact. They said the matter was closed, and they had no intention of stirring things up again. Their investigative ruling will stand."

John Stansbarry stood rigidly staring at his nephew. He couldn't believe what he had just heard. Slowly, almost shuffling, he walked over to his wooden desk chair and sat down. Tovey Stansbarry went to the kitchen and poured his uncle a cup of coffee.

"Here, drink some of this."

"I can't believe the audacity of that so-called medical panel," the uncle stated in whisper tones. He was truly stunned. His nephew had more to say.

"I made some other calls while you were at Taylor's. I found some things out that perhaps unscrambles some of this. This selected panel is pretty much tied to the blood center."

"What are you talking about? How are they tied?"

"I called a friend of mine from college, Chet Lambert. He's a reporter for *The Daily Voice* in Hamilton with some pretty strong ties in the medical community. Chet pieced together bits and pieces of information for me. It seems our own Dr. Silvers is not only the medical director for the blood center, but he acts as a regional laboratory inspector for the NAABC. He has the power to close down a hospital lab operation in a blink of an eye. All three of these docs are beholden to him in so many words. Besides this, Chet dug up a few back pages of dirt from the medical community gossip line. It seems two of the doctors on this panel owe Silvers big time for looking the other way when some pretty heavy stuff came down in their hospitals a few years ago. For one of them, it had something to do with an out-of-state plasma center that the hospital was using to supplement their blood inventory. It seems this for-pay plasma center wasn't too selective in its donor base and was also known for not always running the required standard tests on the blood they were selling to hospital labs at dirt-cheap prices. Silvers caught several batches of contaminated blood products that had already been used for transfusion in his inspection when he showed up at the hospital unannounced. Word has it, Silvers was more furious with catching the hospital using products that didn't come from his center than he was with finding the contaminated blood. Chet didn't really know too much stuff on the other hospital, only that it had something to do with a bacterial fungus found growing inside the hospital's cold storage refrigerators. He could have shut down both labs, but he didn't. They owed him big time all right. It looks like he may have called in his markers."

"If that's the case, these guys knew the truth from the beginning. They knew Silvers's center had screwed up with Taylor's transfusion. They knew there was real negligence involved here. The whole damn group is in bed together."

Tovey didn't answer his uncle.

"I only wish I would have gotten hold of this information earlier. But Chet ran into some trouble with his editor. I guess the editor is related, somehow, to one of the past medical directors who worked at the blood center—a brother-in-law, I think. Chet's been sitting on this for some time. It seems he's heading for a plum spot in Washington, D.C. It's a tradeoff for his dumping the story."

"I didn't think the media did stuff like this, Tovey. I thought it was part of their code to tell the truth."

"Chet's ambitious, Uncle Barry. This isn't the story that's going to nail the Pulitzer for him. But it is the story that moves him out of small town Hamilton and into the big leagues of the Washington Press Corps."

"Can we document any of this on paper, Tovey."

"I don't think so. Chet made it pretty clear he would roll over and play dead if I tried to draw him into this."

"Well by God, if I have to subpoena every one of those sonsabitches, I will. I'm going to nail their asses to the wall. If we're going to get a civil hearing on this, we have to introduce what we've got into public record. We're going to need at least two doctors to go on record on our behalf documenting the center's breakdown in following their own blood bank donor criteria standards. Tovey, can you get on this right away?"

"I think I have found a couple of doctors who live out on the coast who have no ties to this area and might possibly serve as expert witnesses—for a price of course." Tovey said.

"How much are we talking here?"

"The going price for an expert medical opinion can range from $2000 to $10,000, depending on how big a name you get. We also really need someone local, maybe someone we've already got on record. Someone who could look at these errors in the light of day and have the guts to change their deposition statement."

John Stansbarry's anger began to clear from his mind. Anger got him into trouble the last time. This time, he would play their game. All he needed was the right person. An honest person who worked in the industry. Someone who would look at this new evidence and be just as outraged by what they saw as he had been.

"Well, the good doctors are not going to cooperate with us for a call back, and Michael Bryan sure as hell isn't a candidate," Barry stated as he thought through his options. There was one person who came to mind. One single person who could change the course of their long dark road.

"Are you thinking about the same person I am?" Tovey asked his uncle.

"Yes. I think I am. But it's a long shot, Tovey. A one-in-a-million long shot."

"Well, if you ask me, those are the best odds we've had since this whole thing started."

24

The snow was falling heavy now. Roads were closed and traffic was sure to be a mess in the morning. Funny thing about living in Hamilton. You never knew what kind of weather you might face from one hour to the next. It was a little past ten p.m. and the blood center was quiet. The evening lab shift had just wrapped up from a long day of heavy processing and were finally on their way home. It had been an eighteen-hour day for some of them. Reymond Alexander was the last person left in the testing area. For the next hour, Reymond never left his bench. He was waiting for two more people to leave. Herk Golden had stayed to make sure every driver had made it back from his evening run. When Terry Milo finished unloading his wagon, all the drivers had been accounted for. Herk made sure to turn off the lights and to check all the doors. No more unlocked areas. Not on Herk's shift. Not after all the hell he'd raised this morning. On Herk's way out, he ran into Siam Qua.

"You've been working late, again."

"Yes, it seems so." Siam softly answered, fatigue clearly showing in his face.

The two men walked out the side door together. Herk helped Siam brush the heavy snow from his car's windshield. The sound of their engines starting was the signal for Reymond to move to a different location. He had been watching from his now-darkened lab window. Climbing the stairs, Reymond made his way to Dr. Crane's office on the second floor. But it wasn't Dr. Crane's office that interested Reymond, it was her secretary's desk, or rather the computer that sat on top of her secretary's desk. It only took a few minutes to work through the code system set up on this special computer. In a few more seconds, Reymond had gained access to the computer's main menu.

Reymond surprised himself at how easy he had worked through the code system. He had gained access to the secretary's password, giving him entry into Dr. Crane's files. The password was easy to get—he simply watched the secretary log on one day. She used her initials as her password. It was something most of the secretaries did at the center.

"People are so predictable," he thought with a trace of amusement. Dr. Crane had coded her main menu with the code name of NAVY. It didn't take a rocket scientist to compile a list of words that Crane might use for security purposes.

"If more people had minds like mine, what a wonderful planet this would surely be," Reymond mused as he experienced a flush of excitement. He was confident he would find a way to open the system. He needed to find the pathway to the card code that unlocked Siam's inner laboratory door. He had managed to secure the code for the hallway entrance by pretending to one of the new HLA techs that he had simply forgotten the code numbers. Reymond's easy manner carried the scheme off. The tech saw no harm in giving the code to Reymond Alexander. After all, he was a key team member in the testing area and many times brought samples from his lab to theirs. The four digit code, which previously worked on Siam's inner chamber lock, had been changed. Scanning the blue screen, Reymond looked for possible combinations. The palms of his hands began to sweat as he stared at the computer. One of his chronic headaches was coming back. He steadied himself as the throbbing in his temples distracted him. Stopping long enough to extract his pain medicine from his laboratory coat pocket, Reymond pushed the pills down his throat with his finger. He gagged as he always did. Water. He had to have a drink of water. He was burning up and the bitter ingredients he had just swallowed set his stomach on fire. The water cooler was just around the corner from Crane's office. The needed break only angered him more. The taste of the cool water hit his stomach, flooding his senses with relief from the painful thirst and burning. In a few minutes, the waves of pain subsided. As he was leaving the water cooler, the sight of the telephone mounted on the wall caught his attention. The numbers on the dialing plate were extra large. Something clicked in his mind. "Of course," he thought, as he moved closer to the mounted phone. Reymond matched four letters of the alphabet to the phone's corresponding numbers. "7426-Siam."

"She's so predictable—so stupid." Reymond raced back to the secretary's desk. His fingers trembled as he typed in the four digits. In a matter of seconds, the screen displayed Siam's name. It was too easy. But then, Dr. Crane never guessed anyone would be interested in breaking her code system. Things like that didn't happen at the blood center. She controlled the secrets and the system.

Reymond logged off the computer again using the secretary's password. It was so easy. No one would ever know he had been in. It angered him that it had taken this long to break a simple internal code. If he had been feeling better—if his mind could have stayed focused longer—if there were no headaches and. . .

Reymond didn't waste his time with any more "what ifs." His long legs moved him quickly through the executive wing. He took the steps on two at a time. He was in a hurry.

Reaching the lower level, Reymond approached the large maintenance closet that housed the plastic key cards. Using the master key, which he had pilfered and duplicated several weeks before, he quickly gained entry into the pitch-black room. Switching on the light, Reymond went directly to the machine used to make the plastic key cards. His large fingers quickly flipped open the power switch that ran the machine. Unwrapping a blank card, he set it in the housing box that imprinted the codes. His fingers pressed the numbers 7426. The machine registered the code and clicked each number into place. Siam Qua's inner laboratory was now available to Reymond Alexander. Switching off the light and locking the door behind him, Reymond quickly headed down the corridor to Qua's area. In simple motions, he punched in the entrance code. The sight of Siam Qua's laboratory chamber door quickly brought a rush to Reymond's body. He did not turn on any lights. The glow from the many computers with their brightly lit display screens generated enough light for Reymond to see his way around. Reymond's hand tightly gripped the plastic key card. In one easy motion, he guided the card in and out of the special lock. The card, bearing the coded numbers of 7426, unlocked the door.

The room was stuffy and scented with strong chemicals. Reymond had only one purpose here—to find whatever it was that Siam was trying so hard to keep under wraps. To his advantage, he was familiar with the area. The small room was crowded with several pieces of new equipment. Reymond bypassed the bench table and went directly to a closed door on the far side of the room. If luck were with him, the coded key that opened the chamber door would also open this one. It did. His luck was holding. The chilled room was housing the secrets Reymond wanted. In a matter of moments, Reymond had located the liquid samples of the stored test vials. Reymond recognized the coded key words for bone marrow. The samples were each clearly marked with the NAABC's stamped label.

"Whatever Siam is doing is obviously for research," Reymond thought as he continued to look around the chilled room. The frigid air in the chamber caused Reymond to leave the area faster than he would have preferred. Rubbing his arms to generate some warmth to his body, his eyes searched Siam's outer work area.

"There must be a notebook somewhere. Siam always works with a journal." Reymond knew the pattern very well. Siam Qua rarely deviated from his precise work habits. It only took a few minutes of searching before Reymond located a desk drawer that was locked. Working with his swiss army knife, Reymond manipulated the thin lock and the drawer popped open. The black binder that held Siam's notes was pushed to the back of the drawer. For several minutes, Reymond's eyes scanned the lined paper filled with detailed records and personal reflections. Suddenly, a smile spread across his face.

"Here it is—here it is." Reymond was excited—very excited. In Siam's own handwriting, he had outlined Dr. Silvers's direct orders to falsify this bone marrow project.

"I do this with a heavy heart, but little freedom to avoid what I know one day might happen. Dr. Silvers has instructed me to present false information on project 71069A, Bone Marrow Compatibility Coupling, in order to secure the large grant funds from the National Association of Accredited Blood Centers. I am nowhere near the formula to create a manmade substance that will allow a successful joining of human-to-human bone marrow transplantation without donor-specific typing. I can only hope that my journey will take me down the path of success. Many innocent hopes depend on my diligence."

"Silvers is truly the king of bastards," Reymond thought as the words written by Siam penetrated his mind. "When I'm done with him. . ." Reymond didn't finish his thought. He knew what he had to do next. The journal was carefully copied page by page. It took Reymond nearly thirty minutes to carry out this project. Satisfied that he now had enough documentation to catch Silvers at his own game, Reymond placed the journal back where he had found it and secured the lock. No one would ever suspect what had just occurred.

In his hurry to leave the laboratory, Reymond did not realize he had moved the control vials slightly. No one else might notice such a small displacement—but then, few men are as thorough as Siam Qua.

25

The heavy snowfall was now packed to the ground in a dirty gray covering. Bertha White had left her house this morning earlier than usual. The drive to work was less than comforting. The heavy snow had brought traffic to a near standstill. Traffic crawled over the unplowed thruways.

Bertha allowed her thoughts to include moving to a warm climate—to a city where snow never fell. The sight of the blood center's parking lot entrance brought a quick end to Bertha's daydreaming.

A meeting had been scheduled with Dr. Crane for 9 a.m. sharp, and Bertha had hoped to get to her office early. No such luck. It was a little after 8:30 when Bertha opened her office door. She was edgy and feeling out of sorts. The pressures of all that was going on in her laboratory had turned her life upside down. This was not the way she had wanted to start this day in particular.

Discarding her warm oversized winter coat and ankle-high boots the large-boned woman quickly situated herself in front of her computer. Pulling up the coded report, Bertha began scanning the long columns of figures. The numbers gave her a sickening feeling in the pit of her stomach. The research was as complete as it was ever going to be. She initiated the command to print out the startling figures, and the low hum of her inkjet printer slowly served up the report she dreaded ever having to compile.

Sixty units of contaminated blood gave birth to three hundred components of liquid poison. It was all a horrible accident. Such negligence was never supposed to happen on her watch. All the back-up systems in place had failed. How could this have happened? Accident or not, it was now a reality she would have to live with for some time. Dr. Crane had taken the initial report of possible discharge contamination relatively calmly. She had instructed Bertha to do a thorough inventory trace. Such a back trace and retesting effort took time. Bertha and Reymond had worked on this mass project for nearly two weeks. Their actions were as guarded as they could make them without too many people wondering what was going on. Lisa James, a part-time evening data entry clerk, had also been involved in this tracing pattern. Bertha felt sure the young clerk did not have a real understanding of the data she was being asked to compile, and as Lisa was a quiet staff member and not one to ask a lot of questions, Bertha felt fairly comfortable.

As Bertha held the report in her hands, the laboratory director couldn't help but think of the innocent people who were on the receiving end of this deadly report. It was going to take a massive effort to notify these individuals. Getting them to come to the center for a testing of their now contaminated bloodstreams was not to be an easy task. When the center had to retest those who previously had tested in the "false-positive" range for HIV, all hell usually broke loose.

"God help us all," Bertha muttered to herself as she gathered up the rest of the reports.

A tired and rumpled looking Reymond opened her closed door.

"My God, Reymond, you look awful," Bertha said, surprised at his appearance.

"Well, you look beautiful, my favorite lady," Reymond returned smiling at Bertha. "Is it all there?" he questioned.

"Yes, it's complete," Bertha replied, looking at the four-page report. "I want to thank you for all your help, Rey. I know you know how confidential this is."

"You don't need to give me the lecture, Bertha. I'm not going to say anything." Reymond's voice was edgy.

"I know you aren't. It's just something like this could be so damaging to the center and so frightening to the public if it ever got out in a less-than-controlled manner," Bertha stated in a supervisory voice.

She had never been given any reason to question Reymond's ability to keep matters of extreme sensitivity to himself. He had worked long enough at the center to know other such secrets. But none with the consequence of this one. Nevertheless, Bertha had no real doubts about Reymond's loyalty to their operation.

"Look, Bertha, I've never put you or this center in a bad light. You should know by now you can trust me, but if you don't, well, there's not much I can do about that, is there?" Reymond turned away quickly and left the office, slamming the door with his exit.

Bertha was stunned by Reymond's behavior. She had never seen him so cross, especially with her. True, his behavior these last few weeks had shown moments of testiness, but she had connected this behavior to the strain they had all been under. His sometimes strange behavior, which lately included quoting obscure children's nursery rhymes, had not concerned Bertha until this moment. Reymond had become a friend and she cared about him. Bertha's eyes caught sight of the time. She was five minutes late for her meeting with Dr. Crane. There wasn't time to chase after her friend and find out what had set him off. Bertha left her office and walked quickly to keep her appointment. Her knock on her supervisor's door was immediately answered. In less than thirty minutes, an ashen-faced Bertha White exited from the assistant medical director's office. Almost running, Bertha sped down the narrow hallway. As she turned the corner, the distracted woman ran straight into Carter Egan. The force of the meeting knocked Carter back into the stairwell from where she had just emerged. Carter grabbed onto the metal hand railing, stopping her backward fall.

"Oh my God, Carter. I'm so sorry—" Bertha screamed as she reached out to keep Carter from falling.

"It's okay, Bertha," Carter replied as she secured her balance. Carter had not seen the look on Bertha's face as the two had collided, but it only took a few seconds to see that the laboratory director was clearly upset.

"Bertha, what's wrong?" Carter was now the one showing concern.

Tears welled up in Bertha's eyes. Her body began to shake. She made no attempt to answer Carter. Instinctively, Carter reached out and put her arms around the other woman. In small steps, Carter led Bertha around the corner and into her office. Shelly was away from her desk, and this end of the administrative wing was free from curious eyes.

In the privacy of Carter's office, Bertha began to sob. Carter did her best to comfort her, but the shock of seeing such a strong woman in such a vulnerable state caused Carter to remain quiet. For fifteen minutes, Bertha's emotions ran freely. Finally, the distressed woman began to regain control. Carter went to her desk where she retrieved a large box of tissues and handed it to her friend. The soft white tissues were soon matted up to wipe away the falling tears.

"I'm sorry, Carter. This is not like me. I. . ."

"You don't have to explain to me, Bertha. It's okay, really," Carter replied, not letting Bertha finish her sentence. Even between two women, there is a certain amount of embarrassment that takes place when something or someone reduces you to tears. Carter wanted to spare Bertha from those feelings.

Bertha looked like someone in shock, gray-faced, the color of stone. For a few seconds, Bertha studied Carter's face as if trying to make up her mind to tell her what was behind her unusual behavior. At this time, Bertha's troubled mind could not share her heavy burden with anyone, not yet. Not like this—so uncontrolled and vulnerable. The fact that she had collapsed in front of Carter made it all the worse. Carter seemed so innocent.

"Carter, I'm afraid I've worked here too long. It's time for me to move on," Bertha offered, trying to steer her thoughts away from blurting out what had just happened.

"Oh, Bertha. Don't say that. What would we do without you?" Carter said.

"You're always so positive, Carter. I wish I could be more like that these days. It's just—the blood center does something to you if you stay around too long." Bertha had regained her composure and stood up, heading for Carter's door.

"Is it the blood center or the people running the blood center, Bertha?"

Bertha did not answer for a few seconds. Carter's words had hit a nerve. It wasn't the work at the center; it was the evil people who ran it. Carter was absolutely right.

"It wasn't always this way," Bertha thought as she remembered how much she had invested in the center in the way of time and energy and sheer belief in the work they were called upon to perform each day. The last twenty minutes had nearly erased all those memories. The next twenty minutes would test her very soul as a decision had to be made and the time in which to make it was drawing very near. She had to get back to her computer. She had to see if the madness could be stopped.

Bertha turned and looked Carter straight in the eyes.

"Get out of here, Carter. Get out before you are sucked up in all this madness." There was anger present in Bertha's voice. With those words spoken, Bertha left Carter's office. The silence of the moment and the fatal prediction of the lab director's words caused Carter to sit down in a sudden, collapsing motion. So many things were swirling around her. She had spent a restless night pondering over what she should and could do. Grace Tende's findings, or better put, lack of findings, caused Carter even more discomfort. Grace had tried to pull up the center's shipping reports on the main terminal. But she was too late. They had all been mysteriously deleted. The reports showed only local and regional ship-ment dates. The records had clearly been changed and changed quickly to a new format. The center's shipping history had been altered to prevent an easy tracking of resource sharing. Last night, Grace had called Carter at home. The two women talked for over two hours about the situation. With mixed emotions Grace listened to Carter's recounting of her meeting with Dr. Silvers and his veiled threats. She was shocked by what Silvers had said but not surprised. Silvers was intimidating and had used this same tactic on other employees at the center. These same employees would say absolutely nothing about Dr. Silvers in their exit interviews with Grace. With feelings of shame, Grace silently recalled how she, too, had used the veiled power threat of Dr. Silvers's mean side to discourage several nurses from attacking the center publicly because of their involvement with Silvers and his subsequent treatment of them. Together, she, as the personnel director, and Silvers, as the medical director, had acted in tandem to squash those who threatened to break the code of silence that permitted such behavior to thrive and to go unpunished. With her friend on the other end of the phone line, Grace could not help but feel she was, in part, no better than Dr. Silvers. It left a bitter taste in her mouth. If ever there was a time to right her own past actions, it was now. No matter what the consequences, it had to stop.

As the two women continued to recount their suspicions, Grace felt there must be another way to find the documentation they needed. What frightened Grace most was that the executives were aware of the need to cover their tracks. It would not be easy for them to locate reports.

The folder that Grace had left on Carter's desk was barren; there was no evidence to prove wrongdoing on the part of the blood center. What Grace and Carter needed were hard copies of reports with dates and shipment information, to prove the frequency and volume of out-of-state blood delivery during the exact times of false blood emergency media calls. Carter would need to search every available past log file manually. Surely, somewhere, they could find an accounting of shipping that would corroborate their beliefs. Just outside Carter's office door, to the right, stood four large black metal file cabinets that housed past reports. It would take some time, but somewhere in that stack of filed papers, a history of unethical operations just might be waiting. Did she have the time? Carter left a message on Grace's voice mail. She wanted to tell her about Bertha's strange behavior. Something was going on and perhaps Bertha could help. She was careful in her wording, since she now suspected the executives were probably monitoring her every move.

As Carter began looking for material that could be enormously difficult to find, Bertha White was also busy in her office. After leaving

Carter, she went immediately back to her computer. Reaching the sanctuary of her glass-walled office, Bertha took precautions to keep her actions secret. She locked her door and tilted the dusty mini-blinds upward. Quickly, she keyed in the commands that generally brought up a full screen of daily reports with bar code donor test results. She bypassed the general reports and went directly to the sub-directory where she had keyed in all the data on the sixty units of blood with their component breakdowns and test results. Dr. Crane had instructed her to compile all the information in this sub-directory with a special coded password of CIS—Crane Inventory Search. To Bertha's astonishment, the screen now registered only vacant columns. Bertha exited the program, shutting down her computer. In a few seconds, she rebooted the system and keyed in the special code. Again, the special code letters brought up a blue computer screen with empty columns. The reports were gone. Bertha's office was cold but she was suddenly wrapped in warm sweat. Again, and again, the director searched her files for data that held such consequences for so many innocent individuals. It was now clear that Bertha had been set up. Finally, when it was so very clear that her files had been eliminated, she exited her program. She reached for her phone with sweaty palms and dialed Dr. Crane's number. Amy, Dr. Crane's secretary, answered politely as always.

"Let me speak to Dr. Crane," Bertha said.

"I'm sorry, Mrs. White, Dr. Crane has stepped out of her office. Can I take a message?"

"Yes, tell her it is important that I speak with her as soon as possible. She'll know what it's about—she'll know."

Placing the phone back in its protected cradle, Bertha sat almost paralyzed in her chair. There were so many consequences to think about. Dr. Crane had to be the one to delete the information in her data base. No one else knew the code. Deep down, she knew its meaning. They would conceal this information and bury the evidence without any type of notification. True, their earlier meeting had hinted strongly that notification would be done within their own time preference, but a spill of this size had to be reported. But it would be buried just like all the other times. The memory of her meeting this morning flooded Bertha's mind.

Crane and Dr. Silvers were both present. This was a shock. Silvers was rarely present in such meetings. From the moment the meeting began it was clear the road for Bertha was going to be rocky. Silvers paced the room circling her chair as he spoke. He was furious with the foul-up. He couldn't believe the units were all contaminated. He flung stinging and accusatory statements at her that made no sense. He said the error was a deliberate attempt to contaminate the center's blood supply. Sources from the outside must be part of this scheme to discredit him. Him! It was personal now. In the end, he as much as accused Bertha or someone on her staff of sabotage. Bertha was stunned when he yelled in a raging voice that she would have to go.

"Someone is going to have to pay for this and it's not going to be me. You're the director of that laboratory. You should be fired." Dr. Silvers's threat to fire her was completely devastating. It was the most volatile meeting she had ever experienced during her entire tenure with the blood center. She was truly frightened at what steps Dr. Silvers might take next. She was so close to retirement. The thought of being fired was unimaginable and one that Bertha did not want to think about. Not once in this meeting had either of the two doctors expressed any concern for those three hundred and some individuals who had been exposed to bad blood. There was absolutely no talk of a recall or notification. It was a sacrificial lamb. Someone to take the blame. The only concern was for the blood center and how they had to keep a lid on this laboratory mistake.

Fear now turned to rage. She felt dirty. She was just as guilty in all the past cover-ups as the executives she despised. By keeping silent, she had given her approval. If it weren't for her being on a short string until retirement, she would do something. The weakness of this excuse churned in her stomach. It was true that Bertha had less than six months to retirement with full benefits. If she were to quit or be fired, her husband would be without the cushion of paid health insurance. No other insurance carrier would touch him now, and on their limited income, Bertha could not afford to continue the sizable dollar payments on this health plan by herself. She was caught between a rock and a hard place. They needed her retirement dollars and health insurance to live. Without it, there was no secure future for the Whites. This was what kept her silent and constantly looking the other way in her role as laboratory director for the blood center. Dr. Crane had made it very clear to Bertha one Friday afternoon not too long ago that the mistakes of the laboratory were strictly up to the executive level to handle. Dr. Crane and Dr. Silvers would make the decisions in regard to public awareness of any errors, however small or large they may be. Crane also padded her threats to include talking to any board members just in case Bertha ever thought about going over her head. The hand-picked board was indeed controlled. They would not listen to statements against their medical directors. The board would stick together. This method of sabotage had been tried before. It backfired miserably. Bertha had seen it with her own eyes. She was, in many ways, just as frightened of the board as she was of her medical superiors.

"Don't stick your fucking nose in where it doesn't belong or you'll find yourself without a job and those precious health benefits so fast it will make your head swim," Crane said as she dismissed Bertha from her office. Crane had the power to make good on her statement, as she could easily turn the situation around on Bertha and put her into the role of the one trying to cover up her laboratory's operational errors. Crane controlled this situation, and in many ways held Bertha captive. The FDA inspectors, who visited the center maybe once a year, were never able to find any of the center's serious mistakes, thanks to Dr. Crane's expert manipulation of the records and her ability somehow to always be forewarned of the approaching FDA inspectors. Crane was truly a genius at cover-up. Her knowledge of blood and blood banking laboratory operations was never to be questioned when it came to keeping her center free from regulation foul-ups. The FDA did not have enough inspectors to visit the vast number of sites consistently enough to catch them with their regulatory pants down. Dr. Crane was a master at achieving a spotless record for the center. FDA inspectors regularly wrote glowing letters of approval for Hamilton Regional. It was all so mixed up, Bertha thought, as she stared at her blank computer screen. With no data, she had little recourse. There was no paper trail. Besides, she finally admitted to herself that she was a willing hostage to the real truth. She was wrapped up in this foul system beyond a staged innocence. In the end, Bertha White knew she would do nothing to change what had been done. She would look the other way and perhaps, in time, even forget that this incident ever took place. The sharp ring of her phone caught her by surprise. She jumped as she reached for the phone receiver.

"White, Laboratory Operations," she answered.

"Did you want me to call you?" Dr. Crane asked sounding disturbed.

"Did you extract the report data from my sub-directory?" It was a direct question.

"No, I did not."

"Are you telling me you don't have this report in your data bank?" There was a slight smile present on the doctor's face. Information and those who had it were in control of most situations. Especially when the subject dealt with something so sensitive as screw-ups in a blood center laboratory.

"It's gone, Dr. Crane." The message of deliberate maneuvering was apparent in tone.

"Well, perhaps it's for the better, Bertha. We all know how cantankerous our computer system has been lately. I have all the information needed to address this situation. Of course, I expect you to keep this in the strictest of. . ."

"Confidence. Yes, I know Dr. Crane." Bertha finished the good doctor's sentence.

"Tell me, Dr. Crane. Should I expect a visit from the FDA?"

"Not now, Bertha. They were just here, remember?" The smile of absolute control was still present.

"But I thought with this information going to them, a site visit would not be out of the question. Bertha was now a player. She knew there would be no report of the incident.

"I doubt if it will come to that, Bertha. We are proceeding within our regulatory guidelines on this issue. There's no need to stir it up beyond our local responsibility."

"Have you notified the hospitals yet?" Bertha quickly questioned, knowing the answer in advance.

"Notification will be handled by letter, Bertha. From now on, you will not bring this matter up. It is on my shoulders now, and your laboratory errors will be handled accordingly." Dr. Crane's voice carried no emotion except for the threat of reminding Bertha that this situation could be blamed on her.

"Don't worry, Bertha. I will not let you be fired for this. I know how much you depend on your job here. I'm sure I can quiet Dr. Silvers down and persuade him to allow me to handle any serious questions you might run up against. If you are sure only you and Reymond and one other tech have any inside knowledge of this operational error, it's a simple matter of terminating those individuals of lesser status than you. Of course, your loyalty to me goes without question, and I know you will agree that I will handle this matter of notification in due time. Let me see, now. You have less than six months until you can retire if my memory serves me correctly. We wouldn't want to do anything that might jeopardize those benefits at this stage of the game, now would we?"

"No," Bertha answered. What was to come next was pure pain.

"How soon do you want me to let the others go?" Bertha asked.

"Let the part-time tech go tomorrow morning. Get rid of Reymond by the end of next week. Make sure it has nothing to do with this problem. I think you could tell them we are going to restructure the laboratory and are forced to reduce personnel costs. You know yourself that this is a big chunk hitting our overhead budget each month. Your department could downsize and cross-train select personnel. At this point, with all the added costs of testing hitting us, this move makes perfect sense. Don't you agree, Bertha?" Was there a choice? Bertha thought.

"There's no other way to do this, Dr. Crane?" Bertha countered not directly answering Crane's prior question.

"There's no other way, Bertha. Not if you value your position." Crane's voice was cold and to the point.

There was no need to answer Dr. Crane. The phone was returned to its cradle, the conversation had ended. For the rest of the day, Bertha stayed in her office with the blinds closed and the door locked as if trying to lock out the world she was caught up in. Was there no way to stop all of this? The rest of the day was filled with deep and harboring thoughts. Did she have a choice at this point?

Bertha White had not seen the smug smile on Dr. Crane's face as she hung up the phone. Her conversation with Bertha went exactly as she had hoped it would. She felt comfortable her plan would now work. Thanks to Dr. Silvers's sterling and truly frightening performance earlier, she had the leverage with Bertha she needed and the time to buy the outcome she wanted. It was almost too perfect. She would also now be able to accomplish what Dr. Silvers could not—Reymond Alexander would be eliminated. This would surely add points for her in Silvers's book, and she would take all the points she could get at this stage of the game. Lisa James did not worry Dr. Crane as she felt sure the pretty blonde tech was too dumb to put two and two together and cause them any trouble. All blondes were dumb. Wasn't that a given? Besides, it would only be a matter of hours until Lisa's job would be eliminated, and she would never have a clue as to the real reason for her termination. Life felt good to Dr. Alice Crane this morning. As a matter of fact, this whole week had gone better than expected. She had been pleasantly surprised with her reward for the handling of the Taylor Addison situation. The five thousand dollar check Dr. Silvers had handed her the morning after the medical panel ruled in their favor was unexpected, but deeply appreciated. Yes, today had been a good day. Bertha would keep her mouth shut and do her dirty work. It was indeed almost too perfect.

26

The call was placed to Seton Memorial Hospital a little before 11 p.m. The male voice asked to speak to the operations director for the hospital's blood laboratory services. The call was transferred to Dr. Joe Fraser, acting assistant for the Pathology Department at Seton Memorial.

"Dr. Fraser, here"

"You need to check your blood inventory. There's been a tragic mistake and your hospital was on the receiving end of a large shipment of contaminated blood."

"What? What did you just say?" the doctor asked, not quite believing what he had just heard.

The caller precisely repeated his statement.

"Who is this? Who am I speaking with?" Dr. Fraser questioned.

"I'm a cop, Dr. Fraser. My girlfriend works at the blood center. She's been going through hell these last few days with the inside knowledge that bad blood was sent out, but no recall has yet to be issued and she's quite certain now the blood center is not going to notify anyone," the voice stated with quiet authority.

"What are the unit numbers? I can't track this if I don't have some idea. . ."

"I don't have any numbers for you to verify, Dr. Fraser. You just need to know you are sitting in a dangerous position."

"When did we receive this blood? Can you tell me that?" Dr. Fraser asked, trying to calm his own doubts about the seriousness of this call. It could just be a prank caller with nothing better to do on a snowy, miserable night.

"It was shipped from Hamilton Regional a little over eighteen days ago. It came in on your first early morning delivery shipment. You ordered two hundred blood components and you received four hundred and fifty-one. My numbers should match your shipment receipts for that morning's run."

Dr. Fraser felt a sickening feeling in the pit of his stomach. The caller was too precise. Something told him that Seton Memorial was indeed being alerted to a real and deadly situation.

"If it's been over eighteen days, most of the blood has probably been transfused," the doctor stated, hoping to gather more information from the mysterious caller.

"More than likely it has, Dr. Fraser. I wish I could give you more information, but I'm telling you the truth. It's up to you now. Our conscience is clear from now on." The dial tone rang loudly in Dr. Fraser's ear.

"Christ!" The assistant fumed as he hung up the telephone. Without unit numbers to help him track the blood, there was little he could do except file a report of the call.

The next morning, Dr. Fraser's report hit the desk of Seton Memorial's Chief Pathologist, Paul Andrews. The report was staggering. Multiple components of contaminated blood could very well have been dispersed to their hospital patients. A recall would be time consuming, expensive, and embarrassing for the hospital. If such an error did, in fact, prove to be true, lawsuits could lurk just around the corner. Two calls were placed before 9 a.m. One to Dr. Thompson Moran at the State Board of Health, and one to Dr. Benjamin Silvers at Hamilton Regional. Neither of the men was in his office.

Both secretaries recorded Dr. Andrews's call with a notation of "urgent."

Dr. Silvers was the first to return Dr. Andrews's call.

"Hi, Paul, it's Ben. My secretary said you wanted to talk to me—something about it being urgent?"

"Hi, Ben. Yes, I did call. I'm afraid I have received some information that is very disturbing. It seems we have been on the receiving end of contaminated blood; I'm not sure of the number, but I do know it was sizable by shipment standards."

Silvers felt his own blood draining from his face.

"I just need to verify this report, Ben. I'm sure it has been exaggerated, but nevertheless, the seriousness has me very concerned, especially since it has been over eighteen days." The pathologist was direct and his information right on the money.

"How in the hell does he know this?" Silvers thought as he tried to steady his voice before answering.

"Well, Paul, I guess my report was a little scary. But you know how official letters can sound. I'm surprised my letter has just now reached you. Our mail system leaves a lot to be desired," Silvers said in a very sincere and concerned voice. The sweat was building up on the back of his neck.

"What letter, Ben? I haven't received any letter of notice?"

"Well, I sent you one the day after we discovered the error."

"How long ago was this?" There was definite irritation present in Andrews's voice.

"I'm not sure, Paul. Maybe ten days ago. It took us a while once the error came to our attention to go back and verify. Those things can take time."

"I don't have any such letter, Ben. This information came to me from an anonymous source—a cop whose girlfriend works at your center. My assistant filed a report on the call late last night. It just hit my desk this morning." There was silence on the other end of the phone. The pause was long enough to give Andrews a sense that the caller was indeed telling the truth. The chief pathologist pressed on. "Listen, Ben. This puts us in a hell of a situation down here."

Seton Memorial had just settled out-of-court over a messy error that had tragically resulted in a woman's death. Blood that did not match the woman's own blood type had been mistakenly transfused. The woman was O positive, but three units of A negative blood were transfused into her waiting body. It was a nasty death. A death that should never have taken place. Again, human error. The hospital dished out two million dollars to the family. The dollar figure was not released to the public, and the hospital did not have to state publicly to any wrongdoing. It was gracefully settled by Seton Memorial's crack attorneys. The thought of a large patient population of Seton Memorial getting contaminated blood scared the hell out of Paul Andrews.

"I guess you and I need to get together and discuss this with all the details in black and white. We will certainly have to initiate our own notification process. Are you prepared to do the retesting on all of these individuals after we identify them because we're sure as hell not going to absorb these costs?"

"Well, yes, certainly. I stated that in my letter, Paul," Silvers covered, convinced that he had made the right response to this call.

"Well, as I see it, Ben, you need to supply us with the unit numbers and a letter stating the need to contact your center and set an appointment for testing. Keep the letter simple—no broad statements about AIDS or hepatitis that'll scare the shit out of these people. If you do it right, we'll forward the letters to the recipients' physicians."

"Of course, Paul. We're prepared to start the ball rolling. Any feeling for how many we could be dealing with down the road?" Silvers asked.

"It depends, Ben. I'm sure there will be some physicians who won't—well, you know the process, Ben. I suspect we'll round up about half of them at most."

"Well, we'll put a soft sell letter together, perhaps with a research plea for their specific blood type. We certainly don't want to scare the hell out of these people up front. I agree with you on that. We'll begin the retesting process as they contact us." Silvers felt he had done a good job of covering his tracks up to this point. He had one more issue to cover.

"Listen, Paul, just between you and me. This is a very difficult situation to find oneself in—especially in light of what the center has just gone through with that Addison lawsuit. Let's try and keep this as quiet as possible. There is no need to make any public statements here."

"Ben! Didn't I just say this puts us in a sticky situation here. I could care less about your troubles with your own screw-ups. I don't want our name dragged through the mud any more than you do. Of course I want to keep a lid on this." The pause between sentences was short. "Ben, you're certain you sent me a letter?"

"Of course, Paul. Do you honestly think I would not notify you with something this serious." Silvers voice was pitched with just the right amount of indignation.

"Yeah, well. I don't want to make this any more public than you do. It would definitely not be good publicity for Seton. Let's just get on with it."

"I agree," Silvers said.

"Ben, do me one last favor."

"What is it?"

"Send me a copy of that goddamned letter."

"Sure, Paul. That won't be a problem. I'll have my secretary drop you a copy of the original letter in the mail today."

The hospital pathologist had one last statement to issue.

"And, Ben. I guess you should know this. I called the State Board of Health this morning. I'm waiting for Dr. Moran to return my call. As much as I didn't want to do this, I have to follow the hospital's procedure channels."

With that stated, Dr. Paul Andrews hung up.

"That sonofabitch," Silvers cursed as he slammed the phone receiver down. Silvers could not stand Thompson Moran. And he certainly did not want Moran's agency poking its nose in the blood center's business.

Moran was the kind of doctor who loved publicity, and he was very good at getting it. Silvers's mind was racing. So much had happened in the last few minutes.

"An anonymous call from a cop. How in the hell did a cop get involved with this? Silvers was processing as many questions through his quick mind as he could as he nearly ran down the hall toward Dr. Crane's office. The angry doctor almost knocked Dr. Crane's secretary down as he barged into his assistant's office. From the look on Dr. Silvers's face, Amy was glad she was on her way out to the safety of her own desk.

"What's the matter? You look like you've seen a ghost," Crane said as soon as Amy closed her office door.

"We've got a leak. A goddamned snitch. Andrews from Seton Memorial just called me. Some goddamned anonymous telephone call was reported last night—it was from a cop." Silvers was doing his usual angry pacing.

"A cop?" she questioned.

"Yeah, a cop who happens to have a girlfriend working here."

"Lisa James!" Crane said out loud as she pushed deep into her chair with the weight of her large body.

"I'll be a sonofabitch," Crane felt a twitch in the side of her face. Her green eyes narrowed to just slits.

Lisa James was the very person Crane was not worried about last night. As it turned out, this innocent clerk would be the one to ruin a perfect plan—not Bertha White or Reymond Alexander—but the dumb blonde who didn't appear to have a clue. This rattled her. She should have been watching the girl. She should have put the fear of God in her. She screwed up.

Dr. Silvers could see the look of panic beginning to form in his assistant's face.

"I've covered our asses for now," he said, stopping his pacing long enough to stare out Crane's window at the employee's parking lot below.

"How? How did you do that?"

"I told Andrews we had sent a letter out," he answered still not looking at her. "I made him think we were just waiting for him to respond to our notification report, and that we were prepared to forward a letter of explanation. He's all bent out of shape and flinging orders at me over the goddamned phone."

"Yeah, well that's because they got caught with their pants down when they snuffed out a woman by giving her the wrong. . ."

"I know all that shit. That's their problem." Silvers once again continued to circle the room. His dark eyes were focused and his firm body tense. You could see his muscles flexing beneath his tailored suitcoat as he moved around the room. He was like a graceful cat just waiting to pounce on something. Crane wished it could just once be her.

"I told him we were standing by and would soft-pedal our notification letter so as not to cause someone a heart attack. It all depends on how many people are actually notified by their physicians. My guess is, most of the docs won't want to stir up muddy waters—depending on the condition of their patient. If they're on a death's door track, you can bet they won't get a letter. If they're a casual transfusion with a lot of years left in them, the docs will probably forward our letter." Silvers repeated in an animated voice filled with sarcasm.

Alice Crane did not offer any comments. She was deeply disturbed with this turn of events. Silvers had already started to work a safe retreat into place for the center to fall back on. After all, it would still be their word against that of a dumb blonde who had no raw data to back up her claim. Of course the good doctors had followed through with a notification letter. And they were meticulous in the backtracking of all contaminated units. These things take time. No one could fault them for doing the work correctly. Lisa James and her cop boyfriend would not have a leg to stand on. No one could prove they had not sent out a notification letter. The doctors could cover their tracks beautifully. The system would always be on their side. Dr. Crane was thinking rationally again. Of course everything would be okay. Not as they had planned, but okay. They would not get hurt by this unexpected turn of events.

"Alice, I'm going to need those unit numbers. Andrews wants to start a search. . ."

"I'm not sure we can do that, Ben. I wiped out the data from Bertha's system. I thought. . ."

"You've got to get those tracers back, Alice. I don't care what the hell you have to do—just get them back." Silvers was emphatic. He could not be caught without this information. If he couldn't forward the unit numbers for search procedures, Andrews was sure to catch on to the cover-up. Dr. Crane's neck felt moist. The time lapse to go into the computer's back-up system and retrieve the erased unit numbers was now beyond recall. The perfect plan was suddenly not so perfect. Silvers had only a modest knowledge of the computer system. Crane did not respond to the severity of the situation at this moment. She needed time to rethink a course of action. She did not want to lay this on Silvers right now.

There must be a way out. If only she had kept a printed copy—*if only* wasn't worth a hill of beans right now.

"We'll have to bring Carter in on this," Dr. Silvers said, breaking the momentary silence.

"Why?" Crane responded rocking sideways in her chair.

"If the cop called the hospital, he could very well have gotten the fever to call the media. We can't take chances here. Carter is simple. She'll be on our side. I'll handle her."

Silvers quickly left Dr. Crane's office in search of his public relations director. He would find Carter just settling in for the day. She had overslept this morning and had arrived later than her usual 7:30 a.m. starting time.

"Got a moment?" Silvers said in his most friendly voice.

"Of course, Dr. Silvers. Please come in." Carter replied, somewhat startled to see the medical director on her doorstep this morning.

Their conversation began with polite talk about the severe weather Hamilton had been experiencing these last few days. Silvers made sure to stay away from any mention of their stormy meeting which had taken place less than twenty-four hours ago. When Silvers felt Carter was at ease, he began.

"Carter, I need to bring you up-to-date on a confidential situation that has occurred in our laboratory area."

"In Siam Qua's area, Dr. Silvers?"

"No. In Bertha White's area," Silver corrected.

"It seems she had a serious error and several units of contaminated blood left our center. Of course, we have gone through all the proper procedural channels, and I have forwarded a notification letter to each hospital who received suspected blood units. We are now in the process of writing a formal letter to the physicians of the patients involved. In time, this should result in our center retesting those who received possible contaminated units of blood. Obviously, Dr. Crane and I are disappointed with the breakdown in our laboratory system, and we are taking steps to see that such a thing never happens again. It is very distressing," Silvers added, using just the right amount of distressed body language to back up his words.

"How many units are we talking about?" Carter asked.

"Uh, sixty—or somewhere around that figure," Silvers said. "Dr. Crane has the exact breakdown. But at this point, I felt you needed to be briefed just in case the media would get wind of all this."

"Are we going to issue a statement?" Carter asked.

"No! There is no need to make a mountain out of a mole hill, Carter. We just need to be prepared in case this should leak out." The doctor's voice was quick in responding to this question.

"Do you want me to prepare a statement in advance, just in case we need to react quickly?" Carter countered knowing how important it was to be prepared for serious situations involving the public's welfare.

"I guess that would be the best path to take. Yes, go ahead and put something together for my approval. Of course, we'll need our attorneys' input on whatever we say. Have something on my desk by 2 p.m.," Silvers replied as he made his way to Carter's door.

"Carter, it's so good to have you on board," Silver added just before he left her office. "Our center really needs you right now. I'm sure we won't have any problems that you can't handle." For impact he added, "accidents such as this do occur from time to time. It's important to follow all the procedures our system has built in for such matters." Silvers smiled warmly at Carter and closed her door. The doctor's just revealed statements clarified Bertha White's behavior of yesterday morning. Contaminated blood, especially sixty units worth, would cause a lab director to have a considerable amount of anxiety. Carter wondered if Bertha was going to be fired. This revelation, on top of everything else, truly complicated matters.

Part of Carter Egan wanted to simply get up and leave the blood center and never look back. The other part, the professional side, was kicking in with thoughts of action. A statement needed to be drafted. If the center would indeed make a statement, it needed to cover all the bases. Carter would need critical pieces of information to write this technically difficult public response. Who, what, where, when, and why, would all have to be outlined clearly for the public to understand. Carter instinctively picked up the phone and dialed Dr. Silvers's secretary.

"Joyce, this is Carter. I need for you to pull up a copy of the notification letter sent to the hospitals on our contamination incident. I will need to include this in a packet I'm preparing for the media should we respond."

There were several moments of silence on the other end of the phone.

"Joyce, are you there?" Carter questioned.

"Yes, Carter. But I don't remember typing any such letter." Carter felt a twinge in her stomach. It was not a good feeling.

"I'm sure you did, Joyce," Carter stated trying to reinforce her own plunging belief.

"Dr. Silvers was just in my office and told me he had sent out a letter of notification to all the hospitals on the receiving end. I'm sure it's in your computer. Would you mind checking and calling me right back?" Carter asked with an urgent appeal in her voice.

"Sure, Carter. I'll check. But I would remember such a letter if I had typed it," the secretary said as she hung up the phone with just a touch of frustration in her voice.

For a few seconds, Carter tried to recall Dr. Silvers's exact words. Perhaps she had misunderstood him. Maybe he said Dr. Crane's secretary had sent out the notification. Carter dialed Amy's number. The conversation ended up a mirrored reflection of the one she had just had with Dr. Silvers's secretary. Neither one remembered such a letter. In just a few minutes Carter's phone rang. It was Joyce. The secretary told Carter she had gone through all her current files as well as her back-up disks, and there was no such letter in her data bank. If such a letter had been written, someone else must have typed it.

"I even checked with Amy to make sure she didn't type one, but she doesn't have such an animal either. I'm sorry, Carter. Do you want me to ask Dr. Silvers what he is referring to?" Joyce offered not wanting to appear to be uncooperative with the public relations director.

"No, Joyce. That's okay. Don't say anything. I must have misunderstood Dr. Silvers." Carter hung up the phone.

"What was going on here?" she wondered, trying to digest everything that had just happened. Carter decided to go downstairs and see Bertha White. Perhaps Bertha could have been the one to forward such a letter. After all, the error did occur in her area.

Bertha White was in her office talking on her telephone.

"Bertha, can I talk to you for a moment?" Carter asked as Bertha waved her in. Bertha was using a speaker phone.

"I'm talking to my husband—I'll be done in just a moment."

A sudden electric tone of voice grabbed Carter's attention.

"I'-ll s-top -by -the st-ore -and -pick -up din-ner. Tr-y -and -be ho-me -by -six i-f y-ou c-an," the strange voice stated. Bertha said okay and clicked off the phone.

Bertha looked a bit embarrassed at seeing Carter again. The last thing she needed right now was a heart-to-heart conversation about her tearful behavior of yesterday.

"My husband had his voice box removed and he is learning to talk with a voice-assisted instrument." Carter had heard such a voice before, but at this moment could not recollect where. Bertha seemed cool and preoccupied. Carter decided to skip pleasantries and get right to the point.

"Bertha, Dr. Silvers was just in my office and told me about the escape of contaminated blood. I'm in the process of trying to put together a statement we can issue should the occasion arise. I need to have a copy of the notification letter that we sent out to our area hospitals who received the contaminated. . ."

"What letter?" Bertha cut in.

"Dr. Silvers told me he had sent out a letter of notification as soon as you had finished your laboratory verification process," Carter said with a sense of frustration about this whole issue. Just the way Bertha asked the question about the letter said something about the authenticity of Dr. Silvers's words. Was he lying to her again? Was there really a letter sent? Was this just another cover-up of reckless actions?

Bertha did not answer Carter Egan. She turned her chair sideways away from the public relations director as if to put distance between the two of them.

"I really don't have anything to say on this matter, Carter. I feel you would be better served addressing such questions to Dr. Silvers or Dr. Crane. It is out of my hands at this point," Bertha stated in a stilted manner. It was obvious to Carter that she would learn nothing from Bertha White.

"Did he threaten you too, Bertha?" Carter asked as she stood up to leave Bertha's office.

Bertha's eyes suddenly came to life. "What are you talking about, Carter?"

"Bertha, yesterday you gave me some advice. I think it holds true for both of us. We're both sucked up in something that could destroy us if we don't get out of it."

"Wait a minute, Carter," Bertha quickly called out as she motioned for her not to leave. "Come back here. We need to talk." Carter had hit a button that registered inside Bertha's wounded conscience. She had to talk. She had to lay it all out.

Carter closed Bertha's door and sat back down in the metal chair. Her eyes searched Bertha's face. She saw rising anger, pain, and frustration flooding every line in the laboratory director's distressed face. The gates of confession were about to open up. For the next fifteen minutes, Bertha painstakingly took Carter through her own last six years of hell working under this executive command. The shortage calls, the wasteful dumping of blood during emergencies, the processing errors, the laboratory inventory switching—how she used grant money for things other than what the seed money required—all of it came pouring out. She left nothing out of what was, for her, a painful and long overdue unburdening. Finally she went into detail on what had just occurred in her laboratory with the shipping of contaminated blood, and the fact that no recall or notification had been planned as of yesterday morning.

As Bertha was finishing, Carter's eyes suddenly caught sight of a potted plant. It was identical to the plant she saw in the storage room in distribution. It was Bertha's plant. The plant and the remembered voice struck home with Carter. The strange disguised electric sounding voice could have been Bertha's if she were using her husband's electronic voice box. The key was set out for her to find by Bertha. It was now Carter's turn to look stunned. It took a few moments to put things in perspective. Carter's mind chose to focus on the most recent discovery.

"Bertha, are you telling me that this has happened before and we have not notified our hospitals?"

"This is the largest error of shipment that has ever happened, Carter, at least since I've been here. But yes, we've screwed up before on a smaller scale, and I strongly suspect we didn't notify," Bertha stated with belief in her words. Her hands were locked together, moving slowly from side to side as if trying to wipe away pieces of dirt wedged between her fingers.

"Dr. Silvers told me there were only sixty units of blood involved. . ."

"There were sixty units up-front, but you have to understand those sixty units were split into components and—"

"My God, Bertha, we're talking about some three hundred components of blood going out to our hospitals."

Bertha's head rocked back and forth with confirmation.

"That's correct, Carter. It's a serious contamination." There was just a moment of hesitation before Bertha continued.

"I'll also bet you a bundle that Silvers had a sudden reason for bringing you into this circle of knowing people." Bertha said.

"What do you mean?"

"Yesterday morning it was a done deed that we were not going to do anything—at least not right away about notification. No letter had been drafted at that point. And I'll tell you something else, all the data I had compiled in my search was extracted from my computer just moments after I left Crane's office. If I hadn't fallen apart and spent those fifteen minutes or so in your office, I might have been able to pull up a copy of the inventory spill, but. . ." Bertha broke off her sentence as emotions again began to surface. Carter looked away for just a few seconds. The tiny office seemed to be closing in on her. With little fresh air circulating in the room, breathing became difficult. Struggling to regain her composure, Bertha continued to speak.

"Something must have happened since then, Carter, that changed their minds. They were going to bury this. I'd bet my right arm on it. Someone must have pushed a button somewhere. Otherwise, I think we would still be as mum as a mouse on this whole thing. It's how they operate, Carter. Think about it!"

Reymond Alexander suddenly popped into Bertha's mind. "Surely, Reymond would not have pulled the plug on all this?" Bertha wondered. She had been careful to leave Reymond out of the story. No! Reymond was not involved. She felt sure of that. The only other person with any kind of knowledge at all about the break was Lisa James, the system's back-up coding clerk in distribution. Lisa had matched all the tests and blood type data for final shipping. But certainly Lisa didn't know enough to alert anyone. Bertha secretly kicked herself for thinking Lisa James did not have enough sense to realize what was going on. Could she have something to do with this sudden change of heart?

"How can we do this, Bertha? How can we get by with something like this?"

Bertha didn't answer Carter.

"What are you going to do, Bertha?" Carter asked, feeling a ray of hope for the first time that there was now someone of significant importance on the technical side who could join forces with her and Grace.

"Nothing. I can't do a damn thing, Carter." The words slapped Carter across the face with stinging force.

"I can't afford to lose my pension and benefits. Dr. Crane made that perfectly clear to me yesterday."

A look of betrayal was clear and present in Carter's large brown eyes.

"Listen, I know I must seem like just as big a scum as they are, but Carter, I need my pension retirement benefits. My husband's life depends on me. . ." Bertha did not finish her sentence.

"Is that why you tipped me off to the stored blood we are selling out of state during all these emergency calls, Bertha?"

Bertha avoided the question. "Listen to me, Carter, we're sitting in a dangerous situation. Crane and Silvers hold most of the cards in this game. They can make both of us look like out-and-out liars. I've got no raw data to back me up, and believe me when I tell you, they can turn this whole thing around and dump it right back in my lap."

Carter sighed deeply. She knew Bertha was telling the truth.

"Carter, I've have got to keep my mouth shut and go on with looking the other way." The words seemed shallow when spoken out loud. The look on Carter's face made Bertha cringe with shame at having said them. A bit of anger surfaced in Bertha's mind. She felt cornered, exposed, and dirty all at the same time. Carter's own innocence only added to the pent-up rage going on inside her. She resented Carter at this moment.

"You've still got your career ahead of you, Carter. You're young. You've got options. I don't. I've got just six months to keep my nose buried. I can't back you up. And if you try and push me, I will deny everything I've said to you. I have to, Carter. Please understand where I'm coming from on this."

Carter didn't say anything. This was the second time in less than twenty-four hours she had heard this type of a denial statement.

"Listen, Bertha. If this system is ever going to be cleaned up, people who know what the hell is wrong need to work together. I need help. I can't do this by myself. I need information that I can take to the board. . ."

"Forget the board, Carter. They'll gut you as quick as a butcher slices a steer. That board owes Preston and Silvers too many favors. It's a medical brotherhood, Carter. They stick together with their own kind. Besides, too much bad publicity can hit them too. They don't want any part of this to surface and bloody their own goddamn reputations as board members. I've watched others think they can go over the exec's heads only to end up having their own head handed to them on a silver platter. Forget it, the board isn't going to help."

The room was quiet for a few seconds. Sensing that she could not accomplish anything else, Carter stood up to leave. As she reached for the door, Bertha had one last thing to say.

"Carter, you may be the only person here who might be able to stop what's going on. I don't know if even that's possible, but you could use your media contacts. . ." Bertha stopped talking as if she knew her words were useless. "Forget it, Carter. You'd be heading for trouble you can't even begin to imagine if you pursue it. We can't beat this system. Nobody would believe us." Carter didn't bother to turn around and look at Bertha. She couldn't. Not now—not at this moment.

Bertha's eyes followed Carter out of her laboratory. Six months—that was all she had left. She had made the decision to keep her mouth shut, and she was going to stick with it. She was sucked up into the very trap she had warned Carter about. Every day was like an ongoing experience of drowning. She had to go along—her husband's life depended on her. Bertha leaned back heavily in her chair closing her eyes. She had deliberately dragged Carter into the thick of things. It was a mistake to set her up like that and then back away from helping her. The clock on her office wall told her she had six more hours to get through. That's how Bertha's life was now to be measured—by the ticks of a clock on a wall in a laboratory office.

Carter's body felt heavy as she climbed the back stairs. The smell of processing skin from the Tissue Bank operation drifted up her nostrils. For the first time in weeks, the stench bothered her. Each step was made with effort. She felt like a person with a flu—head aching, stomach churning. For one brief moment, Carter thought she had found an ally—someone who could testify with inside knowledge to all the madness. Someone to go to the board with—"forget the board"—her mind screamed. Oh God, just to have a few minutes of peace—a few minutes to digest all that she had just learned. Bertha's confession began to repeat in Carter's mind. The evil of all she had just learned hit her with force once again. She stopped at the top of the stairs and tried to clear her mind. Calling false emergencies was one thing—it was an ethical call. But what Bertha had just told her added so much dirt to the mix she couldn't think straight.

She needed to talk to Grace. Grace was the only person who was with her. Squaring her shoulders, she headed toward her friend's office. The door was open but Grace was nowhere in sight. Carter's mind was filled with so many different thoughts. Bertha's words were ringing in her ears. She had no paper evidence to back up any of these charges. None whatsoever. It would take time to gather it, and each new day seemed to bring with it a new and different dark discovery. She was getting in deeper and deeper each moment with knowledge of wrongdoing that seemed so absurd. Who would believe her? She couldn't prove a thing, and no one was in a position to come forward with her. Carter longed for Patrick. Just to hear his voice. How had all this happened to her. She had just wanted a cause to work for. Something to believe in. When she reached her office, Shelly had put a message on her chair that was obviously urgent. It was from Dr. Silvers. He wanted to see her as soon as possible.

Carter did not hesitate. She had nothing to lose at this point. She went directly to his office. His door was open—most unusual for him. Seeing her standing at the door he waved her in. He was on the phone with what appeared to be his wife. In a few minutes he hung up. There was to be no casual conversation this time.

"Carter, Joyce tells me you have requested a copy of the notification letter?" There was nothing in his tone of voice to tell her which direction he was heading.

"Yes, Dr. Silvers, I need it for the media press release I'm preparing for you." Carter played along with innocence.

"I see. Well, there's been a slight misunderstanding here, Carter, and one that will need your cooperation."

Carter looked interested and nodded her head.

"It seems Dr. Crane did not forward our notification letter as I had instructed her to do. We are now sitting in an embarrassing situation because of her error. I am having Joyce retype my original memo, and I have instructed her to stamp it with a copy marker. I think this approach is in the best interest of the blood center."

Silvers looked hard at Carter searching her face for any signs of disapproval. He knew that Carter had found out that no letter had been forwarded to the hospitals as he had told her earlier. If she was playing a game with him, he would find out soon enough.

"I'm sure this will all turn out all right, Carter, and the important thing to keep in mind here is the fact we are putting together a notification letter. The date really doesn't matter now, does it?"

"I—I guess not, Dr. Silvers," Carter answered. That same feeling of breathlessness was hitting her again. She hated this—all the lying, the fear of pretending and being found out. She had never worked in such an atmosphere.

"Can I go now?"

"My God, Carter. You sound as if you're a prisoner." His statement brought color to her cheeks. His words spoke exactly to her feelings. She was a prisoner.

"I'm sorry, Dr. Silvers. I just feel so. . ."

"I'll tell you what you should feel, Carter. You should feel relieved that I'm telling you about this ahead of time. You should be thankful that I'm preparing you for a situation that could cause us considerable heat. You're a part of this whole operation. As my public relations director, you act for me just the way my attorney acts—you hold certain confidences. It is your duty to protect our name and keep privileged information inside this building. If you can't do that for us—well, I don't think your chances of ever working again in public relations look very bright." The doctor's eyes were narrowed and his voice deliberately soft. It was another threat. He was full of threats. How many people had he run over with this kind of intimidation?

"Don't take me for such a fool, Dr. Silvers." Carter's words erased the slight smile from Silvers's face. "I'm not Anna Cable or, for that matter, any of the other scared robots you have marching around here at your beck and call."

The force of Carter's words stung the air. Silvers made no move to speak. This was a first for him. No one had ever spoken to him like this.

"You've thrown your last threat at me—I don't need this job and I certainly don't need to put up with any more of your lies." Carter's exit was quick and her words seemed to hang in the air. Silvers felt a trace of moisture above his upper lip. A cold chill worked its way down his spine. Carter could be dangerous. He never thought she would bolt. All the others hadn't, at least not until he was through with them. How could he have misjudged Carter's strength like this. He quickly reached for his phone. She was going to have to be dealt with and quickly.

Carter's graceful body carefully moved between the desks in the open area of the administrative wing. Everyone was busy as the day's activity was almost in full force. Only Shelly noticed the difference in Carter's appearance as she headed for Michael Bryan's office. Her boss was moving too fast and her jaw was clenched too tight. Something had happened in Dr. Silvers's office—but then, didn't everyone leave his office at one time or another looking like this? Shelly felt this was not going to be a good day. She was terribly right.

Carter's mind raced over recent events. Everything had happened so fast this morning. The last few weeks had taken a toll on her. She had never expected to find herself in such a dark situation. She had actually been frightened these last few days. Snooping around, gathering files, searching back records. This did not fall under the category of public relations. She was not a trained detective. The thought of such a role frightened her. Last night had not helped quiet her fears as she had located a past employee phone directory and had called the number listed for Anna Cable. Anna's daughter had answered the phone, and when Carter identified herself, there was a long silence on the other end before she responded.

"I know who you are. You came into Gibby's with Grace Tende." The voice was low and very dry.

"I know this call is awkward, but I wondered if I might ask you a few questions."

"I have nothing to say to you." The voice did not hang up but appeared to be waiting for Carter's response.

"I can understand you're not wanting to talk to me, but I've found myself in a situation I thought you might be able to help me with—I mean, I think your mother discovered some of the very same things I have while working at the blood center. I need to know if you. . ."

"If you've discovered something, Miss Egan, you need to get the hell out of there."

"Jody, I'm up to my neck with unethical conduct going on at our center. What I need is documentation. I think your mother has some papers that could help me prove. . ."

"Whatever my mother found out is none of your business." There was a slight pause. "I can't help you. I wish I could, but I can't."

"Jody, listen to me. You can help me. Have you ever looked through any of your mother's personal records she might have brought home with her from the center?"

"I haven't touched my mother's things since the night I found her." The voice sounded distant, almost as if she had gone back into time.

"If we could find whatever it was Anna was using to hold a hammer over the center's head, we could go together to the board or someplace else—like the State Board of Health—and tell our story." Carter's voice was pleading.

"Look, Miss, whoever you are—I don't know what happened to my mom at that blood center; but whatever it was, it put her where she is today." Anger was again present in Jody's voice.

"Jody, will you at least let me come and talk to you?"

"I don't see any reason for you and me to talk. It's too late now to help my mother." The daughter had just one thing left to say to Carter.

"Just get out of there. Get out before they destroy you, too." The line went dead.

Michael Bryan was sitting at his desk putting away a briefcase full of papers when Carter's knock caught his attention. He smiled, waved her in, and continued what he was doing. He did not sense anything out of order. Carter was very good at keeping a pleasant appearance in place. It wasn't until he noticed Carter had closed his door that he even began to suspect that something was wrong.

"What's up?" His voice was upbeat. His trip away to wherever had obviously done him some good. His eyes surveyed Carter's pretty face. Something had happened. What? He was about to learn.

"Michael, I'm afraid I have to. . ." The words stuck in her throat. She had surprised herself just a few moments ago. Silvers's threats had hit a nerve that had never been tapped before. Being threatened was not something Carter handled every day. She was a fool to think she could stay in place and gather information that would cause a change. She should have resigned several weeks earlier.

"What is it, Carter? You look upset." Michael's voice was kind and his eyes reflected concern.

"Michael," she began again. "I'm afraid I have to resign. This just isn't a place where I can work and keep my. . ."

"Wait a minute, Carter," Michael interrupted. "Let's not move so fast here. Why don't you tell me what has happened? I'm sure I can straighten things out. . ."

"Can you stop all the madness, Michael? Can you make them stop?"

"Make who stop Carter? You need to back up and tell me what happened." Michael Bryan could feel the pit of his stomach beginning to burn. This was not supposed to happen—at least not right now. He had been out of town for the last three days. He had flown to Canada to take care of business in preparation for the center's yet-to-be-announced new building fund. Preston was hot to have a new building erected on the land directly behind the employee parking lot. It was to be a state of the art structure and would house all of the technical components of the blood center's operation. It would also be named after Preston. It was to be his monument—his greatest glory. Michael Bryan's good mood was, in part, because of this financial trip. He had started his own life in a new direction. In just a matter of days, he would be out of all this. Carter couldn't jump ship right now. What in the hell had happened in such a short period of time? Michael pressed Carter to sit down and discuss everything from the start with him.

"Carter, I know we work for a couple of assholes, but we really do have a cause in place here. You've made such a difference."

"Michael, I haven't made one damn bit of difference here. In fact, I think you could say I've only added to the deceit that's in place here." Carter's eyes snapped with anger.

"Carter, that's not so. You've done a great job for us under—well—under less than great conditions. I know Silvers is a bear. . ."

"He's more than a bear, Michael. He's a criminal. He lies and bullies people into doing things that are not right."

"What kind of things are you talking about?"

"Michael, quit trying to pretend you don't know what I'm talking about, because you know it all. You're just as involved in all the crap as they are. You know we are calling false blood shortages. . ."

"I thought I explained that to you."

"You just told me another lie to make it come out okay for what's really going on. I know, Michael—I know all of it—the phony calls, the wasteful dumping of blood, the way we misuse grant money and now. . ."

"And now—what?"

Carter's dark green eyes searched her supervisor's face. She wanted to see something in his eyes that told her he really didn't know everything—that he wasn't part of all this madness—that he was just as innocent as she was—just as used as she had been. It wasn't there. She knew it.

"Michael, are you trying to tell me you don't know anything about the contaminated blood that went out of our laboratory several days ago? Are you trying to tell me you didn't know we had no intention of notifying our hospitals and initiating a recall?

"I don't know what you are talking about, Carter." His face did show a certain surprise. Could she be wrong. Could Michael not know?

Michael walked around his desk to his chair. Sitting down he reached up and began rubbing his temples with his hands. His eyes were closed and his face looked drawn. He sighed deeply. Michael gave no sign of answering her. He was silent.

"I'm sorry, Michael. I guess you have your reasons for being involved in all this. But I can't be." Carter moved forward in her chair resting her hands on Michael's desk. "I've worked too hard to turn my back on every ethical standard I've ever learned. I know people have a rather low opinion of people who work in public relations. They look at us as mouthpieces who will say whatever to protect those who sign our paychecks. But that's not the real truth. Most of us in p.r. really do walk that narrow line that separates truth from fiction. But what we're doing here goes way beyond putting a spin on a story." Carter pushed back in her chair, separating herself once again from any close ties with her superior. It was body language at its best. Michael felt Carter pulling away from him. He stood up and approached the side of her chair leaning down to eye-level contact.

"Carter, you can't leave. I promise you I will fix whatever is broken here. I know we can do it."

"Stop it, Michael. Stop lying to me. I thought we were friends. I trusted you in every sense." Carter stood up as if to bolt from the office. Michael's hands gripped her shoulders pushing Carter gently back into her seated position.

"We are friends, Carter. I wouldn't hurt you for anything. . ."

"You've gone beyond hurting me, Michael," Carter said, feeling the release of his strong hands from her shoulders.

"Listen to me, Carter. You don't know what you're in for if you leave now. Silvers can see to it that you never work in public relations again. He will stop at nothing to destroy you and your reputation." Michael's face was close to Carter's. His breath smelled of stale tobacco and coffee. "We can get around all of it if we hang together, Carter. Silvers isn't going to be around here forever, and Preston is just about ready to retire. I can get you more money. . ."

"I don't want more money—that isn't it. I can't work for them, Michael."

"Carter, you don't understand. Silvers will destroy you and your reputation. You'll never work in p.r. again—trust me on this, I know."

"Is Silvers the reason Anna Cable couldn't get another job in public relations? Is Silvers responsible for ruining her reputation too, Michael?"

Michael's face registered an expression of pain as his eyes searched Carter's face for even a shred of understanding. There was so much to tell in regard to Anna Cable. He had gone along with all of the harassment. He regretted it, but he couldn't change it now. Straightening his body, he leaned his weight back onto the edge of his desk. His hands were trembling, and a small bead of sweat had broken out across his forehead. It was time to face the truth.

"No, Carter. Silvers isn't responsible for this one. I am. I'm responsible for keeping Anna Cable out of her field."

His answer clearly jarred Carter.

"You?" The answer hung in the air for a few moments before Michael Bryan went on.

"I don't understand, Michael. How could you be part of something so evil?"

"Anna Cable got involved in matters that clearly could have caused the center some embarrassment. She found out. . .she misunderstood some reports and threatened to use them against us. Whether or not I give a damn about Silvers, it's my job to protect the center. In Anna's case, I was selected to handle the damage control."

"Damage control? For God's sake, Michael, the woman tried to kill herself. What kind of people are you?" Carter's eyes filled with tears of anger.

"I'm not saying any of this was right, Carter. I admit it got out of control. We never should have pushed her so hard, and trashing her personnel references was stupid; but Christ—there's a lot of lives at stake here. Anna Cable just couldn't get it through her head the kind of damage she could inflict on the community. She had to be handled."

"Stop it, Michael, stop it. I don't believe I'm hearing you say these things. Anna Cable was not the bad guy here. . ."

"Listen to me, Carter. It doesn't matter what you and I think. The game doesn't play by any set rules. This is business here, big business, and you and I can't stop the outcome. Anna Cable learned that the hard way. I don't want to see you go through the same kind of hell she did."

"Michael, I don't believe this. How could you ever be involved in such a thing?" Carter responded, clearly shocked at what she was hearing. Silvers would do something like this, but not Michael Bryan. It was such a shock—a painful and shameful shock.

The look in Carter's eyes landed a direct blow to Michael Bryan's stomach. Hurt, disappointment, and, most of all, shame were clearly present in those innocent eyes staring back at him.

Recovering just a little, Carter shot a direct question at her supervisor.

"Did Anna Cable ever try to blow the whistle on Silvers and this operation?"

"She tried once, Carter. It only took a few calls to convince her she was out of her league. Trust me when I tell you, Silvers plays hard ball when it comes to saving his ass. Public relations people don't stand a chance."

"What if someone else comes forward with paper evidence to back her up this time?"

"Carter, don't do this. You don't know what you're in for. I know. Trust me when I tell you, Silvers will take whatever reputation you've worked so hard for and smear it like jelly. He'll paint a picture that will leave you looking like. . ." Michael paused for a moment. He didn't even want to think about all the things Silvers would do if cornered—things he couldn't talk about.

Carter recalled all the warnings she had been given. She should have seen something like this coming. Michael's face reflected the seriousness of the situation. She had never felt so alone. The fear in Michael's words began to settle in, touching her in a most intimate way. She felt stripped—naked in front of him. What was she going to do? The urge to flee was once again very powerful.

"Michael, I can't work here anymore. Not now. I don't care what you try to do to me—it just isn't worth this. I have to be able to look myself in the mirror every morning—something I'm sure you haven't been able to do for a long, long time." Carter's words struck Michael far harder than she ever dreamed possible. She was right. Oh God, she was so right.

Michael stood straight up with the force of Carter's statement. He turned away, walking to the nearest window. His right hand grabbed the cord sending his custom-made wooden blinds upward, letting the strong glare of the winter sun stream in.

Carter swallowed for the first time in several minutes. The fluid in her mouth tasted bitter as it ran down the back of her throat. Her body was still shaking, but not from fear—more like shock.

"Carter," Michael began, "I'll do everything I can to protect you. I promise. I'm sorry for what has happened."

There was nothing for Carter to say. The unspeakable had just happened. As her hand grasped the door handle, she paused for just a moment. Michael had turned to look at her. For one brief moment their eyes met. Carter had no words of forgiveness for him. She had no words left. The sound of the door closing brought an unbearable silence of guilt to his soul. Michael Bryan moved his head forward until his forehead touched the cold windowpane. What had he become? The glare of the sunlight blinded him. He forced his eyes to remain open shearing his eyes with tears. Was all this like some bad dream? Could he really be part of any of this? At any moment he prayed he would wake up and find himself sailing on a white sailboat with the wind at his back. The sky would be clear and the only sound to be heard would be the swiping of the ocean waves as they gently splashed the body of his boat. Michael stayed in this position for several minutes. Finally, he walked to his desk and extracted several reports carefully filed away in his well-organized desk drawers. He folded them neatly, carefully placing them in precise order inside his briefcase. He placed all the paperwork he had worked on the night before in the properly marked trays sitting so straight on the top of his desk. His eyes took one last look around his executive office. All that he had worked for was present.

"It wasn't much," he said out loud. "It wasn't worth all this."

He didn't bother to turn off the lights when he left or to tell his secretary, Michelle, he was leaving the office for the day. It made little difference now. He wasn't coming back.

Carter walked back to her office somewhat dazed. She had a few items of a personal nature to gather up. Just a picture of her husband and a small clock radio—a letter opener given to her by her former staff. Things that a person can accumulate in a office setting to make it all seem like a sort of home away from home. Her office felt cold. It matched her own temperature. She placed her possessions in a plastic blood center bag that was clearly marked with the gift of life trademark. She had helped design the bags for her field reps to pass out at health fairs. Could any of this really be happening? she thought.

Shelly stuck her head in her boss's office.

"Hey, lady. You look a little worn out. Can I order you some lunch in?"

"No, Shelly. I'm leaving." Carter said in a tone of voice that didn't sound right to Shelly.

"Are you sick, Carter. You look sorta pale. Do you have the flu or something?"

"No, I'm not sick, Shelly. I'm going to resign. I'm leaving here for good." Carter's words hit Shelly between the eyes. For a few seconds, she couldn't believe what she had just heard. "Oh, Carter. Isn't there something we can do to change your mind? We. . ."

"Shelly, it has nothing to do with you," Carter said as she finished her short resignation letter. "It's just—I can't work here any longer." Carter looked up from her desk and saw the hurt look on Shelly's face.

"It's nothing you've done, Shelly. You've been a great secretary. I'm glad we got to know one another."

Carter by now had put her coat on and with her gathered things was ready to leave.

"Is there any chance you'll change your mind, Carter?" Shelly asked innocently, truly not wanting to see her boss leave.

Carter looked at her secretary. The worried look on Shelly's face touched Carter. There was so much she wanted to say to this lady, but there was no way to do it in a professional manner. Shelly was going to continue working at the center, and there was little she could do to make things right. The less she knew about why Carter was leaving the better off she'd be. At least, that's what Carter told herself. Carter struggled with what to say. When a person resigns because of a new job opportunity or for something along more positive lines, that's one thing. But when a person is forced to resign because she knows too much and is being threatened daily, well, that's a whole different story. Carter was a whole different story.

"Shelly, I want you to know that I truly believed in what I was doing when I first started here. I thought I had found the right cause for me. But sometimes situations are not what you expect. And in this case, this is what happened to me."

"Carter, you've found out more than you should have—that's it, isn't it. Just like Anna. . ." Shelly did not continue her sentence. Her eyes filled with tears and looked downward, staring at the carpet as if ashamed.

"Shelly, please don't." Carter touched Shelly on the shoulder. For a few moments there was silence. Neither person could find the right words to say goodbye. The circumstances were so difficult.

"I've got to go, Shelly. Take care and thanks for everything." Carter quickly left the room. On top of her desk she left her office keys and silver name tag.

Most everyone was at lunch when Carter made her way down the back stairwell. As Carter's car pulled out of the driveway, Grace Tende came running out the back door. She waved at Carter but it was too late. Carter was gone. Grace had called to see if Carter could go to lunch, and Shelly told her what had just happened. Grace felt a sick feeling as she watched Carter's car speed farther and farther away. Slowly, Grace walked back to the building. She unlocked the door and made her way back up the stairs to her office. She would wait awhile and call Carter later at home. They had to talk. What had happened this morning? Where was all this going? What could possibly happen next?

The car's heater was still blowing cold air as Carter's mind raced to digest all that had just taken place. "It was over," she kept repeating softly, "It was over."

The drive home from the blood center was made in almost a blur of time. The familiar sights of her neighborhood felt strangely protective as she guided her car into the safe harbor of her own garage.

Within the hour, a small black truck would pull up to the curb several houses down the street from her home. The driver turned the engine's motor off and settled deep into his seat. The cold air quickly began to invade the car's interior. The driver lit a cigarette and pulled an old army blanket across his body. Neither Carter or her neighbors would notice there was a stranger in their neighborhood. The cold winter air and the early evening darkness worked to the stranger's advantage just as it had one other time before.

27

Elizabeth Monroe had called in sick the morning after she had opened the blue file folder that contained the donor information on Taylor Addison. She had fled to her mother's house—it was the only place she felt safe enough to try to dry out. Her mother stayed with her, not sure of the demons her daughter was fighting. Elizabeth told her mother she had become addicted to a certain type of pain medication, and she had to pull herself together if she was ever going to get back on her feet.

Withdrawal without medication is not easy or pretty to watch. Myrtle Thomas spoon-fed her daughter warm soup broth. She held Elizabeth's head as those same liquids violently left her stomach. She covered her with blankets and her own body when the chills were so bad the bed rattled, and she sponged her daughter's thin frame with cold cloths when the sweats came in ocean waves. It was difficult for both, but they saw it through. Elizabeth pushed herself to gain control. She had to get back to work. She wasn't really ready to go back, but she had something to do. This goal was burning inside of her—leading her forward. Her hands shook and her body trembled, but she showered, dressed, and drove herself to work. Her face showed the signs of her struggle. Dark circles half-mooned her eyes and her skin seemed pasty white. But there was something else in Elizabeth's face that was now also present—hope. Her eyes were clear for the first time in weeks. She was also hungry. The French toast had settled nicely, and she found herself wanting more to eat. An appetite was new to her. She felt good about feeling hungry.

Her office was hot when she entered. She had forgotten to turn the wall temperature gauge back when she left in such a hurry four evenings ago. The chemistry changes in her body had made her more sensitive to such matters. Before, she was always cold no matter what the thermostat was reading. Her desk was piled high with paperwork—patient charts, personnel requests, scheduling sheets. A nurse's life is filled with paperwork—too much these days. Elizabeth missed the patient contact. She made a mental note to start handing off some of the paperwork to her assistant. From now on she was going to be more involved in the floor work of the center's operation. She needed to get back to being a nurse and cut back on shuffling papers.

"If she had been present, maybe what had happened could have been. . ." Her thoughts once again felt the shame for the actions of the blood center. Her hands began to shake and her stomach knotted as she remembered the envelope she had put in the mail. The intense desire of her addiction was still within. She looked at her desk clock. She had a good hour of private time before the center would be open for business. She began to tackle the mountain of paperwork. The morning would pass quickly. The busy work was good for Elizabeth. It kept her mind occupied from other thoughts that had for so long taken precedence over everything else. She was surprised when her assistant popped her head in her office door and asked if she wanted anything for lunch.

"Elizabeth, can I pick you up anything from McDonald's?" Karen Fisher asked as always. Elizabeth never seemed to be hungry, but the assistant regularly offered to grab her something from a nearby fast food restaurant.

"Yes, I'm starved!" Elizabeth replied. Karen looked startled, but a warm smile spread evenly across her plump face.

"How was your vacation, Elizabeth?" Karen asked as she waited for Elizabeth to gather up the necessary lunch money.

"It was fine," Elizabeth answered as she handed Karen a five dollar bill. "Just get me the works—a Big Mac, fries, and a large milk shake. Is this enough money to cover that?" It had been a long time since Elizabeth had ordered any fast food.

"I think you're okay. If not, you can pay me when I get back. I won't be long."

As Karen left her office, it felt so good to Elizabeth to be doing something so normal as ordering a fast food lunch. Her life had been void of such simple things for so long.

Elizabeth's back was beginning to ache. She'd been sitting all morning. She pushed back from her desk and made her way out to the donation area. The center once again was filled with eager volunteers all wanting to give their share of the gift of life. It felt good to see her techs in action. She went from station to station, visiting with people and observing the technical qualifications of her phlebotomists. Out of the corner of her eye she caught Dr. Crane waddling past the receptionist area. Their eyes met, but as usual, Dr. Crane gave her the cold shoulder. Crane did not like Elizabeth Monroe. The feeling was mutual.

She was surprised when Gerald Preston honored the first floor with his presence. Preston rarely appeared in the donor area.

"Elizabeth, may I see you for just a moment?" he asked.

"Of course, Mr. Preston," she answered.

Preston did not move toward Elizabeth's office, but instead headed for the donor lounge. He quickly poured himself a cup of black coffee and settled down on the vacant lounge couch.

"It's good to see you back, Elizabeth. We've missed you." His words were charming as usual. Preston, for whatever else she might have thought of him, was always polite. Elizabeth's face felt a sudden flush of color. It was nice to be spoken to with kindness—whether or not it was sincere didn't matter at this point to her. It felt good.

Elizabeth smiled and waited for Preston to speak.

"Elizabeth, I need for you to do a sketch of your area as it is now. I think we might be in the process of adding more space to our facility and with as busy as this area gets, you certainly could use more room for our donors." Preston's eyes were almost glowing as he spoke to Elizabeth.

"That would be nice, Mr. Preston. We could use more room, especially in the intake area. We always get so backed up there," Elizabeth said, feeling good about what she had just heard. Preston shook his head in agreement and took a large gulp of coffee from his paper cup.

"We're busy today," he observed as he surveyed the crowded drawing area.

"Yes, we are. Carter's appeals certainly work, Mr. Preston. I guess the center is lucky to have someone who can bring our need so directly to the public's attention. She really does have a way with the media. I've watched her interviews and she. . ."

Preston's smile disappeared. He quickly set his steaming cup of coffee down on the nearby coffee table and moved to get up.

"Yes, she did have a way. . ." He did not finish his sentence, and his large frame moved to leave.

"Elizabeth, if you could just give me a rough outline by, say the end of this week, we'll be off to a good start." With that said he quickly left the lounge.

Elizabeth was taken back. Had something happened to Carter? Surely not this fast. P.R. directors came and went at the center, but Carter was different. Carter knew her stuff and Ben was sold on her. Elizabeth felt a bit disturbed by this conversation. What had happened to Carter?

She wouldn't have time to mull it over as her techs were leading several donors toward the lounge. Elizabeth smiled and poured coffee and cookies and spent the next five minutes making small talk with the volunteers. It all felt so good to her. How she had missed it. How had she ever let so much happen to her? The question was quickly put aside. Ben was now standing by her office door. It was apparent he wanted her for something. She was not quite ready to see Ben, but she knew this moment was going to happen sometime today. It might as well be now.

Elizabeth smiled at Ben as she approached him from the donor's lounge. He did not return it. His face looked tense and his body language was easily read by this woman who knew his body so very well. When they were safely inside her office with the door closed, Ben began.

"Where in the hell have you been? I've been calling you—didn't you get my messages?" He didn't give her time to even answer this set of questions before he launched into the next set. "What the hell is going on with you? I had no idea where you were."

"I just needed a little time to myself, Ben."

"Don't you ever leave again without telling me where you are going. Do you understand that?" His voice was loud and cutting—more than demanding. Elizabeth moved away from him hoping to put a few feet of space between them. She walked toward her file cabinet. The sight of it reminded her of things she wished she could forget. Ben followed her, grabbing her by the shoulder and roughly turning her around to face him once again.

"Ben, don't do this—let go of me," Elizabeth complained with anger present in her voice, trying to pull her shoulder away from him.

Ben dropped his hand from her arm. He turned and walked away from her letting the moment settle.

A powerful surge of adrenaline was now running through Elizabeth's body. She had wanted to pick the timing with Ben. But seeing him this way only cleared her head as to her feelings for him. Ben was a monster. He used people and threw them away. She had seen it happen over and over again. His feelings for her were pure satisfaction for his own pleasures. She didn't count with him—not as a human being. Ben couldn't have such feelings.

"Ben, now that you're here, I want to talk to you about something that's important." Elizabeth opened the file cabinet and extracted the sealed folder. As Ben turned around and saw what she was holding, his eyes narrowed and his jaw clenched. He also displayed a look of being a bit off balance—the blue folder had almost been forgotten. The sight of

Elizabeth holding it made him feel uncomfortable. Ben did not make a sound but chose to answer her with a stare. His look unsettled Elizabeth for a few seconds. She slowly walked to her desk placing the folder on top of it. Her hand rested on its contents. "Ben, I did as you asked me to. I looked at the contents of this folder."

"I didn't ask you to open it, Elizabeth." Ben was quick with his usual lies.

"Yes, you did Ben. Don't stand there and try to deny it. You blamed the whole lawsuit mess on my nurses—does the name Edwin Shell bring back your memory?" The mention of the name brought color to the doctor's cheeks.

Silvers didn't answer her. He made no move to respond. His muscular frame was tense. Something was going on with Elizabeth that he could not quite figure out at this moment. Usually she was passive in behavior. That's what he liked most about his director of nurses. She was not confrontational. He was seeing a behavior surface here that he was not prepared for.

"Shit! what else could go wrong? First Carter and now Elizabeth," the doctor thought as he waited for Elizabeth to spit out whatever was bothering her.

Elizabeth opened the file folder quickly. She held the three separate sheets of paper in her hands.

"Ben. This is our fault here. We made a very big mistake and it cost Taylor Addison and who knows else their lives."

Elizabeth waited for Ben to respond. He didn't. She went on.

"The medical panel that ruled in our favor never saw these question-naires, did they, Ben?" Her question brought a change in Silvers's face. She couldn't read his expression. "Ben, we can't bury this mistake. It isn't right. We were at fault. We did commit a serious act of negligence here. I'll take responsibility for it, Ben, but we have to come forward with this."

Silvers grabbed the donor sheets out of Elizabeth's hands.

"You're out of your fucking mind. We're not going to do any such thing. What the hell's wrong with you? Have you overdosed again. Is your brain fried?" His words were cruel and hit home with impact. "Listen, you dried-up druggy, this is none of your business. It's over. I have no intention of opening up a can of worms that puts me in a. . ."

"You—it's more than you, doctor. A person has died here. We're the cause. We screwed up."

"I should never have given you this file. I thought I could trust you. Alice was right." Silvers reached around Elizabeth picking up the blue folder that had originally housed the donor's questionnaires.

"Trust me? This has nothing to do with trust. It's beyond trust, Ben. This is criminal, and I can't let you walk away from doing what we have to do."

"We don't have to do anything, you bitch, but for you to keep your mouth shut. You're not going to say anything to anybody, do you understand me?" Ben grabbed Elizabeth by the shoulders. His strong hands felt as if they were crushing her arms. He didn't let go when she winced out loud in pain. Moving his face as close as he could to Elizabeth's without touching her, he continued talking.

"I've come too far to let you or any other bitch pull me down. Taylor Addison is buried and forgotten. We went to great trouble to have this settled our way, and I'm not about to let you mess this up. You bloody idiot. Who do you think you are? Where do you get off screaming ethics to me. You're nothing but a goddamned drug addict. You're so strung out half the time you don't know which end is up. You're not a nurse. You should be run out of the nursing profession. Don't you start trying to tell me what I should do. Do you understand me?"

Like a large angry mountain cat, Ben lunged at Elizabeth throwing her body down on the nearby couch. He covered her body with his. She could feel him reaching for his zipper. He had an erection and his hardness was pressing against her body. With his left forearm pressed across her upper body, his right hand pushed up her white starched uniform. He grabbed the top of her pantyhose pulling them down below her hips. Her body was exposed to him now. Only this time she was not a willing partner. Elizabeth began to struggle. Her hands found the sides of his neck. She dug her fingernails in pulling them downward. She reached up and grabbed at his curly black hair pulling at it as hard as she could. It didn't seem to faze him. Desperately, the nurse tried to keep him from entering her. He thrust his body upward with hard movements trying to penetrate Elizabeth. There was no moisture present to help him enter. His penis jabbed at the side of her groin. Her struggling only seemed to arouse him more. He had never raped a woman before. The violence of the act gave him such pleasure he couldn't control it. Semen squirted all over Elizabeth's stomach. The act was not over. Ben wanted more. Shifting his weight, he brought his penis up to Elizabeth's face.

"Take it, Elizabeth. Suck it. I own you Elizabeth, don't you ever forget it." His hands held Elizabeth's head straight as the weight of his straddling body kept her lying flat. She couldn't get her arms free to move his weight. Her eyes saw his limp penis growing in size once more. Shame and disgrace filled her. The act was never like this—never.

The voice of her assistant penetrated the office door. "Elizabeth. I have your lunch. Are you in there?" Hearing no answer, Karen took Elizabeth's lunch back to her own office. Habit had led Elizabeth to lock her office door. Ben's visits usually meant privacy. The insanity of the moment was broken. Ben lost his erection and quickly rolled off her. The release of his weight brought air to her lungs. The choking feeling was still present. Elizabeth's body was now shaking in rolling fits of emotion. Ben zipped his pants up and straightened his shirt and tie. In one more frightening motion he leaned back down on top of her, his chest resting on hers. Pressing his mouth close to her left ear he told her the consequences of her ever speaking to anyone about Taylor Addison. His hand then grabbed Elizabeth's face and his mouth covered hers. He slid his tongue deep into Elizabeth's throat. She didn't fight him. He licked her cheeks and her eyes and took her hand and placed it down his pants. She could feel the hardness waiting. For a moment she thought he was going to finish what he had tried to start just a few seconds ago. He didn't. He pulled her hand out and kissed it.

"You and I are going back to the lake very soon. Fucking you is better than medicine any day." He touched her cheek and pulled down her uniform to cover her body. Standing up quickly, he went to her desk and stopped. He pulled out two small glass containers from his suit coat pocket and left them on top of Elizabeth's desk. With that action completed, he quietly opened her door and was gone. Elizabeth could not move for a few minutes. She felt sick to her stomach. Standing up slowly, she made her way to her desk. The glass containers screamed for her to open them. The liquid inside would erase what just happened to her. It always caused her to forget what she could not face. Her hands trembled as she picked up the vials.

"Knock, knock. Anybody home?" Karen was back with her lunch. "I must have just missed you, Elizabeth. I was just here a few seconds ago, but you were not in and your door was locked. Here's your lunch and you even have some change coming back." Karen laid the paper sack on top of Elizabeth's desk with the change from her five dollar bill.

Color suddenly filled Elizabeth's face. Seeing Karen brought tears to her eyes rather quickly. She could not hide them.

"Elizabeth, are you okay? What's wrong?" Karen immediately put her arms out to her supervisor. They had worked together for the last six years, and although they were not close personal friends, Karen thought the world of her.

For a few minutes, Elizabeth cried on the shoulder of her friend and co-worker. It was a necessary relief. Karen's soft voice and soothing words helped steady Elizabeth's composure.

"I'm so glad you're here, Karen. I need a friend right now." Karen did not answer but instead allowed Elizabeth to talk. "I've been so foolish for so long. . ." Elizabeth stopped short of explaining what her life was like these last few months. Karen didn't really need to know all the dirt. There was too much shame involved. Besides, Karen couldn't help her. Knowing would only complicate matters for the assistant, and there were enough complications in everyone's life at the blood center already.

Elizabeth's tears were over. What she had just been through was something she could not share with anyone. She felt too dirty. Too guilty. She needed time to process her thoughts. Karen offered to stay with her, but Elizabeth brushed the request off.

"I'm okay now. I guess it's just that time of the month." Elizabeth put forth her best smile and hugged Karen. It was a thoughtful hug and one filled with gratitude.

"Why don't you eat your lunch now, boss, and try and knock off early. We can handle things here. We've got it down to a dull roar." Karen laughed as she made this statement. Her eyes told Elizabeth that she could handle the center if she needed more time. Karen was not the kind of a person to ever push her authority around. She was a good floor nurse and the staff liked her. Elizabeth smiled and nodded in agreement as Karen left her office. She would leave early. She desperately wanted a bath. A long, hot, soaking bath. Her hand reached inside her uniform pocket and took the glass vials out. She quickly placed them in her top desk drawer. The lunch was placed in her wastepaper basket. Elizabeth gathered up her coat and turned off her office light. She stopped at the receptionists desk to tell Julie that she was not feeling well and was going home early. As soon as Elizabeth was out of sight, Julie had a visitor at her desk. It was Mary Smith who worked in donor processing.

"Julie, did you hear Silvers and Elizabeth fighting?"

"No, I didn't. What happened?" The young girl asked, eager for any office gossip.

"I didn't hear all of it. Just the part where he told her she would never do something—I couldn't make it all out. All I know is he definitely threatened her."

"Do you think she's gonna get fired?" Julie asked wide-eyed.

"No way. She's got him by the balls." Mary Smith laughed at her remarks and headed on to the rest room. Silvers's and Elizabeth's fight was noted. Silvers's threats were now recorded. Office gossip could prove to be deadly. Very deadly.

28

The blood center was electrified with news of Carter leaving. Rumors were mixed as to whether she resigned or was fired after a stormy meeting with Dr. Silvers. The gossip camps were at war trying to come up with exactly what had happened. Shelly Nisen was being absolutely mum on the subject. A memo was sent to Julie on the switchboard shortly before closing time. It simply stated: "J. Carter Egan is no longer with Hamilton Regional Blood Center. Any inquiries from the media or personnel references are to go to Dr. Alice Crane." The memo was signed by Dr. Benjamin Silvers.

Grace Tende had been summoned to Silvers's office shortly before 4:30 p.m. He was cordial to Grace, as he knew she and Carter had become friends. Grace was told that Carter had resigned shortly before noon, and she did so with mutual agreement with his office. He instructed Grace to prepare the paperwork for termination and to bypass the need for an exit interview.

"Of course, we will miss Carter as she did a fine job while she was with the center. But blood banking is extremely stressful, and the daily demands of her job were just not to her liking," he stated as he continued to shuffle papers from one pile to another on the top of his desk as he spoke with Grace. He was clearly nervous. The personnel director did not press for details at this moment. She knew Silvers would lie about what had really happened anyway. Grace wanted to wait until she could speak directly with Carter. It was the cautious thing to do—but then Grace was a very cautious woman.

Almost as soon as Grace left Dr. Silvers's office, she was confronted in the hall by Gerald Preston. He smiled and told her he had been looking for her. Would she mind stopping in his office for just a moment? Grace did not make many visits to Preston's office. She avoided being alone with him as much as possible. It wasn't that she was afraid to be alone with him—she wasn't. It was simply just a wise decision of prevention.

She knew how he felt about her. That hadn't changed in all these years. All she had to do was look in his eyes and she could see the longing. It made her uncomfortable. It was bearable, but uncomfortable.

"Grace, I'm sure you've heard that Carter has resigned?"

"Yes." She answered, volunteering nothing else.

"It's most unfortunate. Carter was good for the center." He waited for a few seconds to see if Grace had anything to say. She didn't. "To be honest with you, I'm not sure of all the details that led to Carter resigning today. I understand she and Dr. Silvers had a major—well, shall we say, they had a large misunderstanding. Dr. Silvers is a driven person, and I'm afraid his personality just overwhelmed Carter." Preston's face expressed his own displeasure over losing Carter. "Silvers was such an ass," he thought as he tried to conceal his feelings. This never should have happened. They needed Carter and Silvers blew a good thing again. Seeing no visible signs of interruption from Grace he continued.

"Grace, I know you and Carter were good friends. . ."

"Carter is a friend, Mr. Preston. I respect her a great deal." Grace said just enough to confirm his statement. No more.

"Yes, yes of course. We both do, Grace." Preston's body squirmed slightly in his executive chair. His fingers softly began to tap the edge of his desk. It was a nervous habit he developed many years ago. It helped steady his thoughts. To others present, it could be very annoying.

"Grace, I believe it would be in all our interest if we were able to somehow. . ." he paused. This was going to be difficult. "I think it might be best for Carter if you could speak to her about the confidentiality statement she signed. I mean. We are a closed industry, and some of the information she was privy to could be easily misunderstood, if it was ever to become public." His words were weak and he knew it. Grace was no fool. Preston was well aware that she possessed a tremendous amount of personal insight about their operation—resource sharing and all. He did not know exactly how much she knew, but he knew she was no dummy. Preston also knew that Grace had worked at the center long enough to make waves if she had wanted to. She hadn't. And as far as he was concerned, she never would. Grace was loyal. Grace would never try to hurt the center or him. In his heart, he felt Grace was attracted to him. But he was married and she was. . .

"Mr. Preston, Carter is a friend. As far as the blood center goes and why she left, I'm in the dark the same as you are. I had no idea Carter had resigned until I spoke with her secretary."

"Will you be speaking to Carter?"

"Yes, I plan on calling her this evening. As personnel director, it disturbs me to lose good employees. Carter was a good employee. There are two sides to every situation, Mr. Preston. I believe Carter may have some legal recourse on her side, especially if Dr. Silvers stepped out of bounds as you and I both know he can do." Grace cut to the core. She knew Preston was just as upset with Silvers as she was most of the time. Preston had class and handled staff members in a fair manner. Silvers was not on such a level. She knew it and Preston knew it. They both had to work through his messes.

"Grace, I'm sure you will handle this in just the right manner. If there are to be any problems, I would appreciate it if you would let me know as quickly as possible." Preston smiled at Grace. For the next several minutes, the conversation was held to small talk—the weather, music, holiday plans. In due course it was time for Grace to leave. As she stood up, Preston asked one more question.

"Grace, do you have any idea how much Carter really does know?" It was a direct question and one that Grace did not see coming.

"I'm not sure I know what you mean. . ."

"Forget it, Grace. It was just a thought. Forget it." Preston's cheeks reflected the slip-up. Grace nodded and left his office. For several minutes, Preston sat quietly at his desk. The air still carried her aroma. Such times alone with Grace were few and far between. He cherished them dearly.

Carter woke up feeling just as tired as when she had gone to bed. It had been a restless night. So many memories from yesterday kept flooding her thoughts. A lingering hot bath had taken away some of the strain, but the touch of yesterday was still covering her.

She had left her answering machine on. Grace Tende had left several messages. Carter just could not bring herself to speak to anyone—not yet. If only she could talk to Patrick. She had called his outpost office several times. He was out in the field and not expected back for several days. For the first time in all their married life, Carter resented Patrick's job. She needed him and she needed him now.

The sound of the telephone snapped her thoughts. Instinctively, she reached for the phone. Patrick usually called early in the morning. Maybe, just maybe, the voice on the other end would be his. It wasn't.

"Hello," she answered with a touch of sleep still in her voice.

"Is this Carter Egan?" She recognized the gravelly voice of John Stansbarry.

For a moment, Carter did not answer. He repeated his question.

"Yes, this is Carter Egan."

"Mrs. Egan, this is John Stansbarry." Carter started to hang up the phone. Stansbarry sensed her actions.

"Carter, don't hang up. I have to talk to you. It's very important." His voice was almost pleading. It upset Carter but she found herself staying on the line. John Stansbarry knew he had just a few seconds to gain her attention. He pressed forward.

"Listen, Carter. I know you don't want to talk to me—that you're a loyal blood center employee and all. . ."

"I don't work there anymore." Carter was surprised by her own statement. Stansbarry was stunned.

"You don't work at the blood center anymore?"

"No, I don't."

"Listen, Carter. I'm not sure what is going on right now for you, personally, but I do know I have something you must see."

"If it has anything to do with the blood center, I'm not interested."

"It has everything to do with the blood center, Carter. Taylor Addison should not have died the way she did, and I have proof."

"I'm not interested, Mr. Stansbarry. I just want to. . ."

"You have to be interested, Carter. The blood center was negligent and I can prove it. . ."

"I don't want to get involved with anything else. I gave you my statement, and I have nothing more to say. I told you the truth."

"You told me the truth, Carter. But the guys you work for didn't. They're a bunch of liars and an innocent girl died because of it."

The click of Carter hanging up rang clearly in John Stansbarry's ear. He quickly redialed Carter's number. The answering machine greeted him this time. He left a short message and his office number.

"Listen, Carter. I don't blame you for not wanting to talk to me. But right now, you are the only person who can help us bring these guys to justice. All I want to do is show you the proof. If you already know the truth and don't want to talk to me—okay. I guess I misjudged you. It will only take half an hour. You owe Taylor Addison that much. Give me a call—913-356-8970."

Carter got up and put on her warm robe. She needed a cup of coffee and a few minutes to clear her head. When would it ever settle down? Her whole life had gone upside-down since she started work at the blood center. So much had happened in such a short period of time. And now this call from an attorney telling her there was some other dark secret she needed to know about. The coffee couldn't perk fast enough. She pulled the glass container from its receptacle and poured the half-filled pot of brewing coffee into her china cup. She went to the front door and retrieved her morning paper from her doorstep. The black truck was no longer parked out front. She tried to read through the sections of the national news of the newspaper, but she couldn't concentrate. Nothing was making any sense. Her hand impulsively hit the message response on her answering machine. John Stansbarry's voice again repeated his urgent plea for her to call him. Carter hit the replay button several times in a row—almost as if she could not believe what she was hearing and she had to listen to it over and over until the message sank in.

Her shaky fingers dialed the numbers. The attorney's voice was once again on the other line.

"Stansbarry."

There was a pause. A long pause. John Stansbarry knew it was Carter. He had an inner feeling.

"Carter, is that you?"

"Yes. What do you want me to see?"

"Can you meet me today? How about lunch?"

"Where?"

"I'm not real familiar with Hamilton. Why don't you tell me where to meet you. I'll find it."

Carter thought for a few seconds and finally gave him the name of a small restaurant on the far side of town."

"Gates Grille is just off I-65. I could meet you there."

"Great! What time?"

"12:30."

"I'll be there." Stansbarry hung up the phone and prayed that Carter would not change her mind. She was the key. A light in the valley of shadows.

Carter did not change her mind. She was fifteen minutes early for the meeting. Her face clearly showed the strain of these last few days. She was dressed in blue jeans and a white sweat shirt. She wore little makeup and no lipstick. It felt good not to be in business clothes at this time of the day. She took a booth in the far corner of the cozy grille. She gave the hostess a description of her expected luncheon guest. John Stansbarry was easy to describe. John and Tovey arrived right on time. The pretty blonde hostess recognized the senior Stansbarry and quickly ushered them to where Carter was waiting.

The attorneys got right to the point. The donor's health question-naires were retrieved from Tovey's briefcase. It only took Carter a few seconds to see the tragic error. Her hands began to shake and tears were edging out from the corners of both eyes. Carter felt sick to the very fiber of her soul.

"I never saw these documents. I had no idea. I was told they all met the criteria."

"Who told you that?" Tovey asked softly.

"Dr. Crane and Dr. Silvers. On many different occasions," Carter stated.

"You had no knowledge concerning donor number three?"

"No, I did not. I told you, I never saw the health questionnaires. I took their word. . ." Carter didn't finish her statement. Her eyes stared at her salad. The color had drained from her face and she was as white as her sweat shirt.

"Carter, are you okay?" The elder attorney asked touching her on her arm.

Carter didn't answer for a few seconds. Tovey moved his glass of water in front of Carter.

"Here, take a drink of this. You don't look so good at this moment, Carter."

Carter sipped some of the water. Her hand was shaking as she raised the glass to her lips.

"Carter, I'm sorry to upset you like this. It's obvious to me you didn't have a clue concerning this donor and his state of health at the time he donated the blood for Taylor. We just got these clear copies in the mail a few days ago.

"The blood center just now sent these to you?" Carter asked uncertain of the chain of events.

"The blood center didn't send these to us, Carter. They came from someone else. To be honest, we don't know who sent them to us."

"Did the medical panel see these?" she asked.

"They saw them, but they didn't have clear copies. We had requested clear copies several times from Dr. Crane's office, but the copy machine was supposedly always out of order."

Carter could not remember any trouble with the copy machine. It was just a passing thought, but it added to all the cover-up.

"You don't need me, I mean—the medical panel will. . ."

"We've already spoken to each of those panel members and they will not reconvene."

Carter looked stunned once again.

"What is it you want from me?" Carter finally asked.

John Stansbarry looked down at his folded hands for just a brief moment. This next part of their meeting was not going to be easy.

"Unfortunately, Carter. I want more from you than you should be willing to give me."

"What do you mean?"

"I need for you to go way out on a limb. I need for you to possibly put your professional career in limbo for maybe quite some time. Hell, if this case gets as much local and national publicity as I think it will, Carter, you may very well. . ."

"Publicity?" Carter's eyes looked suddenly like a frightened deer caught in the bright headlights of an approaching car.

"Carter. The evidence we have now should help us move forward to a public trial. We're going after the blood center—not just for negligence but for deliberate cover-up activities. We've got information that connects the medical panel straight into bed with the blood center. We have the doctors on tape telling us they will not reconvene even though we now have evidence that should have been of considerable interest to them as medical professionals. I also intend to get Silvers and Crane for deliberately covering up key information from our court requests. They knew all along this donor was a mistake. That's why we never received a clear and legible copy of his health questionnaire." Stansbarry's face was moist now. His blood pressure was working overtime.

"Carter, if you will agree to letting us take an additional deposition statement, as a witness for us this time, and agree to be part of a group of witnesses testifying for Taylor Addison and against the blood center in a court trial, we have a good shot at getting a just settlement for Taylor's family. And trust me when I tell you there's no way that jury can rule against Taylor Addison. Not this time. The law and the facts are clearly on her side, Carter."

Carter had listened to all that John Stansbarry had just said. Tovey could see the many questions running through her mind just looking into her eyes from across the table. There were a few things he wanted her to really think about.

"Carter, you need to know what you're going to be up against. The blood center's attorneys are going to subpoena you for their purposes of holding your first deposition statements on record. They will do their best to make you look like anything but an expert witness if you try to retract any of your previous testimony. Their questions could get personal and down and out mean during the deposition. We want you to state on record that you were told by your superiors there was no negligence, and that they directed you to present this statement to the media." Tovey spoke slowly waiting for Carter to interrupt him with any concerns. It was now time to ask the question they had yet to ask.

"Carter, we were surprised to hear you say this morning that you no longer worked at the blood center."

Carter flinched ever so slightly. The subject was not going to be easy to cover. She did not look at him but instead stared out the window. Her face was a reflection of raw nerves.

"I just resigned yesterday afternoon." Carter's words were dry.

"Why did you leave, Carter?" Tovey was direct. At this point there was no other way to be. Time was a key issue here.

No response came from across the table. Carter continued to look out the window. Tovey and John Stansbarry waited. Their patience would be worth the wait.

When Carter's deep brown eyes finally met John Stansbarry's, they cracked with pent-up anger. Maybe it was because Patrick was not there and she felt so violated by all that had happened. Maybe it was because the attorneys seemed like the first decent individuals she had spent time with, in God knows, oh so long. But for whatever reason Carter decided to spill out all that had happened to her and all that she now knew about the operations of the Hamilton Regional Blood Center.

For almost two hours she talked. Slowly, in precise sentences, she described in detail all the events that led up to yesterday's fateful resignation.

The Stansbarrys did not move. Their attention was riveted to Carter's story.

Finally, when she was finished, the table of three was silent. John Stansbarry was the first to speak.

"Jesus Christ, Carter. I never would have believed it." John looked at his nephew and Tovey shook his head in agreement.

"It's unbelievable," he said again as if still trying to digest something that was never meant to be digested.

"Nobody will believe it, Mr. Stansbarry. Nobody. But it's true—it's all true, so help me God." The words were stated in fear. A fear she really felt.

"We believe you, Carter. We've had just a small taste of what you've been through. I have no doubt whatsoever that everything you've just told us would hold up on a stack of Bibles."

John Stansbarry's words registered with Carter. To feel that even one person would believe her story was worth so much to her right at this moment. Tears surfaced in Carter's eyes. She reached for her napkin and held it to her face. Tovey experienced a wave of emotion for Carter.

"Carter, we're with you from now on. With what we have already uncovered, and with your inside knowledge. . ."

"All I have is inside knowledge. There's no paper proof to back up anything I've said, Mr. Stansbarry."

"Carter, is there any way you can get paper?" John asked.

"I was trying to gather some of it right before I left. I don't know if there's any possibility of getting anything out now."

"Is there anyone inside that still works there that can help you?" Tovey asked.

"One person, maybe. I'm not sure if I would want to put her in such a situation."

"We don't want to put you in any situation you don't feel comfortable with, especially if it involves asking someone on the inside to put themselves in jeopardy."

"Carter, you are really important to our case. But knowing what we know now, I'm sure the blood center would stop at nothing to discredit you—especially if they've used personal character assassination to back off other past employees who threatened to expose them. You could be in for a tough ride if you decide to testify for us. You also need to know that everything you just exposed to us will be viewed as hearsay and not easily presented in a courtroom. There are exceptions in hearsay evidence, but it is difficult and depends a lot on the judge. We would try to get it all out in a deposition statement as discovery just to put the pressure on the blood center crew. If they even thought we might put you on the stand and that the media would hear any of this on the record or off the record, they just might want to change their tune."

Carter felt a little sick to her stomach. She could not imagine telling this story and all that she knew in an open courtroom, a room that would be filled with media.

John Stansbarry felt sorry for Carter Egan. She really was alone. With her husband out of the country and no close family to turn to for support, this was certainly not going to be an easy time for her. But Carter was key to his case, and he was going to do whatever it took to move her to his corner. He had one last thing left to impart to this key witness.

"Carter, Taylor Addison died with one thought burning in her brain. The blood center had caused her death. She was right. There's a little boy being taken care of by a set of brokenhearted grandparents who had to stand by and watch their youngest daughter go through hell. All the while, your precious blood center physicians lied through their teeth and even celebrated at her death. They got away with it, Carter. You can't let them continue to walk all over Taylor Addison's grave. Will you help us?"

Tovey looked at his uncle. The words stung. Tovey's neck muscles tightened. In the next few seconds they would have their answer. It could go either way, Tovey thought. Carter had been put through the wringer. She was obviously still afraid of the center's doctors and with good cause. His gut told him she did not have the courage to go through with what they were asking of her.

"Yes, I will help you. It's what I have to do. It's what I have to do."

Tovey's intuition was wrong. This time it was very, very wrong.

"Carter, you must know you may march yourself right out of your field. You may be labeled a whistle blower and several other titles that we both know go along with someone turning over information about a former employer. I want you with us, Carter. God knows I really want you on our side, but I want you to understand the consequences of your actions."

"Mr. Stansbarry, I've been in public relations for a long time. Everything that it stands for in principle has always been very important to me. I don't have a choice. My silence would mean I support all that the blood center has done. A person died and other innocent people will probably die. It wasn't done on purpose; I truly believe that, Mr. Stansbarry. But a horrible error took place, and it should be admitted, and Taylor Addison does have the right to her day in court. If I never work again in public relations isn't the point here. The truth of the negligence that occurred is the point. It could have all been handled so differently. The blood center could have done the right thing. It's unbelievable to me. It's all so unbelievable." Carter's statement was good enough for John Stansbarry. This lady would be okay. She would come through this and teach them all a lesson about character. The trio left the restaurant together. Carter was told they would get in touch with her soon, and that she should expect a subpoena within the next two weeks from the blood center. The handshakes were recorded by the driver in the small black truck who had arrived at her house just before she left to keep this appointment and had followed her to the restaurant. Carter went straight home. The truck parked down the street in its old spot.

The phone messages were stacked up. Grace had called several times. There was a call from Shelly and one from a salesperson wanting to sell Carter new blinds. The last caller was Madison Boggs. Just a simple message of "call me."

Carter wondered how Madison Boggs got her home telephone number. After a few seconds Carter realized how easy it was to find her number, especially if you're a reporter. Carter decided to call Grace. It wasn't easy. The situation was awkward. Grace knew so much, but she didn't know everything. That was the difference. Carter knew everything. What should she say? Should she break off her friendship with Grace? Was it the right thing to do? So many questions ran through Carter's mind as she waited for Grace to answer her phone.

"Grace Tende, may I help you?"

"Grace, it's Carter."

"Oh, Carter. I'm so glad you called me; I've been worried sick. How are you?" Grace motioned for her secretary who was walking by to close her door. With it shut, she felt closer to Carter.

"I'm okay, Grace. I feel funny about calling you at the center."

"Don't feel that way, Carter. I'm so glad to hear from you."

"Grace, I'm not sure what kind of paperwork you need for me to fill out. . ."

"Don't worry about it, Carter. And don't worry about coming here. I can handle everything for you from this end."

"Good. I don't think I could ever come back there." Just the way Carter made this statement told Grace something awful must have happened to Carter with Dr. Silvers. Grace and Carter spoke only for a few minutes. Grace would leave the blood center early that evening and go straight to Carter's house. Her arrival would be recorded. The two women consumed several pots of hot tea before Carter was finally able to tell someone close to her all that had happened. She had left Michael Bryan's behavior out of her conversation with the attorneys. It was just too personal for her to recount. It seemed to serve no real purpose. She did not leave Michael's warnings out with Grace. Grace was shocked. Truly shocked. It was like something out of a horror movie. One thing that did make sense now to Grace was Silvers's direct order that any calls concerning Anna Cable be turned immediately over to Michael Bryan, including personnel references. She normally handled such calls from inquiring companies. It was almost impossible for Grace to see Michael in such a role. Slander was not a role that suited him.

Carter told Grace about Madison Boggs, including the fact that she had called her this afternoon. Grace surprised Carter by telling her to return the call. Grace's reasoning was simple. Carter was going to need someone on her side with enough influence to open the wall of silence. Grace was aware that Madison had contacts inside the center. As personnel director, she knew just about everything that was going on inside, including who would pick up the phone and place calls to the media. Madison could be an ally. This reasoning sounded logical to Carter. She would call her back later this evening. She could at least see what Boggs wanted.

Grace left Carter's house a little before 8 p.m. At 8:30 Carter's phone rang. It was Madison Boggs.

"Carter, Madison Boggs. I just heard through the grapevine you are no longer at the blood center."

Carter confirmed her question.

"Why'd you quit, Carter?" Reporters rarely beat around the bush.

"It's just not someplace where I want to work, Madison." Carter was honest but not totally forthcoming in her answer.

"Listen, Carter. I'm not going to waste time here. I've got individuals from inside the center who have given me quite a story. I need you to help me unravel it and sort out all the technical stuff that I have no idea how to sort through. You're the only one that can make this happen." For the second time today, Carter had been told she was the only one who could make something happen.

"Madison, I don't want to get involved in all this. I have enough going on right now with Taylor. . ." Carter caught herself. Madison did not miss a beat. Taylor Addison was maybe not such a dead issue. Madison's radar was active and working overtime.

"Listen, Carter. I know you don't want to get involved publicly. I need you to come down to the station and look at some of the testimony I already have on tape."

This statement surprised Carter.

"You've already got people taped?"

"Yes, Carter, I do. I've been looking at you guys for some time now. I have some pretty credible inside information on tape. I need for you to look at it. Don't worry about your co-workers; we've screened out their faces. I'm going to camouflage their voices before I run with this, but I won't be able to do that when you're here. You probably will recognize most of these individuals, Carter. I will need for you to sign. . ."

"Madison, I have no intention of coming to your station. Please understand and please just leave me alone." Carter hung up the phone. She was so confused. Everything was happening so fast. If Madison had people on tape, who were they? What were they telling the reporter? Carter was bone tired. It was almost 9 p.m. She went straight to her bedroom and retrieved her warm flannel pajamas from the storage chest and headed for the shower. The warm water felt good to her. She stood with her back to the shower faucet and let the steaming hot water pour over her shoulders. The bathroom was warm and steamy. In a few minutes, Carter emerged with wet hair and warm pajamas. She was just finishing up her dinner when the front doorbell rang. She wasn't expecting anyone. At least not this late at night.

The porch light revealed the very pretty face of Madison Boggs. Carter was stunned to see her standing on her front porch. Carter unlocked the door and Madison came through it before Carter could recover enough to tell her no, she wasn't welcome.

"I know I'm barging in where I'm not wanted, but you have to look at this, Carter. I think you need to see what I've got here." Madison was holding a cassette tape in her hand.

"Do you have a VCR?" Madison's eyes were already searching for Carter's television set.

"Madison, I don't want to see anything on that tape. I don't want to get involved. I thought I made myself clear earlier." Carter was still a bit taken back by Madison's presence. It's one thing to do taped interviews with a reporter in your work place, but it's a whole different feeling to have her standing in your private living room.

Madison spotted Carter's television set and VCR player. Walking straight to it, Madison continued talking.

"Carter, I have some stuff on here that I think will shock even you, depending on how much you know about what's going on down there, and I think you know quite a lot. You need to see this and then tell me you won't help me." Madison made a commanding figure of herself. Carter knew Madison was not going to leave until she got her way.

"Madison, don't you have to be on the air in a few minutes?" Carter was searching for anything to back Madison off.

"Carter, if I have to miss this show and tomorrow's newscast I will. I'm not leaving until you at least give me a chance and look at what I have to show you. I need your help, Carter. Now are you going to turn this thing on or am I going to have to waste more of your time trying to figure out how to make it work?"

Carter had not yet closed her front door. For a few brief seconds she debated with herself on demanding that Madison leave her house. She had that right. But did Carter have the right not to look at what might very well be something critically important to her own future, let alone that of the community's future?

With a deep sigh, Carter closed her front door. Madison felt the relief of Carter's action. She took a chance coming to Carter's house and bursting in on her the way she did.

Carter walked over to Madison and took the tape out of her hand. She turned the set on and flipped the channels until the dial showed Channel 3. The VCR was turned on and the cassette popped in. Madison backed away and sat down on Carter's couch. Carter continued to stand in front of the television. The rainbow colors of stations QUES filled the screen. In seconds, a blackened silhouette of a male appeared on the screen. He was in the middle of talking about blood shipments. Carter recognized his voice. He had been a clerk in distribution. He usually helped pack the blood for the drivers. His statements were confirming evidence of the blood center having more than enough blood during times when they were calling media appeals. He told of being ordered to hide the blood inventory before every blood shortage call. His taping ran into another figure, also disguised. This time Carter matched the voice to one of the telephone recruiters. The woman gave in-depth details documenting the pressure she was under to call donors and get them in for donations. Her rehearsed script told the prospective blood donors there was a little boy with leukemia who desperately needed their blood. The hospital had never issued such a plea to the center because there was no emergency. There was no little boy needing blood that the center did not have an adequate inventory to handle. It was a pressure call using a make-believe little boy as bait. She ended her statement by documenting that the blood donated for the fictional child with leukemia went out of state on the next afternoon's blood run. "Such stories were a common practice," she stated. A common, everyday pressure practice. Carter also heard statements documenting activities at the center she knew nothing about—the disposal of contaminated blood straight into the city's sewer system and the dumping of blood in dumpsters by unhappy drivers hoping to leverage their position at the center with a union. At this point, Madison asked Carter to stop the tape.

"Carter, this next individual has some pretty strong statements. I need to know if you were aware of any of this. It's pretty incredible. With that said, Madison hit the play button.

"I can attest to the negligence in our laboratory. We have had a break in control, and a large amount of contaminated blood was forwarded to our hospitals. We have yet to begin a recall. This wasn't the first time such an accident has happened with no recall procedure being enacted by my center."

The disguised woman's voice took Carter's breath away. It was Lisa James. Madison could see the total look of surprise in Carter's face. Carter sat down on the nearest chair. She was shaking her head back and forth. Madison hit the stop button.

"Carter, I had a long talk with Lisa James today. She was fired early this morning. It seems she had been working on this project for the past several days, and when all the data was confirmed and entered in the computer, her data entry code was changed, and yesterday morning she found herself locked out of the back-up system. I guess when she heard you quit, she decided to join the others and do what was right. Carter, I believe Lisa James is telling me the truth. Can you verify her story at all?"

"Madison, I don't want to get involved with all this. I have enough going on right now without being dragged into the press. I just want to get on with my life. I need to find another job and forget all about working at the blood center."

"How can you forget all about the blood center? Those guys running the place are clearly walking way over the line. Real people are getting hurt here, Carter. How can you look yourself in the mirror ever again if you don't try and stop it?"

"I can't stop it, Madison. And neither can you. There's no proof—we don't have any documentation. . ."

"We've got signed statements from several different current and former blood center employees, Carter. If Lisa James is telling the truth, and you can back up her statement from personal, inside knowledge, I've got enough to go to the air."

"Without me and any paper documentation to back you up, will you still take this story public, Madison."

"I'm going to take it to the air, Carter. It's just a matter of time. You can help me keep it all together from a factual side. Just tell me you will help me sort through all this. Lisa James has given me the names of other people to call. She thinks we might just be able to get a few more to testify about what they know is going on inside those protected walls. The paper trail will come; I'm sure of it."

Carter felt trapped. This afternoon she had agreed to help the attorneys for Taylor Addison. Right now, at this very moment, she felt so relieved to know there were others who knew what she knew, to some degree. On the other hand, she also knew the blood center would have answers for every accusation—every charge would be met with a statement. They would also have the dollars to defend themselves. And last but not least, when the story died, and it would, those individuals who put their job security on the line by coming forward would be labeled whistle blowers and turncoats. They would face disbelief from outsiders, and they would face resentful co-workers on the inside. It was not a situation where any of these people were going to walk away easily.

Madison spoke first. "Carter, I know you don't want any part of this right now. But you are the link in this whole story that would serve as our stabilizer. You could help me keep on the right track.

"How can I do that?"

"You can review these tapes and tell me if you agree from your experience and inside knowledge. . ."

"I didn't know about several of the issues these people brought to you, Madison. I don't know if I'm the right person to help you with this." Carter made an honest statement. Madison easily recognized it.

"Carter, just tell me you will help me. I need help in putting this story together."

"I don't want to close the blood center down, Madison. We need it. Our communities depend on blood."

"I have no intention of shutting them down. I promise you that."

"What is your intention, Madison? Are you going to help these employees if they are recognized in your broadcast and get fired? Are you going to be there for them then?"

"Yes, I will be there."

"Will your station put that in writing?" Carter was angry. Not so much at Madison, but by the whole media situation. She had seen innocent people get caught up in the glamour of working with a television reporter on a whistle blower story. But so often, when the headlines were over, the reporter wouldn't even return a phone call. Suddenly, they're not so important. It only lasts as loong as an afternoon headline. "That's what these people had better know in advance," Carter thought to herself as she looked across the room at Madison.

"No, Carter. I'm afraid I can't promise you that. It's a chance we have to take."

"You. I don't see you taking any chances here, Madison Boggs."

"That's where you're wrong, Carter. I am taking a chance. I'm taking on a huge medical industry here. They're not going to take this lying down. I risk losing my job, too. If they get hold of my newscast sponsors, they can put a ton of heat on my station. Trust me when I tell you I think they will stop at nothing to stop me from putting this story on the air. I intend to. With you or without you, Carter."

Carter's damp hair had soaked the back of her pajamas. She felt a chill from the trickle of moisture running down her back.

"Madison, I know you mean well. It's just right now, I'm so tired, and I have so many things on my mind. Can you give me a day or two to think about all this?"

"Sure, Carter. I have about two weeks of filming and interviewing to do before I bring this to the air. You need to know, I am also giving the blood center executives a chance to answer all the charges in advance that I will be bringing against the center. I want to be fair here, Carter. But to tell you the truth, if even half of what I have on tape is true, the best thing that could happen to this center is for these guys to be deep-sixed."

Carter smiled for the first time today.

Madison left Carter with an understanding that Carter would think about her role of working with her. Madison needed to ask Carter a ton of questions about blood banking, questions she'd never even thought of before. The whole system was foggy. Madison needed Carter's expertise to make the story flow in a technically correct presentation. And if she could convince Carter to come before the camera, not disguised, but in a direct interview, it would seal the credibility of the story. The public knew Carter's face. They had bonded with her during some very hectic times. They would believe this lady and the inside information she could divulge from firsthand experience.

Madison left Carter's home just in time to make her last evening newscast. Her visit was also recorded.

The next morning, when Carter opened her door to retrieve her morning paper, she thought it seemed rolled differently than the standard paper boy-tucked corner wrap. When she removed the rubber band, a small plastic doll fell to the floor. Looking closer at this strange figure lying on her living room carpet, Carter could see that some type of battery acid had been poured over the doll's face. Its arms and legs were broken and crudely twisted backwards for emphasis. There was a note pinned to the back of the doll. "If you know what's good for you—you'll keep your mouth shut." Carter more than got the message. This was the first threat. It was not to be the last one. But sometimes threats do backfire. Instead of frightening the victim into submission, they move them forward to action. In this case, the acid-scarred plastic doll gave courage to Carter Egan to stand up for what was right. Carter went straight to the phone and left a message on Madison Bogg's voice mail to call her as soon as possible. Five minutes later, Carter placed a call to Dr. Thompson Moran. Sometimes threats do backfire.

29

At five o'clock that afternoon the winter storm in its seventh straight day was showing no signs of letting up. The city of Hamilton could not dig out from one day to the next, and the roads were still a traveler's nightmare.

Thompson Moran was early. It was rare for him to be away from the office at such an early hour. But he liked this feeling of escape. His car's engine was idling softly as he sat in the parking lot of The Breakaway and waited. In a matter of minutes, the lot began to fill. It was a popular eating spot in Hamilton where the trendy over-thirty crowd wined and dined.

A glance at his watch told him he had a few minutes to review some of the paperwork he had brought with him from the office. If there was one thing Moran did not like about his job, it had to be the paperwork. "My God, our government is obsessed with forms," he thought as he began the process of reading a report from one of his "infectious control" staffers. He didn't see the car pull in behind him. The knock on his window caused him to jump, spilling the paperwork from his knees to the car's floorboard.

The pretty woman standing next to his car brought a smile to his face. "Grace Tende was indeed a pretty woman," he thought as he reached across his front seat to open the passenger door for her.

"I'm sorry. I'm a few minutes late. I got stuck in that traffic on Emerson." She brushed the falling snow from her hair and shoulders. Her eyes were warm and her full lips looked soft and moist as her carefully applied muted red lipstick reflected her smile. The sight of her sitting so close only stirred the intense longing Moran felt for her.

"That's okay, Grace," the doctor smiled at her. "I was occupying myself with all this government bullshit my office gets to play with on a daily basis," he answered warmly. His face was even more handsome than Grace had let herself remember.

As Thompson and Grace continued to talk, another car pulled in behind them, parking two rows back. A slender figure approached the car on Grace's side. A quick knock on the car's rear window immediately gained entrance into the back seat of Moran's expensive black BMW.

Carter was chilled from the short walk. The warm air greeting her from inside the car's interior felt good as she quickly settled herself in the soft leather seat.

For the next hour, the trio sat in the parked car with the engine running. Thompson Moran listened as the two passengers talked. After a while, he began taking notes of their conversation. He interrupted many times, asking one question after another. But many of his questions could not be answered. His face reflected his interest and his amazement. What he was hearing was a surprise—not a shock, but a surprise.

Thompson Moran could make no promises. His agency had virtually no jurisdiction over the blood center. Yes, he had power to bring about pressure from a public health standpoint relating to the contaminated blood shipments; but no, he could do little about all the rest of the madness Carter had carefully described. They had no paper trail to back up most of their allegations against the center. It was all just hearsay at this point. Disgruntled employees at it once again—all issues the blood center could easily counter.

It seemed little consolation to Carter and Grace who had sought his help. He wanted to be there for them, but it would have to be in the form of moral support only at this time.

As Carter was preparing to leave, Thompson Moran told her one thing that made the whole evening seem bearable—he believed everything she had told him.

As Carter's car pulled out of sight, Grace broke the silence that had settled between them.

"Thank you, Thompson, for listening. I know we may have put you in a difficult position."

"Not at all, Grace. I received a call from Paul Andrews from Seton Memorial a couple of days ago. He told me about the contaminated blood shipment. But his accusation could not be backed up with any concrete evidence. I would bet money that Silvers could explain this story if he were pushed up against the wall. I mean all we have on record is an anonymous phone call by a part-time evening clerk who was just fired. They can make it look like revenge from a disgruntled employee if they want to, and the public would probably buy it. If we're going to stand a chance at nailing Silvers, we need a paper trail to catch him at his own game. As for these other allegations, I didn't know any of the rest of this, but nevertheless, hearing how Silvers operates really doesn't surprise me. He's a pompous, sick sonofabitch. I've always known that. I feel sorry for Carter; and to be honest, Grace, I feel sorry for you. How do you stand working for such a jerk?"

It was an honest question. Grace did not really give Thompson much of an answer. But then, Thompson didn't expect her to. Many people work for difficult and even corrupted people, and they stay put in their jobs year after year. Sometimes it's the money and sometimes the job just becomes a comfortable habit. It's easier to stay than to face the prospect of moving somewhere else and starting all over again with others, who could turn out to be just as bad.

Grace declined Thompson's offer of dinner. It didn't seem like the time or the place in light of the conversation that had just unfolded. She asked for a rain check and was immediately told there would be one.

The snow was falling even harder now. Thompson got out of his car and helped Grace clear off her windshield. He stood by the side of the slow warming car making small talk as the car's engine struggled with the cold. Grace had cracked the window just enough to allow Thompson the opportunity to render a gentle touch to the side of her cheek. It was a goodbye gesture issued with affection and hope. Thompson Moran was in love with Grace Tende. He had been for some time. He only realized how very much he had missed her when he ran into her at the restaurant. He was not going to let her go again.

As he watched her car pull away, he made up his mind to keep his eyes and ears open, and if there was anything he could do to help turn the evil Dr. Silvers out on his ear, he would gladly do it. This was going to be a nasty situation with the media mounting a public exposure story aimed at the closed world of the blood center. The medical brotherhood was not going to stand by and see the blood supply cut off to their hospitals by sensational news stories. Even if the story was dead right, the doctorhood would rally around and protect one of their own. Silvers was a power in the medical industry and one not to be misjudged. Thompson Moran was enough of a politician to know he would have to walk a fine line. A very fine line.

Carter would probably come out of it the loser, he thought. She was no match for the mighty blood industry, as she could be set up so easily as a whistle blower by the medical gods with their deep pockets and endless contacts. He hoped she would stay off the camera and out of the headlines. It was one thing to help Madison understand the ins and outs of blood banking, but it was a whole other story to step in front of the camera and hurl accusations at the very respected blood bank industry. The whole situation was indeed going to ruffle a few feathers, especially those physicians who served on the blood center's board. Moran was personal friends with several of these doctors, and he knew they would not cotton to all the bad publicity in store for the center. The accusations would reflect on them as well, and they would be ripe to take some kind of action. He figured it could go one of two ways: They would rally around Silvers and hang tight against the incoming flack, or they would jump ship and demand his resignation. The latter was an appealing thought to Thompson Moran. Appealing because the position of medical director would have to be filled rather quickly. The thought of such an assignment triggered a new interest within him.

"The next few days would be very interesting," he verbalized out loud as he steered his car out of the parking lot.

"Yes, this whole situation was to be very interesting. Very interesting, indeed."

Siam Qua checked his notes for the third time. He had recorded his inventory placement in a precise order. This afternoon, at exactly 5:30 p.m., Siam discovered the vials were now out of order. Capsules one and two were moved to position three and four. Five and six were now sitting in position one and two.

"How could this be?" he thought as he retraced his steps mentally. His methodical placement had a strict order. On the bottom of each capsule a small number was marked. The vials had never been moved in any other manner.

"Perhaps I was tired and made the error myself in recording," he thought as he stood in front of the glass containers. A dark thought suddenly passed through his mind.

"Had someone else been inside this area?" Chills rolled down the scientist's thin spine. Only three people had access to this locked room. He knew Silvers and Crane would not be involved in such tinkering. But someone was, and it was not in the best interest of the project. He would have to run a liquid scan to see if any of the vials tested below the exact inventory level of current usage. It would take time, time he did not have to spare. But he had no choice. The secrecy of his project depended on him. Silvers would not react well to such news. Siam Qua had one other dark thought. He moved quickly to his desk. He pulled on the locked drawer. It did not open. His key quickly released the lock. His eyes immediately scanned the drawer for his private journal. It was still there—safe within his locked drawer. He breathed deeply for the first time in several seconds. Picking up the leatherbound journal, his eyes began to scan the secret pages. A sudden dark feeling gripped him. The pages had been disturbed. His unique method of turning the corner of the last entry page showed that his secret journal had been tampered with. The corner of the right side of his last entry was bent forward, not backward. His first instincts were to notify Silvers immediately. As he reached for the phone, he had second thoughts. Perhaps it was Silvers who had violated his space. If it were, he would wait for Silvers to approach him. Knowing the doctor, it would only be a short time before Silvers would come forward. If it weren't Silvers, whoever it was would let his motive for invading his office be known soon enough. Right now, he would do nothing. Time would take care of all of this—the secrets, the lies, the fears. Time always took care of such matters. The project report had already been forwarded to the grant committee. The center would soon know its fate. For the first time in his life, Siam Qua hoped to be passed over. It was a new feeling for the scientist. A feeling that weighed heavily on his shoulders.

It was nearing 6:30 p.m. when the phone rang at Herk Golden's house. Herk Golden didn't like taking calls at home from people he worked with. But tonight this caller would be an exception to his rule.

"Are you sure you have all this straight?" he asked as he wiped his mouth with a paper napkin.

"Your food is going to get cold," his wife called out to him, angry at the interruption of their evening meal. He motioned for her to be quiet as he continued to ask questions.

"All these people have been in and out of her house? Hmm—yeah— I see. How long did the news lady stay? Interesting," he repeated softly holding the phone close. "We expected Tende to go over there, but Boggs is a surprise." There was a pause in the conversation, but the report was not over yet.

His face held the look of real surprise. "Are you sure it was the attorneys for that girl? Yeah, well I saw them on television, too. Where did she meet them? You're right, that is out of the way. Yeah, well maybe we'd better double up. Put someone on Boggs. I want them both watched. We need to know what's going on. If any more of our people start showing up at the house or around Boggs's station, I want to know about it right now. Do you understand?" The caller definitely understood what Herk Golden meant. It wasn't the first time they had to watch people. If Carter Egan was up to something, Herk Golden would be the first to know. The very first.

By 7:05 p.m. that same evening, Michael Bryan was just finishing his packing. It all had to be timed. Nothing could set off any alarms before the time was right. Bryan's suitcase contained only a few items of clothing. He wouldn't need much, just a few pairs of jeans and a couple of his favorite flannel shirts. The house seemed so quiet. Betsy was in New York. It was her annual shopping trip to the big city. The timing for her trip was just perfect. It would mean no questions nor interference. There was only one thing left to pack—a silver-framed picture of Michael with his parents. It was downstairs sitting on top of the piano. Betsy would never notice it was gone. The silver frame was retrieved and carefully wedged between the heavy shirts and the underwear. His packing was complete, and now all he had left was to grab a quick hot shower and change. Michael headed down the hall to the guest bathroom, which he had been using for the last five years. The water felt good as it rolled across his shoulders and down his back. The thick terry cloth bath towel quickly absorbed the warm dripping water from his compact body. This time he would spend a few minutes picking out just the right business suit. It needed to look expensive and executive. He settled on his blue, double-breasted wool pinstripe that Betsy had spent a fortune on last year for his Christmas present. A starched white linen shirt with a striped red and blue tie was selected. A quick shave and a comb run through his straight dark hair finished his grooming. There was just one last thing for him to do.

His office was just down the hall from their bedroom. Switching on the light in the small cozy room brought him face to face with all the treasures he had gathered over the years. The model sailboats, the old high school football awards, the college diploma. It was all present in this room. None of it could go with him. None of it. For just a few seconds, he had doubts. He quickly shrugged them off. It was too late to turn back now.

Walking over to his desk, Michael lifted the small table clock and retrieved a key from underneath that would unlock his desk drawers. Betsy never bothered his office. It all bored her long ago. It wasn't a very good hiding place for a key, but it had worked well enough. He opened the desk drawers and began to skim through the alphabetized folders. His eyes scanned the various reports whose contents he knew so well. He carefully extracted certain sheets, placing them neatly in a pile on top of his desk. In a few minutes, he had all he needed. The sheets of gathered information were folded once and neatly placed in a letter-size envelope. His hand was steady as he carefully printed Carter's name and home address. He blew on the ink to hurry its drying time. Stamps were applied and the envelope was slipped into his suitcoat pocket. He took one more look around the room where he had spent so much time these last several years. All the memories were burned into his mind one last time. A picture of himself hanging next to the window caught his eye. His father had taken the picture at his college graduation. Michael walked to the wall and removed the picture. The image was painful now—innocence, ambition, and an attitude of determination. It was all right there, stamped across his face for all to see. He wanted to succeed in the world of big business, and he wanted it big time. To be more successful than his father was his goal. When did it all get out of hand? When did he crawl into the black hole that led him to the person he now was? Could he ever get back that innocence? He was going to try—he was going to try. Michael placed the photo in the bottom drawer of his desk and locked it for the last time. The memory of his past would be put away-nicely and neatly. It was Michael's way of doing things. Habits are hard to break.

On the way to the airport, Michael stopped at the post office. As his hand opened the blue mail box receptacle, he paused for just one second. A small smile spread across his face. It was the right thing to do.

The subpoena was delivered to Carter at 7:30 p.m. The attorneys for the blood center wasted little time once they received notice of Carter's intent to be a witness for Taylor Addison.

"Defendants Alice Crane, M. D. and Benjamin Q. Silvers, M.D. by counsel, file Motion To Strike Affidavit of J. Carter Egan with certificate of service." It was a scary piece of paper to have handed to you by a stranger through a chained door. A hearing was scheduled for 10 a.m. the following Tuesday in the courtroom of the Washington Circuit Court, Hamilton County. J. Carter Egan had never stepped foot in the courthouse as long as she had lived in Hamilton. It was not going to be a happy experience for her.

When the attorneys for the blood center received notice of Carter's intention to testify for the plaintiff, they quickly circled their wagons around Silvers and Crane. The doctors were to make one significant mistake. Their arrogance led them to tell their attorneys less than the truth.

They spoon-fed Philip Jarvis a tale involving Carter and her superior, Michael Bryan. The attorneys wanted to question Michael also but were told he had gone out of town on blood center business and would not be back for several days as he had asked for some vacation time at the end of his road trip.

Philip Jarvis sensed that he was being misled. But even after close questioning, the doctors would not change their story. Silvers was more than upset. He flew into a rage calling Carter every name in the book. But Philip Jarvis had spent enough time with Carter, when he was preparing her for the first deposition, to feel that something was wrong with this picture.

Alice Crane surprised her lawyers. Jarvis was stunned at her vile language. The two of them made an amazing pair. Jarvis's gut instincts told him Carter could most certainly be the molehill that turned into the mountain. Whatever she knew, the doctors were afraid of. So afraid, they chose to lie to those hired to protect them. Jarvis did his best to make them understand that if there were any dark secrets, he needed to know them now. Both Silvers and Crane swore an oath that there was nothing beyond what they had shared. Carter Egan was an evil woman, spurned by her boss, and now out for revenge. She would stop at nothing to maim all their reputations and cause the blood center hardship. Sara Lawford, a junior partner in the law firm, had been assigned as Dr. Crane's personal attorney. She was present for these briefings. She said little, but harbored the same feelings Jarvis did. For some reason, Carter's resignation had terrorized these two doctors. What did Carter know? What had happened these last few months to cause this public relations director to resign, and the two doctors, who sang her praises only recently, to speak about her in voices laced with sheer hate. Was it hate or was it fear? Lawford wasn't sure. Personally, she did not care for either doctor. Carter, whom she had met earlier, seemed very good at what she did and very much a believer in the blood center. What had gone wrong would be a question that could come out at this second deposition. She only hoped they would be prepared for the chain of events that could follow. What Carter knew, and what she could introduce into the court records would be discovered. That was what this hearing was all about.

Philip Jarvis was very near to filing a motion for a summary judgment when he received notice from John Stansbarry that Carter Egan had agreed to speak on behalf of the plaintiff. Stansbarry had dug up something, but just what he didn't know.

When the court date arrived, the Stansbarrys met Carter on the steps in front of the courthouse. With a courtesy handshake and a few words of encouragement spoken, they were on their way inside. The beautiful lines of the old and stately architecture made her feel small and unimportant. Courtroom A had been assigned for the hearing. Three sets of attorneys were present when they entered. Polite exchanges were made and the room became silent once again. Carter felt her body shaking ever so slightly. She was nervous. All her fears of facing this day were present. Her adrenaline was working overtime. When all the attorneys were gathered and the court stenographer seated, Philip Jarvis, lead counsel for the blood center, started the questioning. The deposition was started at exactly 10:15 a.m. For over an hour, Jarvis asked questions about Carter's background and education. John Stansbarry objected to the line of questioning several times for the record. Finally, Jarvis turned the questioning over to Stansbarry. Stansbarry stood up and slowly circled the table. In a deliberate motion, he removed a sheet of paper from his suit pocket.

"Mrs. Egan, I would like for you to identify this piece of paper for me, if you wouldn't mind."

Jarvis leaned forward in his chair—his attention glued to the mysterious piece of paper.

Carter took the paper from Stansbarry.

"It's a donor's health questionnaire."

"Have you ever seen this information before?"

"Yes, one other time, just a few days ago, when you showed it to me."

"I would like for the record to show that this paper is a clear copy of the health questionnaire of donor number three, whose blood was given to one, Taylor Addison."

"What in the hell is going on here?" Jarvis thought as he waited for Stansbarry to continue.

"Now, Mrs. Egan, you testified in an earlier deposition statement, that the donors in question were all in good health, and did, in fact, pass all the criteria standards of the NAABC. Is that correct?"

"Yes, I did—but that statement was based on information I had been given by my former medical director and his assistant."

"Dr. Benjamin Silvers and Dr. Alice Crane?"

"Yes."

"Am I to understand you had never personally reviewed this health questionnaire of donor number three?"

"That's correct. I asked to see it, but was told I could not. Dr. Silvers and Dr. Crane told me everything was in perfect order, and that the donors all passed the criteria for donating blood." Carter's voice was low but forceful. Philip Jarvis leaned over to Sara Lawford and whispered in her ear.

"When did he get a clear copy of that donor?"

"I don't know," she replied.

"Mrs. Egan, it is my understanding that you have left the blood center. Is that correct?" asked Stansbarry.

"Yes."

"Were you fired?"

"No. I quit."

"May I ask you why you left—I mean, when I took your first deposition statement, you seemed to be completely happy at the center."

"I left because I found the center to be engaging in unethical conduct that I could not condone."

Jarvis started to object, but instead he leaned back in his seat. If Carter was going to be a problem for the center's case, now would be the time to hear it all out.

Carter Egan took in a deep breath and once again started her testimony. It would take nearly two hours before she completed her reasons for leaving the blood center. She left absolutely nothing out.

Jarvis felt his own blood pressure rising. It was now very clear to Jarvis why Stansbarry had recalled Carter and why she was now on the side of Taylor Addison. "When the blood center execs read this deposition statement, they're gonna run to their checkbooks to keep this kind of testimony buried," Jarvis mused as he kept all emotion out of his face. "No wonder they were so upset with her. She's got them by the nose hairs."

Of course, in a courtroom, Carter's testimony would appear as hearsay, unless she could produce documentation to back it all up. The blood center's current operational practices did not have much to do with Taylor's lawsuit, but if Stansbarry used Carter as he was using her now, she could show the tendency to operate a less than tight screening pattern, plus she would have an impact on the media who would obviously be there in force.

Step by step, Carter had pointed out the clear negligence of the center in accepting this donor.

"We bypassed our own rules and our medical doctors had to have known it from the moment they first reviewed this donor's health questionnaire. It was sheer negligence. Negligence that should have been admitted when first discovered." Carter made her case and made it very powerfully. Her words rang with outrage.

"The blood center officials knew from the very beginning Taylor Addison had been right in expressing negligence in her transfusion process," Carter stated. "They lied to me about the donors in question and used my ignorance—an ignorance set up by my superiors—to manipulate the truth away from their guilt. We should have done the right thing in the beginning. The public could have accepted our human failure. We should have apologized to Taylor Addison and taken steps immediately to prevent another such incident. As it is, there are other people who received blood components from this same donor who are also going to die. They shouldn't have to die. It could have been prevented. If we had followed our own criteria, we could have prevented this. We didn't. But worst of all, we tried to cover it up. The whole system failed from the very beginning. Taylor Addison was given blood that contained a deadly disease. It could have been prevented. It could have all been prevented." Carter was close to breaking down. Her voice was shaking.

Philip Jarvis began his redirect. His young associates had scribbled notes fast and furiously while Carter was speaking.

Names, places, exact conversations were all noted. Sara Lawford also took notes. What she had just heard turned her stomach. In a courtroom with a jury present and the gallery packed with media, as this case would surely draw, Carter's personal account of what she had been through in her official role as public relations director would open up a can of worms for the media. They would have a field day each night for weeks. Carter's testimony would be shocking and scandalous for the blood industry if it ever got to court. One thing was sure though. It would be a long, messy lawsuit with many billable hours. It also became clear that the defense would not be asking for a motion of summary judgment. That tide had definitely turned. John Stansbarry was clearly within his rights to request a trial by jury.

It was now approaching four o'clock in the afternoon. Carter Egan had been answering questions for nearly six hours. She looked pale and very tired. Philip Jarvis was asking questions about blood center policy and her knowledge of physician guidelines regarding acceptable medicines before donation. John Stansbarry interrupted Jarvis this time.

"I think our witness is in need of a break. Could we not allow her fifteen minutes, or even better, continue your questions at another time?"

"I think you're right. I believe I have covered all the ground necessary at this time. Perhaps we could mark our schedules and continue this deposition at a time convenient for all of us?" Jarvis was surprisingly pleasant. Stansbarry felt relieved. Carter had held up better than he thought she would; but still, situations such as this are hard on those put into the position of defending their every word. Carter had shown courage and spunk. She didn't let Jarvis push her around. She refused to be categorized as a spurned woman gone awry. Jarvis had hit her with this as soon as she finished her testimony concerning why she left the blood center. She kept her cool and turned his loaded questions back with thoughtful and sincere answers. If she ever met Jarvis in a courtroom, Stansbarry felt certain Carter could handle him in a manner that would be believable to a jury. Stansbarry sensed Jarvis felt this as well. He was all too agreeable at this point.

As Carter was leaving the courtroom with John and Tovey Stansbarry, her eyes met Sara Lawford's. A look passed between the two women with each recording a mutual respect. Philip Jarvis did not see this exchange. He was too busy gathering his notes and rattling off instructions for his associates. Sara Lawford was given no assignments.

"How about getting a bite to eat, Carter?" Tovey asked.

"I'm not really hungry, but I would love a cup of coffee."

The trio walked across the street to a small but cozy restaurant frequented by more than one struggling attorney.

"You did very well today, Carter. I know this whole day was rough, but nevertheless, it certainly changed the tide as to how we were doing," John Stansbarry said with a look of appreciation in his eyes.

"I'm afraid the only thing I can back up with proof is the donor's health questionnaire. The false shortages, dumping, and everything else can't be backed up with any concrete evidence."

"You don't understand, Carter. What you just put into public record today is almost mind-boggling to the average person. John Doe would never dream that some of these things could ever exist, let alone be happening in their own back yard. I don't think the blood center officials will want you anywhere near a public courtroom, paper trail or not. Besides, we have all the real evidence of negligence we need with this clear copy of the donor's health registration sheet. You know, I still don't know how we got this copy. I'm sure Crane didn't send it to me. But somebody did. I only wish I could thank them in person whoever it was."

Carter asked the obvious question. "Do you think the center will offer to settle out of court?"

"I don't know for sure, Carter. But I'll tell you what. If the shoe were on the other foot, I'd be thinking about a nice quiet settlement right now. I sure as hell wouldn't want you up on any witness stand bringing up all that dirty laundry, paper proof or no paper proof. You'd make a believer out of me, Carter, if I were in earshot of hearing your ordeal at the blood center."

John Stansbarry's words hit a raw nerve with Carter. Tears came to her eyes. Tovey was the first to see them.

"Carter, what's wrong?"

"You pretty much used me for leverage today. You didn't really need me to put that donor's health questionnaire into public record—you could have done that for yourself. Don't get me wrong; I understand. It's just what you said about me just now—how I could make a believer out of you. Funny, Mr. Stansbarry, but the blood center thought of me as a kind of pied piper—making people believe. I guess I did make a believer out of a lot of people. Only now I have to stand up and tell the world it was all a lie. I'm not so sure they will ever believe me—it's all so. . ."

"Carter, I'd be lying to you if I told you these next few days are going to be easy. God only knows what tactics they'll use to paint a less-than-rosy picture of you within the minds of the public. And they certainly have the clout and the means to do it. But if it's any consolation, you showed more courage today by doing this deposition than anyone else I've met in quite some time. I know you're worried about the outcome of all this on your career, but, certainly, doing the right thing should work in your favor."

John Stansbarry believed his words. He also knew that Carter Egan was out on a limb with him. Never before had he placed someone in such a situation. Every word of Carter's testimony would be gone over with a fine-toothed comb by Philip Jarvis and company. They would weigh every statement, every accusation she hurled against their clients. Stansbarry felt confident a request for an out-of-court settlement would be coming to his office in the near future. But there was one fear tucked away in the back of his mind. What if the blood center got to Carter? It was a fear he didn't want to address at this moment.

When Carter arrived home shortly after six, she felt totally exhausted. The day had taken its toll on her. She took a long shower and then headed for the kitchen. Perhaps she would feel better if she fixed herself something to eat. The flashing message light on her telephone answering machine finally caught her eye.

She hit the rewind button and waited for the recorded messages to play.

"Carter, this is Madison. Give me a call when you get home." Carter made a mental note to do just that after she put some food in her stomach.

"Carter, it's Grace. I was just wondering how today went. I hope you're all right. Give me a call if you feel up to it. I'll be home after six."

The sound of Grace's voice added cheer to the lonely evening. A friend's voice can do that, and Grace had turned into a good friend. She was glad this had happened. It was perhaps the only positive experience that had come from her working at the blood center. She would return Grace's call as soon as she heard all her messages. Perhaps Patrick had called and was to be the next voice she would hear. Patrick hadn't called and the next message would not be recognized as a friend.

"If you like your face the way it is, Mrs. Egan, you had better keep your mouth shut and stay away from Madison Boggs."

Carter reached for the phone instinctively. A faceless caller has so much power. The call made Carter angry at first. In a few moments, Carter was hit with a second emotion—fear.

"How far were they willing to go to scare her?" Her thoughts were turning to the dark side of all that had happened.

Carter did not return any calls this evening. She disconnected her answering machine and took the receiver off the hook. She went from one room to the next in her spacious home, checking all the windows and turning on all the lights. Across the street in the shadows of the evening, the driver of the small truck was watching. He smiled as he saw Carter turning on the lights. "She got my message. She got my message," he repeated as he started the truck's engine. He was confident that Carter Egan was going to go nowhere else tonight. She would be too scared to leave now. He had done his job well. It was so easy to scare a woman all alone. So easy.

Carter finally settled down in the living room. She would sit up all night watching and listening. Every strange sound caused her heart to skip and her body to freeze in fear. How could all this be happening was a question that kept repeating itself.

As the sun was just peaking through, Carter Egan finally fell asleep. Sheer exhaustion had finally forced her eyes closed. It would be a long time before Carter felt comfortable with darkness. A kitchen knife was still clutched in her hand as her tired body slumped in Patrick's favorite recliner. Anna Cable's daughter was right when she said to Carter that bad things do happen to people who try to do the right thing—bad things.

30

"Hey, Madison. Do you have a minute?" The chief photographer asked.

"Sure, Stew. What's up?" Madison said as he caught her in the hallway across from the editing booth.

"Listen, Mad. I don't want to raise any red flags, but there's been a van parked across from the station most of the afternoon. I saw it when I first came in, but I didn't pay any real attention to it until just a few minutes ago."

"What's wrong?" Madison questioned, not sure where Stew Henderson was going with his concerns.

"There's some guy over there taking pictures of everyone who comes inside. I'm just wondering if there's any connection with the center and the people you have coming in and out of here for the interviews?" It was a good question.

"Listen, Stew. I have three more blood center employees scheduled for late this afternoon. If there is a connection, I think we should test it before they get here." Madison had a point. For the last week she had been taping blood center staff who were now more than willing to talk on camera. All it took was one person to come out of the closet and the rest followed. Madison had lucked out when she received a call from Lisa James's boyfriend. It was because of his support that Lisa had come in to see Madison. She gave Madison a list of blood center personnel that she thought might also come forward if the popular TV news anchor called them personally and promised to keep their identities a secret. Madison now had seven blood center employees on tape, all with different kinds of information to contribute to her story. The testimony was a combination of amazing, shocking, disgusting, and also at times, unbelievable. What she didn't have was a paper trail. She needed it desperately.

Carter Egan was spending almost as much time at the station these last five days as Madison. The anchor was getting a crash course in blood banking from Carter. Her story could not be kept on the right track without this lady's help. Yesterday was the first day she had not been in. She was doing something more important than teaching Madison the rules and regulations of blood banking—she was giving her deposition statement. Carter had not returned Madison's call that evening. For just a second, Madison had strange thoughts. Carter was very good about returning phone calls. Could she be in trouble? The thought passed. The incident with the plastic doll on her doorstep was cause for concern. Madison couldn't believe it meant anything more than just a warning, a kind of prank. After all, this was a blood bank they were dealing with, not a Mafia-infiltrated industry.

"But someone taking pictures was ominous," she thought as she walked toward the front entrance with her chief photographer. To her knowledge, the blood center did not yet know of the story she was mounting.

"There's the van."

"The white one?" Madison asked as she peeked through the blinds.

"Yeah. That's it. See. You can see the driver scrunched down in the front seat."

Stew could see this clearly because he was using his telephoto lens on his small camera to bring the van up close.

"Madison, I'm going out with my camera. If this guy's a plant from the blood center, I may be able to scare him off or at least let him know we are on to what he's doing." Madison didn't say anything but nodded her head in agreement.

Sure enough, the sight of the approaching cameraman jarred the van driver into action. With squealing tires, the van pulled out of the lot and drove quickly down West 16th Street. The photographer could only make out three digits of the license plate.

"I didn't get a whole set, but maybe I got enough for some of my friends at the license bureau to run a trace on the plate."

"This is wild, Stew," Madison said as they walked back toward the editing booth. "I need to get hold of Carter right away. See if you can find Ed. Tell him to meet me in my office in twenty minutes. I think we've lost our window period and we need to go with the story." Stew nodded and set out to locate the station's news director. There was something exciting about this story, and the sight of the van racing away from the news station was captured on film. It would make a great intro.

"God! I love this business—I love this business," the chief photographer exclaimed as he raced down the hall.

Madison quickly pulled up Carter's home phone number and dialed. A busy signal. "Damn it—why doesn't Carter have call waiting?" For the next ten minutes Madison repeated the action.

Ed Morton appeared as requested at Madison's doorway. The news anchor waved him in.

"Ed, I think we have to start running with this story. I'm pretty sure the blood center is on to what's going on. There was a van across the street—Stew spotted it—with a guy taking pictures of everyone coming in our front door. I'm not sure how long this guy's been out there, but I can't take the chance of losing the upper hand."

"Do you have enough documented?" Ed was being cautious. He had seen the preview tapes and some of the revelations were pretty amazing. A news director had to cover all bases. They couldn't risk a sensational story with no hard copy proof to back it all up.

"I'm working on the paper back-up, Ed. The incidents we have on tape from the center's employees all fit together, but if you're asking me, do I have clear copy to hold up, the answer is not yet. But it's coming, Ed, it's coming."

"How soon till you get some of it?" Ed questioned.

Madison took a deep breath. "Ed, I'm not sure."

"Damn it, Madison, the suits upstairs are not going to want to hear 'it's coming.' They want to see it in black and white."

"Ed, I'm as sure as I've ever been on a story. These people are telling the truth."

"Truth in our industry doesn't count unless you've got a picture of it or a paper trail. Hearsay is just too dangerous, Madison." Ed's face was serious.

"Are you telling me to trash this story?"

"Have I ever pulled you off a story since you took the chair?"

"No, Ed. You haven't." The room was quiet for several seconds.

"You know, Ed? These guys are lower than snakes. How in the hell did they think they could get away with this kind of crap?"

"They've got that shield, Madison—that medical sheepskin. They used their power to bully a system. It's not the blood center that's rotten—it's the jerks they've got running it right now. Your story should change that."

"I hope you're right, Ed. I hope you're right."

Ed winked at his anchor. As he turned to leave, he stopped for just a moment to say one last thing.

"Madison, I'm going to front for you with Edwards, but do me a favor and please get my ass off the hook as soon as you can. Okay?"

Madison smiled and nodded her head. Ed disappeared from sight leaving Madison alone. The reporter knew it was a tough situation to go to the air with only so-called testimony from faceless witnesses. That Carter could confirm that the center was using her to call false media alerts, gave a certain level of comfort to Madison. She was a very credible source. Dumping blood, high pressure tactics to secure donors, false blood alerts, and last but not least, the forwarding of contaminated blood with no recall effort was indeed a story worth going out on a limb for. She still had time to bag it all up nice and neat. It would come—the paper would come. The one element that still bothered Madison was Carter's physical presence in the story. She had to convince the ex-public relations director to come forward at some point in this exposé. Carter was the story's ace in the hole; but right now, the key witness was still standing firm on staying out of the television lights. Madison understood where she was coming from, but her mindset had to change as the story's air date was moving forward.

Madison tried dialing Carter's number again. Same result. Busy signal. Madison was out of time. The next number she dialed was that of the blood center. She asked for the Executive Director.

"Mr. Preston's office. May I help you?" the executive assistant asked as she continued typing.

"This is Madison Boggs, Channel Eleven. I would like to speak to Mr. Gerald Preston." Madison's voice was immediately recognized. A bit flustered by the unexpected and famous caller, Nancy Houston almost disconnected them.

"Yes, Miss Boggs, please hold while I see if Mr. Preston can take your call."

The elevator music immediately blared in Madison's ear.

"God, I hate this music," she thought as she waited.

"Gerald Preston." The voice was older than Madison expected.

"Mr. Preston, this is Madison Boggs from Channel. . ."

"I know who you are, Miss Boggs. I have the pleasure of watching you every evening. You're my favorite station for news." Preston was smooth-sounding over the phone.

"I want to be up-front with you, Mr. Preston. I am preparing a story that will feature your operation in a very frank and less than flattering position. I would like to give you the opportunity to know in advance what some of the charges are that are going to be leveled against you." Madison did not pull punches.

Preston moved his chair from side to side. The impact of what she was saying had not hit him.

"Well, Miss Boggs, I'm sure we can straighten all this out and correct any misinformation you might have."

"Mr. Preston, I'm not dealing with misinformation. The information I have is accurate and backed up from reliable sources. Your center is being charged with calling false emergencies for the sake of generating a financial gain. We have documented statements showing you deliberately hid blood during these calls in order to convince your personnel and the media that a real blood shortage existed."

"Now wait a moment, Madison. I guess you could say that we did do this, but. . ."

"Are you telling me you ordered blood to be stored out of sight and directed your public relations person to call a blood emergency when there really wasn't one?" Madison was pushing. She heard a direct quote from the executive director that she couldn't believe she would hear. He had documented Carter's statement. The executive director admitted the wrongdoing as plain as day.

"Miss Boggs," Preston was formal now. "Yes, I guess I did do that, but you have to understand, Carter did not understand blood banking. We are working on many co-op situations here. We have to help our neighbors—that's what resource sharing is all about. I'm sure when you understand all of this, we can come to an agreement and forget this whole situation ever happened."

"Well, first of all, Mr. Preston. I did not mention Carter Egan's name, and second, I have several inside sources who have come forward to document those phony calls. And just now, you clearly admitted to engaging in such conduct."

Preston was quiet as Madison's words were beginning to sink in. His lighthearted attempts to pacify the reporter had backfired.

"Mr. Preston, I want to make sure you understand the seriousness of these charges. I understand resource sharing and trust me when I tell you that is not how the system works. You are being charged with deliberate attempts to dupe the public into believing our community has a blood shortage, when in fact, our community has donated far more than their rightful share, and your company is taking advantage of it morally and financially."

Preston's cheeks were turning red. His palms were sweating. Madison Boggs was not going to back off. God, how he hated these media people. Who did they think they were talking to him in such a caustic manner—trying to stir up trouble on a subject they knew nothing about. The whole situation was just getting way out of hand. Preston's usually controlled temper was just moments from exploding.

"Listen, Miss Boggs, I'm telling you that you cannot put this story on the news."

"You're telling me what?" Madison countered hearing the anger beginning to surface on the other end.

"I'm saying I want this story killed. You have no right to try and stir up a bunch of hogwash. We have done absolutely nothing wrong. Do you realize how many people might die if you go through with this?" He was trying to intimidate Madison. It was the best kind of intimidation.

"Mr. Preston, my story is running. I would like to give you a chance to appear on camera and give your side to all the accusations."

"I have no intention of appearing on camera—and I'm telling you right now—you will never air this story. I'll bring your station to its knees if you try and. . ."

"Mr. Preston. I consider your remarks threatening in nature. I don't like to be threatened. If you have nothing to hide, why not let me come down and get your side of all this?"

"You will never step foot in my center and we'll see if you air this story, Miss Boggs." Preston slammed the receiver down.

Madison's could feel the tension. The timing of this story was not the best for her pregnancy. But the story had become very personal to Madison. She now had a glimpse of how Taylor Addison must have felt.

"He had no clue. He really thought he could sweet-talk me into dumping this story. It's as if he was offended. I'm in the wrong for telling the truth! Hell, this guy wouldn't know the truth if it jumped up and bit him in the ass." Madison's thoughts were running hot and heavy. She had just heard the executive director confirm the calling of false blood shortages. She checked her notes to make sure she had copied down his exact words. They were going to make a hell of a lead sound bite. The story was going to air. It was beyond stopping. Madison would spend the rest of her day locked in an editing booth.

Ed Morton was called up within the hour to his boss's office. It seems that several prominent physicians had called the station. There were concerns. "The charges were absurd. All this could be explained. What was going on was a group of disenchanted employees, all wanting higher salaries, trying to stir up trouble." The physicians promised that more than one hospital would pull its big buck ads if the station did indeed move forward with this sensational story. Preston had wasted no time in calling in some of his past debts. He wanted to put pressure on the station from the outside.

Jack Edwards, the station's general manager, had been briefed on Madison's story from the very beginning. He was pissed as hell with the audacity of those medical gurus who had called him. Not once could he get them to even listen to the documentation Madison had captured on film. They didn't care what she had; their concerns were on a different level. The story couldn't air. It would damage the flow of blood to their hospitals. The public would stop donating. People were going to die. Edwards had heard all this before. One physician threatened Madison. He said that Madison had better think of herself. He knew she was pregnant and just might need to have a Cesarean section. What if she needed blood? If she put this story on the air, she just might not get the kind of blood she needed.

That threat settled the issue for Jack Edwards. Madison Boggs would get the green light to bring this story to the airwaves. Ed Morton had assured Edwards that Madison was just minutes away from securing the paper documentation needed to back her witnesses' statements. In doing so, Ed placed himself in the boiling pot with Madison. The story could air in segments. Whatever overtime might be needed for crew or editing was cleared. Madison was more than pleased to know Jack Edwards was backing her.

The thought of losing advertising dollars had more than once crossed Madison's mind. No one knew how the advertisers would react to this story. Their reaction could affect Madison's ability to air the whole week's segments on the center. If heat were applied to the station's pocketbook, cold water could be poured on her story. Madison knew she still stood a chance of having her story pulled. A few calls wouldn't stop her story at this point, but a combined pullout of financial heavy hitters could do so. But Jack Edwards hadn't made it to the top to be pushed around by advertisers—at least not yet.

Carter finally called Madison. As she conveyed the latest threatening phone call, Madison felt her own anger mounting. As a reporter, she was, in a way, insulated from such direct fear tactics. She would get an occasional call, but always at the station, never in the privacy of her own home. She admired those people who put it all on the line with no such protection in place for themselves. The public would only hear the headlines. They wouldn't know about all the threats that could go on behind the scenes when important people were about to be exposed. Threatening calls to their homes, job intimidation, loss of wages, and most devastating of all, not being believed was what Madison's witnesses had ahead of them.

Carter kept her word and came to the station early. Madison greeted her at the front door. She glanced across the street as she opened the door for Carter. There was no white van. For the next five hours, the two women sat glued in front of TV monitors. They were looking at what was to be the first installment of Madison's story. She would lead with the false blood shortages and over the course of the next five days cover the rest of the allegations. The faces of the witnesses were blacked out and their voices altered, a time-consuming process. Carter also brought a copy of Taylor's donor questionnaire.

"I brought this in to show you. I wanted you to see it firsthand to know what we're saying is absolutely true. Right now, it's the only paper evidence I can show you."

"Listen, Carter. I hope you know I believe every word you have told me about your experiences at the center. I'm not sure when this part of the story will air—probably toward the end of the series. But I need to have a copy of this in my hands—just to lay any demons to rest that such a piece of evidence does exist. Of course, I won't reveal where I got this information, but it is a big part of what's wrong down there. My God, if they tried to cover up something like this, how far would they go?"

Carter smiled slowly. The color in her face was almost gone. "Is there anyone who can bring us some kind of documentation—reports, shipping statements, anything like that?" Madison asked with the urgency of the situation showing in her voice.

Anna Cable's daughter came to Carter's mind.

"I'm not sure if it's right to tell you this—I mean I have no proof. But I do know the lady who held my job before I did left the center under a dark cloud. I've been told she had papers with her, and that the center was terrified she would use them against them."

"Can we talk to her? What's her name? Do you have a phone number?" Madison fired back at Carter.

"Madison, we can't talk to her."

"Why in the hell can't we?"

"She's in a coma."

"What?" Madison's face showed bewilderment.

"She tried to kill herself."

"For Christ's sake, Carter. This whole story gets sicker and sicker. Why did she do that?"

"I'm not sure. I tried to talk to her daughter, Jody, a few days before I quit, but the family wants nothing more to do with anyone from the blood center."

"Do you have any idea what kind of papers—what's her name?"

"Anna. Anna Cable."

"I remember her. She was a nice lady, different personality, but nevertheless, she seemed sincere. What kind of information could she have pulled out of there?"

"I don't know. All I know is it was enough to make them play hard-ball with her. I think the center's actions may have led to her attempted suicide," Carter said with a certain fear now present in her own voice.

"Carter, can you give me the daughter's telephone number? Maybe if I called her, there might be just enough bitterness to help me get my foot in the door."

"I'll call you with it as soon as I get home."

"Carter, you know I have to ask you this. Will you let me interview you—put you on the air face to face—no shadows. You are a strong witness to speak to the truth of this story. Everyone knows your face—they believed in you every time you came on the air asking for blood. Will you do it?"

Carter took in a deep breath. "I can't, Madison. I just can't. I promised I'd help you keep this story on track, but I don't want to take it any further. You've got more than enough without me."

Madison didn't reply, but smiled softly. She knew Carter was having a rough time. Right now she didn't need her on camera, but she also knew that without the paper reports to back up the accusations, there would come a time when she would desperately need the face of Carter Egan on camera. Madison would not ask again today.

"Ok, but please call me with Anna's number as soon as you can."

Madison walked with Carter to the front door and watched as she walked to her car. This week had taken its toll on Carter Egan. But the next week would be worse. In just a few more days, all of Hamilton would be hearing information that she had been living with in the most intimate way for several weeks. It was painful and frightening. Very frightening.

Madison tried several times to reach Anna Cable's daughter. A recorded message was as far as Madison could get. She also tried to interview the blood center executives. They would not return her phone calls. By the end of the week, the story was ready to go. Her channel would use special promotional teasers over the weekend to generate interest for the coming Monday night newscast. The teasers were tagged at the high end of suspense, complete with dramatic music, and the moment they started to air, the station's switchboard lit up.

The blood center's switchboard also came to life. Silvers was livid. Silvers, Crane, and Preston would spend the weekend in conference with a new public relations firm they had quickly hired, a firm that specialized in crisis communications. The trio agreed to let the firm handle all public statements and to be cooperative to a point. But Silvers still wanted to be in control.

Swabuck and Associates was a young firm, but already known for their aggressiveness in explosive situations. Their services were expensive, but the center had to face this story with the best consultants working on their side. The staff had been briefed as to who the troublemakers might be. The van had recorded several center employees entering the television station. Personnel records were pulled and all identified center turncoats were given profiles. It was easy to create a negative impression of these individuals. The personnel records were secured without Grace Tende's consent. The agency pushed aside her stern warnings of employee civil rights. Frank Swabuck estimated the kind of a response to prepare initially, though he did not know all the issues Boggs might hit them with. Swabuck would go with the angle of disgruntled employees seeking revenge. Preston was adamant in not returning Madison's calls, and Silvers would not let the agency meet with her. Swabuck felt confident he could use the strategy of whistle blower to combat most of the explosive headlines as they were aired. They were also counting on a lack of physical evidence. All Madison had to their knowledge were faceless employees making statements that could not be backed up with documentation.

Swabuck was counting on the blood center's solid and stainless reputation to counter the charges. And the medical community had already started to circle their wagons. Swabuck quickly took statements from past blood center board physicians with high community profiles. The agency would use countering quotes from these physicians in their press releases. The Swabuck staff was excited by this assignment. It was a prime opportunity to enter the big time world of medical crisis. If they did their job and turned the expected public outrage to the blood center's favor, there would be many future lucrative contacts at their fingertips. Swabuck also knew one other thing. Time was on their side. Sure, the publicity up front would be sticky, but Madison Boggs and Company were not going to be able to carry this story indefinitely. There would be a start, and there would be an end. When the end came, that's when Swabuck could press their healing tactics best. The blood center would have many future media advantages at their fingertips. The need for blood could be conjured up in so many different story appeals. They would shoot quick commercials, and use children stricken with leukemia as spokespersons. There would always be a need to donate blood. It would be a warm and touchy-feely campaign. Crisis communications was really so simple if you knew how to work the system, and had big bucks to fund the cost.

By Monday evening the citizens of Hamilton were glued to their television sets. Even the local bars switched over to carry this broadcast. The story was given a long air space. It covered nearly twenty minutes of straight broadcast time before a commercial was aired. The headlines lived up to the promotion. The information Madison had assembled was startling and believable. The eye witnesses were credible, even with their identities screened out. The Swabuck team sat huddled together in their downtown office, while Dr. Silvers and Crane had gathered in Preston's office to view the newscast on a TV set brought in from the first floor lounge. The truth hit the blood center execs between their eyes.

"How in the hell did these employees have so much access to our private business matters," Preston roared totally out of touch with the way the center had flaunted their actions these last several years. Their own arrogance had caught up with them. They never believed that their staff, whom they so controlled, would divulge such secrets to the media. A palpable tension filled the room. They knew the story's documentation was right on the money. False shortages, dumping blood, errors in the laboratory, the pressure on the telemarketing crew to highhand donors into donation screamed with the real truth of their operation.

The broadcast was devastating. Madison Boggs delivered her story exactly as she promised. The physicians who initially called to pressure the station into not carrying the story squirmed nervously as they listened to blood center personnel describe the various situations presented. Several of the doctors remembered Dr. Silvers's advance calls to warn them of a scheduled blood emergency. He had also told them not to worry—there was plenty of blood available—their supply would not be interrupted. They knew this tactic was widely used by the industry, but as long as it kept blood on their hospital shelves, who was to be hurt. It was harmless. It was good marketing. It could all be justified. Only tonight, it didn't seem so harmless. The ethics of the story cried out to be heard.

By Tuesday morning, Madison's station had received hundreds of calls. The public was outraged. But most important, the public seemed to believe the individuals who had come forward. By Tuesday afternoon, Swabuck and Associates were ready with their counterattack. Dr. Silvers was put on tape. He was well briefed on how to act and what kind of hand motions to use and when to look into the camera. The medical director denied everything. "It was all out of context. Resource sharing could be so easily misunderstood, especially by employees who were not privy to all the pressures of the industry." He also quickly addressed Preston's admission of guilt in ordering blood to be hidden. Looking directly into the camera's red eye he stated:

"Gerald Preston never made such a statement."

It was short and sweet. Silvers's handsome face conveyed a warm image, an image deeply upset by the actions of Madison Boggs and blood center employees who did not have the courtesy to come forward and state their concerns and misunderstandings to him. He was indeed hurt by this story and worse than that, he, acting as medical director for the center, was deeply concerned personally that the community's blood supply would be affected by this untrue and slanted news story. "What you have seen presented by Madison Boggs is reckless and sensational journalism. At this very moment, I am preparing to turn over all blood center records to a medical panel for review. I welcome the outcome of such an investigation. I know you will continue your support of the center as you have for the last twenty years. Our reputation is above reproach. Please, for those citizens in our hospitals right now, please continue to give blood. Don't judge us until you have heard all the evidence."

Silvers gave a strong performance. His words hit home with the faithful donor population. Sawbuck was counting on their support to help with the press statements. Silvers's taped response was delivered to all the competing media outlets. The other media affiliates, who had been locked out of this story, jumped at the chance to compete in the news ratings.

Confidence was beginning to surface at the executive level.

"After all," the young media agent related, "when the public learns the true reason for resource sharing and the position the center found itself in— having to deal with whistle blowers and all the other nonsense, they too would stand behind the cause. Madison Boggs would be forced to back off this story."

The Daily Voice carried Madison's story on its front page Wednesday morning. A photo of Silvers and Preston ran next to the headline: "Center

Officials Deny Everything." The story carried the pull quotes from the supporting medical community and loyal blood donors. The words, "whistle blowers," ran in the body of the text no less than fifteen times. The story was definitely slanted in favor of the blood center. Chet Lambert smiled as he read the story. He didn't like the smug look of Silvers, and Preston looked like an arrogant son of a bitch.

"I could have made mincemeat out of those jerks. It just goes to show you how a brother-in-law connection with an important editor can bleed a story. Poor Madison, I could have backed her up royally." Oh well, it was no skin off his back now. He was moving up in the world. Loyalty could bring about certain advantages.

By Wednesday afternoon, the community was getting its share of sound bites from both sides. Swabuck was counting on the response interviews from the supporting medical community. The center executives knew they had to keep denying all the charges, and most of all, they had to get to those advertisers in the medical field. If the calls of advertising cancellations could be stepped up, Madison Boggs's air time could be cut short. In the meantime, Dr. Silvers was booked on every talk radio show the agency could arrange in a twenty-four hour period. Over and over, he denied Madison's charges. Several hospital administrators accompanied the center's medical director, each giving support to his testimony and casting deep doubts on those individuals who spoke from behind shadowed faces.

The agency also spent time on the phone with Madison's competition. If they could challenge Madison's witnesses, they could begin to influence the way the other media picked up on the story. Madison's credibility had to be attacked. Was there an ax to grind by these witnesses against their center? Why had they not come forward before? Anything that spoke to a troubled past relationship between these witnesses and the blood center was pulled from the files and used. All Swabuck needed was for one reporter to question the validity of any of these whistle blowers, and the story could be moved in their direction. Swabuck also felt there was one major issue that now required attention. He asked to meet once again with the three blood center executives.

"So far, Madison Boggs has run with just the testimony of faceless employees. She has not produced one single piece of paper backing up the shortages or the confirmation of shipping bad blood. Is there any such evidence to be found?"

Preston shook his head and looked at Silvers. Silvers eyes were glued on Dr. Crane.

"Of course not," Crane answered. There is no paper proof. No one can prove any of these statements because it simply didn't happen." The doctor smiled broadly, knowing full well that she had personally erased the data reports on the contaminated blood incident. As for calling false media alerts, no one could really document that either.

With those statements out, Swabuck felt it was time to press for a "prove it" attack. Dr. Silvers would be booked on WGLE, a top-rated radio show on Thursday morning. He would press for the story to be proven with hard evidence. Silvers liked the idea and agreed to the plan. Later that same afternoon, Silvers remembered a conversation that sent him straight to Dr. Crane's office.

"Alice, we may have a problem with Andrews at Seton. If I go on the air and deny such an incident, Andrews could fuck us up."

"Have you called Andrews?"

"Not yet. I wanted to get with you first. If I can't convince him to go along with me, I may have to cancel that radio thing tomorrow." Silvers was more than just a little nervous at this point. "Are you sure there is no paper trail here, Alice?"

"Trust me on this one. It was erased from our system. It's as if it never happened. All the media has is unsubstantiated accusations from Lisa James."

"Lisa James?" Silvers was again agitated at the mention of her name.

"We've got Lisa James on camera entering Madison's station. I also took a taped copy of the broadcast to Video Technology and had it unscrambled to the point where I could clearly identify Lisa James's voice."

"I didn't know that could be done," the medical director answered approvingly of Dr. Crane's investigative actions.

"Did you get the rest of those bastards' voices unscrambled? He quickly asked with vengeance surfacing in his mind.

"They're working on it right now."

"What about Carter? Is she on tape? Are we in any danger of her coming forward?" Concern was present in his voice. Carter Egan was a threat—a very big threat. She had credibility.

"I don't think Carter Egan would risk her lily-white reputation at this point. She knows if she blows the whistle, she would kiss goodbye to her career." Crane made her statement with utmost belief behind it.

"Get Andrews on the phone for me right now. I had best see where we stand on his keeping his mouth shut."

In just a few minutes, Seton Memorial's chief pathologist was on the other end of the phone.

"This is Dr. Andrews."

"Paul, this is Ben Silvers. How are you?"

"Well, I'm probably better than you are right now," Andrews answered, twisting the knife just a little. The thought of Silvers squirming a bit with all the media publicity shining on his doorstep gave a bit of warmth to Paul Andrews as he personally didn't like Silvers. He was a pompous jackass—an overpaid pompous jackass at that. Silvers also made more money than Andrews.

"Yeah, well it certainly has been less than a dull week," Silvers answered, keeping his sharp tongue under control. He could not afford to ruffle Andrews's feathers right now. He needed a favor. A big favor.

"Listen, Paul. I'll get right to the point. I need you to stand behind me."

"In what way?" Andrews interrupted.

"I have to back down all this crap about our center, or you guys are going to find yourself canceling all those surgery dates down there." The warning was clearly in place.

"What do you want, Ben?"

"Paul, at this stage in the game, I have to issue a denial about shipping out contaminated blood. Right now, there is no way in hell to prove it ever happened—the records have been erased."

"Wait a minute, Silvers. I'm not about to get mixed up in your troubles down there. I don't want any part of this rubbing off on my hospital," Andrews roared.

"Look, Paul. If I don't bury this contamination crap, your hospital will be up to its armpits in major lawsuits. Anybody and everybody who has ever been given a blood transfusion will be up your ass so far it will make your head spin. We've got to stand together here. All I'm asking of you is to keep your mouth shut if any goddamn reporters start nosing around and asking questions. One thing we have going for us is nobody, on either end, can prove this. I'm asking you to forget our conversation and to muzzle your assistant about that late night call he took."

The phone line was quiet.

"What happened to your unit report you were supposedly forwarding to me?" Andrews asked still not giving Silvers an answer.

"Dr. Crane erased it from our data base."

"Was this done before or after you called me?"

"What difference does it make now—it's gone."

"Are you trying to tell me you knew you had dumped bad blood in our laps and were not going to recall or notify us?"

"I'm telling you accidents can happen, Paul. You should know this better than anyone. It seems to me you and I have been down several dark roads together, or should I take this time to refresh your memory?"

Silvers had shifted the hook to Paul Andrews's back. Seton Memorial had its fair share of cover-ups. Silvers had been privy to just enough to be able to hold a damaging club over Andrews's head at this very regretful moment.

"Look, Dr. Silvers. I find this conversation to be very distasteful. I do not want to be a part of any of this." Andrews had suddenly become formal.

"Will you keep your mouth shut, Andrews?" Silvers was at the boiling point now.

There was another long pause.

"Let's hope it doesn't come down to that, Dr. Silvers," the chief pathologist answered.

Ben Silvers took in a deep breath as he hung up the phone.

"He'll forget the conversation," he stated out loud for his assistant. "Listen, Alice. I need you to pull Lisa James's personnel file. . ."

"I've already done that," Crane answered.

"How did Tende react to your messing in her records?"

"She doesn't know it yet. I let myself into her office last night and retrieved Lisa's file. I've already dummied up two personnel incidents that show Lisa making coding mistakes in QA, complete with her signature and Bertha White's on the warning report. There's also a letter in her file stating she has been a disruptive employee in her area and would face termination if she did not change her professional work habits. I think there is enough on record now to paint a pretty dim view of Lisa James. I will hand over the file to Swabuck this afternoon if I have your permission?"

"Alice, you amaze me sometimes," Silvers stated as he felt the tension in his neck relaxing. We just might come through all this after all. It would take some effort, but with the medical community's backing to pull their precious advertising dollars from Boggs's station, and the counter blows of real credibility about to be landed by Swabuck— Madison Boggs might just have to kiss goodbye to her reporting career.

"Alice, just one more time here. You're sure there's no data proof of our laboratory errors?"

"Trust me, Dr. Silvers. There is no proof. I wiped it away myself."

"Tell me something, Alice. If all this hadn't happened, how were you going to furnish me with a copy of those forwarded units that I needed to satisfy Andrews?"

"I can't answer that question. I guess some things do happen for a reason," Crane answered with a smile.

"Let's hope so, Alice. For your sake, let's just hope so."

The next morning, Silvers kept his appointment to appear on radio station WGLE. Jumping into the thick of it, the station had promoted Silvers's appearance with hyped statements about new revelations in this dramatic exposé of the city's blood center.

Silvers handled himself like an expert. The cocky early morning radio host, Jeff Majors, quickly jumped on the bandwagon of the blood center, painting the employees who had come forward as "whistle blowers." Swabuck had done an excellent job of orchestrating the interview. Silvers waited until the end of his air time to drop the bombshell.

"If Madison Boggs has any solid proof concerning her desperate attack on my blood center, then I challenge her to produce it on the air. What she has done amounts to reckless journalism in undocumented accounts made by troubled employees, some who were dismissed by my center because of poor work habits. If she can't produce such evidence, then I demand she apologize to the blood center and to our community."

Jack Edwards heard the radio interview in his car as he was driving to the station. The last several days had indeed been tense. The blood center story had placed his advertising department at direct odds with his news department. Ad reps were screaming for Madison to ditch the story—Seton Memorial had made a very real threat to pull the plug on their sponsorship of the station's very popular Medical Updates. St. Gray's had followed suit with a firm deadline threat to cancel their advertising sponsorship of the station's popular Sunday Morning In Review talk show. On top of that, a long-standing advertiser with deep pockets had called in threatening to pull all his commercials, which amounted to a pretty hefty chunk of ad dollars for WIXL if this story were allowed to continue. Jack Tunes, who owned Tunes Auto, was a long-time blood donor and had served on the center's foundation board for several years. He strongly supported the blood center and could not believe what he was hearing. His loyalty was fierce and his anger very real.

The calls of support were narrowing for Madison's story. This latest challenge to produce positive proof of wrongdoing had indeed left Jack Andrews feeling uneasy. Andrews knew Madison was short on documentation. He had allowed her enough rope, but perhaps it was time to sit down with his anchor and re-evaluate. This story could very well turn into a nightmare. Jack Andrews pressed his car's gas pedal down harder. Thoughts of a libel suit were not the best way to start off his day. For the first time in his career, Jack Andrews faced a real threat of buckling under to station advertisers. It was a powerful wall to hit.

Bertha White had also heard the medical director's challenge on the morning air waves while she was driving to work. His words made her feel sick to her stomach. She felt caught like a small fish in a big net of sharks. She had dismissed Lisa James as she had been directed. The look in James's eyes reflected the loss of respect the clerk held for Bertha. Lisa had done nothing wrong and did not buy the downsizing in Quality Control as a reason for her discharge. Bertha had also gone along with Dr. Crane in the rearranging of personnel records that belonged to the part-time clerk. It was frightening how easily records could be altered. The second dismissal of Reymond Alexander was now on hold. Dr. Crane had called Bertha at home late last night and told her to put off firing Reymond until she got back to her. It was decided that Reymond was to be retained as they did not want to give him any reason to join the Madison Boggs bandwagon. Reymond, as an employee, would keep his mouth shut—his loyalty to Bertha was assumed. It was this loyalty that ate away at Bertha White.

Grace Tende was furious when she discovered Lisa James's personnel records had been removed and tampered with. As personnel officer for the center, she had found herself placed in a very awkward position. She knew very well Silvers and company were working to cover their asses. The Swabuck people had made it very clear they were in control now, and Grace needed to back off and do whatever it took to keep the image of the blood center from being tarnished.

To make matters worse, Grace had received a call from Carter yesterday evening. Carter was in tears and was obviously very frightened. When Carter had heard about the van parked across the street from the television station, she started paying more attention to her own neighborhood. It wasn't long before she spotted the truck parked outside her house. Seeing the driver slumped down in the front seat was all the evidence Carter needed. A call to Grace quickly hatched a plan to slip Carter out from under the watchful eyes of whomever was sitting in the parked vehicle. Carter set her living room lights on an automatic timer set for five minute intervals. She did the same thing in her bedroom and upstairs guest room. Packing a bag with just a few items, she slipped out the back door unseen and made her way across her neighbor's yard to Grace's waiting car. Grace could hardly believe that Carter was being followed and threatened by the very people she had worked with day in and day out. Grace had hired these people. She had to confront her bosses. She had fifteen years of service in at the center. It was not going to be easy to walk away from this job and start all over again. Her reputation could be smeared by the powers above her. It could be done. Her bosses could throw up red flares to an inquiring personnel officer. Most of the time, a job-seeking candidate is never told why his application for employment was denied. Standard letters of "your qualifications did not match the preferred job duties" are forwarded as front letters for rejection. Grace Tende had worked in this field long enough to respect it. Today, though, she was more than just a little bit afraid of it.

Dr. Crane was prepared for Grace Tende's visit. She and Silvers knew it would only be a matter of time until Grace tried to stick her nose in where it didn't belong. They also knew they had to tread thin ice when dealing with Grace. Her knowledge of Dr. Silvers's flawed character hung heavy over their heads. But Grace only held the reins to Silvers's personal reputation; his professional reputation had never been an issue.

The meeting was short. Grace sensed immediately that Dr. Crane would lie through her teeth to protect her superior. Crane had documented reasons for intervening in Grace's department. Seeing Bertha White's and Lisa James's signatures on a letter of warning in James's personnel file could not be denied. Grace did not have the answers to take her case any further. Crane clearly had manipulated the records, but with Bertha's signed, sealed, and delivered signature backing her up, Grace had no evidence.

Grace left Crane's office and headed straight for Gerald Preston's. Seeing her standing in his doorway brought a smile to his face.

"Come in, Grace. It's good to see you." He stood up and made his way around his large desk to help Grace with her chair. His manners were impeccable even in this time of obvious stress.

There was a tense look about Grace that Preston immediately observed. He knew her face well, and this was a look he had not seen before.

"How can I help you, Grace?"

"Jerry, you can tell me the truth. What are we doing with Lisa James's personnel file, and why are you having goons sit outside Carter Egan's house?"

Preston shifted his eyebrows to a questioning expression.

"I don't know what you're talking about, Grace."

"Since when have you gone along with lifting personnel records from my office without my knowledge?" Grace wanted to tackle Lisa James first.

The executive director had never been in a confrontational situation with Grace Tende before—it made him most uncomfortable.

"I have no knowledge of any such incident happening, Grace. None whatsoever. Lisa James was dismissed as part of a restructuring of our laboratory. Dr. Crane felt she could utilize a substantial amount of savings. . ."

"Lisa James was let go because she had inside information concerning contaminated blood that had been shipped to our area hospitals without any intention of a recall," Grace said with a hard edge in her voice.

"Lisa James is a loose cannon whose sole purpose is revenge for being let go. There is no truth whatsoever to shipping contaminated blood to our hospitals without a recall. It just didn't happen, Grace." Preston spoke his words with conviction.

"My God, Jerry. Are you being led down the garden path by Silvers and Crane? Can't you see what is happening all around you?" The eyes begged Preston to hear her.

Preston stood up and walked the short distance across his office to close his door. His hands were slightly shaking and his heart was beating very fast. Grace's questions had hit their mark. He didn't know this part of the plan. What in the hell were Silvers and Crane up to? It could cost them dearly in the long run.

"Grace, I can't tell you how unsettling all this is to me. I mean—I don't know where you're getting such information?"

For the next thirty minutes, Grace took Preston step by step through all she knew concerning Lisa James and Carter Egan. When Preston continued to deny his participation in such happenings, Grace stood up. She had made up her mind.

"Jerry, I simply cannot stand by and pretend not to see what is going on. I intend to resign my position with the blood center."

"Now wait a minute, Grace. You can't do that. Not right now with all that is going on. You must at least allow me the courtesy to look into the allegations you brought to me and see if there is any documentation to prove you right or wrong. Give me a week, Grace. That's all I ask." Preston was stalling for time. He could not afford to let Grace walk out in this state of mind.

Grace's hand rested on the brass door handle of Preston's office door. Turning around to look squarely into the eyes of the executive director, she gave him her answer.

"You have my two week notice. It would be a waste of my time, Mr. Preston, to even consider staying here past this professional obligation because you and I both know the truth. You may not have been aware of what went on with Lisa James or what they've been doing to Carter Egan, but you know about all the rest. The false emergency calls, the dumping of blood, the high-pressure donor tactics, the cover-up of contaminated blood shipped out of here from time to time. We both knew. It's something we can't run away from anymore. We're both guilty as hell."

Preston felt his blood pressure skyrocketing as Grace closed his door. He never in a million years expected this. Grace Tende had gone along with all the other upheavals in the past. Why would she pick this time to walk out on him? He felt deserted—betrayed. He loved her; she clearly knew this. It was because of her that he stayed at the center. Silvers had brought all this on. Silvers had crossed over the edge and was doing things on his own that were not part of the agreement. The absolute stillness in his office was deafening. Gerald Thomas Preston could not imagine a day going by without seeing the face of Grace Tende. He had to get her back. It couldn't end this way.

31

The phone call to the blood center from Philip Jarvis came late in the day on Thursday. The attorney asked for Dr. Silvers to return his call as soon as possible. Silvers had spent the better part of this day giving out radio and print interviews. All in all, everything had gone very well, especially his appearance on WGLE. This one interview had been heard by a large audience. The challenge to prove wrongdoing certainly seemed to indicate the center had nothing to hide. The tide was turning and Silvers could feel it. Jarvis's requested call was at the top of his phone messages.

"Philip, it's Dr. Silvers. I have a message you needed me to call you as soon as possible."

"Thanks, Dr. Silvers. I'll get right to the point. I'm sorry I didn't call you sooner, but my office has been very busy sorting through Carter Egan's second deposition statement. After careful review, I believe we are now in a situation with Taylor Addison's lawsuit that needs immediate consideration for a settlement."

The word settlement jumped right out at Silvers.

"What do you mean by 'settlement'?"

"I think the blood center needs to offer an out-of-court settlement to Taylor's family."

"Like hell, we will. I have no intention of paying them one damn. . ."

"Dr. Silvers, clear copies of the donor's health questionnaires were entered in court records today. I think John Stansbarry has some very strong paper evidence on his side at this point in time."

"How in the hell did Stansbarry get clear copies?" Silver asked.

"I'm not sure, Dr. Silvers. Perhaps you're in a better position to answer that than I am," Jarvis quickly replied.

Silvers's mind was racing to figure out this mystery. The copies were buried. Suddenly Elizabeth's face popped into place. The pit of his stomach burned. Elizabeth Monroe had double-crossed him.

"Listen, Dr. Silvers. I do believe you would be best served to settle this whole matter quietly. Of course, if you are intent on fighting this case in an open courtroom, I think you need to read Carter's deposition very carefully. She brings some very heavy baggage with her. I think you must know what I'm referring to. Of course, we can limit most of the heresay evidence, but nevertheless, Carter would be free to talk openly to the press should she choose to do so. In light of all that's going on in the media right now, I'm not sure the timing is right to. . ."

"Pay the fucking settlement. Get her out of my hair. I want those court records sealed, and I also don't want to admit to any negligence. Can you do that?"

"If we offer them a full settlement, I'm sure the family will agree not to discuss this matter for an agreed period of time. And we can get a clause that exempts us from admitting negligence. It can all be worked out. Stansbarry seems like a decent man who just wants. . ."

"I could care less what any two-bit lawyer wants. We've already spent a fortune—for what? Now we're out another half million," Silvers spit out.

Philip Jarvis felt his ears burning. The arrogance of this man was beyond anything he had ever heard before.

"Perhaps if you would have followed your own rules, Dr. Silvers, you wouldn't have found yourself in this situation. As it is, I think you are getting off pretty easy. I mean—there are a couple of other people out there who got the same blood that killed Taylor Addison. In my opinion, you could have faced several more lawsuits for this negligence." Jarvis did not mince words with his about to be ex-client.

Silvers's instincts told him to pull back from his attack. "What do we do now?" Silvers asked in a more respectful tone of voice.

"I'll contact Stansbarry and feel him out. If he agrees, we'll draw up the settlement and begin to process the papers. It will take several weeks before any funds exchange hands. Do you need to confer with Dr. Crane or Mr. Preston before I start the ball rolling?"

"I'm sure they will agree to this decision," Silvers answered.

Sitting at his desk, Silvers ran through all that had just occurred. He sure as hell did not want to open up another can of worms right now. If Taylor's lawsuit was going to bring Carter out of the closet, it could only end up hurting him. At this point, Silvers felt confident that Carter was not going to join the bandwagon of turncoats that Madison was using against him. Silvers was putting his money on Carter's knowledge of what happens to public relations people once they get involved in messes concerning former employers. Carter Egan was pushed out of Silvers's mind by a more powerful presence—Elizabeth Monroe. She would have to answer to him for her actions. This time, he was not going to be so easy on her.

Port Smith—5:30 p.m. John Stansbarry picked up the phone on the second ring. Philip Jarvis's voice on the other end was indeed a pleasant surprise.

"The blood center wants to settle out of court. They felt it was time to put this all behind them and move forward," Jarvis said with his articulate voice dripping honey. The center was prepared to offer a full settlement—five hundred thousand dollars—the highest monetary award allowed because of the capped ceiling for such lawsuits against a blood center. Of course, there were certain minor stipulations to accompany the agreement. The blood center would never publicly admit to any error or negligence, and the dollar figure of the settlement would be sealed in court records. John Stansbarry listened quietly. Philip Jarvis could not see the smile spread across the small town lawyer's face, but he could feel it. The words were nearly choking in Jarvis's throat as he went over other minor stipulations his firm was requesting on behalf of the center.

Stansbarry thanked Jarvis for the call, and related he would meet as soon as possible with the Addison family. He would call him back tomorrow morning.

The phone had not hit its cradle when John Stansbarry let out a holler that could be heard across county lines. Tovey nearly dropped his coffee cup at the unexpected yell.

"What's the matter?" Tovey cried as he came racing out of the office kitchen.

"Nothing, Tovey—nothing," his uncle said as he grabbed his nephew in a bear hug.

"They want to settle, Tovey. We did it. The sonofabitches want to settle."

A feeling of pure joy ran through Tovey's body. For just a few seconds the two men stood together in an exhausted embrace.

Finally, John Stansbarry stepped back a few inches to look directly into Tovey's eyes and smiled. "She was right, Tovey. The law is supposed to protect the innocent. By God—every now and then it all works."

Tovey smiled back at the face he had come to admire so much. John Stansbarry was not a flashy lawyer, but he was an honest lawyer. The time for celebration was over. The two counselors had work to do. The first thing the senior Stansbarry did was place a call to Taylor's parents. He would be at their home within the hour. The second call went to Carter Egan. Carter had given him Grace's home phone number for him to contact her there should the need arise.

"Carter, it's John Stansbarry. Are you sitting down?"

"What's happened, Mr. Stansbarry?" Carter held her breath.

"They want to settle, Carter. You did it. You pushed them right out on a limb." Stansbarry's voice was almost giddy.

Carter closed her eyes and leaned back against the kitchen wall. For the next few minutes, the attorney shared with her only those things he could. She was not told the amount of the settlement, only that it would ensure the baby's future and make things just a little bit easier for Taylor's mom and dad. He felt certain the parents would accept the offer. It would be a few weeks before any of the dollars actually showed up in their bank account, but nevertheless, it was over.

Carter hung up the phone and sat down. No matter what happened to her professionally, some things were worth the pain.

Later that evening in the quiet of his office, John Stansbarry would take out the gray linen envelope that had brought him the evidence he needed.

"Whoever sent this to me—God bless you. God bless you big time."

On his way home that night, John Stansbarry, attorney at law, would drive over to Grandville. He wanted to stop by the cemetery where Taylor Addison had been laid to rest. With the moon full and the ground covered with white, glistening snow, he placed a copy of the evidence Taylor had never seen at the base of her tombstone.

"It's over, Taylor. We did it. You won. Maybe we can both rest now."

32

It was well past midnight when Elizabeth Monroe drove into the blood center's vacant parking lot. These last few days of sensational news headlines had slowed the incoming donations considerably, and there was no extra crew working on their own time to process a heavy donation day. It would be several weeks before blood donations returned to their normal intake levels.

It only took a few minutes to reach her darkened office. She was still in a state of shock. The rape had affected her deeply, and she had not been to work for several days. Elizabeth had confided the whole terrible act to her mother. Mrs. Thomas was outraged and wanted Elizabeth to call the police. For reasons not clear to her mother, the nurse refused. Mrs. Thomas did all she could to support her daughter though she did not understand her daughter's action.

Elizabeth Monroe had chosen this late hour to return to the center purposely. She did not want to run into Ben Silvers. Not now—not ever again. She wanted to process her request for a leave of absence through the proper channels and to gather some personal items she had in her office. There was also the matter of the blue folder she had left on her desk. Silvers had not picked up the folder when he walked out of her office. This she clearly remembered. What she found was a shock. Her desk was completely empty of paperwork. Karen, her assistant, had left Elizabeth a note: "Elizabeth—I'm earning my keep for a change. I've gone ahead and processed all the waiting forms. Everything else has been signed, sealed, and delivered. Dr. Silvers picked up the report he said you had prepared for him. It was the one in the blue folder. He said it was the one he needed. Hope you're feeling well. This has been some week!!!"

There was nothing Elizabeth could do now. Silvers had the blue folder and the evidence she had hoped to turn over to the State Board of Health. A feeling of sheer frustration and failure wrapped itself around her shoulders. Elizabeth had no way of knowing that her single act of courage in forwarding clear copies of the health questionnaires to Taylor Addison's attorney had resulted in a settlement. The office suddenly seemed to close in on her. She could still feel the weight of Silvers's body as she looked across the room at the old leather couch where she had been physically violated. Steadying herself, Elizabeth sat down at her desk and turned on the small lamp. She pulled a sheet of letterhead stationary from her right desk drawer.

She addressed her request for a leave of absence to Grace Tende with an explanation of her drug abuse. As her hand glided across the white stationary, the entire story of her relationship with the center's medical director and the final outcome which had resulted in rape poured out. She clearly stated her intentions to divulge the rape to the authorities at the rehab center where she was about to check herself in. In her own handwriting, she conveyed her sense of humiliation and fear. She stated she wanted no one else to suffer the same abuse. She knew that her actions could place Dr. Silvers's medical career in jeopardy, but she felt he, too, was ill. In his own way, he was as out of control as she was. She also documented that it was Silvers who started her on the road to drug addiction, and that he supplied her with the liquid morphine to which she had become so addicted. She explained to Grace her decision to enter a rehab house was the only way she could face everything that had happened to her these last several months. She told Grace that as soon as she could, she would be in contact. She ended her statement by documenting the fear she now was living with, and that she still truly felt that Ben Silvers was capable of even more violent actions. Elizabeth signed the statement, dated it, and placed it in a company envelope addressed to "Grace Tende—confidential." She then set the envelope in the message distribution center just outside her office. She knew the records clerk would pick it up in the morning and deliver it to Grace's office in a normal routine manner.

In a few minutes she had gathered everything she wanted to take with her. In a matter of hours, Elizabeth had an appointment to check herself into Central Rehab. It was not going to be easy to kick her habit, but she knew she could not do it alone. She also knew it could be the end of her nursing career.

Elizabeth wanted her life back. She wanted to look in the mirror and respect herself again. She wanted to be able to look at Kitten's picture and feel the love she had known for such a short period of time. This office held nothing for her now but bad memories.

The night air seemed so sweet as Elizabeth stepped outside the rear employee entrance. The sky was pitch black and dotted with tiny, shining white stars as far as the eye could see. For the first time in many months, Elizabeth Monroe walked away from the blood center with her head up.

33

Madison was in her office early Friday morning. The heat of producing paper documentation was clearly putting pressure on her story, and she was expecting to be called upstairs to Andrews's office at any moment. It was no secret at the station that Madison's story was putting heavy pressure on the advertising department. Caren Dillion, who was in charge of advertising, was trying to keep several big accounts from canceling. The informants' promises to produce a paper trail had not come through. Madison had never become so personally involved in a story before. Some of the tales she had on tape were chilling. At the same time, she could understand how the public could be confused as to who was telling the truth. They wanted to trust their community blood center. It made her angry to think of the greed and misuse of the public trust she had uncovered. She just couldn't get the story out of her mind. What had happened to Taylor Addison was the evil culmination of this whole situation. Silvers's recent challenge to document her story with paper had upset Madison more than she let on to her co-workers. At this point, she couldn't answer that challenge.

When the phone rang, Madison almost didn't answer it, but her hand instinctively picked it up.

"Boggs here."

"I told you there would come a day when you would need me," the haunting voice answered.

"Red Man. Is that you?"

"I'm always so flattered that you remember me."

"How could I forget you, Red Man?" Madison played along.

"You seem to be in a bit of trouble with your story, lovely one. Could you use some help?"

"It depends on what kind of help you're referring to," Madison countered, not sure where this was going.

"What would you do if I told you I could hand you proof of all those poison blood babies that the center says never existed?"

Madison's heart started to pound.

"Can you really do that, Red Man, or are you just stringing me along?"

"I would never do that to you. You are my redemption. You are the one to get rid of the evil one." His voice was louder now.

"Red Man, tell me what you have. If you're just pulling my chain here, you're wasting both of our time."

"Don't get angry, Madison. I can help you if you let me. I have the data sheets you need. I've had them all along."

Madison was breathing heavily. Her gut told her this man was not playing.

"When can you get them to me?" Madison asked, hoping not to push him too hard.

"You will have to come to me, pretty lady."

"Okay. Tell me where can I meet you?"

"You are anxious, aren't you?" The voice was clearly enjoying this game.

"You're right—I am anxious. I mean you may just be pulling my leg and heading me off on a wild goose chase," Madison said, trying to pull back a little.

"Now why would I waste my time doing that. You need what I have. The evil one has you backed into a corner, Miss reporter. You could be the laughing stock of the news world if you can't meet his challenge. Tell me—if I don't help you, who else can?"

"Why do you want to help me?" Madison was pushing. There was a story here as well, and it wouldn't hurt if she could dig just a bit deeper.

"I know what you're doing now—and I don't like it."

Madison bit her lip. "Damn it, I don't want to lose him again. He just might be the key to unlock this whole puzzle."

"You're right, Red Man. I'm sorry. I guess it's just the reporter in me. Listen—where can I meet you?"

"Do you know where St. Claire Street intersects with Town Avenue?"

"Yes, I think I do. I can look it up on a map just to be sure."

"Come alone in your pretty red car—pull in behind the liquor store on the corner of Town. Don't look back. I will find you." Without hesitation he added, "If I see anyone with you, Madison. I won't give you what you want." That this faceless caller knew what color of car she was driving, proved to be very unsettling.

"What time should I be there?" Madison asked.

"When the sun sets. That should give you enough time to prepare for your grand late night finale. It's been a pleasure talking to you, Miss Boggs with the beautiful mouth."

Click. The line went dead.

Madison's hands were shaking as she hung up the phone. This was a very serious situation. She was not about to go to that section of town alone to meet a man she wasn't sure was operating with a full deck. This was real life—not the movies. Madison took chances, but not this kind—at least not now—now that she was pregnant. Ed Morton was suddenly standing in front of her. He was just the person she needed to see at this moment. It was beginning to come together. Now all she needed was Carter Egan and someone else to do the five o'clock news in her place.

"Ed, you've got to pull Ryan from the streets and plug him into my chair for the five o'clock segment tonight."

"What the hell are you talking about? Since when don't you anchor the news?"

"Since I just got a call from Red Man telling me he can produce the paper trail I need to nail the blood center story shut."

"What did he say?"

"He told me he had the papers I needed on the blood center, and to come alone at sunset to St. Claire and Town Avenue. We're meeting behind the liquor store."

"This is not a safe situation here, Madison. For all you know this guy could be really warped. I'm not going to let you. . ."

"Ed, do you think I'm out of my mind. Of course I'm not going over there alone—you're going to be with me. I'll just stuff you down in the back seat on the floor. We'll cover you up with a blanket or something—just as long as he can't see you from a distance. It can work, Ed."

"Madison, this isn't Hollywood. Besides, I think we've gone over the edge here. Andrews wants to see us upstairs at four."

"Let's go up now. I'm telling you, Ed, I'm this close to having all I need to tie it all up." Madison's face was flushed with excitement as the pair made their way up the back staircase to Jack Andrews's plush office.

Madison could tell from the look on the GM's face that he was not in a good mood. This was one of those rare moments for Jack Andrews. He was generally very upbeat, very supportive of his news personnel. But this time, the situation was anything but normal. Madison, as much as she didn't want to, could understand where he was coming from. The station was faced with an immediate loss of revenue and a possible libel suit if her story didn't come down with positive black and white.

Five hospitals, all heavy investors in the station's advertising budget, had jointly issued an ultimatum for a retraction earlier that afternoon. The idea was not prescribed by Swabuck and Co. The ultimatum was spawned by Dr. Silvers who had called in a few markers from key hospital administrators with powerful advertising budgets.

Ben Silvers had called a meeting of selected CEO's of area hospitals. He opened the meeting with carefully chosen words. Words he knew would get their attention quickly.

"We all have skeletons in our closets, gentlemen, that are, shall we say, better off left alone. If Madison Boggs is successful at rousing up "disgruntled" employees against me and my operation and you allow her to get away with it with no proof other than faceless accusers, well, it's only a matter of time until you all will be faced with the same situation."

"Dr. Silvers, perhaps you should tell us how much of Madison's story is accurate?" Greg Steinburg, CEO for St. Gregory's asked.

"It's all been blown out of proportion. Have any of you ever suffered for lack of blood? Hell no, you haven't," Silvers emphatically answered. "The public wouldn't understand what we have to go through to keep that red pipeline flowing to all you guys on a daily basis. And frankly, it's none of their goddamned business. The media has crossed the line on us, and if we don't shut Madison Boggs down, who's to say she or some other half-baked reporter won't come creeping up your asses one day." Silvers's voice carried the threat of what could very well happen.

"Ben, I would like to know if the contamination incident is. . ." Bill Stidwelch, CEO for Union City Mercy Hospital, was cut off in mid-sentence by a very angry Silvers.

"It never happened. She can't prove it did either. You all have heard my challenge to Boggs—prove it. She can't. I'm not going to say any more. I have every intention of suing her and her station for libel. They can't prove any of this. All I'm asking for is your support. If the blood center doesn't get this support, it's only a matter of time until the operation we've built together on partnership comes tumbling down. Hamilton has never left you high and dry. We've kept you supplied in times that have crippled other areas of the country. You all know that. I shouldn't have to stand here and remind you. Your surgeons have never been put on emergency standby either. I might ask you to reflect on how that would feel to your purse strings, though." Silvers paused long enough to look across the table at Bud Mybeck, Seton Memorial's aging CEO. Mybeck didn't return the eye contact.

"We all operate on the human factor, gentlemen. Our employees hold a huge stick in their hands and up until now, we've been able to control their asses, but if we give in and allow the media to sort through our trash and talk to those individuals on the inside who have a privileged view of our operation. . .well, I don't think our world will ever be the same. I'm sure none of you want me to rehash some of the—let's say—errors of regret that we've all suffered through from time to time." The room was quiet as the administrators shifted uncomfortably in their seats. Silvers's words laced their thoughts with just the right amount of pressure.

"I need your commitment, gentlemen. If our operation goes public and is at the continued, unchecked mercy of whistle blowers with inside information and grudges on their backs, then it's only a matter of time until you will be faced with the media knocking at your back door. God help us all if you allow it to come to that." With that said, Ben Silvers stood up and left the room. For a few quiet moments the administrators did not speak. Finally, Bud Mybeck, Seton Memorial's powerful leader broke the silence.

"Gentlemen, whether we like it or not, we all are in this slime pot with Silvers. Personally, I can't stand the SOB, but he gets the job done over here, and my hospital isn't on any short rein when it comes to scheduling surgeries. He's right in reminding us of how much revenue surgeries bring to each of our hospitals. And if we let this go unchallenged by our silence with no show of support for our blood center, we all could face lawsuits by anyone we have pumped blood into during the last six weeks. If Silvers says the contamination shipping never happened, well, surely he wouldn't be stupid enough to publicly challenge Boggs to prove it on the air like he's been doing. I, for one, am going to back him up on this. If Madison Boggs had any real proof of these accusations, she would have plastered it all over the screen by now. I don't think we can lose anything by using our advertising dollars to leverage an end to a story that threatens us all. Like it or not, the sooner this story is pulled, the sooner the public can forget it."

"Bud's right on this," Roger Bush, CEO for Hamilton University Hospital, chimed in. "The media has no sense of boundaries anymore. I, for one, do not want to be held hostage by my employees. If Madison Boggs gets away with this story, we all could face some pretty uncomfortable moments in the future."

"Let's look at it from another point of view," Stidwelch jumped in. "We have nothing to lose by standing behind one of our own at this point. Silvers has walked around in all of our hospitals and there's dirt on the bottom of his shoes from our floors. I don't think it's any secret to anyone in this room that I don't trust the sonofabitch. He's a loose cannon as far as I'm concerned. If we let him get cornered, he could turn tail and drag us all down with him. If the television reporter has the goods on him and can produce, then he's sitting at his own table and we can all cry foul loud and clear after it's out. But, if she can't, we've killed two birds with one stone. We've backed her off and shown Silvers the support he's asking for from us."

The nervous administrators continued their debate on how to handle the situation for several more minutes. Finally, it was mutually agreed the hospitals would jointly issue a cancellation of advertising later that afternoon in a show of support for the blood center.

Jack Andrews was on the receiving end of their fury. Madison was a good reporter, but perhaps he had let her go too far out on a limb with this story. With no paper proof to back up the accusations, the story wouldn't hold in the long run. Facing a libel suit was nothing to sneeze at either. It was a difficult position to be in, and unlike the movies where the media is pictured as fearless at the scent of a good story, this was the real world where advertising dollars and the absence of libel suits were carefully watched.

Madison did not wait for Andrews to begin. She laid it on the line with what had just happened in regard to her call from Red Man.

"Madison, I have never pulled you off a story, but this time I don't think. . ."

"Jack, don't say it. Listen to me. I know this story is here. I can feel it."

"I can't run a television station based on your gut, Madison."

"Since when did you let advertising run the newsroom, Jack?"

Madison's words stung a bit too much. Andrews had all he could take from his anchor at this point. He was wrong in letting her air the story before she could back it all up. Faceless accusers were not enough in today's news market.

"Madison, you're off this story. I'm pulling the plug. You're going to go on tonight at five. . ."

"I am not going on tonight at five. I'm going to meet my contact and bring you back the best damn story you've ever aired on this station." Madison was out of her chair and heading toward his office door. Ed Morton stood up to follow her.

"Jack, give us the first set. We've got nothing to lose here if Madison isn't on the air at five, and we say nothing about the story. The hospitals will feel they can back off. If we get what I think we're going to get, we can be back at six and nail their asses. If it doesn't pan out, we'll do a retraction and the whole thing will settle down." Morton's words were not spoken with anger, but solid logic.

Madison stood at the door, her eyes were glued on Jack Andrews. Andrews thoughtfully rubbed the side of his face as he quickly considered his options.

"Jack, I know it's there. All we're asking for is just a couple of hours to bring it back," Ed added. Jack Andrews looked across his desk at his news director for one long moment before his eyes shot across the room to his anchor. She was angry and the emotions of the moment flooded her face. Andrews knew that look. Madison Boggs could be one of the most difficult women ever put on this planet, but aside from that, she was a good reporter. If this story could be nailed shut, it would complete this exposé that truly served the public's best interest. But Andrews didn't like what he was feeling at this moment. He and Boggs had never gotten sideways before. Her instincts on a story had always been on target. It was this "gut" thing that bothered him. Nothing was on paper, but those people he had watched on tape were all tied together with a story that begged to be aired.

"Bring it back, Madison—goddamnit, bring it back by six."

When Madison and Ed Morton emerged from their General Manager's office, their ears had been clearly pinned back, but the time to go after their lead was granted. Ed and Madison had seen the look on Andrews's face. They had gone way out on a limb with this story, and the branch was now in danger of breaking. Madison Boggs had never issued a retraction on a story. The thought was difficult to face. Red Man held the outcome in his hands. Would he show up? Or was he to be Madison's downfall?

34

The last four days had been difficult for Carter Egan. Displaced from her home by fear and out of touch for weeks with her husband, Carter had learned a great deal about herself. There seemed to be more to life than ambition or challenge. What she wouldn't give to go back in time. But she couldn't look back with regret. She had to face today.

She knew it was only a matter of time before Madison called for her to come out of the shadows. Watching the story unfold every night at Grace's house was not easy, especially when Carter listened to the different media outlets giving contrasting versions. She knew firsthand how wrong some of the information was, but there was no way to contradict it from the safety of a spectator's seat. The newspaper had clearly launched an attack on Madison's witnesses. A strong editorial came within a hair's breath of painting the faceless accusers as liars, out to settle a sour revenge on the management of the blood center. Carter could not understand how the paper could print a story so one-sided, but then, she wasn't aware of the editor's relationship with the center. The blood center employees had even offered to meet with a *Daily Voice* reporter face to face to tell their side again, but the offer was never picked up.

Swabuck and Company had made a huge difference. Their efforts planted just enough doubt, especially with the support of the medical community who had predictably risen to the center's defense. The paper proof, which Madison so badly needed, was just not there to back up the accusations. "If only" just wasn't good enough this time, and Madison and her band of blood center employees had their backs up against a very hard wall.

Carter knew that her appearance with verifying testimony could calm the waters for Madison. Her biggest fear at this moment, however, was the thought that the blood center would once again sidestep the challenges and win another round. All the pain that went into this story, with blood center personnel risking their jobs and reputations, could very well be lost with Silvers's challenge for paper proof, a proof that seemed slim in materializing.

Carter decided to check her phone messages before she placed the call to Madison. The first message was as far as she got.

"Mrs. Egan, this is Jody Cable. Please call me as soon as you can."

The voice sent a chill down Carter's spine. Jody's home number was quickly dialed.

"Hello."

"Jody, this is Carter Egan. I'm returning your call."

"Listen, Mrs. Egan, I've been watching Madison Boggs story, and I've been thinking about what you asked me a few days ago. I think I may have something you need. I mean—I'm not sure if it could help, but I really don't know what I'm looking at. I mean, Mom has some papers in her briefcase, and I don't know if they're important. Madison Boggs has been calling me, too and. . ."

"Listen Jody, if it's what I think it may be, you're right, it could help. I'd have to look at the papers. Can I come over to your house?"

"Sure. I'll be here for the rest of the evening."

"Give me your address—I'm not sure where you live."

Carter started to write the directions when Grace Tende opened her front door. She could see from the look on Carter's face something serious was happening. Hanging up the phone, Carter asked Grace to drive her over to Jody's house. Just before they left, Carter placed a call to Madison. When she got the reporter's recorded message, Carter left a brief message of her own.

"Madison, this is Carter. I may have something. Jody Cable wants to see me. She may have the papers you need. If this works out, I'll bring them to you myself tonight. And Madison, I think it's time I come out of the closet."

Reymond Alexander looked at the wall clock in his laboratory. For the last forty-five minutes he had been placing calls to the hospitals that had received the bulk of the center's contaminated blood. His calls were directed with one purpose: to alert them to the dangerous product that still might be sitting in their hospital refrigerators. His initiative was met with placid results. It made him angry to be put on hold. He knew why they were doing it. They didn't believe him. Over and over he tried to give the bar code numbers out for them to check, but each time he was told his call would have to be transferred to another administrator. It was infuriating to the tech who couldn't believe the indifferent response he was experiencing.

"Jesus, they act like I'm trying to sell them something," he thought as he glanced up again at the large clock in his laboratory.

"I won't have enough time to complete the calls this afternoon. I'll have to work on it tomorrow." He smiled suddenly. Tomorrow would probably be a better day. "They'll listen to me then. Oh yes! Tomorrow will be a different story."

Reymond cleared the top of his bench and turned off his light. There was only one more thing to do before he left. The tall, lanky tech took the stairs two at a time. He felt a bit out of place on the executive level at this time of day, as all his visits to this floor usually came after hours. Dr. Silvers's office was straight ahead of him as he walked down the hall.

There was no secretary in sight, but Silvers office door was cracked just enough for him to see the medical director was still present.

Silvers looked startled to see Reymond Alexander standing in his doorway. His dark eyes narrowed.

"What do you want?"

"I need to speak with you, Dr. Silvers."

"Whatever it is, take it up with your supervisor. I'm busy right now."

The brush-off did not work this time. Reymond smiled and stepped inside the office, closing the door behind him.

"Oh, I think you will want to hear what I have to say, Dr. Silvers." The voice was filled with contempt.

The brashness of Reymond's actions sent Silvers's blood pressure rising.

"What the hell is this all about?"

"It's about deceit, Dr. Silvers."

Silvers looked puzzled. He sat back in his chair and waited to see where this tech was going.

"I believe you owe Bertha White an apology. In fact, I think you owe this whole community an apology."

Silvers slammed his fist down on the top of his desk and stood up.

The action only widened Reymond's smile.

"Get the hell out of my office, you—"

Silvers stopped suddenly when Reymond reached inside his jacket and extracted the data sheets produced from Bertha's computer before the information had been erased by Dr. Crane on that fateful morning. Silvers hesitated before he reached across his desk. Whatever Reymond had in his possession gave the tech too much confidence. If it were not something damaging, he would never have confronted him so squarely.

Red was circulating up Silvers's neck. Small traces of moisture ran through the palms of his hands.

"Where did you get this?" Silvers questioned as he looked at the exposing data sheets.

"From our system, Dr. Silvers. The same system that doesn't work half the time."

Silvers felt a sick feeling in the pit of his stomach.

"This doesn't mean anything to me. I've never seen this report."

"That's bullshit! You and Dr. Crane are in this together. You held this incident over Bertha White's head, making her fire Lisa James and holding her pension as ransom for your sick actions of deliberate cover-up. You just don't want to ruin your perfect reputation by admitting your laboratory is pushed to the limit and driven to commit errors. But because of you and your insane push for blood, we did commit an error—a deadly error, doctor, that you're trying to push under the rug now by pretending it never happened. There could be blood sitting out there right now on some hospital shelf that is filled with disease. We still have a slim chance at getting some of it pulled. But you sure as hell won't do the right thing, so we're going to do it for you. And after we do, good doctor, you're through here. As soon as this gets into the right hands, you'll be out on your ass in the cold driven snow. It couldn't happen to a nicer person." Reymond sneered as he reached for the documents.

Silvers grabbed Reymond's arm, shoving him away from his desk. Reymond quickly recovered and lunged at the medical director. His powerful hands sent the smaller man reeling backwards. The executive chair caught the doctor's falling body. The strength of Reymond surprised Silvers.

"You're scum, Silvers. I've waited a long time to tell you this. You've pushed people around for the last time, and, oh yeah, doctor, I don't think you're going to get that little research project you so counted on either. I don't think the NAABC cottons too well to dummied up research grants." Reymond didn't wait for the doctor to respond as he turned and quickly made his exit. He had a meeting to make and the sun was just beginning to set.

Benjamin Silvers mind was racing. Reymond was obviously going to turn the information over to someone. How in the hell had he gotten his hands on all this information? Where was he going with those documenting reports? "Goddamn Alice Crane. Goddamn her." The thought held in Silvers's mind as he quickly dialed Herk Golden's office.

Golden was just about ready to walk out of his office for the day when the phone rang. He hesitated for a moment before answering it.

"Golden here."

"Silvers. I need a quick fix for a situation that is headed out."

"Who?"

"Reymond Alexander. I think he is on his way to the media with some reports that aren't in our best interest. I need them back here tonight."

"Where is he now?"

"I think he's coming down the back stairs to the parking lot."

Golden didn't say goodbye as he raced from his office. He found just the right person for the job standing at the time clock.

"You've got a tail tonight for the boss. Alexander's got some paper and you need to make sure it doesn't get into the wrong hands. We need them back by tonight." The driver slowly nodded his head. He had been given this kind of assignment once before. As they were speaking, Golden spied Alexander sitting in his car. "He's out in the lot right now. See what you can do and give me a call later at home. Whatever he's gotten hold of has to be buried one way or the other." Golden's words would have been subject to interpretation by anyone who might have overheard them. To this driver, though, they carried only one message.

Reymond's car was slow to warm on this cold winter's evening. Herk Golden had the time he needed.

Nervously, Reymond gunned the car's motor as the defroster struggled to clear the ice-covered windows. His hands were cold, but his body felt strangely warm. It was a good feeling to finally get a piece of the pompous doctor who had made his life so miserable. Glancing at his watch, Reymond saw there was just enough time to make his rendezvous with Madison. He didn't see the small truck pull out behind him as he left the center. The roads were wet and beginning to ice up again as Reymond carefully approached the intersection of St. Claire and Town Street. The liquor store's parking lot was strangely empty for this time of the early evening. Madison's red Buick was nowhere in sight yet. The feeling of what was about to take place felt good and the anticipation of exchange heightened.

Reymond pulled his car across the street in a side alley from where Madison was told to go. From this vantage point, he could see both ways up the street for the reporter's arrival. Something inside Reymond told him Madison was not foolish enough to come to this meeting alone. She'd put someone inside her car or position another car nearby. He knew this in advance, but all that mattered now to Reymond was a clear shot to turn the information over to her. She was his redemption at this point. As a team, they could accomplish the removal of the evil now present at the center. In a few more minutes, it would all be over.

There were two clearly marked blood center envelopes resting innocently next to Reymond on the passenger seat of his car. One was addressed to Madison Boggs. It carried all the computer data information concerning the blood center's shipment of contaminated blood to their county hospitals plus a surprise piece of information written in Dr. Crane's own handwriting. The second envelope was addressed to the NAABC Research Committee. Siam Qua's secret diary notes would make very interesting reading for Fritzsimmons Garret and Company. Ben Silvers's days of glory were surely numbered.

The sun was just setting when Madison's car rounded the corner and pulled slowly into the side street behind the liquor store.

"She seems to be alone," Reymond gauged as he waited a few minutes before pulling out.

Cautiously, Reymond drove his car across the street, positioning himself just a few inches behind the reporter's car. He could see the anchor straining to catch a look at him in her rearview mirror. He flipped his car's bright lights on. The harsh glare took away her view. In graceful strides, Reymond quickly approached the driver's side of the red car. Cautiously, Madison cracked her window downward a few inches.

"Just keep looking forward, Miss Boggs. There's no need to strain those beautiful eyes of yours."

"Red Man, if these are bona fide reports, I owe you big time," Madison replied keeping her eyes looking straight ahead as she was instructed. Her hands were shaking as the cold air quickly drifted in through the half-open car window and chilled her face and shoulders.

"This won't cover all the charges, but it should clear you on the contamination issue, my lovely. Once you can prove him a liar on this, the rest should fall into place, don't you think?"

Reymond passed the sealed envelope through the cracked window space. His hand for just a few seconds lingered on Madison's as she accepted the envelope.

Madison did not get a chance to answer his question as the roaring sound of the approaching truck's engine immediately captured the attention of the lone figure standing next to Madison's parked car. The headlights caught the surprised look on Reymond's face as the truck raced toward him. A smile was present on the driver's face as the gas pedal was pushed down even harder.

Just as the speeding vehicle made contact with the parked car, Reymond managed to hurl himself up on Madison's car hood. The sideswipe impact threw Madison forward into her steering wheel and the jarring impact sliced open her nose at the bridge. Her forehead absorbed the rest of the impact, slightly dazing the anchor for the moment. Ed Norton, who was huddled down on the floor directly behind Madison, was startled by the sudden jolt, but his curled up, compact position saved him from injury.

Reymond, dazed and shaken, rolled to the ground, scrambling as quickly as he could to reach his own car. He was trembling with anger as he backed up his car in pursuit of the driver who had just clearly tried to kill him. The squealing of his tires filled the air.

"Are you okay, Madison? My god, what just happened here?" Ed yelled as he struggled to upright himself in the back seat. A sudden twinge of pain ran down his right shoulder.

"I'm okay, Ed. I think I've just got a bloody nose."

"Jesus, look at you—are you sure you're okay? What just came off here?" Ed struggled to reach the front seat. Madison was holding her neck scarf up to her nose, blotting the steady stream of flowing blood.

"I'm not sure, Ed." She paused a second. "It could have been someone trying to run Red Man over. Jesus, would they go that far?"

"What happened to Red Man?" Did he get hit?" Ed asked as he pulled out his handkerchief and began to dab at the blood smeared across Madison's forehead.

Madison pulled her head back. The touch of Ed's hand on her cut and bruised face was painful.

"He's gone. The truck just missed him. He pulled around us, I think." Suddenly Madison felt a bit lightheaded. As her head fell forward, Ed caught her.

"Madison, we need to get you to a hospital. You need to be checked out by a doctor." Ed eased Madison's body back in her seat.

"No! I'm okay—really, Ed. Just give me a few minutes."

As she let her body relax, the thought of the envelope suddenly returned. "Ed, where is it? Where is the envelope?" Madison sat upright and began to search her lap for the evidence.

Ed reached up and turned on the car's overhead interior light. The clearly marked white blood center envelope was lying at his feet on the passenger's side of the car.

"Here it is, Madison." Ed handed the envelope to his anchor.

"Do me a favor, Ed. Open this up. Things are a little blurry right now."

Ed's index finger served as an opener across the top of the envelope. Five sheets of computer paper with columns of printed data were in place. The blood center's name was visible across the top of the information, as was the date and time of day the report was run. As Ed pulled the rest of the sheets out of the envelope, a single sheet of yellow, legal size paper fell in his lap.

"What's this?" Ed said as he strained to see what was written on the paper.

"Well I'll be damned—a personalized note from one Dr. Alice Crane to her lab supervisor." Ed's eyes quickly scanned the information. "This is it, Madison. This seals it."

"What is it, Ed. What do we have?" Madison impatiently demanded.

"We have the computer report with enough documentation to show the severity of the laboratory error, and we have a note from the assistant medical director ordering the data about the contaminated units to be stored in a separate data entry bank out of the system's normal data base. There's no doubt about it now; this break was a damn serious situation." Ed's voice carried the tone of excitement and relief. He looked across the seat at his bleeding and bruised anchor.

"Are you sure you're okay, Madison? Seton's only a couple of blocks away. Why don't I drive us over there and have the doctors look you over?" To his surprise, Madison agreed.

Madison slid across the seat as Ed entered the driver's side of the car. He couldn't help but notice the damage inflicted on the left side of Madison's car.

"We were pretty lucky with this one, Madison, but your insurance rates are gonna go up, though, after you file this hit and run report."

Madison forced a smile and continued to hold her head back, trying to stop the flow of blood draining from her nostrils. "Maybe we'll take on the insurance industry next, Ed," Madison replied, her sense of humor still intact. She was beginning to feel a bit stiff from the heavy jar she had just taken and a sudden low pain in her back was now surfacing. Her thoughts were focused on the baby inside her. She didn't remember hitting her stomach, but nevertheless, this time, she could not afford to tough it out. She needed to see a doctor, but her reporter's instinct was fighting for control.

"Ed, maybe we need to follow Red Man's car—I mean if someone just tried to bounce him off the wall, perhaps we should follow. . ."

"Madison, if you weren't pregnant, I'd floor this gas pedal and join the chase, but not this time, lady. You're going to the hospital. We've got what we came for. This chase is going on without us, Mad."

Ed was right. Things were different now. She had the story. If there was going to be more, it would have to unfold without her. She felt a bit sick to her stomach and her face was beginning to swell. Her right eye was just about closed, and she could barely see out of her left one. Maybe the impact damage was more than she originally thought.

"Oh God, let our baby be okay," she prayed as she held Ed's handkerchief up to her nose. She could feel the wet sticky feeling of blood soaking up the cotton cloth. Her hands were trembling slightly. For the first time in a long time, Madison felt there was something more important to her than a story and a deadline. It was a very different feeling.

As they headed their car south toward Seton Memorial, Reymond's car was traveling north at high speed. The fast cruising truck was directly in front of the blood center tech, and Reymond clearly recognized the vehicle and the driver.

"That sonofabitch—sending one of his flunkies out after me. When I catch up to that fat, bald punk, I'll pound his ass into the ground, and then I'm going back for Silvers." Reymond's anger was pounding at his insides as the chase continued to gain speed.

Terry Milo was cursing to himself. He had screwed up again. Damn! It wasn't the first time, either. The driver's mind flashed back to another incident of getting caught. When Anna Cable had surprised Milo in her garage, he reacted violently. He hit her hard across the back of the head as she ran toward the phone. The vicious blow rendered the small-framed woman unconscious as she fell to the floor. Why did she have to open that door? Milo was beside himself with fear. Cable had clearly recognized him, and if she had reported the incident to the police, as she had threatened to do, he would have had a one way ticket back to prison for a long, long time. Terry Milo just couldn't let that happen. When he discovered the note on her kitchen table, the intruder shaped the seemingly perfect out to his screw-up. The police officers, eager to close the investigation, accepted the probable cause of attempted suicide. They never suspected Anna Cable was knocked out before she was placed behind the wheel of her car. It was not her hand that turned on the car's engine that night, but Terry Milo's. It was made to look like a suicide and it worked. No one even suspected a crime had ever taken place at the house of the former public relations director for the blood center. Terry covered his actions with Herk that night by inventing an excuse that would clear him of any involvement.

"She was already slumped over the wheel, Herk, when I got there. I wasn't going to stick around and wait for the cops to come." Herk agreed that Terry had done the best thing by getting out of there when he did. The situation had taken care of itself. It was a subject never to be brought up again. It would be their secret—one of many to be kept.

Terry's foot pressed the gas pedal down harder as Reymond's car was just inches away from his rear bumper. The tree-lined street was beginning to narrow, and a hard curve was just in front of the speeding cars. When Milo hit his brakes, he realized too late the road was a solid sheet of ice. His truck had just begun to spin when Reymond's car rammed it just behind the driver's door. The high speed slide joined both cars together, sending them crashing sideways into the solid oak trees. The collision was so powerful the gas tanks of both vehicles exploded on impact. Heat from the flames sheared the bark off the trees, sending sprays of yellow orange fire upwards toward the black skies filled with crystals of falling, freezing rain. There would be no survivors. The secrets of both men would be carried with them to their graves.

Carter and Grace heard the shrill sound of responding fire engines and police cars in the distance as they slowly negotiated the icy streets in Grace's compact car. Anna Cable lived on the west side of town and the ride was slow.

The yellow porch light of the small brick home greeted their arrival, and a soft knock on the door brought a quick response.

Jody's face carried the strain of the situation as her two guests entered the neat home. The pair followed Jody to the kitchen, where a large, well-used briefcase now lay on top of the formica kitchen table.

"This belongs to my mom," Jody said as her hand reached out to touch the leather case. "I don't know if any of these papers or reports are what you're looking for, but someone once wanted them."

"What do you mean by that?" Carter asked.

The daughter hesitated a few seconds before answering Carter's question.

"All I know is Mom told me that she thought someone had gone through our house one afternoon. She wouldn't tell me any of the particulars. I just know that after this incident, Mom was afraid to come home to a dark house."

"Do you think someone broke into your house, Jody?"

"I don't know. Mom never used to lock the doors, but after that, she started to lock everything up around here like Fort Knox. I couldn't get

her to talk about it. I guess it's too late now for me to know what happened. All I know is Mom kept this case locked up in the trunk of her car
under a bunch of blankets."

"Can I look inside, Jody?" Carter asked timidly, aware that the case
belonged to a woman whose job she taken not too many months ago.
What secrets would she find? Maybe there was nothing hidden away in
the case. Maybe it was all just a wild-goose chase, but then again. . .

"Help yourself," the daughter replied stepping back from the table.

Carter quickly spread the contents of the briefcase out onto the top of
the kitchen table. There were several reports folded together. Grace and
Carter began to separate the sheets of paper.

The two women anxiously pored over the papers now in their hands.
These were clearly blood center documents. What secrets did they contain? Could these innocent looking papers have caused Anna Cable to put
her life in jeopardy?

Grace was the first to speak.

"Carter, these are airport shipping receipts. Look, Anna attached the
daily report sheets to them."

Carter, almost at that same instant, had found something else. "Look
at this," she said as she held out stapled together press releases which
documented an emergency appeal for blood donations while Kiley's
attached detailed inventory reports showed a healthy five-day supply in
reserve. The levels in both reports clearly proved a sufficient supply of
blood was available on the center's shelves while the center was calling
false blood shortages.

"Kiley Matson has never shared these damaging reports with
other staff members. I wonder how Anna got hold of these?" Carter
questioned.

"I don't know. I've been going to morning flash meetings for years,
and I've never seen either of these reports before," Grace answered,
amazed at the information Anna Cable had in her possession. Suddenly,
Grace picked out another report. Her eyes grew wide with excitement.

"Carter, look at this—I've never seen this documented before,
either. It's the Glass account. It shows an inventory of several thousand
units of O's, above and beyond the daily call sheets." The two women's
heads were only inches apart as they began to spread the various reports
across the kitchen table. Anna Cable had somehow compiled enough
evidence to prove the center was engaged in unethical activities. No hard
laws were broken, but they were clearly using a false media alert for their
own profit.

"No wonder Silvers was panicked about Anna. She had the paper proof to do some real harm."

"Jody, do you know if your Mom ever tried to turn these reports over to anyone?"

"No—well, I mean yes. All I know for sure is Mom called some board members shortly after she left the center, but they wouldn't meet with her, and she was very upset with whatever they said to her on the phone. After that, she just didn't talk about the center any more—at least not to me. She was always trying to keep up a good front for me—you know. I only wish she would have told me what was going on in her life. I could have been there for her." The daughter's words trailed off. A slight flush was present in her cheeks and a look of deep sadness filled her yellow-green eyes.

"Jody, will you let me have these papers?" Carter asked.

"I guess, I mean if they can help you, they certainly won't do my mother any good now. If any of this was responsible for what Mom did—then maybe it's best. I have no sympathy for the blood center. Mom worked so hard for that bunch and what did it get her?"

Grace felt the impact of Jody's statement. Anna Cable had indeed been wronged by her company. That was abundantly clear now. Why hadn't she pursued Anna's situation? So many things were now coming back to haunt her. It was a painful moment for the personnel director.

"Jody, I am so sorry for all that happened to Anna. If I had known. . ."

"There's nothing that can be done now, Miss Tende—about the past. But you sure as hell can make a difference in the future, if you guys just have the guts to stand up to them. Mom didn't have anybody to go to bat for her. You all turned your backs on her." Jody's voice trailed off. The emotions of all that had past were now very much alive again.

Carter sensed the situation could go no further. She had to get these papers to Madison—time was running out.

"Jody, thank you for calling me. I can assure you these papers will come to good use. I promise you that." Carter touched the daughter on the shoulder and walked toward the front door. Grace lingered for just a few seconds. Once more she apologized to Anna Cable's daughter. The bitterness was not present this time as Jody slowly nodded her head in a kind of understanding. The gesture reached out to Grace.

The cold air penetrated their winter coats as the two women walked as fast as they could on the ice-covered sidewalk to Grace's parked car. Ice had again covered the windshield. They sat in stunned silence as they waited for the car to warm up and the defroster to clear the tiny crystal chips of frozen rain from the windshield. Grace spoke first.

"I probably shouldn't say this out loud, Carter, but I just can't believe Anna tried to kill. . ."

"Don't say it, Grace—don't. I don't think you and I could ever get through all of this right now if you do."

Carter was right. There was no use in thinking out loud. The thought was just too unbelievable.

Carter elected to change the subject. "I need to run by my house if you don't mind. I want to change clothes. If I'm going to be on the news tonight, I should try and look presentable. Blue jeans and this sweat shirt won't cut it."

"Are you sure you want to do this, Carter. I mean you know what you could face in this community if you. . ."

"I know what I'm getting myself into, Grace. It doesn't matter to me anymore. No job is worth your self-respect."

Grace nodded in agreement and turned the car in the direction of Carter's house.

The street crews were out in force now, spreading salt and sand on the slick roads. The tedious trip was negotiated in half the time it had taken them to reach Anna's house from the other side of town.

As the car moved slowly down Carter's street, the two women strained to see if the parked truck was still present. It wasn't. The sight of her own home brought a warm feeling to Carter as the car moved cautiously up the slick driveway, coasting to a stop directly in front of the garage. On her way inside, Carter retrieved her mail. A blood center envelope immediately caught her eye. She quickly opened the envelope and withdrew its contents.

"Oh my God! Grace, look at this," Carter said as she sat down on the nearby couch holding several papers in her hands. Grace quickly came to her friend's side, and her eyes began to scan the papers Carter was holding.

"These look like some sort of profits sheets based on quarterly sales reports." Grace's eyes raced across the columns.

"Look at this, Grace. Here are copies of checks—my God—these look like bonus checks paid directly to Silvers, Preston, Bryan, and Crane. They're listed under "debt retirement and service fund in this account report."

"These are some pretty hefty checks, Carter. I guess the business of selling blood under resource sharing does pays off."

"Yeah, if you're at the executive level. No wonder we've got such a push on all the time to recruit blood."

"Look at this—this report clearly backs up what Anna Cable had. It's a tracking of some kind. It shows a reserve level of blood in place every time we've called an emergency."

This sudden turn of events prompted other questions.

"Who sent these to you, Carter?"

"I don't know."

"Let me see the envelope." Grace asked.

Grace recognized the near perfect printing.

"Carter, this is Michael Bryan's handwriting. He's left-handed and he prints at a backward angle. I would know it anywhere."

Carter felt a catch in her rib cage. The last thing Michael Bryan had said to her was, "I'll do my best to protect you."

Was this his way? Carter felt tears welling up in her eyes. Where was Michael Bryan? So many thoughts began to flood Carter's mind. Michael Bryan was indeed involved in all that was wrong at the center, but he didn't seem to have the same motivation as the others. Power and money linked Silvers and Preston. But there was something different about Michael. There was just something that didn't fit. A trace of decency was still alive inside him; Carter could feel it, see it. How could Bryan have gotten so mixed up with all this? It was no secret to her now; he was very much aware of the machinations that were going on at the blood center, but what did the co-directors have on him to pull his strings the way they did? What evil secrets were hiding in his closet? Michael Bryan was a decent human being. Bright, and yes, ambitious. He had shown more than he was given credit for at the center. The good changes were brought about through his efforts; but still, how could he have been a part of all this? Who was Michael Bryan and what had he become?

"If I had stayed and looked the other way, would I have ended up just like Michael?" This thought made Carter uncomfortable. Carter Egan wanted to share just one more conversation with Michael Bryan. It was a wish that would not be granted.

"Carter, we've got to get this information to Madison." Grace felt blood rush to her face. Carter nodded, dropped the papers in Grace's lap, and walked quickly to her bedroom to change her clothes. The house seemed so quiet, so empty. So much had happened so fast. Carter felt a mixture of excitement and exhilaration, but mixed with fear and not a little anxiety. Thoughts of the last few hours pounded her consciousness. Grey dress, green dress, the colors seemed to blur. . . Three hundred units of blood, not the red dress, no. Those patients need your blood, the little girl—her transfusion. The bank account totals. She put on the green dress. . . Am I ready? Get to the mirror, quick. Am I okay?

Suddenly Carter was downstairs. Grace was waiting with the all-important letter. They left the house and drove quickly to Blair Street and the TV station parking lot. The evening receptionist told them Madison was running a bit late and would they mind having a seat until she arrived. In less than fifteen minutes the receptionist received a call from Ed Norton. She transferred the call straight to Jack Andrews with the news that Madison had visitors in the lobby.

"Jack, this is Ed."

"Where in the hell are you, Ed? It's ten minutes till six."

"We're at Seton Memorial—there's been an accident."

"What kind of accident? Are you hurt? Is Madison okay?"

"She's okay, Jack. She's getting some stitches right now. She just wanted you to know we've got the papers; we've got way more than we need to prove our case against the blood center."

"Ed, I don't understand. How did Madison get hurt?"

"It's a long story, Jack. I'll fill you in when I get back." "Jack, you need to get Ryan ready for the six and eleven news. Madison is not going to be able to make it. The doctors want to keep her quiet for the next few hours. She wants Ryan to get over here after he finishes the six. She said she could brief him enough for him to take over and finish the story at eleven."

"Ryan take over Madison's story? I mean, Ryan can fill in at six, that's no problem, but my God, Ed. Are you sure Madison wants to turn this story over to someone else to finish?"

"Hell no, Madison doesn't want Ryan to finish her story, but she's not got much of a choice, Jack. Her face is pretty banged up; both her eyes are almost swollen shut and her nose is the size of a banana. And besides that, the doctors are worried about the jolt she took. They aren't going to let her out of here tonight, that's for damn sure. Madison had about thirty minutes to get used to all this, but Jack, it was her call and she made it. The story is the point here. It's not the reporter, it's the story."

It took Jack Andrews a few seconds to digest what Ed Morton had just relayed. Ed continued.

"As soon as Ryan's through at six, you can wheel the promos for the eleven o'clock news. Stew can program them up with the new bites. Have Ryan do a voice-over and drop in the background music.

"Are you sure, Ed. I mean our ass is way out over the line here. I don't want to get in deeper if there's. . ."

"Jack, I'm looking at the documentation now. It's in my hand. We've got computer printout sheets and a handwritten memo from Dr. Alice Crane that backs up every one of Lisa James's accusations."

"Yeah, well Ed, you may have another bonus here at the station that you don't know about."

"What's that?"

"Carter Egan and a Grace Tende from the blood center are downstairs in our lobby waiting to see Madison. I'm sure Carter wouldn't be here at this time of night unless there was a pretty good reason for her showing up. Maybe Madison has her ace in the hole to back her up—and if what you have in your hand is bona fide information, we've got that whole group right where we want them. Ed, is Madison's baby okay?"

"Yeah, the doctor thinks everything is okay, but she took a jolt and just to be safe, they want to keep her overnight. I called her husband at work, and he's on his way to the hospital now. Madison's not being the best patient, but she's minding the doctors at this point. I'll tell you what happened when I get back."

Jack Andrews immediately made his way down to the lobby. He greeted Carter and Grace and asked them to accompany him to the news room. Feeling comfortable after a few minutes of conversation, Carter handed the information she had obtained from Anna Cable's daughter and Michael Bryan over to the General Manager. A dark look of disgust covered Andrews's face as he scanned the pages of information he now had in his possession. The sheets of information were given to Madison's chief photographer to scan into video for the evening news broadcast.

Andrews excused himself and walked down the hall to production. The order was given to start the promotion teasers for Madison's late news program every fifteen minutes across the bottom of the screen. When Madison didn't appear on the five and six o'clock news installments, Swabuck & Company read it as a victory.

"She can't prove it and she's been yanked." But the victory celebration would be short-lived. When the promotion teasers started rolling at eight-thirty, there was no doubt in Frank Swabuck's mind that something was very wrong. Had Silvers and Crane lied to them about the documentation? No matter, Swabuck thought. It would only be a temporary setback for the public relations agency. He knew there would still be a need for his services after this story ran tonight, no matter what revelations were revealed. A new image would have to be created, and his agency had the inside track. There was still money to be made, and the center would feel comfortable using his firm to rebuild whatever damage was about to happen.

A nervous Ryan Patrick began the late evening news broadcast with a brief statement. "Yesterday, Dr. Benjamin Silvers, Medical Director of the Hamilton Regional Blood Center issued a direct challenge to Madison Boggs to back up her taped witnesses' statements with paper documentation. Paper documentation he said didn't exist. But the truth of the matter is, it does exist, and Madison Boggs, who was injured earlier this evening in a hit-and-run car accident while securing this information, can prove it."

Slowly and dramatically, Patrick began to read a prepared statement that Madison had scribbled out on the back of a patient's food order form. It was a personal address unlike any she had ever scripted before.

"Every now and then, a reporter finds a story that cries out to be heard. This story was one of them for me. I was issued a challenge yesterday to prove the accusations presented over the course of these last few days were true. The individuals who came forward to try and right a system that has obviously gone haywire, were promptly labeled as "whistle blowers and disgruntled employees," out to intentionally cause harm to the management of the Hamilton Regional Blood Center. I believed these individuals and the story they had to tell, and the documents you are about to see should haunt this community for some time. I stand by my story and the individuals who risked so much to expose what has been hidden for so long."

Patrick shifted his weight in the anchor's chair. Looking directly into the camera's red eye he continued.

"We will also include in tonight's news segment, a live interview with Carter Egan, former public relations director for the blood center. Her story, and what she was asked to do by the center's officials will shock you and rightfully so."

Patrick recounted the story, touching on each accusation and following each revelation with the paper documentation Silvers had challenged the station to produce. Carter's interview was devastating to the center, and her appearance reinforced the story's credibility. Madison Boggs had produced the evidence and sealed it with a personality the community had come to recognize and trust, Carter Egan. Madison Boggs's most difficult story came to a conclusion without her, but the evening viewers could feel her presence, even if they couldn't see her face. Within minutes after Patrick signed off with a personal get well quick to Madison, the switchboard was jammed with calls from a worried public. Madison watched her story from her hospital bed with her husband, Whit Sisson, by her side. Within minutes, Ed Morton was on the phone to his anchor.

"Hey lady, you did it."

"We did it, Ed. Tell Ryan he's too damn good looking and too damn young to be sitting in that seat."

"Yeah, well, he said to tell you that chair felt comfortable," Ed returned with a chuckle. "You were right on with this one, Mad. Listen, how are you feeling?"

"Like a truck hit me," she stated slowly. "I wonder if Red Man saw the story? Have you checked my voice mail to see if he's called?"

"No, Madison, I haven't. I just got off the air and I haven't had the time. There was a bit that came in about a fatal car accident, though. The police haven't given out any identification yet on the drivers. It's probably not connected to your Red Man, but it did happen close to the time. . ."

"Do me a favor, Ed. Stay on top of this. I think there might be a connection here. Listen, how is Carter? She did great tonight. We couldn't have done this story without her. Did you tell her that?"

"She knows it, Mad. I hope she's going to be okay. You and I both know how long p.r. people last when they get a "whistle blower" attached to their résumé."

That thought had run through Madison's mind several times in the last few days.

"Listen, Mad, I've got a thousand things to wrap up right now. The switchboard is going crazy with your fans wanting to know how you are. We've pulled two interns just to keep up with the calls. I want you to settle in and get some rest. I'll be down first thing in the morning to see you. Tell Whit if he needs anything to give me a call at home."

As Madison was hanging up the phone, her doctor appeared in her doorway.

"You gave us a little bit of a scare, Madison. But the tests all show everything to be okay. I'm going to keep you for a couple of days, just to make sure you stay down."

Madison did not object, which greatly surprised her husband. The last few weeks had taken a toll, both physically and mentally, on the newswoman. She knew Ed would run the story again on tomorrow night's broadcast, and Ryan Patrick would do a good job with it just as he had tonight. What mattered to Madison Boggs was centered around the story's accuracy and that the public had been served in its best interest. That was what news was all about to Madison—not the person reading the TelePrompter. Nevertheless, this was her story and it hurt not to be able to deliver it in person.

As Madison was allowing herself to relax, she squeezed her husband's hand and slowly began to share thoughts she had been keeping from him.

"This story got to me, honey. You know how I always tell you I just read the lines? Well this time, this story was different. It took away some of my trust in human nature and maybe even what was left of my innocence. I never thought to question this company, Whit. I just trusted them like everybody else did. If it hadn't been for those people on the inside who saw what was happening and couldn't live with it. . ." She moved her head gingerly on the pillow as she struggled to finish her sentence. "I'm never going to forget what I've learned these last few weeks." Her battered features spoke to the pain she was feeling.

"It's over now, honey. You can put it to rest." Whit covered her hand with his.

"No, it's not over. That's what scares me the most. It's not over. People will always need blood, and they have to trust an industry that has gone on record putting profits over safety. Look at what's happen globally. Hemophiliacs relied on the manufacturers of their blood clotting agent to safeguard their product and look what happened to them; over forty-five percent of that population was infected with this disease from the medicine they took to clot their blood because the industry they depended on and trusted resisted heat-treating donated blood for years despite the plain as hell evidence that the process was capable of killing the HIV virus. Why did these companies allow that to happen? Profits. This was just a regional story, Whit, but the problem reaches out way farther than I care to even think about. Only the public doesn't realize it, and the media can't get inside to expose it except on rare occasions such as this one. Blood is power and money all mixed together. Can you imagine what we don't know about this product, or even worse, what we do know about blood but pretend we don't? There's no way in the world this industry should be allowed to state in any way shape or form that blood is safe. It isn't, and people should be very aware of it every time they come face to face with it. We need more laws on the books regulating this industry. We need more FDA inspectors out there doing unplanned drop-bys. Hell, the government makes no sense. At a time when disease is gaining on us, what do we do? We cut the funds to the only process we have at safeguarding and regulating. The Centers for Disease Control can't keep up with it, and the FDA has been hacked back in personnel to the point it's almost a joke. No, Whit. It's far from being over." Madison's thoughts were all running together faster than she could speak."

"Madison, I don't think you can solve all these problems tonight. Let it go for a while and get some rest. You've done more than most in taking on this story But right now, our baby needs for you to let up a little. We can talk about this tomorrow." Whit hoped to calm her agitation.

"That's the trouble with all of us, Whit. We won't talk about this tomorrow. We'll just lie back and put our heads in the sand and pretend such things can't happen in America. It isn't over—maybe it's just starting." The green in her eyes deepened as her anger exploded in a torrent of bitter pent-up words.

Her husband gently began to rub his wife's temples. His familiar touch took away some of the angry energy that had built up and she began to relax. The last words she said to him before she gave in to sleep were words Whit Walker never thought he would hear.

"Maybe I need to call it quits, honey. I've seen enough crap to last me a lifetime, and I'm so tired of living and breathing all the bad things in life. Maybe I need to get on with all the good things, like you and our baby. Maybe it's time—-Ryan Patrick did look pretty good in my chair. Maybe. . ."

As Madison was drifting off to sleep across town, Gerald Preston's home phone rang. The executive director of the blood center knew who it was before he even answered. Madison's late newscast had sealed his fate. He was expecting the call.

"Preston here."

"Jerry, this is Francis," the president of the blood center's board began.

"I'll get right to the point, Jerry. We need to make a move to settle this whole unfortunate situation down. Madison Boggs had some pretty raw stuff on tonight, and I'm afraid Silvers has gone too far this time." Preston was glad to hear his co-director's name used and not his own.

"I'm afraid I have to agree with you, Francis. For the sake of the community, we need to put closure on this whole affair." Preston's voice carried the tiredness of his thoughts.

"Listen, Jerry. Let's do this in a civilized manner. You don't need these headaches anymore, and it was just a matter of time until you decided to take your retirement package. I'm sure I can negotiate an early release on your contract. You can help us make an easy transition as soon as we find a replacement for Silvers. It's time we looked at this situation and gave the reins fully over to a medical person with a good community profile—I mean, it's going to take time to settle the public down and build up a trust level again. And I think I have the man to come in and get the center off to a clean start."

"Who are you looking at, Francis?" Preston asked curiously.

"Thompson Moran."

"Do you think he'd take it?" A surprised Preston asked.

"Yes, Jerry. I think he's ripe for the change. We had lunch yesterday and, well, I'm pretty sure Thompson is just the breath of fresh air we need right now."

"How are you going to handle Silvers?"

"I think we can work our way through it by stating that the good doctor wanted to move on to other interests at this time. Of course, we won't admit directly to the charges, but then we won't have to if we handle it right. I'm sure Frank Swabuck can come up with a strong recovery statement for the center."

"I'm not so sure Silvers won't fight you on this, Francis. I mean, he won't take this lying down. He called me earlier when the station began running the damn news preview, saying he knew nothing about the contamination problem, that it was Dr. Crane and Bertha White who cooked up the whole damn mess. I'm sure he's going to try and have the Swabuck group save his ass. It wouldn't surprise me if he tries to set all of us up."

"Jerry, don't worry about that. I've got a call in to Fritzsimmons Garret. Hopefully, Silvers's ambitions will be cut off at the ankles from both ends if I can get Garret to intercede. Silvers can either leave the blood center with a cover story and a glowing personnel recommendation, or we can turn the tide and use the public headline to show we fired his ass in light of Boggs's revelations. He won't want that kind of publicity attached to his résumé. If he goes peacefully, he can lay low for a while, and when this all dies down, surface again and start back up the ladder. I mean, he didn't break any laws here, Jerry; he just used very poor judgment. It's just so unfortunate that all this had to happen, but we can't be seen as a nonresponsive board here either. It's best to meet it head-on and get it all out of the way. The community's blood supply cannot be disrupted."

Preston hung up the phone and finished his scotch. It would be a long night for the executive director. At seven-thirty the next morning, Gerald Preston was in his office waiting for Dr. Silvers. The wait was short.

"Ben, did Francis get hold of you last night?" Preston followed Silvers into his office and closed the door behind him. This conversation was meant to be private.

"If that sonofabitch thinks I'm going to step down, he's crazy as. . ."

"We don't have a choice at this point, Ben." Preston interrupted.

"Maybe you don't, Preston, but I've done nothing wrong, and I'm not about to let a stupid mistake by Crane tarnish my reputation. As a matter of fact, I'm calling a press conference this afternoon."

"You're doing what?" A stunned Preston reacted.

"I'm going to clear my name—and don't think for a minute of interfering."

"Ben, you can't do this."

"Watch me. This whole mess is going to be dumped in Alice's lap. She has nothing to lose at this point in her career. The press can't disprove it, and Frank Swabuck's group will wash it all down like a fine glass of wine." Silvers's voice was strong and determined. His mind would not be changed. He was confident that another lie would save him.

"If you go through with this, Silvers, I want you to know I will do everything in my power to back up Alice. You and I both know she was following your orders to cover up the errors in our laboratory. How in the hell can you do something like this? What kind of a person are you?"

Preston's threat didn't register with Silvers. "Just an empty threat," Silvers thought. "Preston wouldn't go down in front of a group of reporters. He has as much to lose as I have."

Suddenly, a familiar voice spoke up.

"I can't believe you would do this to me, Ben." Dr. Crane was standing in the doorway of Silvers's office. The emotions of the moment had kept the two men from hearing the assistant medical director's entry. She had heard just enough to know. Never had she felt so betrayed, so impotent. There was a part of her that worshipped Ben Silvers. How could he forget her loyalty to him. It was Ben's idea to keep the break under wraps, and she of all people understood why. But now she felt weak, sick to her stomach. Was she seeing Ben Silvers for the first time? His evil side never meant anything to her before because it was never directed at her. She had always been his favorite, the one person whom he always said he could count on.

"Alice, this is nothing personal. You are at the end of your career, and it won't hurt you. Besides, I'm not about to let some half-assed reporter take away my reputation because you screwed up and didn't do your job the way it should have been done. If you had covered your ass and made sure that report was eliminated from the computer as you said it had been, you wouldn't be in this fix."

Crane's eyes were riveted on Silvers. His words cut like a knife and the pain of his betrayal entered her body with severe force. She could feel her blood pressure rising and her heart pounding. A burning sensation crept up her neck and passed through her jaws. The sudden pain radiated sharply down her left arm. She recognized the symptoms immediately.

It had taken the two men a few seconds to react to the sight of a sturdy Alice Crane crumbling to the floor. She had kept her heart problems a secret for years. Silvers reached her first. He searched for an absent pulse and immediately began compressions over her chest area. By the time the medics arrived, there was a faint pulse. She was alive, but just barely. The ambulance roared away from the blood center with Alice Crane less than fifteen minutes after Gerald Preston dialed 911.

As Silvers and Preston watched the ambulance pull away from the center's parking lot, very different thoughts were running through each of their minds. Preston was devastated at what he had just witnessed. Silvers felt a relief. Dr. Alice Crane would not cause him any problems for the moment, and her condition would prevent any questioning from the pack of noisy reporters who were sure to attend his press conference. Once again, Dr. Alice Crane had come through for him. "You couldn't ask for a better assistant," he stated as he walked back to his office.

Grace Tende was stunned when word reached her about Dr. Crane. She had arrived at work this morning later than usual and had missed the commotion. It was a little after ten when the phone rang in her office. It was the police. They had just received an identification trace on the license plates of the two cars involved in a fatal crash last evening. As peculiar as it seemed, both men were employed by the blood center.

"We're sorry to inform you, Miss, but it was a double fatality. Both vehicles were traveling at a high rate of speed when they hit a patch of ice. They were killed on impact." The officer's voice seemed distant to Grace. All of this was just too much to handle at one time. It took Grace a few minutes to pull her thoughts together. She called Herk Golden first to inform him of Terry Milo's death. He listened quietly as Grace explained there were two blood center employees involved.

Herk quickly inquired, "Who was the other person?"

"Reymond Alexander," Grace sadly answered the Fleet Chief.

There was little response after that on Herk's end. Grace attributed it to a masculine way of handling shock. Terry Milo was known to be Herk's favorite driver. Grace placed her phone down and pushed back deep into her chair. These last few weeks had been unlike any other for

Grace. People that she cared about had gotten hurt. Others had deeply disappointed her. What was the connection between Reymond Alexander and Terry Milo? Why were they speeding? How in the world could they have been involved in a fatal accident? Slowly she picked up her phone. It was a call she dreaded to make.

Bertha White did not take the news in the same fashion. She broke into tears. Bertha had tried to call Reymond several times last night. He had not returned her calls, which was most unusual. Her concern deepened when he failed to report to work this morning. Now she knew why. There was only one person in the whole world who could have given Madison Boggs the computer data information. She should have known Reymond would be smart enough to print out a copy. It was so like him. Reymond always backed up his work with print-outs. Why had he not told her? If only he would have shared this one secret with her. At least he had the courage to do the right thing. That was far and above her own actions—actions she would have to live with for the rest of her life.

Her laboratory phone line was jammed with calls from pathologists of the sixty-five hospitals they supplied with blood. The hospitals were deluged with calls from patients, all wanting information on whether or not they had received contaminated blood. The pathologists had never seen a reaction like this before. People were scared to death. Half of the callers had not even received blood, but they were taking no chances.

Bertha was caught in the middle. All she could do was confirm. She had no way of tracing. It was going to be a nightmare to get through this situation. When Bertha opened her side drawer to retrieve a small package of tissue, she saw an envelope with her name on it. She recognized Reymond's handwriting immediately. It seemed so strange to be opening something left for her by a man who had been a friend and whom she was never going to see alive again.

Her fingers trembled as she pulled out a copy of the data sheets. Reymond had made her a duplicate. Whether it was fate or not would now never be clear. But one thing was sure. Reymond Alexander had given Bertha White the opportunity to save the lives of innocent people. It might not be too late to get out a recall, especially for the smaller hospitals that did not use blood as fast as their larger counterparts. It was a small window of hope but it counted. It should have been done days ago. An accident had happened, but a deliberate act of the most unspeakable kind had followed. Bertha White had a long day in front of her, and for the first time in a long while she didn't bother to call upstairs for a clearance to do her job.

Sitting back in her chair, Grace tried to sort through the last few days. Her eyes suddenly caught a letter in her in-box marked "Grace Tende—Confidential."

Sheer habit caused her to push aside her personal thoughts and reach for the envelope. Elizabeth's handwritten request for a leave of absence was more than shocking. "Oh my God—how could he do such a thing?"

Quickly Grace pulled her employee directory from her desk drawer and dialed Elizabeth's home number. When it was apparent Elizabeth Monroe was not at home, she quickly pulled her employee file. Her mother's name and home phone number were listed as nearest of kin to be called in case of an emergency. This was surely such an emergency.

"Mrs. Thomas, this is Grace Tende, director of personnel for Hamilton Regional. I need to talk to Elizabeth—is she with you?"

"No, Miss Tende. Elizabeth is away for a while," the mother answered reluctantly.

"Is there any way I can get in touch with her?"

"I'm afraid not for a few days."

"Mrs. Thomas, Elizabeth wrote me a very disturbing letter requesting a leave of absence. There were several statements made that I really need to talk to her in person about."

"Miss Tende, my daughter has gone through hell. I'm not sure if they will let you talk to her yet, but she's checked herself in to Central Rehab."

"Thank you, Mrs. Thomas. I'll call her there."

Grace looked up Central's number and quickly dialed. The intake person would not release any information or even confirm that Elizabeth was there, but she did promise to have someone return her call. Just as Grace was leaving her office for Gerald Preston's, she passed Frank Swabuck and company in the hall. They barely acknowledged her presence. Grace was unaware that Silvers had called a press conference. The media were beginning to gather in the main conference room.

"What's going on, Julie?" Grace asked as she approached the main receptionist.

"All I know is Dr. Silvers is holding a press conference. He's announcing something, but I don't know any more than that."

"Is Michael Bryan back yet?"

"No, I haven't seen or heard from him in several days. I'm not sure when he's getting back from vacation."

Grace walked up the front stairwell just in time to see the Swabuck group going into Silvers's office. The door closed behind them immediately. Gerald Preston was not part of the group.

"God, let him be in his office," Grace thought. His office door was ajar, and Grace could see the commanding figure sitting in his large executive chair. He appeared to be staring out his window in deep thought.

"Jerry, can I bother you—it's important," Grace asked as she moved through the doorway.

Preston didn't answer her. His eyes looked tired and there was a certain droop to his shoulders that Grace had not seen before.

"Jerry, I don't want to disturb you—I know this is not a good time with all that has happened in the last few days, but I have something you need to see."

"What is it, Grace? Couldn't it wait until tomorrow?" His voice was pitched deeper than Grace had ever heard it.

"I don't think so, Jerry. It's a very serious situation and one that you need to know about immediately as I'm not sure if the authorities will be getting involved."

"Grace—please. We may have done a few unethical things in these last few weeks, I'll admit, but we have broken no laws. . ."

"This has nothing to do with what's just happened, Jerry, it concerns the possible rape of one of our directors by Dr. Silvers."

"What in the world?" The color that was left in the older man's face suddenly evaporated with Grace's last statement.

"Jerry, please read this." Grace handed Elizabeth's letter to her supervisor.

It only took a few minutes of reading to grasp the seriousness of what had happened to Elizabeth Monroe. As he read Elizabeth's handwritten explanation, he repeated over and over, "My God, I had no idea—no idea."

The letter was slowly released page by page from his hands to the top of his desk. For a few moments, the pair sat in a disbelieving silence. Finally Preston regained his composure.

"Grace, this is extremely distressing. It could cost Dr. Silvers his medical license and his. . ."

"If Dr. Silvers is guilty of any of this, that would only be the start of what it could cost him."

"There were no witnesses to such an attack, Grace. This could be a matter of her word against his."

"Jerry, at this point, I haven't been able to speak directly with Elizabeth. She has checked herself in to Central Rehab. It may be a few days before we hear anything. But I do know that Elizabeth intends to report the rape and her drug use to the authorities. She also intends to point the finger at Dr. Silvers as her supplier in her official statement."

Preston's eyes suddenly moved past Grace as he caught sight through his half-opened door of Silvers and the Swabuck people exiting the doctor's office.

"My God, there's got to be a way to stop all this," Preston slowly muttered as he stood up suddenly and called out Silvers's name loudly.

"Dr. Silvers—wait a minute. I need to see you before you hold that press conference."

Silvers looked back over his shoulder but kept going. He waved Preston off. The brush-off triggered something in Preston. In swift movements the large man caught up with Silvers and the public relations party just as they reached the stairs.

"Silvers, I need to talk with you, and I mean now." Frank Swabuck turned toward Preston and motioned for Dr. Silvers to continue on. He would see what Gerald Preston wanted. Dr. Silvers could not be late for his own press conference. The press was gathered downstairs, including Ryan Patrick from Madison Boggs's station, and Swabuck knew far too well, the press does not like to be kept waiting when they've been summoned, especially with the bombshell story Patrick had laid out last night.

"What's the matter, Mr. Preston? Dr. Silvers is going to address a very serious situation for the two of you—I mean, Dr. Crane really put both your asses in the sling with her shoddy behavior around here. If you would please just cooperate, we can turn the tide for the two of you and save both your jobs here."

Preston stopped in his tracks. Silvers was really going through with it. He was going to dump it all in Dr. Crane's lap and God only knows who else. Swabuck stood in Preston's way, blocking the executive director's entrance to the stairs. Silvers had told Swabuck that Preston would try and stop this conference. Frank Swabuck had bought the doctor's explanation of why his co-partner would try such a thing. Swabuck had once again been duped by the cagey medical doctor.

When Preston made no move to go forward, Swabuck took that as a good sign. He patted the older gentleman's arm and told him to just go on back to his office and let Silvers and himself handle the press conference.

"It's better if the two of us face the media, Mr. Preston. And we both know you're not as good at this as your partner."

The word "partner" hit Gerald Preston squarely between the eyes.

As he watched Swabuck continue down the stairwell, a thought suddenly entered his mind. "This has to end. It has to." Quickly Preston returned to his office. Grace was standing just outside his door. She had witnessed the Swabuck incident and was not sure what was going to happen. She did not know why Silvers was holding a press conference.

"Jerry, is Dr. Silvers resigning—I mean, what is going on here?"

"Yes, Grace. Dr. Silvers is resigning, and I'm going to do what I should have done years ago—I'm retiring." Preston brushed past Grace and looked at the top of his desk. Elizabeth's letter was not there.

"Where's Elizabeth's note—where is it, Grace?"

"I have it here," she said holding the three page letter out to him.

"I need this, Grace, for just a few more minutes. I promise you, after that you can have it back."

Preston nearly tore the paper out of Grace's hand as he swiftly moved down the hallway toward the stairs. He paused just as he reached the top of the stairs.

"Grace, would you do me the honor of accompanying me to this press conference? Just the way he said it told Grace something strange was about to happen. When they reached the bottom of the stairs, Preston turned toward her and whispered a few words in her ear.

"This is for you, Grace. And for all those other people I never meant to hurt."

His words didn't make sense right now. His actions soon would.

Silvers was positioned in the front of the room behind the speaker's table. A bank of microphones was spread across the top of the wooden conference table. The television stations were there in force. Their bright lights were blinding.

Ryan Patrick was standing to the left of Dr. Silvers in the front row of the gathered news hounds. He had taken quite a bit of kidding on what happened to his anchor from her counterparts who still did not know the whole story.

"Hey Patrick, did you take out Boggs last night to get those headlines? Or did she duke it out with Silvers?" Chet Lampert laughingly teased Boggs replacement as he settled in behind him. Patrick smiled but gave no blow-by-blow report. It was all part of the job.

The media had been kept in the dark about the purpose of the press conference. No pre-written statements were passed out before hand, only

Frank Swabuck's brief comments that a clearing statement was about to be made.

At this point, Patrick and the other reporters could only guess what Dr. Silvers had in mind. Silvers's forehead now carried tiny beads of sweat. The palms of his hands were moist, and he felt his starched shirt beginning to stick to his body. In just a few minutes, it would be over. He would place the blame on Dr. Crane and issue a humble, pleading-for-forgiveness, apology to the community. He would be forgiven and Crane would carry the stain. Her chances of surviving, as he had judged her heart attack to be massive, were little if any. Her weight, age, and state of mind almost ensured her demise.

"Ladies and gentlemen of the media, I want to thank you for coming on such short notice. As you all know, my center has faced some very serious charges by certain members of the media."

Patrick shifted his weight only slightly, not knowing what words were going to follow this statement. All eyes in the room were now focused on Silvers. What was the doctor going to say?

"I want all of you to know I have only just recently learned the charges were true. It seems my assistant carried out a plan behind my back. . ."

"Dr. Silvers, I believe you need to read this before you say one more word." Preston's words jarred the gathered crowd of reporters as he moved forward from the back of the room. Silvers's face suddenly flushed and Swabuck seemed stunned.

"Jerry, what in the hell are you doing—what are you trying to pull?" Silvers's words were unprotected and being recorded in force by the bank of microphones lying in front of him.

A rumble of whispers swept across the room. The reporters sensed the drama was real and they were eyewitnesses at the scene.

"Jerry, get out of here—don't you dare and. . ."

"You're the one who needs to get out of here, Doctor. This belongs to you—now read it before I read it out loud." Preston's words thundered in Silvers's ears. Feeling trapped, the doctor quickly pulled the papers out of Preston's hand. As his eyes focused on Elizabeth's recognized hand-writing, the color drained from his face. The television cameras captured the guilt.

"That bitch—it isn't true. She's just trying to frame me." Silvers whispered as his eyes shot across the room searching for Frank Swabuck. Swabuck was as emotionally wrapped up in the actions of the blood cen-ter personnel as the reporters were at this point. He made no move to interfere. Whatever Gerald Preston had in his possession was more powerful than the statement Silvers was about to release. Swabuck couldn't weave any damage control now—it would have to play itself out in full view of the media. That was always the trouble with live press conferences. If something went wrong, you couldn't stop the camera and rework it.

Silvers was beside himself with anger and a new emotion, fear. Preston positioned himself quickly in front of the doctor, moving Silvers away from the eavesdropping bank of microphones.

"You lying sonofabitch—you're not going to say one more word or so help me, Jesus—I'll read Elizabeth's letter word for word to this pack of hungry wolves. You're a rotten SOB, Silvers, and this time you're going to pay for your actions. Now get out of this room while you still can—do you understand me?"

"I'll get you for this, Preston. If it takes my last breath, I'll get you. If I go down, so will you."

"So be it, doctor. So be it."

Silvers raised his arms and shoved the larger man back from him. It would be his last act of defiance for the day. As he slowly began to weave his way past the reporters, the beads of tiny moisture crystals on his forehead turned to a flood of sweat.

"Get out of my way—" he shouted as he quickly picked up his pace, pushing the body of reporters out of his way as he made his exit toward the conference doorway. The reporters were riveted on the behavior of these two men. Whatever it was that Preston had in his possession certainly controlled the doctor and the atmosphere of this strange news conference.

Just as the crowd was beginning to recover and shout questions at the doctor as he left the room, Preston's loud and commanding voice recaptured their attention.

"Ladies and gentlemen, please forgive our actions here today."

The reporters quickly turned toward the front of the room, allowing the doctor to reach the doorway of the conference room. Suddenly Silvers was standing directly in front of Grace Tende. The sight of her face only added to his rage. He lashed out at the woman he had always thought of as his enemy—right from the very start he knew she would one day be trouble. His words were kept low, so that only Grace could hear.

"You're part of this whole scheme to ruin me—you bitch. I'll see you again—you can count on it," Silvers slurred as he stepped around the personnel director.

"You're right, Silvers. You will see me again—in court."

Her words hit Silvers in the stomach. His whole body seemed to shake as he quickly picked up his pace to exit the blood center. Preston's voice pulled Grace's attention back to the front of the room.

"Dr. Silvers was about to tell you of his intention to resign and my intention to retire. There will be no further statements made here today. Please accept our apology and please do not stop supporting our cause. Saving lives is our business. We will need all your support to regain the public's trust during these next few months of rebuilding."

The room erupted in a sea of mass confusion. Gerald Preston was immediately surrounded by the reporters who had just witnessed the most unusual press conference ever held in the city of Hamilton.

Grace Tende's eyes suddenly filled with tears. It was over. It was finally over. She would wait in the back of the room until the last of the reporters surged past her. Gerald Preston seemed surprised to see Grace waiting for him. The sight of her helped quiet his thoughts. As he took hold of her arm, the pair quietly walked up the front stairs. When they reached his office, his hand dropped to his side.

"Grace, I'm sorry for. . ."

"Please don't say anything more, Jerry. It's over. I wish things could have been different." Tears came to Grace's eyes.

"I wish you a happy life, Grace. I'm going to miss seeing you more than I can ever tell you." Preston did not wait for a response. He walked inside his office, closing the door behind him. Dignity and regret once again filled the air.

The sun was just beginning to set as Grace Tende left the center on this most unusual day. So many things had happened in such a short period of time, including the resignation of Kiley Matson. The Distribution Director told Grace he had been offered a job with East Coast Alliance, the nation's largest blood center, operating out of New York City. Alliance had dangled the carrot in front of Kiley many times before, but this time, the climate seemed right to accept. Kiley's timing was perfect.

As Kiley turned to leave Grace's office late that afternoon, he was in a reflective mood.

"It's been a hell of a day, hasn't it, Grace?"

"Grace shook her head sadly. "It has been a hell of a day. But I think things will change for the better. . ."

"Don't count on it, pretty lady," Kiley interrupted. "Don't count on it. Some things are too good to change. Some things."

35

It was unusually warm in New York City for this time of year. Thomas Hampton was carrying his heavy wool overcoat when he walked into the National Bank of America. The bank's rich-looking interior reminded Thomas of a place where old money would be right at home.

Thomas walked past the marble teller cages and around the side to the desk of what he thought must be the floor manager. He was promptly greeted.

"May I help you, sir?" The young man asked in a hushed tone of voice.

"Yes, I would like to open my safety deposit box." The bank official smiled and said, "Of course. Right this way please."

The two men walked toward the rear of the building. A bank of elevators was now clearly visible directly in front of them.

"If you will just take the elevator to the second floor, someone will be able to help you."

In a matter of moments, Thomas was standing in front of a row of safety deposit boxes. The bank official used his key to unlock the lock on the left—Thomas slipped his matching key in the lock on the right. The silver box was pulled out and handed to him. He was escorted to a room nearby where comfortable desks with green glass shades gave privacy light for the select clients to conduct their business.

Thomas's hand trembled just a bit as he removed the papers from the box. Two envelopes were extracted. Thomas chose to open the small envelope first, leaving the manila legal-sized envelope lying on the top of the richly polished mahogany desk top.

He unfolded four sheets of expensive stationery bearing his father's name and started reading.

Thomas Hampton, my only son:

   *It is no secret to you that I have not turned out to be the kind
of father I had so wanted to be. Because life has shown itself to
be short, I find I must unburden my heart and share with you
words I will never be able to say out loud. You and I were never
to be close—the pain of looking at you and seeing Annie kept us
apart. This I feel in my heart. But there is a part of me I must
share with you—for whatever it is worth when the time comes.
You must know your father for all that he was, and for all that he
was not. When you read this, I will not be with you to answer in
person for my deeds acted out so long ago. I can only tell you
that my actions were motivated by my desire for a woman you
will never know as I did—your mother, Anna Lingermond Hampton, and a position in life that I could never have obtained without the power of money. In no way do I hold Annie responsible
for my actions. Quite the contrary, she would serve as my saving
grace. But by revealing what I am about to reveal, you, my son,
will have the power to do something about my regrettable
deeds—if you choose to do so. First, let me tell you as much
about your heritage as I can. You must know, family history
never really mattered to me. Let me tell you what I know of your
mother's background. She was an orphan. Anna never mentioned
her early years as they were too painful for her to speak about.
She was raised in a dreadful orphanage on the East side of New
York City, where little love was shown to her. Annie needed love
and surroundings that spoke of anything but the bleak atmosphere she ran away from as soon as she could. As for my family,
I never really knew my parents. They died shortly after arriving
in America from England. It was a fever of some sort that took
their lives. I have no idea if they were a happy couple or just
bound together with paper that is supposed to signify happiness
ever after. I was given to a distant aunt and she raised me with a
stern hand. She did see to it I had an education, an education
that opened doors for me in areas that now seem so foreign. I
studied chemistry and physics and labored over research that no
one else really wanted to be involved with. This empty pattern of
diligence led me to discover a formula for producing pure artificial blood that some wanted to buy, not for humanitarian purposes, but for purposes of power. My formula and patent for*

artificial blood was signed over to these power brokers with an agreement to be kept secret for a period of thirty-five years. I sold my formula after twenty-five years of research, research that produced failure after failure, until one day blind luck unlocked the critical process I had spent the better part of my youth searching for. I set out to offer my findings to an industry that I thought would welcome my discovery. Instead, I was made an offer not benefiting mankind, but serving the masters of greed. I accepted their offer without a whimper of protest. The price they paid was handsome, twenty million dollars. It offered a chance for a new life for your mother and me. One filled with love and all the opportunities that go with great wealth.

To the corporate executives who elected to conceal my discovery, it meant they could continue their hold on a public so dependent on them and their powers of control. The production of artificial blood would surely bring the elimination of the deep-seated power base for the NAABC and its multiple levels of income generated from all the support factors. It would more than just hit their pocketbooks; artificial blood would put them out of business. Power, my son, is the key here. As for GENCO, a pharmaceutical and medical supply house, they too would take a tremendous loss in income because it would eliminate their lock on untold profitable divisions responsible for supplying testing kits, laboratory equipment, and all such related medical supplies that the blood industry relied on for the processing, testing, and distribution of humanly supplied blood. This would also hurt GENCO's research divisions that used the excuse of searching for the formula of artificial blood to divert huge government funding grants to other, more profitable areas of production. Paying me twenty million dollars was small change to their pockets of income generated from the liquid gold assets found in the production of human blood. All it took was an agreed silence—silence well paid for and to be honored by all parties concerned for thirty-five years, at which time, my formula for artificial blood was to be announced jointly by the National Association of Accredited Blood Centers and GENCO. Tonight, my son, the anniversary date has passed and there is no intention of carrying out the agreement. I now know that my formula will stay buried forever. Therefore, I am taking steps to see that our agreement is lived up to, if you, Thomas, so choose to proceed.

For purposes of control and bargaining power, I have been buy-
ing stock in GENCO under a blind front for the last ten years.
You are now listed as sole heir to my vast stock holdings at my
death. At the rate I was able to purchase, you are the largest
stockholder in GENCO. I also instructed my brokers to buy large
shares of stock each year in all of GENCO's competitors. These
shares will again be in your name and shall continue to be
amassed until such a time as directed by you to stop. This should
give you the leverage you need with GENCO, just in case they
are not willing to proceed as promised. I placed my detailed
patent formula for producing artificial blood, and the original
sealed documents signed by NAABC and GENCO, outlining the
agreements of sale for my formula in this safety deposit box some
thirty-five years ago. Today, I will add this letter, which I have
written to you, my only son. I have set up a trust fund to pay the
rent on this safety deposit box faithfully until such time as you
decide to close this account. Thomas Erin Hampton, you are in a
position to do for the world what your father chose not to do.
The wealth that you have always known places you in a different
position than I was so many years ago. God only knows how
many lives my formula would have saved had I the guts to go in
another direction. God also only knows how many other patents
like mine are also buried away in the deep pockets of greed.

I do not think NAABC or GENCO will ever want to face the
world with questions concerning their decision not to produce a
formula which could have safeguarded the world's blood supply,
especially in times troubled with the discovery of so many human
diseases. But alas, diseases newly discovered, also bring about
the need for more tests, more equipment, and more supplies, cre-
ating the perfect circle for an industry whose products are devel-
oped and sold based on human suffering. Each new disease
found in the river of blood creates a new opportunity for industry
and scientists like myself to make a profit. My patent would touch
this empire in their pocketbook. But in the world of science, my
son, you must also know that discoveries are made every day and
bought every day by the same kinds of individuals like myself
and those whom I have now revealed to you. We are not evil men,
Thomas, but men driven by dollars, pounds, and francs. Perhaps
it is my own bitterness and disappointment in myself that is now
speaking out. My shame at being a part of what I most detested. I

realize you may decide to burn this letter and forget what I have shared only with you. I also know that during these next few months, someone else may come forward with a formula for producing artificial blood. If that happens and they are successful at finding a buyer who will put this formula to good use, my secrets will be old secrets and of no interest to anyone except you. You need to know that your father had a weak side to him. A side that he is not proud of. I do not know what decision you may make, Thomas. I want you to know that your mother never really knew what I had done to obtain our new start in life. She just knew that I had created something that was of great importance to someone else. I did not know that our life together would be so short. When she died after your birth, my heart simply stopped beating. I knew I would never be able to look at you without seeing her. The pain of such a sight was unbearable for me and so destructive for you, my son, who surely felt my neglect. You cannot ask someone to forgive you for not showing love, so I will not. I can only tell you that you were created out of the purest form of love. I hope that this is comforting to you, and that you will one day find a way to understand. I want you to find a love such as I found with Annie. A love pure in heart with no regrets attached. The decision to force a giant company and a respected national institute to do the right thing is at your disposal. Do with it as you wish.

With love and regrets,

Your father,
Walter Hampton

Thomas did not take a cab back to his hotel. He needed fresh air to help him with his thoughts. His father had created a formula for artificial blood thirty-five years ago and sold it for a sizable fortune. But that fortune condemned hundreds of thousands of individuals to a death that, maybe, could have been prevented if they had access to safe blood. The walk to the hotel was only three blocks. Thomas agonized over his choices. He was appalled by the thought of what his father had done. His father's money had cushioned his life with nothing but emptiness. But he had never known anything but luxury, luxury paid for by the sufferings of others. Thomas tried to place himself in his father's shoes. As he walked, his anger shifted from his father to those who had dangled the pot of gold in front of the struggling chemist. The manila envelope tucked under his arm felt heavy with secrets and shame. Thomas Hampton began to walk through the steps in his mind that needed to be taken. He had reached a decision. He had all the names and numbers he needed. His father had gone to great lengths to give it all to him in precise detail.

The brass doors of the Parker-Meridian hotel were a welcome sight. When he reached his suite on the tenth floor, Thomas shed his suit coat and placed a long distance call to Quinn Careton. It would be a lengthy call. Early the next morning, Thomas would receive a call back from Careton. The meetings had been arranged for early the next morning.

"I have to tell you, Thomas, the GENCO executives are eager to meet with you. They have no idea what's in store for them. They think you will show up for their annual board meeting day after tomorrow. The timing couldn't be better, Thomas."

A slight smile spread across Thomas's face. Surprise was always the best plan of attack—if you could achieve it. Quinn Careton arrived on the redeye flight from England the next morning. They were ten minutes early for their scheduled 10 a.m. meeting with the executives of GENCO who greeted them like long lost relatives.

The two were taken on a quick tour of the headquarters. The GENCO building was impressive. Rich furniture balanced with original artwork touted the company's successful financial standing. The tour ended at the door of the main board room. Thomas and Quinn were quickly introduced to the waiting president of GENCO, Hutchinson Franks. "Hutch" as he was called by close friends, had been the company's CEO for the last twenty years. He had replaced Morley Habing, his long-time friend and mentor. Shaking this man's hand sent a chill down Thomas's back—Frank's sprawling signature was one found at the bottom of the documents he was carrying in his briefcase. This was one the men who had helped orchestrate the secret agreement with his father so many years ago. There were four conspirators, all of whom signed the contract drawn up for Thomas's father. Franks, Habing, and Gerald Thomas Preston represented GENCO, with Fritzsimmons Garret signing as head of the NAABC. These were the brokers of record on a contract of power and greed.

Hutch seemed nervous as he clung to Thomas's hand just a bit longer than the normal handshake allows. The room came to order when everyone was finally seated. Hutch Franks started the meeting, as the powerful CEO was accustomed to asserting his control.

"Mr. Hampton, I can't begin to tell you how delighted we are to finally have our largest shareholder attending what we think will be one of our best annual meetings. Times have been good to us, and dividends are to be paid at their highest earnings ever," he stated with a nervous mix of pride.

Thomas did not respond. He smiled a bit and continued to hold his gaze steady upon the CEO. The silence of Thomas caused the others to shift a little in their seats, especially Avery Cummins, vice president and second in control at GENCO.

"Something is not right here," Avery thought as he sensed the tenseness of his superior. Hutch continued.

"I once knew a gentlemen by the name of Hampton—Walter was his first name I believe," the CEO casually stated trying to be discreet in his probing. "He was some sort of a chemist, I believe," he added.

"Walter Hampton was my father, Mr. Franks. And yes, he was a chemist. A very good chemist."

The meeting was no longer in GENCO's control. At this point, an impatient and very direct Thomas Hampton decided to speak up. He presented all the background material, complete with signed documents he had brought with him—documents with age and shame clearly showing. Quinn had prepared copies, and they were quickly distributed among the GENCO executives. Franks did not open his packet. He remembered all too well what they contained. Avery Cummins felt his ulcer burning deep inside his stomach as he read the sealed and all but forgotten documents. Franks's signature on the bottom was real—Avery had seen it too often in his career at GENCO not to recognize it as authentic. This was no game. Thomas Hampton was no impostor.

A buzz of whispered conversations took over the quiet of the room. Finally, as the shock of what had just happened cleared, Franks spoke again.

"What is it you want, Mr. Hampton?"

"My wishes are simple, Mr. Franks. Very simple," Thomas answered as he began a lengthy explanation of what had to be done. As GENCO's controlling stockholder, as well as their main rival, TARMAC, Thomas was in a position to press his points. He wanted GENCO to move forward with his father's patent for producing artificial blood. If they decided to fight him, he would simply sell his shares in GENCO to TARMAC and proceed with a leveraged takeover at which time they would all lose their jobs. It would be messy with huge amounts of press coverage included. Resistance from GENCO at this point would require an immediate release of all the documents now contained in their personal packets. Hampton made it perfectly clear he was ready to go the distance if push came to shove. Franks squirmed in his chair. He did not want to face the world with his actions of thirty-five years ago—not in an age of AIDS.

"Gentlemen, think of it this way. I am giving you the opportunity to do the right thing. You will be the saving grace for your industry. Your names will go down in history. GENCO will move into a new age—an age that will require new leadership and direction," Thomas stated looking directly at Franks.

"I believe we should be able to work through whatever discomfort is needed to put my father's patent to work as soon as possible."

Thomas and Quinn gathered up their documents and stood up. The body of executives present remained seated. "I look forward to tomorrow's meeting, and to what I hope will be a long-heralded announcement. You can reach me at the Parker-Meridian, gentlemen. In the meantime, if you have any further questions, please don't hesitate to ask them of me now while I'm here."

"Mr. Hampton, I had hoped to save this news for our annual meeting, but I feel you should hear it now," Franks said as he rose from his chair in response. "Our research division has just discovered a method of washing the AIDS virus clean from donated blood. The blood supply of the world will at last be protected from such a tragic disease. As a stockholder, you should know how profitable this discovery is for our company. To move forward with your father's patent at this point is cause for GENCO to lose millions of dollars in our support divisions. Surely you would not want to see the demise of all that we have accomplished these last thirty some years, now would you, Mr. Hampton?"

"Can all the money in the world bring back the thousands of innocent people who have died from receiving bad blood, Mr. Franks? My father's patent would have saved their lives. Money is not the issue here—at least not this time. Can your new discovery clean out all the other diseases carried in blood?"

"Well, no. Not yet, but given time and the dollars involved. . ."

"Not one more person should be subject to a death sentence because of dollars, Mr. Franks. Artificial blood guarantees a safe blood supply, Mr. Franks. Are you telling me you want to bury this patent again?"

Hutchinson Franks didn't return an answer. This time he couldn't. There were too many witnesses.

As Thomas reached the doorway, he turned back to address the Genco executives with one last statement.

"Gentlemen, this could be very messy for all of you, especially you, Mr. Franks. Be careful with those packets; I would hate for the media to accidentally get hold of the secrets they contain. We all know how the media loves secrets."

The stunned executives were quiet for several seconds. Finally, Avery Cummins spoke. "Hutch, I believe you and I should have a few minutes alone." His words immediately sent the others to their respective offices. They would wait to be summoned.

Alone, the two top executives shared a long, difficult, and sometimes emotional discussion. At 12:30 they came to a difficult decision, a decision that neither wanted, but both knew was now beyond their control.

A press conference was arranged for 3:30 that afternoon. GENCO's public relations department hurried to set up the board room for the arrival of the puzzled, but eager press corps. The faxed press release contained only enough information to whet the media's interest. "GENCO was about to make an announcement that would be felt worldwide. AIDS and the blood supply were involved." The coverage would be intense.

At 5:30, Hutchinson Franks would quietly announce his retirement to the gathered group of GENCO board members. Avery Cummins would take over until a successor was appointed. It had been a long day. A very long day.

It was close to 7 p.m. when Thomas Hampton realized he was hungry. The pressures of the day and jet lag had sent Quinn Careton to his suite early. Thomas passed through the revolving door of his hotel and started walking toward a small deli three blocks west. His thoughts were heavy and mixed with so many emotions as he turned the corner at 7th and Lexington. He did not see the figure directly in his path. With considerable force, his body ran squarely into a petite young woman carrying an arm load of books. The impact sent her sprawling. Surprised and stunned, he immediately moved to assist her. Her deep brown eyes looked gentle. She smiled hesitantly at this stranger. She liked his obvious shyness—a trait she had seen so little of in New York since she had arrived from Iowa just a few weeks earlier. She was a student at Columbia. The girl volunteered her name. It was Annie—Annie Sherry. Thomas was stunned with the coincidence.

Within minutes, the two strangers had begun a conversation— one that would keep them together for the rest of their lives. The son's loneliness was about to end. Thomas Hampton and Annie Sherry would never have secrets between them. Secrets had destroyed too many lives. This Thomas Hampton knew for a fact.

36

He was early for his flight. He could hear the small plane's engines warming up through the frosted plate glass window as he took a seat waiting for the first call for passenger boarding. He was tired but surprisingly relaxed. Everything had worked. His life was starting over. He wanted a cigarette so bad he could taste it. His hand reached instinctively inside his jacket. The familiar package of tobacco was not present. Instead, his hand retrieved his passport. His new passport. Opening it, his picture stared back at him. His moustache was gone. For ten years, Michael Bryan had carefully cultivated the perfect lip fuzz. It was gone now, just like the cigarettes. He looked again at his new name. "Jack McGuire." He liked the sound of it.

Michael Bryan had spent the last few days in Montreal. Through a series of wire transfers, he had withdrawn two hundred thousand dollars from each of the blood center's ten accounts, wiring the deposits directly to a bank in the Netherlands Antilles, where he had flown the week before to open an account in the name of Michael Bryan. When the money was safely deposited, Michael wired the money to the Queen's Bank in Montreal. As he signed the withdrawal request for the funds, he met no resistance at the Queen's Bank. In today's world of high finance, actions for such businesses with deep pockets are rarely questioned if all the presenting credentials were in place. Michael's signature was verified, and a certified check for two million dollars soon cut.

Michael walked down the street to another bank where he had opened an account in the name of Harry Winston the day before. He told the bank's trust officer he would soon be depositing a substantial amount of money in his bank. The trust officer was delighted to be of service. His signed endorsement checked out and the deposit was made. Michael loved Montreal. The wire service instantly transferred $1,000,000 to the account of Jack McGuire in The First of America Bank in Seattle on Harry Winston's signature. He cashed a check for $500,000 and left the rest of the money in this account. Once he had cashed out his account in Seattle, Jack McGuire would vanish. None of this was as easy to accomplish as it sounds. But all of this was possible.

Michael had held his breath. He had not been questioned at the Queen's Bank since his name was listed as a certified officer of the blood center. He had arranged this by having Preston sign an authorization. Preston rarely bothered to read the papers Michael set in front of him to sign. The executive director's signature set Michael up as a legal financial officer for Hamilton Regional Blood Center. The rest required the services of an individual who was handy at creating new identities. Michael learned about such a person from Herk Golden. Armed with the proper passports and social security numbers, Michael Bryan was able to assume the identities of Harry Winston and Jack McGuire. So far, Michael was in the clear. He knew it would only be a matter of time until his actions would be uncovered, but if things went right, he had that small window of opportunity to disappear. He was not expected back at the center until late next week. He knew nothing of the recent events at Hamilton. If he had known, well, no one could say what Michael Bryan might have done.

The sound of arguing interrupted Michael's thoughts. A young man, dressed in an expensive suit and overcoat was hassling the ticketing clerk. The flight to Seattle was sold-out, and the next flight wasn't until six o'clock that evening. The young man almost shouted that his entire career depended on his securing a seat on Flight 145A. When it was clear to the distressed traveler that the ticketing clerk could not help, he turned away in disgust. Michael Bryan clearly recognized the young man's panicked look. For a few seconds his hands gently fingered his boarding pass. The name Michael Bryan was clearly stamped on the ticket. It would be the last time he would use his real name. When he heard the clerk announce the impending boarding, Michael made his decision.

"Excuse me, sir, but I couldn't help but overhear. I have a seat on this flight, but if you can cough up the price of the ticket, I'd be glad to sell it to you."

"Jesus! There is a God," the relieved young man replied as he quickly reached for his wallet. "You don't know how much this means to me—I mean, I'm up for a job, and this is a one-time shot at an interview I've been working to get for six weeks. It all came down at the last minute, and I never dreamed I'd have such a time getting a flight out."

"Yeah, well I've been there myself," a smiling Bryan said as he accepted the currency for his ticket.

"I wish you luck," Bryan added as he picked up his briefcase. He had already checked his luggage through, but a few hours of delayed arrival time was not going to make or break his life. After all, Jack McGuire had no timetable at this point in his new life.

Michael Bryan watched the small plane lift off gracefully from the frozen ground. A strange feeling suddenly touched him. As the plane began to bank as it changed course, one of its engines sputtered, and a strange grinding and popping sound emerged. A small burst of red light appeared above the right wing as the plane struggled to gain altitude. For an instant, Michael thought the pilot had corrected the problem. But in less than fifteen seconds, the small commuter plane rolled hard to its left. The wings of the plane seemed to wave at those observers watching the sight from below. The piercing sound of a rapid and uncontrolled descent paralyzed Michael Bryan as he suddenly realized the fate of the plane. With its nose pointed straight down, the plane descended rapidly. It was over in a matter of seconds. The stranger had used his ticket in his name.

Flight #145A from Montreal to Seattle burst into flames upon contact with the ground. The heat was so intense Michael could feel it through the terminal window. There was no way anyone could help the plane's passengers. Their deaths were recorded in a ball of rolling fire. It had all happened so quickly.

Fate had control of the situation now. A fate that truly gave one Michael Bryan a clear shot at a new life.

37

Michael Bryan had been listed among the passengers identified as killed by the airlines. His family was notified and a brief obituary ran in the newspapers. The embezzlement would not be discovered for several months, and when it surfaced, it was kept quiet by the current board members who did not want to deal with another scandal. No investigation was launched as the money was thought to have perished in the intense fire that claimed the life of the center's assistant executive director. It had been just a little over six months since Hamilton Regional Blood Center had suffered the mayhem. The city of Hamilton was just beginning to recover from the shock of all that had happened. Gerald Thomas Preston retired with full benefits from the blood center, handing the reins of control over to Thompson Moran. Dr. Moran's reputation was spotless, and he was highly regarded in the community. It was the best way to show a dramatic change to the public.

Elizabeth Monroe's accusation of rape and her drug involvement at the hand of her medical director was reported to the police. The prosecutor's office filed charges against Silvers who denied everything and immediately hired the best attorneys money could buy. The testimony against him was presented forcefully as the director of nurses painted a dark picture of herself and Dr. Silvers. Her testimony about the rape was a painful journey to revisit. The defense attorneys cross-examined Elizabeth relentlessly. The lack of physical evidence and the time lapse in reporting the rape weakened her case. But her drug use and his part in it were documented through prescriptions for liquid morphine that were traced directly back to the medical director's pad. It was damaging evidence. Silvers's occasional wild outbursts could not be controlled by his attorneys. His rambling statements during cross-examination clearly worked against him with the jury as he all but admitted his supplying of the drug to his mistress. His angry, "she-didn't-have-to-use-it" outburst was the final nail in his coffin. It did not take the jury long to find the defendant guilty as charged of drug misuse. The rape charge was dismissed.

Silvers was sentenced to seven years in prison at Hardington Penitentiary in West Grandville, Illinois. The prosecutor's office filed a complaint with the Attorney General's office and recommended the repeal of Silvers's medical license. The complaint was processed before the local Board of Medical Licensing that suspended Silvers's license for a period of seven years.

Benjamin Quinn Silvers would never realize his aspirations to head the most powerful association in blood banking. This was the ultimate punishment for the man so driven by desperate and unholy ambition.

Madison Boggs was honored with a Knight Award—the highest award that could be bestowed on a journalist. This time, Madison hung the plaque in her office. She was also offered a top anchor job in Chicago, but she declined the offer. Hamilton was her city, and recent events had modified her driving ambition. The approaching birth of her child and the happiness she had found with her husband gave her reason to rethink her lifestyle. Ryan Patrick was now her co-anchor. It was her idea and it seemed to fit. They made a strong team, and the break in duties would allow Madison to spend more time with her family. Family was now a priority with Madison Boggs. It suited her.

Carter Egan's husband returned earlier than planned. His wife's experiences at the blood center seemed almost too hard to believe at first. It was only after he had seen the taped interviews and had shared a supper with John and Tovey Stansbarry that it all began to sink in. He was furious and heartsick at what his wife had endured during the course of her employment with this agency. He felt her mental health as well as her hard-earned professional reputation had been more than damaged from this frightful experience. With his encouragement and support, Carter filed a civil lawsuit against the blood center for intentional infliction of emotional distress. John Standsbarry served as her attorney. It was settled out of court in less than two months. All court records would again be sealed and no dollar judgment would ever be revealed. There was one last surprise in store for Carter Egan. It was a personal call from Walter Adams, the new president of the board for the blood center. He wanted to offer Carter her old job back.

"The center needs you now, Carter. If you come back, we can begin to rebuild, and the public will see us once again through your eyes." His offer was politely refused.

Grace Tende would stay on at Hamilton Regional until a replacement was found for her position. As the wife of the center's new Medical Director, she violated the company policy of nepotism. This was a policy she had helped to create, and she was more than happy to follow the rules. Before she left the blood center, she terminated Herk Golden. He was caught falsifying his driver's expense reports and collecting the difference. He was turned in by his own staff members.

Bertha White's husband was showing signs of relapse, and she was allowed to use her accumulated sick and vacation time to retire early.

Thompson Moran was well-suited for the role of medical director at the blood center. He would act as the sole executive, as his administrative background was more than sufficient to handle the center's dual needs. Bright and more than charismatic, he was excited by his new role as he began initiating many changes in his first few weeks on the job. The morale of the staff under his warm leadership slowly began to rise.

The announcement of the development of artificial blood was met with a certain amount of skepticism by the blood industry as a whole. Time and the slowness of the FDA to approve the patent would be on their side for several more years. The NAABC would use its power to demand stringent testing of the new patent. Power is never easy to give up, and time and a powerful political lobby behind them were again on their side.

It was late on a Friday afternoon when Siam Qua stopped by Thompson Moran's office for the first time. Siam closed Moran's door as he entered. For over an hour Siam Qua outlined the research project he had been working on with funds obtained from a large grant from NAABC. The funds had come in just after the madness took place. For the first time Siam spoke of the deceit that was applied to secure the grant.

"How close are you, Siam?"

"I could be sitting on top of it right now or it could be light years away. I'm working as hard as I can, but these things take time. In the meantime, I need to buy more equipment. If I forfeit this grant money, I cannot move forward. In fact, several other projects would suffer."

"Siam, this puts us in a rough spot." Moran couldn't hide his frustration.

"There is something else you should know, Dr. Moran, that's even more important. I have identified a new strain of hepatitis. It is twice as virulent as anything I've ever seen before. Our current screening methods are helpless at identifying. . ."

"Christ, you've got to be kidding? Don't tell me our screening procedures don't work on this."

"No, they don't. I'm sorry to upset you with such news so soon, but this is part of my job."

"Look, Siam, I'm not upset with you—it's just the situation. A new strain of hepatitis is most unsettling. Where did you pick up the strain?"

"It came in through a donor whose blood was part of the contaminated blood accidentally shipped out to our hospitals last month."

"Are you telling me we've shipped out a new strain of hepatitis? Jesus Christ, we've got to notify—Did we notify?"

"I called on this one myself as soon as it came to my attention, but unfortunately the donated blood was broken down into components, and there were several patients involved for notification. I'm not sure what the hospital has done to notify."

"Are they aware of the strain? Did you tell them it's a new strain?"

"I told them I could not identify all the markers, but that it was definitely in the hepatitis family. Dr. Moran, I'm sure you're aware that this is as far as we are required to go. The hospital must follow through."

"Hospital hell, Siam. This is serious stuff we're dealing with here, and we could be dealing with a panic if the public or the media becomes aware of this new danger in blood."

"Dr. Moran, there is nothing we can do at this point. I'm sure our hospitals will follow through, and besides, I need time to work on this. I have sent a sample to the CDC. Until we can spend time in research, there is no sense in causing another panic in our community. I'm sure you're aware of how easily our public can be spooked. We have a certain amount of responsibility to contain information until we can respond in a proper manner. If you are going to work in blood banking, you must know we discover new diseases every day. We can't be constantly putting out an alert on every single one of them. We have a system in place, and we need to follow that system for the good of the whole." Siam's words were spoken with conviction and experience. Moran understood what Siam was saying. His work on the Board of Health dealt with all kinds of daily crises that never made it to notification levels, and he sure as hell kept a lid on possible epidemics from the media. Science has its own code of ethics, and the public was way down on the list when it came to revealing serious situations. There was a time and place for everything.

"Ok, Siam, I hear you. I'd like a copy of your notification to the hospitals for my files. In the meantime, go ahead with your research on the bone marrow project. The money's here, and you're as good as they come. Keep me posted on all of this, but let's keep it between the two of us. Do you understand?"

"Yes, Dr. Moran. I do understand."

Thompson Moran sat down at his desk after Siam Qua had left. There were some ways that did work best. Maybe he didn't agree with it personally, but he had to look beyond the moment. It was the only way. It was the way it had always been done. The public wouldn't understand. There would be just too much pressure to deal with and still keep the blood center operating. It was for the good of the whole. Siam Qua had convinced Thompson Moran of their divine right. *Adjusted prevarication*, the right of the medical gods to decide what the public should and should not know would live on. As it began—so it would end—some things never change.

PARADOX

A statement or event that seems contradictory, unbelievable or absurd, but that may actually be true in fact. . . .